Before, During, After

A NOVEL

Richard Bausch

ATLANTIC BOOKS
London

First published in the United States in 2014 by Alfred A. Knopf, a division of Random House LLC, New York, and in Canada by Random House of Canada Limited, Toronto, Penguin Random House companies.

First published in Great Britain in 2015 by Atlantic Books, an imprint of Atlantic Books Ltd.

10 9 8 7 6 5 4 3 2 1

A CIP catalogue record for this book is available from the British Library.

Trade Paperback ISBN: 978 1 78239 395 5
E-book ISBN: 978 1 78239 396 2

Printed and bound by CPI Group (UK) Ltd, Croydon, CR0 4YY

Atlantic Books
An Imprint of Atlantic Books Ltd
Ormond House
26–27 Boswell Street
London
WC1N 3JZ
www.atlantic-books.co.uk

This book is for Lisa and Lila

. . . do not understand me too quickly.

—ANDRÉ GIDE

Before

Ms. Barrett and Father Faulk

I

Not to be lonely, not to look back with regret, not to miss anything, always to be awake and aware. And to paint. Beautifully.

Natasha Barrett had written this in her journal when she was seventeen.

Favorite watercolorists: Sargent and Gramatky. Favorite sculptors: Bernini, Donatello. Favorite book: The Age of Innocence *by Edith Wharton. Favorite music: rock, particularly Men at Work, the Police, Dylan; and also for music: jazz, especially Chet Baker and Billie Holiday. Biggest fear: rejection. Biggest ambition: to travel and to know the world by heart.*

Seventeen. And she had come upon it this past winter, years away. You could be a little proud, looking back. You could even find some comfort in the recollection.

In early April of the year she was to turn thirty-two, what she thought of as the chastened later version of that young woman attended a fund-raising dinner hosted by her employer, Senator Tom Norland of Mississippi, at his mansion in Arlington. The mansion was on a high bluff overlooking the Potomac River, and from the road it was just visible at its roofline after you crossed into Virginia—an immense redbrick Colonial. She had visited several times before, and there was always something warm and welcoming about it in spite of its imposing size. Behind the house was a flagstone patio, and walking paths wound through the tall oaks that stood at the edge of the bluff above the river. Along the paths, iron benches were placed decorously amid flower beds and statuary. People would gather in this wide shady space when the senator was entertaining guests.

This evening she arrived late and was greeted by Norland's tall pretty wife, Greta. "Come right in, darling." Greta smiled her white smile and then frowned. "Are you all right? You look a bit downhearted."

"Oh, no, I'm fine," Natasha said. "Just tired."

"Well, good to see you, honey. Go right through."

The younger woman reflected that there were people for whom cheerfulness was a trait, something they were blessed with like good bone structure and silky blond hair. She went along the polished hardwood floor of the hall and stepped out onto the patio. Cocktails and wine were being served to the left of the entrance, a young dark man standing behind a table there. Natasha asked for red wine, and his gaze went over her. She could have imagined this.

Moving away from the crowd and out onto the lawn, she walked among the statues—small, delicate-looking angelic figures in supplicating poses. *Please*, they all seemed to be saying.

The winter had been long, colored by the aftermath of the end of an affair. She was in no mood for a party and had wanted very badly to find an excuse not to come. But it was Friday, still part of the workweek, and her presence was required: the gathering was for the benefit of the Human Relations Conference, one of the senator's pet projects. She was his chief organizer.

Wandering back to the patio, she stood sipping her glass of wine, surrounded by people whose evident curiosity about the senator's "assistant"—two people actually referred to her that way—made her irritable and cross. She wasn't there five minutes before she found herself desiring with adolescent fervor to disappear into the rooms of the house. She kept forcing a smile, listening politely to what was said to her. The guests, many of them local celebrities, were talking about the upcoming conference and about politics—the new president's withdrawal from the Kyoto Protocol on global warming. It was a signal, someone said, about where things were headed with the Republicans back in power. Others speculated about all that. Someone else remarked on the perfect weather, trying to change the subject. To Natasha it all began to

seem depressingly automatic, like the chatter of birds on a shoreline. Species noise.

The weather was indeed fine: clear and cool, breezes stirring
like whispered secrets in the leaves of the oaks bordering the property, the new leaves gold daubed with sun, nearly translucent. The
gravel and flagstone walks skirting the edge of the bluff afforded a
lovely view of the dark green river far below, with its ranks of scull-
ing boats from Georgetown. The air was flower scented.

Norland approached through the confusion of others, grasping the upper arm of a man who seemed reluctant to be handled in
that way. She saw that the man wore a clerical collar. "Natasha,"
Norland said. "You grew up in Memphis."

The senator had a gift for tautology.

She nodded and smiled at him.

"I'd like you to meet Father Michael Faulk, pastor of Grace
Episcopal Church in Memphis, Tennessee."

Father Faulk was tall, solid looking, bulky through the shoulders. She saw his dark brown eyes and, when they shook hands, felt
the roughness of his palm.

"Actually, I grew up in Collierville," she said to him.

"Collierville. I don't get out that way much."

"In Memphis people decide not to go somewhere if it's more
than five minutes away. I had Memphis friends who would talk
about Collierville as if it was Knoxville, four hundred miles down
the road instead of fifteen."

"You say you *had* Memphis friends." His black hair was reced-
ing. He looked to be in his late forties or early fifties.

She said, "Former friends, yes."

"I won't ask."

"They all moved to other cities?" she said in the tone of someone speculating.

"I'm still not asking."

They talked a little about Graceland and other attractions. It
was the usual informal kindness of social occasions. She did not
feel up to it.

"I've never really thought about the distance to Collierville,"
he went on. "*Is* it fifteen miles?"

"Fifteen miles from Beale Street to where I lived growing up."
She turned to acknowledge the greeting of a coworker, Janice
Layne, who was the senator's press secretary. Father Faulk moved
off, having been pulled in another direction by one of the donors
to the event—and perhaps having sensed her reluctance to chat.
Janice frowned slightly. "Mmm. Who's the one in the pretty collar?" That was Janice, boy crazy by her own account, and probably,
secretly, nothing of the kind. Natasha had an indulgent sense of
knowing affection for her.

"I've just been introduced. You don't know him?"

"He does look a little familiar. And he's *hot*. And Episcopal. I
already got that much. And so if he's single, he's fair game. I'll find
out for us."

"Go, girl," Natasha said automatically. She was already beginning to forget him.

But they got seated next to each other at the dinner, and he
turned a charmingly sidelong smile her way, talking about how he
could never get used to the grandeur of places such as this—with
its atrium and its wide entrances and the original Rembrandt on
the wall in the next room. He had been raised in Biloxi, in a decidedly middle-class environment, though his mother, just after he
turned seventeen, was the recipient of a large inheritance from a
great-uncle who had made a lot of money building houses. "Most
of my boyhood," he said, "was spent so far from this. Anyway, I
don't think I'll ever get used to it."

The humor in his face and the rich timbre of his voice brought
her out of herself. He asked, through the smile, if she liked Washington. "I do," she told him. "Mostly."

"Exactly how I feel about Memphis."

"How long have you been there?"

"A long time, now. I went north out of high school. College in
Boston—not Harvard." The smile widened. "Went to seminary in
Saint Louis, and then down to Memphis."

"Your family still in Biloxi?"

"My mother died three years ago," he said. "My father lives in
Little Rock. I have an aunt here in Washington."

She leaned toward him and murmured, "The, um, senator's press secretary wants to know if you're married."

He looked down the table toward Senator Norland and Janice Layne. "You mean Ms. Layne."

"The very lady."

He grinned. "Divorced."

"I'm sorry. But she'll be glad to hear it."

"Not interested."

This occasioned a pause, and they watched the others talking and sipping their wine. She thought she might have stepped over some line. He was gazing at the room, evidently far away now, hands folded at his chin.

She said, "Did you like Biloxi?"

And he seemed to come to himself. "I did. Very much. Yes."

Another pause.

"How about you?" he asked. "Does the senator's press secretary want to know if *you're* married?"

"Janice was just curious," Natasha told him.

"I was joking."

"She was, too—a little."

He grinned. "Actually, my former wife is getting remarried. It's happening in the next couple of days."

"How's that make you feel?"

"It's—as we say—in everyone's best interest."

Natasha nodded, unexpectedly on edge now. She thought of excusing herself. But there wasn't anywhere to go in this place without being seen leaving. She watched the senator talking to a big florid man about Virginia horse country and drank down her wine. It left an almost-syrupy aftertaste.

"I never feel comfortable at this kind of gathering." Father Faulk spoke softly, only to her.

"I can't help seeing it all as a series of gestures," she said. "Makes me feel judgmental."

"Not us. We're too cool."

It was pleasurable to be included in that way, even jokingly.

"Want to talk about Collierville?" he asked.

"Sure."

He waited.

"Do you like bluegrass?"

"Don't know much about it, but I like it."

She described summer evenings when people would gather in the charming old town center to play music.

"I have seen that," he said. "Wonderful. I like the antiques shops, too, and the old train station museum. I should go out there more often."

"I guess it's different if a person lives there."

"You couldn't wait to get away."

"No," she said. "Not really. It was just—you know—it was home."

He had an appealing weathered look. Realizing her own growing interest in him, she experienced a surprising stir of anticipation. It had been months since she had felt much of anything but weariness. She sipped the ice water before her, and her hand shook a little when she set the glass down. She wanted more wine. He was talking across the table about the Rembrandt to a narrow-faced middle-aged woman who had spectacles hanging from a little chain around her neck. "I joked about all the cracks in the original painting," he told her, "you know, going on about them to this fellow who—doesn't seem to be here now. Hope I didn't frighten him away. I told him that I have one just like it that has no cracks at all in it and that I bought it at Walgreens for less than five dollars. He was not amused. I'm pretty sure he thought I was serious."

The woman across the table was not amused, either.

"Forgive me," Natasha said to her. "I didn't get your name."

"I'm Mrs. Grozier. My husband is on the board."

"Oh, yes, Mrs. Grozier. I've worked with your husband."

Mrs. Grozier nodded civilly and then turned her attention to the other end of the table.

Father Faulk turned to Natasha and said, low, "I keep thinking it was funny about the Rembrandt."

She smiled. It was as though the two of them were in cahoots, looking at all the others. She felt herself calming down. She saw warmth in his eyes, a sort of reassurance radiating from them.

"What about you," he said. "You still have family in Memphis?"

"My grandmother. She's responsible for my having this job. She worked in the mayor's office in Memphis for years, and she knew a lady who came here to work for the senator."

"Is the lady still working for him?"

"Retired a couple of years ago and moved to California. Somewhere near L.A. I didn't know her very well."

"And your grandmother? Do you still go to Collierville to visit her?"

"We moved into the city the year before I left home. A little house in the High Point district. I visit her there, of course."

"I know a woman in High Point who used to work in the mayor's office. Iris Mara."

This gave her a pleasing little jolt. "That's my grandmother."

"I worked with her on a project to make books available to schoolkids in some of the poorer neighborhoods. Iris Mara from the mayor's office. Retired. Right?"

"Yes. All that—but she never mentioned a project."

"She comes to my church now," the priest said.

"*Church?*" Natasha said. "Iris?"

Grinning, he said, "Hmm." Then: "Yes. The very lady."

"We talked on the phone two days ago. We talk a couple of times a week. She's never said anything about going to church."

He was silent.

"Well. I've been away so much since I left for college."

At the head of the table, the senator stood and clinked the end of a fork against his wineglass until the room grew silent. He thanked everyone for attending and introduced some of the principal organizers of the event. He congratulated Natasha for her work on the project. Then he sat down, acknowledging the polite round of applause.

Faulk turned to her and said, "I didn't know you were so important."

"Hmm," she said. "Sarcasm in a priest."

His face betrayed no sign of amusement. "I wasn't being sarcastic. Honestly."

After a pause, he said, "So Iris didn't mention going to church." And they both laughed. There was something so incongruously familiar about the remark. His soft baritone voice when he laughed rose wonderfully to another register.

He held up his water glass and offered it, as for a toast. She lifted hers, and they touched them and drank.

"I'm probably slandering her by my reaction," Natasha said. "But she's always been so secular."

"She's been coming for several months now."

"You notice when someone starts coming to your church?"

He gave forth another little laugh. "In *her* case, yes. She came to see me first."

"It's so strange—Iris going to church. She never went to any church. *We* never went to any church. As far as I know, my parents never did either."

"You say as far as you know."

"They died when I was three. I never knew them."

"Oh, Lord—forgive me," he said. "Of course. I should've remembered—I knew that Iris lost her daughter and son-in-law."

"And Iris just goes on through the days being Iris."

"She's a brave lady."

"I can't wait to talk to her about *you*," Natasha said. "And church. I'll spring it on her. Be fun to hear her reaction."

"Please don't tell her I'm as stupid as I must have seemed just now."

"Don't be silly."

The man on his left began talking to him loudly about the unseasonably hot weather in the south. And then the waiters were circling the table, pouring wine in everyone's glass. Each held a bottle of white and a bottle of red.

Father Faulk asked for water. Natasha held her glass out and indicated that she wanted the red.

"When do you go back to Memphis?" she asked him.

"Probably tomorrow. I've been visiting my aunt Clara. She's the senator's mother-in-law."

"Then maybe you'll see Iris before I do," Natasha said.

"Oh, well, in that case, I'll remember *you* to *her.*"

The food was arriving. She felt a pull of nausea at the pit of her stomach. For months she had been miserable; and here, completely unforeseen, was something like light pouring in. And he would be gone tomorrow, and she would never see him again. She drank half her glass of wine, nearly gulping it. He was listening to the man go on about humidity. The man owned a bookshop in Leesburg, and business was slow. Finally he grew quiet; Faulk turned to her and asked how she liked the wine.

She held up the nearly empty glass. "Evidently too much."

She was not thinking of him in a boy-girl way but simply as a possible friend. And she did not want him to go back to Tennessee. "You should have a glass," she said.

"I think I will at that." He signaled one of the servers.

"Is your aunt Clara here?"

"She was supposed to be—she knows this crowd pretty well, of course. But she developed a migraine this afternoon. She doesn't get them often, but when she does they're fairly incapacitating."

The waiters were bringing the food. Two choices: a vegetable medley, with butternut squash and kale, or medallions of beef, with arugula salad, red potatoes soaked in olive oil and sprinkled with candied garlic. She asked for the beef, and he followed suit. Her glass had been refilled. He had a little wine, too, now.

"This is very jammy," he said, with a slight smile.

She said, "Maybe too much so."

2

Her parents were lost in the *Meteor* cruise ship fire near Vancouver in 1971, their remains sepulchered somewhere in the waters off that coast. The recitation of this history never failed to make her wish herself far away, and her grandmother still occasionally mentioned it as a reason that Natasha possessed such an old soul.

Natasha, in her early twenties, took to thinking of her own beginnings ironically. After all, it was just who she was. There seemed something faintly snobbish or even smug reporting the calamity to people like some sort of pedigree. But the accident was the dividing line of Iris's life, so the fact of it would be mentioned in talk with new acquaintances, and often enough this would lead to Iris using the phrase "old soul," meaning it in the best way, about her granddaughter. At times she would elaborate a little more, pointing to the watercolors Natasha did—depictions of faces from piles of photographs found in bins at antiques stores, families long gone, staring out in the light of those rainy-looking scenes.

Natasha felt like an old soul, all right, but not in the way Iris meant it. Through the past winter all the shifts of her mind and heart seemed frail and elderly to her, and she endured the purgatorial hours of each day, walking around in a haze of penitential worry about minutia, experiencing an immense lethargy and a recurring fearfulness. Fear of others, the sounds outside her apartment at night, the shadows in the cold streets when she walked home, all the possible harms of the world, and, most terrible, the fear that this darkness might last all her life. Night panics, dread wakefulness, fierce dreams when she could manage any sleep. During the days, nothing had any taste. Everything seemed dismally the same, the same. Her own thoughts oppressed her. The voices of others were demoralizing and dull. Friendships lapsed. The young women she had studied with in France and the group of friends and acquaintances she had made in Washington drifted to their own concerns, stopped calling or writing, acceding one by one to the silence. All but two: Marsha Trunan, a Paris friend with whom she had traveled in Italy and who was also from Memphis, and Constance Waverly, who lived in Maine now and was twenty years older than Natasha and sometimes treated her like a daughter. Marsha continued to call and leave messages, apparently having decided to ignore the difference between Natasha before and Natasha now. Marsha wanted to know what was wrong. Natasha kept insisting that nothing was wrong. She was overwhelmed with work. Just awfully busy. And this was partly true when you added to the daily responsibilities in the senator's office the necessity of keeping up appearances.

Perhaps the thing that tormented her most was the banality of it all: a squalid little cliché of betrayal and being the other woman. Surely regret was supposed to be reserved for mistakes on some grander scale than this—yet regret was what she felt, so deep that it sat under her heart, a physical ache.

She had thought he was the love of her life.

His name was Larry Mackenzie, a photographer she met through her job arranging appointments with journalists and news services for the senator.

She had spent almost a year sneaking in and out of hotels with him, and taking trips to other cities for false reasons, lying to everyone, including herself, holding on to the hope that he would leave his wife for her, end an unhappy marriage, a loveless disaster. He had described the misery in his house: a wife sinking into fanatical pursuit of the supernatural, believing in her ability to read minds and predict the future. Natasha had felt sorrow for his pain, mingled with desire that he stop talking about it and do what he kept saying he would do: find a way to make the civil arrangements. No one had to remain in a marriage he no longer wanted.

The day after Thanksgiving, she got a phone call from the wife.

Mrs. Mackenzie was confident and strong and spoke from a great height of scorn and moral superiority. She had confronted her delinquent husband with what she had known "for some time," and he'd told her the whole story, had answered all her questions, being courageously forthright, explaining everything to her satisfaction. "I've already forgiven him," she said. "As my faith dictates I should."

What Mackenzie had done, it turned out, was convince the poor woman that Natasha was the instigator of the affair and was now stalking him.

Ugliness all around.

Natasha confided this to Constance Waverly, and Constance responded in a tone that expressed how sordid *she* thought it was.

Well, Constance was right—no use denying the fact.

There had followed a series of blurry evenings, of being out by herself in Adams Morgan and Georgetown—boozy hours and instances of dalliance with unknown men. She had stopped painting altogether, and she began to drink alone, in the predawn, in her apartment, often going to sleep drunk, half clothed, on top of the blankets of her bed. This desperation had slowly turned into the interior gloom and ache that had brought her to a doctor and a prescription for bupropion.

She confided in no one else. When she spoke to Iris on the telephone, it was their usual pleasant back and forth. When Iris asked about her plan of saving money to go back to France and spend a year putting together enough work for a show, she pretended that things were still on track. Senator Norland, who kept a proprietary interest in her and saw her nearly every day, was nevertheless too absorbed to notice that anything was wrong, and somehow she continued to keep up with her work. She had in fact gotten better at it, had buried herself in it.

But the days were long, and filled with dejection.

Now, in the soft evening in the senator's house in Virginia, she was surprised by her own lifted spirits. She finished the medallions of beef, sipped the last of the wine in her glass, and went with Father Faulk to look at the new flowers clinging to the trestle bordering the patio. Blessedly, she felt no pressure to speak. The two of them were quiet. They strolled contentedly together along the gravel path above the river.

3

Father Faulk had seen an intimation of gloom in the young woman's eyes—not quite definable, yet there, like a shadow on water. Well, she was lovely, bracing up against something, and evidently not particularly eager to be introduced. Senator Norland, with characteristic, ham-handed, well-intentioned gregariousness, had barged through the moment like someone hoping to get them together as a couple. It was nothing of the kind, of course: Norland had merely realized the Memphis connection and, as was his nature, acted upon it, wanting everybody to be comfortable. Anyway, Faulk was grateful for having been pulled away in the middle of small talk. It was clear that this young, darkly beautiful woman had scarcely noticed him.

He was struggling with his own shadows.

The fact that his former wife, Joan, was getting remarried and was also expecting hurt him in a surprising, steady, aching way. He could not plumb the reason for it. The marriage ended three years ago. Joan had wanted a child and they had not conceived, but this was secondary: what bothered her most was what she called his moodiness; she believed that he had no sense of joy. Whereas she saw joy as an emotional goal and resting place, he had always looked upon it as something lovely that nevertheless contained awareness of the possible darkness all around—the rush of delight gazing at a sleeping baby, for instance, while also noting the little blue veins in the cheek, those minute tokens of mortality.

Moreover, the progress of her leaving had to do with her admission to herself that she found little rest in the daily rounds of work, of supporting the life, his ministry. Eleven years of the troubles of others, including his own peculiar form of darkness. She said everything drained her, his needs, his inability or refusal to see her, *her*, as someone separate from him. "First thing in the morning the calls and the needs and your needs and the work and more calls and I just can't breathe. It's driving me crazy." The accusation surprised and weakened him. He did not know how to change things. It was like trying to change one's skin and bones. And so she went to visit her mother, who lived in an old house in Portland. It was supposed to be a break, time and space to gather herself. But then the stay lengthened, and when she finally came home, it was to pack and leave for good.

In the end it wasn't quite clear how much of her discontent came from his work and how much of it came from himself. She wanted to leave. She claimed she felt no anger. And since, now, he was indeed considering leaving the priesthood, he had come to imagine that her restlessness and her wish to depart were early reflections of his own trajectory.

In his vocation, he had lost something unnameable but necessary.

This came to him one afternoon not long after she left. He was visiting a man in the hospital who had fallen in his own kitchen and hit his head. Sitting at the foot of the man's bed watching him go in and out of sleep, he had the unpleasant thought that this visit was his job. Across from where he sat with his half-conscious parishioner was a woman with a man whose demeanor showed that he hadn't gone mentally past the age of three. Father Faulk saw the shape of her face in shadow, the devotion in her light blue eyes, her loveliness as a woman. He looked back to the sleeping patient, but the image of this woman played across the surface of his thoughts. He would speak to her, get to know her, offering solace, at which of course he was practiced enough. She turned into the light from the window, and the light showed the lines of her face. For some reason he hadn't seen those lines before. She held the man's hand—this man, her son, with some injury to his leg, and all the cost of her reality was in her features. Suddenly Father Faulk knew he had nothing to tell her that she would want to hear, and he experienced the strongest sense of having awakened from some dream of life.

For a time he resisted negative considerations like these. He put them away like temptations—that was what he thought they were—and went on. And on. There wasn't anything else for it. You did your job and you accepted the bouts of despair as part of the normal run of experience in the life of a priest. Since the divorce he had settled into a zone of gray calm, performing the tasks of his calling—an efficient, uninspired servant of his vocation. Now and then he saw one woman or another and felt lonely even when he was with them. He was no longer fit for the work. Or so he expressed it recently to a friend, Father Andrew Clenon, the warden of the vestry for his parish. Father Clenon wasn't yet aware that Faulk wanted to leave. The talk had been confined to the dissatisfactions of the life. Clenon thought the trouble was spiritual dryness and told him to pray about it and went on to speak about the perils to the spirit when one was suffering through some change, as Father Faulk was with the news of Joan's pregnancy.

"It's been three years, Andrew."

"You're going to sit there and tell me that her getting remarried—the baby—none of that's bothering you at all?"

"I don't think it has anything to do with Joan. Except that I think maybe she knew I wasn't up to it before I admitted it to myself."

"You've dealt with it, though. Haven't you. You're a fine priest."

"I'm telling you it has nothing to do with Joan."

But of course it *did* have to do with Joan. And it had also to do with that life he once thought he was building, the changed life he was leading now, a chain of barren habit and avoidance and all the complications of being only marginally present in situations that deserved more from him. Through the winter, he had been carrying around the conviction that he must leave, must break free. The journey to Washington and a visit with what was left of his family, the senator's mother-in-law, had been something Father Clenon suggested.

It hadn't helped, hadn't changed anything. In fact it had strengthened the feeling that his priesthood was a failure.

But strolling along the gravel path above the river on that spring evening with Iris Mara's granddaughter, Natasha, he saw the unselfconscious pleasure she took in the new flowers, tulips and daffodils and wisteria, and he sought to break out of his own self-absorption. The flowers were indeed lovely and sweet scented, and when she looked at him, her dark sad eyes took him in, and for the first time he thought of leaving the clergy not as a capitulation but as a chance at some kind of happiness.

He did not return to Tennessee the next morning. He got his aunt Clara to ask for Natasha's number from the senator and called her to ask if she would accompany him for a stroll along the Tidal Basin, to the Jefferson Memorial.

4

She was curious, exhilarated, and even so she declined.

"Come on," he said. "It's just coffee and a stroll on a fine Saturday morning. What's preventing you from that? I'm just going to call you tomorrow and ask you the same thing."

"I thought you were going home."

"I'm staying on for another week. Come on. A little walk."

They met at a coffee bar on Wisconsin Avenue. He wore a white shirt rolled above the elbows and tan slacks, and she thought the civilian clothes made him look younger. She wondered if you called them civilian clothes and almost asked him, holding herself in check and smiling under her hands as they walked into the little café. They each had an Americano and pastry. His talk was gratifyingly fanciful. He wondered where she would live if she had unlimited funds, and what climate would be best for her, what countries—advantages and shortcomings of the several candidates for home, as he called it.

"France," she said. "I've been trying to save money to go there for a year and live."

They talked about Iris a little. He paid for the coffee, and they took their walk. An image came to her mind of clouds lifting. She paused to appreciate the quality of light through the cherry trees. He bent down to pick up a blossom and then tossed it.

"You didn't name any of the states as a possible place to live," she said.

His smile was slightly sardonic. "Somewhere far away. California? Alaska? Hawaii?"

"Not Alaska."

"Too cold," he said. "Right? I wasn't serious."

"My mother was a bit, well, crazy. I mean that's the only way to describe it. She had an idea that my father and she should find some way for us to live in Alaska. Anchorage. Think of it."

"A lot of nice happy people live there," he said.

"I wonder if she would've been happy. I don't know that I would've."

They went on a little.

"So she got my father to get a job on this Norwegian cruise ship to Alaska. My father was a trained chef. They were going to make the money to move. But there was an explosion, and the ship caught fire, and they jumped into the ocean. Several people did that to get away from the flames."

"Iris didn't tell me any of this, of course."

"She didn't tell me the real specifics of it until I was out of her house a couple of years. All I knew was that they were gone, lost at sea off Vancouver. I never knew them. Iris is—well. I used to wonder sometimes what she was thinking. And she never complains. It could be pretty quiet in the house, and anybody might think we were angry, or sad, but it was both of us sitting within four feet of each other reading. Perfectly glad of the quiet. I used to imagine her raising my mother alone. What *that* was like. And I guess it must've been like it was with me."

"And your mother wanted to live in Alaska."

"She actually wanted the cold. Loved snow, Iris says. I don't think much of her survives in me."

"Do you think Iris would say that?"

"Probably not."

Presently, she said, "But really, I'd like to go back to France. The southern coast. I went to school there. Let's say I like to imagine living in France and—painting."

"Making enough money to live on it?"

"Sure, why not?" She smiled.

"You paint every day?"

"I don't paint at all just now. But I have done some watercolors. But this was about fantasy, right?"

"Did you study painting?"

"Studied art."

"What would you say is your best trait?"

She had the feeling that he was talking now just to talk. "Doing the watercolors."

"That's your best trait?"

She decided to change the subject. "Is Clara your mother's sister or your father's?"

"My mother's half sister."

They were quiet for a few paces. The Tidal Basin was awash in blue shade with patches of sun, and on the fresh-cut grass shirtless young men threw a Frisbee back and forth. Only yesterday she would have seen them as cruelly separate from her, spending a carefree morning.

The day was growing lovelier by the minute. The white linen slacks she wore were comfortable and cool. She had tied her hair back in a chignon, and the breezes pleasantly brushed her neck. Butterflies flew around her.

"I think they're drawn to your pink top," he said.

At the water's edge they stood, watching the ducks glide by and several geese that kept honking. He reached over and, in a way that seemed natural and uninvasive—like the gesture of an older sibling—undid her hair. "I didn't know I was going to do that," he said. "I was appreciating the shine of it in this light, and I wanted to see more of it. Sorry. I don't usually do that kind of thing."

"It's fine." She was a little surprised at how much his worry about it pleased her.

They walked along the bank of the river. Sailboats glided past out in the brightness, and one motorboat sped by heading the opposite way, creating a white wake that churned at the banks. He placed his hand gently at the small of her back as they moved to the lane, into the cooler shade. A woman came by, pulled along by two large black dogs whose panting and striving—long nails clicking on the pavement—were the only sounds in the stillness. At a stone bench near the memorial, with its classic circle of columns and the tall shadow of the statue inside, they sat together and talked idly about the dinner party the evening before and about Senator Norland.

"Ten years dry now," he said about the senator's famous alcohol troubles. "But when they handed the presidency to Bush, that was tough for him."

"We're not allowed to mention that."

"I remember John Mitchell saying the country was going to go so far right it would hardly be recognizable. And here we are, not even three months out of the Clinton administration, and Mitchell, that crusty old bastard, looks like a prophet. It's so strange that the very people who are hurt most by them are their most vociferous supporters. An unforeseen flaw. The Founding Fathers couldn't have imagined television. What to do about a duped population."

"Do you talk about any of this from the pulpit?"

"Actually, I'm leaving the, um, pulpit."

She turned and waited for him to explain. But he sat back and sighed.

"You can't just say that and leave it there."

"Well, I'm not a very good priest. I feel like I'm lying."

"You no longer believe in God."

"No, I do. Very much. You don't have to leave the *religion*, you know, if you renounce your vocation."

They walked over to the memorial. Staring at the sculpted face, he murmured, as if out of respect for it, "This is one of my favorite places in the city. He's actually an ancestor on my mother's side, I'm told."

"Tell me about your aunt Clara."

Thinking about the woman gave him obvious pleasure. "She's lived here all her life. My mother's younger sister by twelve years. Got a big old pretty house in Cleveland Park, and it's constantly filled with people. She's not slightly involved in politics, either."

"And you?"

"I'm fairly insulated in Memphis. My coming into town to see her and her husband is usually as close as I get."

"I've lived here for years," said Natasha, "and I've never come to this memorial. A lot of this town I've never seen. And these are places people travel thousands of miles to see."

"What did you paint when you did the watercolors?"

"Not this."

He was still gazing at Jefferson. "There's a lot of places here I've never been in, too."

"How old are you?" she asked.

"I won't make you guess. I'll be forty-eight in June. And you?"

"Thirty-two in July."

They went back toward the Ellipse and on to the Lincoln Memorial. School buses were lined up, emptying out, children gathering to go in. The air was full of diesel exhaust.

"Tell me the happiest you've been," he said.

She didn't have to think. "When I was in France. Aix-en-Provence. One day I was standing in a little café waiting to order a baguette. I'd come on my bicycle down a long mountain road overlooking the Mediterranean, and it was cool and sunny and I realized I'd never felt so much at home, and I was happy. Really happy. And I'd been happy for weeks."

"Ever been back?"

"Not to live. Had a few days there a couple of times, taking pictures."

"Not painting them."

"Working for a travel magazine. And now how about you? What's the happiest you've been?"

"Actually, I'm pretty happy *right now*."

"Not fair. Come on."

"I don't know. Maybe I've never been really happy. Maybe that's why I asked the question. I'm still trying to figure out if it's possible."

"You're a little old for that kind of questioning, don't you think?"

"I know." He laughed. "Even at my age, I'm incomplete."

5

They spent the rest of the day together, looking at the famous sights of the city that neither of them had ever gotten around to—the Washington Monument, the National Archives, and some of the Smithsonian. It was a lark, a sweet game. For her it seemed a charm against having to part ways. In the evening they had dinner at a small French place she knew in Georgetown. The day's experience had made clear to her—it was a disconcerting little revelation—how rarely she had been herself with any of the men she had known. It was as if she'd always had to labor through some unspoken contest of wit. The insight made her hesitate. Perhaps it was the age difference. She got quiet while they ate and thought about finding an excuse to go on her way. Suddenly the whole gloomy history of the past two years blew through her. She sat straighter, attempting to fight it off. She had taken to calling this feeling the white sustenance, except that now she felt anxiety, too. She took a long sip of her wine and finished it, keeping her eyes on him.

He ordered two more glasses, then said, "Be right back." He rose and went toward the restrooms. The server, a long-faced, grouchy-seeming old man, set the glasses of wine down, and she took a small drink from hers and breathed deeply, wanting to calm down. It had been such a good day. She possessed the necessary detachment to admit that her emotions about it might be sentimental, that she could be producing them in some way, a self-deception born out of where she had been and what she had been through. She looked across the room at the bar, where a man and woman sat close, murmuring.

People got along in the world. People provided comfort for one another.

She took the rest of the wine and signaled the server for another. He brought the bottle over and poured more for her, without saying a word. She saw the wrinkles across the back of his neck as he moved away. Faulk came back to the table and sat down. He was an interesting man, and she could just enjoy him. He was not that much older: sixteen years. But they could simply be friends. She could leave it there.

He sipped his wine and looked at her, and she looked away.

"Something hurt you a minute ago. Did I say something wrong?"

She touched the back of his hand. "No."

"This is fun," he said.

She found herself talking more about Iris, how it had been growing up orphaned in that old house. "Of course I never thought about it then, but I was being raised by a woman who had lost everything except me. Her husband had gone off, and she never heard another thing from him or about him until news came from a cousin that he'd passed away on a street in San Antonio. I still don't know what made him leave, except that she was pregnant with my mother. But, you know, I don't feel deprived. Life was—well, itself. And then I went off to France. And of course we don't—she doesn't live in Collierville anymore. Not since my last year of high school. But I always had a sense of this—this sad past I couldn't know about, and Iris has a thing about time. There's a pillow she embroidered that she keeps on the piano bench. It says, *The dark backward and abysm of time*. I don't have any idea where it comes from."

" 'The dark backward and abysm of time.' "

"I was fourteen when she did it."

"Strange thing to embroider on a pillow."

"So tell me about you," Natasha said. "Your parents."

"My father's Leander. Lee. From Gulfport, Mississippi. He used to practice what he calls small-town law. His joke is that all he's ever missed in life is the *n-e-r* at the end of his name. Then we'd be Faulk*ner*s. We have what you might call a complex relationship, since he thinks the religion, um, makes me a fool. He and my mother argued about it and about *me* all the time, and finally they broke apart when I was in divinity school. Basically she believed and he didn't. And in his mind she coddled me. And I guess she did. In his mind, anyway, that explains my being a priest. Her obsessive piety."

Natasha took a little more of the wine. "Still?"

"I guess. He's retired and he has a new wife I haven't seen."

"He doesn't visit you in Memphis."

Faulk shrugged. "Something about his peripheral vision makes it so he can't drive anymore, but he talks of getting the new wife to drive him over one day. They were married this past fall, and of course he was glad to have me know it was a civil ceremony. Her name's Trixie. I've talked to her on the phone. Soft, sweet voice. And I've seen her picture with him on the Christmas card." Sitting back, folding his arms across his chest, he sighed. "I'd like one more glass of wine, I think."

"Yes," she said. "Let's."

As he signaled the server, he said, "By the terms of my mother's last will and testament, I have a trust fund, really enough to live on if I don't go crazy with it. So if I leave the priesthood I won't—"

The server came and poured, still without saying anything, and they sipped the wine.

A little while later she said, "I think I'm getting blotto."

So they ordered coffee and stayed until all the other patrons were gone from the place—the old grouchy server and the bartender talking quietly at the bar.

She was telling him about being eighteen years old and arriving in France with only the vaguest ideas of what she might do with her life. The world was wide and welcoming. As she talked she was suddenly aware of the coarseness of her hands, the bitten fingernails. She folded them under her chin and looked out at the street. Then, slowly, with a small soundless breath, set them down on the table between them, fingers spread, in plain sight. "Anyway, it was a good time. I felt like I'd found the place on earth where I belonged. I took a job as an au pair for a Dutch liquor wholesaler and his wife and two children after I graduated, because I didn't want to come back to the States. I met my friend Constance Waverly working for them. My rich lady friend. She's older. So you see, I have experience, I guess because of Iris, really, being friends with—" She stopped.

"You were going to say 'with people who are so much older'?"

"With people who are a good deal older, sure."

"That's—reassuring."

She sipped her coffee and sought something else to talk about. "And how old is Constance?"

"Fifties. I'm supposed to spend some time with her in Jamaica in September. A little vacation she's offered me. All I have to do is pay my way down."

"Ever been there?"

"No."

"Nice place." He stared. "I hear."

"I'm sorry if I said something wrong," she said. "I didn't mean anything by it."

"It's all right, really."

Deciding to pretend that she'd already forgotten about it, she said, "What're people saying about you leaving the priesthood?"

"Well, you're the first person I've told other than the warden of the vestry about my—difficulty. And *he* doesn't really know I want to leave."

She said nothing.

"I've been thinking about it for a while. But you're the first one to know all of it."

"Not Aunt Clara?"

"No—not yet. But I don't think it'll matter much to her."

"Why me?"

Something changed in his eyes, a very slight narrowing; it could've been the light. "I don't know," he said.

He walked her to her car, and they exchanged a hug before she got in behind the wheel.

"Good night," he said. Then: "Let's go somewhere else tomorrow."

"Call me," she said.

He stood under the streetlamp and watched her go, and she saw him in the side-view mirror.

In her apartment she had a whiskey, trying to offset the coffee and the nervousness she felt. Marsha Trunan had called twice and left two messages. Natasha reflected that her last remaining friend in the city might soon go the way of the others. She made herself return the call.

"What," Marsha said, her voice thick with sleep.

"I woke you. I'm sorry."

"I knew it would be you. I wasn't asleep."

"You called me today?"

"Where are you?" Marsha wanted to know.

"Home."

"Want a visitor?"

"Marsha, I'm really fried. It's so late."

"Busy, busy."

Natasha said nothing.

"I've got tickets to something called *Hamlet* at the National Theatre way in June. Way, way off in June. And I hear it's a pretty good play by this English dude named Shakespeare."

Natasha sighed. "Sounds interesting."

"But you can't say that far ahead."

"I'm sorry, Marsha. I'm just so—"

The other interrupted her. "Busy, right. I get it. I'll stop calling."

"Please don't do that."

"Well, anyway, I've got news," Marsha went on. "Guess who's divorcing his insane wife and marrying some Ph.D. sociology student at GW."

Natasha waited. She could not remember when the other would have learned about it all, and then she felt she knew: Constance.

"You remember your photographer friend. Mackenzie."

She expected to feel a sting, but it didn't come. "Why would that mean anything to me?"

"Oh, come on. I know all about it. And I haven't divulged it, either, like someone else we know. But a lot of people saw that you were pretty thick with him."

"Well, anyway. Good for him. I'm sure it was love at first *sighting*."

Marsha laughed, and coughed, and said through her sputtering that she was going to steal the line.

"You can have it," Natasha told her.

"God! I miss you. You *are* amazing. If it was me, I'd be a hopeless mess. But you—"

"Marsha, he's so gone from me."

"You're strong. I wish I was strong."

"Tell me."

"Oh, things're cool with me, really. I wish I had your troubles sometimes."

"I'm supposed to go to Jamaica with Constance in early September. Why don't you come with us? We could split the cost of a room ourselves."

"Constance wouldn't speak to us for decades."

Natasha heard her light a cigarette. "Listen, Marsha, I really should get to bed. I'll call you tomorrow, I promise."

"Bye," Marsha said, and hung up. Something like a song note sounded in her voice: two syllables. "*Bye*-eye."

Natasha listened to the dial tone for a few seconds, feeling the separation. She would call her back, say she loved her. She punched the number, then felt too tired for the talk that would follow. She pressed the disconnect and put the handset down.

Sitting at her small night table, she opened a book. Nearly midnight. She heard sirens out in the night, someone shouted in the street a block or two over. It was the sound of a Saturday night in this part of the city. Without even quite attending to it, she put the book down, undressed and got into bed, and lay there in the light from her reading lamp, gazing at the ceiling and going over the day, afraid to think forward.

So the photographer was breaking up his marriage after all.

Willing herself away from any thoughts of him, she conjured the picture of Michael Faulk as he appeared in her side-view mirror, standing under the streetlight. She went to sleep with this image in her mind like a ghost outline after looking into bright light.

Love Life

I

The weather had been breezy and a bit cooler than usual, and then it warmed up, and you knew real spring had arrived. She took the week off and saw him every day, making sure they went to places where it was unlikely they would encounter anyone from her office. He showed that he had divined this when they were on their way to dinner at his aunt Clara's, explaining that long ago he'd extracted a promise from her not to talk about his comings and goings.

Her tall old house in Cleveland Park was reminiscent of the house in Collierville where Natasha had grown up, with its wide front porch and its Italianate windows. Going up the sidewalk in front felt like coming home. Here were the same worn steps, the same spindle-shaped wooden supports for the railing. Aunt Clara stood in the doorway with arms extended in greeting as they came up the walk. She was thin, sharp featured, with dark auburn hair and brilliant light blue eyes. Natasha thought briefly of the daughter, the senator's wife, Greta. The eye color was the same, and you saw something very similar in the jawline.

"Can I call you Tasha?" Clara asked. "When I was a girl I had a friend Natasha and we all called her that. Do any of your friends call you Tasha?"

"Well, no—but I don't mind at all. If you want to."

"Sorry I'm so forward."

"No," Natasha hurried to say. "Really."

Aunt Clara's husband, Jack, was Italian, and he kept a wine cellar and was proud of it, happy to show it off. At dinner, he told about being a young man ignorant of anything but the taste of beer and pouring down the sink a gift bottle of Château Lafite Rothschild 1956 because it wasn't sweet. "Well, I was only twenty-four. Grand cru, worth about two hundred seventy-five dollars *back then*. I lied to the nice guy who gave it to me in gratitude for helping him get his car out of a ditch. Said it was excellent, and of course he was stunned that I'd opened it."

Aunt Clara said, "The deepest regret of the man's life."

"That makes him very lucky," said Natasha.

After dinner, they all sat out on the porch, and Jack smoked a pipe. They remarked about the hot weather that would arrive soon, the town's unbearable humidity. Clara said her daughter had recently decided to take up yoga in order to help her relax.

"She always seems so relaxed," Natasha said.

Clara smiled. "She's as nervous as the very *idea* of nervousness. And I think I did it to her, too. I was such an anxious mom. Saw threats everywhere. The poor thing was bearing up under a catastrophic imagination way before she became the senator's wife, no kidding."

"I think a person's character is probably there at birth," said Jack, blowing smoke.

Clara turned to Faulk and said, "Have you spoken with your father lately?"

"Not too long ago. Couple weeks."

"I wonder how he's doing."

"He said something about stopping to see me on their way to visiting Trixie's family in Tuscaloosa next month. I'm pretty sure it's Trixie's idea."

"Don't be so hard on him."

"Well."

They sat breathing the spring air, the fragrance of Jack's tobacco. A bird sang in the nearest tree, and Clara whistled at it, making almost the same sound.

"That's good," Jack said, smiling without removing the pipe stem.

It was a pleasant, calm evening, and Natasha watched them,

wondering at their ease together. Faulk had said nothing of his plan about the clergy.

As they were taking their leave, Clara said to Natasha, "I hope I'll be seeing you," and embraced her. Then she kissed Faulk on the cheek. "We'll keep the light on, as usual. But you know we always do that anyway."

"Thanks, darling," Faulk said. "Thank you very much." He put his arm around Natasha, and they walked down the sidewalk toward Thirty-Sixth Street, where he'd parked the car. The street-lights made shadows of the laden tree branches across the sidewalk. She felt pleasantly sleepy. "That was such fun," she said. "What cool people."

"I stay with them every time I come to Washington. Since my divorce, Aunt Clara's been worried about my well-being. I think she's convinced you'll be good for me."

Natasha hooked her arm in his. "She's wonderful. I want to be like her when I grow up."

"I know that feeling."

"It's funny. Politics didn't come up at all."

"Cousin Greta came up. That's politics in a way. Her nervousness. It's all about what she has to do with her days."

"But you know Greta always does seem so comfortable and at ease. Like she was born to it. She was glowing at that Human Relations dinner."

"Yeah, well, she claims Clara's house is the only place in the city where she doesn't have to be the senator's wife. You should see her and Clara together. Clara talks to her so tenderly, like she's eleven years old and still living under her roof. And of course no mention is ever made of the, um, business. It's like furniture: always there, but you never talk about it."

"I thought you might say something about your plans."

It took a moment for him to respond. "I'm not sure why I didn't. I'll tell her sometime before I go back to Memphis."

They went along the walk to the corner. The concrete was uneven, a tree root having forced it to buckle. He tightened his grip on her arm as they negotiated this and then let go when they crossed the street. Opening the car door, he said, "So where'll we go tomorrow? It's your call, I believe."

"I want to make love," she said. "Tonight. Now."

He stood shuffling with the car keys.

"Did I say something wrong?"

"I'm thinking where we can go."

"My apartment," she said.

So their first time was in her bed in the small room with one window overlooking East Capitol Street. Before they went in there, though, they sat for an hour on the sofa in her combination living room and kitchen, sharing a snifter of brandy. She liked that he was not in a hurry. At one point she lay her head against his shoulder. She told him about wanting to grow up to be an artist.

He looked at the little square frames with the watercolor faces in them on the wall. "Are those yours?"

"Yes."

He got up and went to them and stood gazing. He took his time in front of each one. Finally he said, "They're *amazing*. Truly. You must know how good they are. Who're the models?"

"I don't know. Except, you know, I *do* feel like I know all of them. I buy old photographs from antiques stores and try to paint the faces, and you do get a feeling for a person, painting a face. I haven't done it for a while."

He came back and sat down. "You have to start again. These really are quite amazingly good."

She felt the need to change the subject. "What will you do when you leave the priesthood?"

"Haven't thought about it much," he said. "Some kind of social work? I've had to write a homily every week, and not having to do that is going to be good. I can get to some of the reading I've been too busy to do. I've been rereading Thomas Aquinas. And I'm not trying to impress you with my erudition. Really, it's calming."

"It's Catholic."

"Well, we're English Catholics, right?"

"I went to that church down in Charlottesville. A big metal statue of him out in front of the place. A very podgy, disgruntled-looking aluminum monk. And a building that looks like a spaceship."

"I spent some time reading in his big book when I was a kid. Something reassuring about having everything laid out in that orderly way. I liked that. Still do. It might've been what led me to life in the church. Not his, of course."

"Let's not talk about church," she said. Then: "Will you wait until I can put things away?"

"Of course."

He sat on the sofa in the light of the one lamp, legs crossed, a magazine open in his lap, looking like someone in a dentist's office. It was endearing, and sweet. She went into the other room and worked behind the closed door, putting dirty clothes into the bottom of the closet, stacking books neatly on the nightstand, and changing the bed. She worked hurriedly, and when she came back out to the living room she found him standing at the bookcase, hands clasped behind his back, gazing at the titles.

"We've got some of the same books," he said.

She took him by the hand and led him into the little room. He moved as if worried about waking someone, padding to the window and pulling the curtain aside to look out. "Nice view of the Capitol."

"Yes."

He came back and put his arms around her, kissing her neck, the side of her face. His mouth tasted of the brandy. They were standing beside the bed. They sat down and looked at each other.

"I'm nervous," he told her.

"Me, too."

They made love, saying little, and she came very quickly, holding tightly to him. He kept going, and she spread her legs wider to take him deeper, murmuring his name.

"I'm going to come in you," he said suddenly, loud.

"Do. Oh, yes," she said. "Yes."

Afterward, they lay in the tangle of sheets, saying nothing for a time. Finally he leaned up on one elbow and gazed at her. "That was glorious."

"Can you stay?" she asked.

His expression was faintly bemused. "I'm not going anywhere, if it's all right."

This gave her a distressing sense that he might suppose she had done this often enough to wonder. She said, "I don't know what the protocol is. I've never done this."

"Here?" he said.

She answered simply. "Here, yes."

"I'm glad I'm the first. Here." He smiled.

She reached up and brought him to her, then rolled over on top of him and began softly to move down. When she took him, still a little flaccid, into her mouth, he moaned, "Oh, lover." She felt him harden, and she tightened her lips and pulled, and then ran her tongue slow along the shaft, and then straightened and straddled him, guiding him into her, sinking and rising on him, head back, hands gripping his shoulders. It went on. It was very good. She paused, bending to his face, kissing him, tightening the muscles of herself around him, then straightened, moving her hips back and forth, rising and sinking. "I'm going to come," she said, and did, and held him tight inside her, hands still gripping his shoulders, her head drooping so that her hair was in his face.

Later, they went into her small bathroom and took a shower together, moving gingerly in concert because of the small space and the clutter of the bottles of shampoo and conditioner. He held her in the rush of warm water while she let it cascade over her hair. They stayed until it began to get cold. Then they toweled off—he dried her and she him—and returned to the bed. She lay back and opened her legs, and he kneeled before her, paused, moaned, lowering his head. He began kissing her inner thighs until, with tantalizing slowness, he licked her. And when she was about to come, raising himself, he pushed deliciously inside. She felt the easing, the falling through, without quite going over, and he went on, apologizing for taking so long, until at last he, too, was finished.

"So lovely," she murmured.

"It's been a long time," he breathed. "Too long." He was still out of breath.

"Let's sleep now. Or do you want something else to drink? I have some wine in the refrigerator."

"I don't want to move."

"Can I get it for you?"

"I don't want *you* to move."

She snuggled closer, put one leg over his middle, and felt him running warm out of her—how good to have this sensation without the attendant stab of guilt or aversion; how wonderful to feel so clean and clear.

"Where do we go tomorrow?" he said.

2

She chose the Corcoran Gallery. Though he had driven or walked by the building many times during visits to the city, he had never been in. They spent a pleasant couple of hours looking at an exhibit of Impressionist paintings on loan from the Louvre—and then they went across the river to Mount Vernon and Arlington Cemetery, those somber, gentle slopes, row upon row of white crosses and six-sided stars. At the Kennedy grave site, they stood quietly among other visitors and read the words of the speeches.

She said, "Doesn't seem fair."

"What."

"Lincoln wrote the words on his memorial."

He stared for a moment, unable to decide how serious she was. "You've been working in politics too long, I think."

"It's the truth. Right?"

"I think JFK wrote his inaugural himself."

She shrugged. "He had help."

"You don't like him."

"I don't remember him," she said.

"Well, I was ten when he died. I remember him. And I remember *that*. Everybody remembers where they were that day."

She said, "For me it's the *Challenger* disaster."

They made their way down to the parking lot and drove back across the river, to Georgetown. He noted that she appeared almost passive about the evening, but then he realized that this came from a form of relaxation: her smile was both playful and compliant, the expression on her face giving forth a lovely intimation of gratitude, perhaps not for him, particularly, but for the fineness of the day. He kept the talk light, and the way her dark eyes seemed to narrow very slightly when she concentrated on something delighted him.

The next morning, they drove out to Middleburg for a long leisurely afternoon of thrift shopping. They stayed there that night. And the following morning they traveled down to the Old Town section of Fredericksburg to look at antiques. He watched her negotiate with a dealer about a set of old pewter cups for Iris, and together they rummaged through old postcards and photographs in a bin. She bought thirty of them in a packet. One family's photos going back to 1913.

It was gratifying to discover that they had the same fascination with the individual details and concerns of past lives.

He wanted to look at Civil War battlefields in the area, and she agreed to this with an enthusiasm that warmed him; it was an interest of hers as well. They went to Marye's Heights, and over to Chancellorsville, then on to Manassas and even out to little Ball's Bluff, in Leesburg. This necessitated intervals of travel on the highways and the country roads, too, and they were quiet for long periods. When they spoke, it was mostly about the battles that had thundered back and forth in these peaceful hills and fields. He was impressed with her knowledge of all that, her comprehension of the politics of the time, and when they were standing at the little monument to the action at Ball's Bluff, he told her so.

She bowed her head. "Thank you, Mr. Professor, sir."

"Well, I *am* impressed."

"You just can't believe someone my age could be at all knowledgeable."

"That's not how I meant it."

"Just teasing you," she told him. "I did a lot of reading growing up because I was alone so much. I even knew about Thomas Aquinas."

"Hey, I don't feel there's anything about you I have to compensate for."

"I was being silly. Okay?"

"Okay." He put his arm around her. "Let's forget it."

But that night, in her bed, lying awake in the dark with the sound of traffic out the window, he couldn't sleep, and while she moved and murmured, dreaming, he kept thinking about the numbers: when she was five years old, he was already old enough to vote; when she was ten, he had been married for two years. He quietly got out of the bed and went into her little living room. It was chilly, and he pulled the afghan that covered the sofa around himself. Looking through more of the books, he found a volume of Shakespeare. He took it to the kitchenette and had a glass of water, then poured himself some of the sauvignon blanc that was in the refrigerator. Most of the flavor was gone from it, but he thought it might help him sleep. Finally he sat on the sofa with the afghan over his shoulders, looking through the Shakespeare. The line she had told him that Iris embroidered on a pillow rose to his mind. The phrase was vaguely familiar. He had seen two Shakespeare plays in the last three or four years. He looked through *Hamlet*, and then *The Tempest*.

And there it was, in the second scene. He closed the big book, satisfied, as if he had won some kind of contest, and abruptly felt foolish for it.

He crawled back into her bed and was very still when she turned and put her arm over his chest. The feeling of intimacy, the slight sourness of her breath in sleep, the warmth of her body, so close, caused something to collapse in his heart. He told himself that he'd had the wine, and therefore could sleep. But sleep did not come, and he lay there doing the math, worrying all the more about it because he knew now that he was in love.

3

Friday morning at Harpers Ferry they hiked up beyond the old ruin of Saint John's Church and the grass-overgrown, tumbledown two-hundred-year-old graves adjacent to it, to the big flat boulder where Thomas Jefferson reportedly stood and declared that this view of the conjoining rivers and opposing bluffs was worth the grueling journey across the Atlantic. They stood together on that rock, a light breeze moving over them, and held hands, watching the waters course and mingle in currents and eddies far beneath them.

"I'm beginning to feel like this touring is a pretext," he said.

"Explain."

"I don't really care so much about it now. I just—I want to be around you. We could've stayed in bed today, at your apartment."

"The air-conditioning doesn't work that well. We'd be miserable there in the heat all day."

They watched the white folds of the water below and saw two people—a man and a woman—high on the cliff across the way. The two people were wearing backpacks, and it looked like they had dry-tooling axes and ropes. Apparently they were serious. There seemed something ostentatious about all that equipment. Except that now the man dropped something shiny, and it bounced terribly off an outcropping of rock far below. Natasha gave a little cry of alarm.

"A long fall," her companion said.

She covered her eyes. "I can't watch them." A second later, she peeked through her fingers.

"I did a little climbing in Colorado when I was in my twenties," he told her. "Well—once. I didn't mean to make it sound like more. It was just once. Very *supervised.*"

They watched the couple move across the face of the cliff.

Suddenly he said, "It's from Shakespeare. The line embroidered on the pillow."

She looked at him.

He shrugged. "It sounded familiar when you told me about it. I was up last night, looking through your books. It's from *The Tempest.* I saw it done last year in the park."

" 'The dark backward and abysm of time.' "

"It's part of something Prospero asks Miranda. 'What seest thou else in the dark backward and abysm of time?' He's asking her what she remembers."

"I should know the play, but I don't."

"I'm in love with you," he said evenly, straightly, as if answering a question.

She pressed herself against him, looked up, touched his cheek, and kissed him. It was a long, exquisite kiss. Then she gazed into his eyes and murmured, " 'What seest thou . . . ?' "

"I want to marry you and have a family and raise a bunch of kids," he said.

"Yes. The answer's yes."

"But I'm a little worried."

"People will find things to say anyway."

"Then it doesn't bother you," he said. "Sixteen years."

She kissed him. "Does that answer your question?"

"It answers everything in my life. When do you want to?"

"In Memphis—in September. After I get back from Jamaica. Something small. Very few people. I don't want a big deal."

"Can I say the words?"

She smiled.

"Will you marry me?"

"Yes."

They stood close, gazing at the country below and around them, and then others came rushing up the hill out of the cut path, children with older boys and girls, teenagers showing off for one another. Natasha looked at them with that sense of pity a lover feels for the less fortunate of her kind.

4

In mid-August, she gave notice that she would leave her job with Senator Norland and return to Memphis. Iris had suffered a fall and hurt her knee and had required surgery. She was healing slowly. Natasha was needed at home. This was the truth but, of course, not the whole truth.

She and Faulk had not announced their plans to marry yet; she was keeping to her determination not to divulge anything at work about her personal life. Since the first days of the affair with Mackenzie, she had maintained a strict rule about it.

She had kept the present news even from Iris until the second week of May.

Faulk came to Washington every other weekend through the summer months, and they traveled to the Maryland and Virginia beaches or visited with Aunt Clara and Uncle Jack and sometimes Marsha Trunan, too. It was a splendid summer, full of laughter and wide-ranging talk and long walks on the shady streets of the city. They went sailing off Annapolis and picnicking at Great Falls, and they visited the galleries and saw concerts and went to restaurants, and it was as though she were recovering something lost, that adventurous young someone she remembered.

On the muggy, oven-hot afternoon of her last day at work, Senator Norland tried to talk her into remaining in Washington. She could consider this a long vacation. She listened politely to him, sure now that Faulk had done as she asked and kept it to himself: the senator would not be talking to her about staying if he knew why she had resigned. She was going home and taking her private life with her.

Anyhow, that was how it felt.

The air conditioner whirred in one window, and the other was foggy with inside moisture. She experienced a moment of disorientation, pretending to consider his words. He emphasized that she could come back anytime. He stood over her with arms folded. On his desk were photographs of him with Greta, and Clara and Jack, too, and his own parents—two very jolly-looking people standing on a porch. The wall was festooned with framed photographs of him with presidents Reagan, Bush Sr., and Clinton, and there was a letter wishing him well on his reelection signed by the current president. But no picture of the senator with him. Tom Norland had fought hard to keep George W. from being given the office by the Supreme Court, and he had been outspoken in his criticism of the whole affair. Natasha had typed some of the letters and had contributed wording for them, too.

But she had never wanted to be the person people saw her as being, in that office. The work interested her, but she had no enthusiasm for wearing the smart little business outfits and the jewelry; never wanted to be the type—with no strand of hair out of place, the senator's administrative person, the one everyone depended on for practical matters, and about whom they all made easy assumptions, without any inkling of the nights she had spent in other parts of the city. Even before the affair, their picture of her was far from who she really was, sitting in that fluorescent light behind the desk while her thoughts turned on places she had wandered before she was twenty-five years old: Paris and the Loire Valley; Nice and Florence and Rome; Greece, Cyprus, Turkey, and Africa. From her earliest conscious life she had experienced the sense of being held back by her own skin and bones, confined in space. This feeling had carried her across the world.

Now, with Michael Faulk, she was full of the old thrilling sense of freshness, on the verge of a new life, and in this last week of work the days crawled, reminding her of the tremendous unhappiness she had endured here. She and her new husband would spend next spring in the south of France. It would indeed be like getting her twenties back.

When she lived in Provence, she went on day trips, biking the roads lined with plane trees and walking the paths above the sea at Beaulieu-sur-Mer. Her thoughts about it were delectable. She could be in those places again, and with the time to take it all in, and to paint. She was beginning to believe she might manage to do something consequential, something people might remember. The idea delighted her, though she recognized that just now, since she had not painted anything in many months, it was a form of daydreaming. But she would work to realize it. She felt the resolve like a rush of adrenaline. Life was gorgeous; she would make it so.

Working for the senator, with the daily requirements and the little satisfactions of being on the inside, all that was over now, and she felt detached from it and from the thin, stooped, gaunt man who stood before her, talking. His face was blue veined from the years of alcoholism. He wore a lapel pin with the word HOPE on it.

He was a humorous, decent, quiet man whose voice, when he was serious, had a way of making her feel drowsy. "None of this is getting through to you, is it." He grinned. It was not a question.

"I'm flattered that you've taken the time," she said. "I really am—and I'm grateful. It's been a wonderful adventure, Washington." Though in some important ways this was true, she still felt as if she had said something deceitful.

"Well, I couldn't let you go without at least expressing what I hope you'll take as my friendly concern."

"I do. I have."

"And you're sure I can't give you some money to tide you over until you find something out there."

"No, really. I'm fine. I've actually saved some. You've already done more than you should."

"Ah. It doesn't amount to much." He had made the arrangements with the storage company and the movers, thinking they were for Natasha alone. All her belongings, which as of that morning were in a storage bin on Georgia Avenue, would, the week of September 10, be headed by truck back to Tennessee.

She rose from her chair and offered a handshake. "Thank you so much for everything. And thank Greta for always being so kind." They embraced, and that was that.

She would spend the time with Constance Waverly in Jamaica, then join Faulk in Memphis on the twelfth (they had joked about how it would be their own Twelfth Night).

Jamaica was the vacation Constance had offered her in the unhappiness of last winter. People were so kind. She walked along Pennsylvania Avenue in the bright sun and looked at the faces, everyone showing consideration, negotiating the traffic without stopping to realize what a fine thing it was, this organized hurry and bustle of a summer afternoon.

Back at her empty apartment, the phone had not been cut off yet, and she called Faulk to tell him about her conversation with Norland.

"Did you tell him the news?"

"Yes. I just said."

"About *us*, sweetheart."

"Oh, well, he was so kind about storage and the movers, I—I just couldn't do it. I mean, he wanted me to know I could consider this a long break."

"Well, of course marriage is such a deeply embarrassing thing to have to go through."

"Stop it, Michael. I can't help how I feel about it. I didn't want my private life bandied about in the halls of that place. You knew that. Aunt Clara will say something to him anyway."

"No, she won't. It's our business."

"Well, exactly," Natasha said.

He sighed, and she sighed back at him.

"Are we having a fight?" she said.

"I hope you have fun in Jamaica," he told her.

"Do you want me *not* to go? Because I'm going."

"Go."

"Bye," she said, and hung up.

Out the window, sun blazed on the façades across the street and the people strolling by, the cars gliding past. She turned and looked at the empty rooms and then walked through them one more time, pausing in the bedroom, that small space where they had first made love. It looked barren now with its faded places on the walls where the pictures had hung.

5

She had met Constance in Nice while working as an au pair for the liquor wholesaler and his wife and their two overindulged children, a girl and boy only eighteen months apart. The six-year-old, the girl, was verbally quite advanced and already showing signs of a fundamental dishonesty, and she had been giving Natasha a hard time. Her name was Elga. The couple was from Utrecht, but they spoke perfect French and English, and Constance, back when she lived in England, had purchased art from the wife, who was a ceramist. Natasha was introduced—the lady of the house took some pleasure speaking of her young *American* servant, or so it seemed to Natasha—and in the polite talk that followed, Constance said she had spent time in Tennessee and still had a small house in East Memphis, which she was trying to sell. Memphis remained the subject of their conversation, in English, while Natasha tried to keep Elga from taunting the boy. A moment later, when the Dutch couple had gone to prepare snacks, Constance murmured that the pretty children were decidedly not pretty when considered from the inside. "Selfish, spoiled little buggers, if you ask me," she said, and the mild obscenity made Natasha laugh. It became a jag. Constance got lost in it, too, both of them unable to speak to the Dutch couple, who waited impatiently for them to subside.

The increasing awkwardness fed the laughter, of course, and it also made them friends.

They saw each other several times that week and kept the connection, though Constance was perpetually moving back and forth from one city to another. Through the six years Natasha was living in D.C., the older woman spent periods of a week or two at a time in the city, really only to see Natasha.

The bond was complex. At times Constance exhibited a form of intolerance for Natasha's other friends, little asides in conversations, a certain tone when speaking about them, often preceding the name with the word *that*.

She would say *"That* George" or *"That* Marsha" or *"That* Kelly," like a schoolteacher discussing unmanageable students, and she could be critical regarding Natasha's history—seeing herself as a kind of arbiter, especially concerning the younger woman's relations with men. Her disapproval about the affair with the photographer had been both unsurprising and at the same time intensely dispiriting.

Indeed, they didn't speak for several weeks after Natasha told her about it. Constance sent vaguely petulant notes wondering who was in Natasha's life now. It was almost as if she wanted Natasha only for herself. She had a grown daughter with whom she didn't get along very well, and on occasion Natasha wondered if the other saw her as a kind of surrogate.

So she worried some about the Jamaica trip.

Constance's money was from her father's side of the family. The old man had bought a four-mile strip of shoreline that nobody wanted near Pensacola, and in his last years he often talked about this one lucky chance of his: buying a piece of swampy lowland property that he ended up selling, acre by acre, to the hotel chains. Constance herself was in possession of a large house in Malibu, where her daughter lived alone, and a condominium in Manhattan overlooking Central Park. She was renting that to a city official. She now lived temporarily in an apartment near Old Orchard Beach, on Maine's southern coast, where she was having a house custom-built for herself. Jamaica was a yearly trip for her.

That afternoon on the last day of August, Natasha left her apartment for good and headed for National Airport. While waiting for her flight, she called Faulk to apologize for her sharpness earlier.

"I'm happy about us," he said. "And I want people to know it."

"But it really wouldn't have been the right time to say anything, Michael. I think it would've made the poor man feel silly after all his talk about my career in politics."

"He's going to feel silly anyway, when he knows."

"Well, just tell him I didn't have the courage or something like that. In a way I *didn't* have the courage."

Faulk's sigh this time was not pronounced, nor intended to be anything but itself. "You have fun, darling," he said. There was so much he did not know about her, and just now it made her anxious.

"I'll call you each day," she said.

"You don't have to do that. Just be careful."

"I will. You, too." He would fly to Washington at the end of next week and then take a train to New York on Monday for the wedding of a family friend. How strange, he had said, to know that he would not be the one conducting the ceremony.

"I'll only be in town the one night," he said. "But the wedding's in the afternoon, and since it's down where the World Trade Center is, I just might go in the morning and have a look at the city from one of the towers. Be fun to get breakfast a hundred floors up."

"I have to call Iris now."

"I'll look in on her before I go. And I guess I'll have to try like hell *not* to see Tom Norland when I get to D.C."

"Michael."

"I'm taking an Amtrak express up to New York Monday, to make the rehearsal dinner. Dad and Trixie will arrive around two in the afternoon. The wedding's midday Tuesday, so I'll be back in Washington late that night."

"I'll call you from paradise," Natasha said.

"Be careful in those waves. Promise?"

She promised. Then: "And you don't go dancing in the clubs down in the Village."

"Not much of that on Monday night, with two elderly people in tow. Anyway, there's no riptides down there. I'm going to be with Dad, Trixie, and the wonderful Ruhms of Brooklyn, New York, very generous but devoutly conservative Christians. We'll be downtown. Rehearsal dinner Monday evening, wedding and recep-tion the following noon, with the real possibility that all of it will have to be endured in the absence of anything but fruit punch to drink because the groom's elderly old aunt Linda gets upset at the sight of anything stronger. Probably won't be any dancing, either. Maybe just a couple pictures of the city from high up."

"I'll miss you," she said. "Even being in paradise."

After they hung up, she sat in a small airport café, drinking cof-fee, feeling strangely bereft. It would be good to see Constance, in spite of the older woman's occasional tendency to be magisterial.

Poor Constance was like that with her grown child as well, and it was the reason the daughter wasn't coming to Jamaica and Nata-sha was. The daughter, against her mother's wishes, had purchased an antiques store in Malibu, using money given her upon gradua-tion, last June, from law school at Yale.

The two were scarcely speaking.

Natasha thought about being with Constance in the middle of this complication.

Out the window to her left, beyond the line of planes at their gates, she saw the Washington Monument, small in the distance, with two stripes of shadow on it, the shadows moving up and dissolving in sunlight. She reflected that she would not miss this city as much as she had thought she might when she first started thinking of leaving it. Well, she was about to enter a whole new life, a different way of being in the world. The wife of an ex-priest. She sighed, thinking of it. "Help," she said, low, under her breath. It was as close as she ever got to prayer. She started to order another coffee but then thought better of it and asked for hot water instead. She sipped that, warming herself from the inside. And she called Marsha Trunan. There was only Marsha's voice: "You know what to do after the beep."

"I'm at the airport. Getting ready to fly down and see Constance. Be back in Memphis in a couple of weeks. I'll call you from there. I'm sorry I've been so stupid about spending time. I'll do better." She broke the connection and felt suddenly so sad that she had to fight back tears. She went to the bar and ordered a whiskey and tossed it back, standing there.

The bartender was a tall round-faced man with arching bushy eyebrows and dark red lips. He stared.

"Flight nerves," she told him, picking up her bag.

The plane was boarding.

In Jamaica—happily absorbed by the fresh charms of the place, the lovely aqua-colored waters of the Caribbean out her window, and the soft tropical evenings spent in surprisingly relaxed chatter, drinking cool rum cocktails and eating wonderful spicy meals of jerk chicken and ackee with salt fish—she realized again how pervasive her unhappiness had been, and she remembered reading somewhere that the most terrifying thing about despair was that it was unaware of itself as being despair.

The resort was near Kingston, a complex of bungalows ranged around a single hotel-sized building that stood like a sandy-colored fortress above the beach. It was all owned by an elderly German woman named Maria Ratzibungen and her two sons, each from a different father—the older from an industrialist named Dieter Ratzibungen, and the younger from a lover of Maria's as her marriage was ending. This man had tried suicide when he couldn't have her and had ended by deranging himself with years of drinking, living on the island within sight of her and his growing son. He was still a figure in their lives, surfacing now and then, looking like someone who had come to the island from a shipwreck. His name was Lawton. Constance had pressed Mrs. Ratzibungen to tell the story on the night she and Natasha arrived. Mrs. Ratzibungen and Constance were friends from Constance's earlier visits. Neither of the German woman's sons seemed to have any other family. They were both in their forties and looked like twins, though they were separated by four years. Their mother's speech was pleasantly accented, but they spoke impeccable English, having been raised among relatives of their grandparents in London—German Jews on their mother's side who'd had cousins in Manchester and had fled to England in 1934. The older one was forty-eight and went by the nickname Ratzi. Neither Constance nor Natasha saw Ratzi's brother after their first day on the island.

All Mrs. Ratzibungen's employees—cooks, waitstaff, those who kept the rooms—were Jamaican, and they dressed according to the traditions of life in the tropics: colorful skirts, blouses, and headscarves made from calico for the women; light shirts full of designs with flowers, loud colors in patterns, or depictions of sailboats, rising fish in the surf, or palm trees in the sun for the men. The men all wore shorts, even in the evenings. Mrs. Ratzibungen's sons had taken to the island way of dressing.

Natasha got a tan and spent hours swimming. She called Faulk on the third day, and he told her that his father had decided not to attend the Ruhm wedding after all, because a mild case of gout had made it painful to walk. "So it's only going to be me there, and it's just as well, I guess. But, you know, I'm actually going to miss the old apostate."

"We'll go see him. As soon as we're settled. Let's."

"You sound very happy."

"It's beautiful here. I wish you could see it."

"Maybe I'll take you back there one birthday."

"I mean it, you really will love it."

"And we will go visit the old man in Little Rock. Though he'll be insufferable about my leaving the clergy, you can bet on that. Vindication. He'll use the word."

"I'll listen for it."

He laughed. "Think of it. We'll go visit people, a married couple going around and shining for everybody."

"And we'll spend weekends in Jamaica," she said.

"We'll be island people half the year."

"We'll smell like coconut oil all the time."

"You're wonderful," he said.

They began a pattern where they talked every other morning. He would call her, and the sound of his voice on the other end of the line was a warm reminder of the new life.

Her twelfth day there, she arose and looked out her window at the sea. The morning was gorgeous, white sand and emerald ocean stretching on into dark blue distance, the wide sky without a cloud, showing all the shades of the one color.

Fire

I

Faulk woke before light on that morning with a headache from too much wine. The airlessness of the room wasn't helping. With a familiar sense of taking his punishment, he got up and swallowed some aspirin and a lot of water, then took a cool shower, and, without feeling any relief, lay back down to try reading for a spell. The wedding wouldn't take place until noon, more than seven hours away, at Trinity Church, but he would not go down to the towers for breakfast. In the first place, he lacked the appetite, and finally he was too hungover to do much of anything but lie there and suffer it. The Marriott Downtown, three blocks from the church, was where the rehearsal dinner had been and where the groom's whole family was staying. Faulk had booked himself a room uptown, and before the rehearsal evening was over, he was glad of this.

He had been unready for the well-meaning but essentially prying talk arising from the fact that he was not conducting the wedding ceremony. It placed him at a slight remove from everyone, as if they were all wondering about him.

Theo Ruhm and Faulk's father had gone to college together; they had been friends for fifty years. Theo considered Faulk another son, and, when they were all boys, his four sons were like brothers. The groom, Charlie, was the youngest and the last to be married. Faulk had performed the ceremony for the three older ones, each in turn.

Everybody was solicitous of him—a couple of people called him Father Faulk and then blanched from embarrassment—and they all wanted to know how he was doing. He could not help hearing a note of concern in their voices, doubtless stemming from the belief that leaving the clergy involved something more complicated for him than the wish for a change. In any case, it seemed unpleasantly clear to him that to these kindly people the very idea was in need of some kind of explication: a man in his late forties leaving a twenty-year vocation for any reason, even if it was only to "seek happiness elsewhere."

Theo Ruhm was particularly interested and wanted details and wasn't shy about asking. He cornered Faulk at the entrance to the large ballroom where the rehearsal dinner was to be held, handed him a glass of wine, and said, "So tell me."

"There's really not much to tell."

"Hey—this is *me* you're talking to."

"Well, but there really *isn't* much to tell."

Ruhm merely gazed at him, smiling.

"It stopped meaning anything to me, you know, Theo? I can't explain it beyond that."

"You turning into an atheist, like your old man?"

"Oh, no. Not at all."

"He's the most religious atheist I ever saw. Been arguing with God his whole life. I still get pissed at him when he starts in about it. And I still love him like a brother."

"He'll think he's *won* something with my leaving the priesthood."

"So," Theo Ruhm said. "How do you—*quit*, exactly, in your line of work."

"I went to see my superior. The—the senior warden of the vestry. Who's a friend."

"And what did he say?"

Faulk looked at him. "You don't really want to hear all this do you? *Today?*"

"You don't think I'd be interested about what you go through?"

"You're a good man, Mr. Ruhm."

"Well," Theo went on, raising his drink, "the prohibitionist aunt didn't come, so we can have as much as we want of this. And it's a happy time. I'm sorry Leander's missing it. I was looking forward to meeting Trixie and having her meet my lady."

"I was looking forward to seeing them, too," Faulk said. "I've only spoken to Trixie on the phone a couple times myself."

"I hope you're happy, Michael," said Ruhm, patting his upper arm.

"I am. And I'm happy for you, too, Theo."

The Ruhms had been together only a couple of years, the boys' mother having left Theo a decade ago to pursue happiness elsewhere. The phrase went through Faulk's mind, an evil little turn, and he grasped the other's hand and congratulated him on the marriage of his youngest son. The boys' mother, Cheryl, was on the other side of the room celebrating with her side of the family and her new husband, who was a football coach. The new husband's capacity for this kind of cheerfulness was a cause for worry, and even now he lifted a cocktail and drained it. Faulk saw this, wondering at the failure of kindness in everything he felt, standing there with his glass of wine in his hand and his changed life showing in his face. He wished Natasha could be with him, and the thought of her soothed him.

"You'll like Natasha," he said to Ruhm, but the older man was already distracted, greeting a business associate whose bushy red mustache looked as though it had been glued on, completely covering his mouth.

Faulk moved to another part of the room. A band was setting up, five young men with the apathetic look of being hired for the purpose of background music.

Faulk watched them, wishing he was in Tennessee. Or Jamaica. He had a glass of bourbon at the cash bar, then switched back to wine.

And he faltered through the afternoon, repressing the bad temper that troubled him when his new circumstance surfaced in the talk, striving for patience with his own wearisome explanations, the same anemic phrases others used over and over, phrases he hated—*self-fulfillment, new challenges, time to move on*—phrases that, discouragingly enough, contained an element of truth. He drank several more glasses of Burgundy before the sit-down for the rehearsal dinner. It was not noticed, particularly, because there was plenty to drink and no one was holding back. But when, at dinner, he realized that the alcohol was having an effect on him, he removed himself quietly and took a cab back to the hotel, where he had another whiskey and went to bed with the room spinning.

There, sleepless, he thought of his last meeting with Father Clenon, where he actually said the words "I want to renounce my vows." He had come back from Washington, and Natasha. He went over the failures of his priesthood, and talking about it was like getting out of jail. Father Clenon stared at him for a long time. Finally he said, "Take a month? For me?"

"Let me do it now," said Faulk. "For *me*."

The other continued to stare, and there was something bitterly forbearing in his gaze. "Write the letter when you're sure," he said. "Let's just put it that way."

And so Faulk had waited through that following week.

Now, in the dark of predawn, he tried to read and couldn't. His mind kept wandering to the strangeness of being outside the fold—someone had used the term—and to random images from the evening before. He had seen so many wedding gatherings. The blur of them made his mind ache.

How tired he was of being the one to whom others felt free to unpack their sorrows. Recognizing the self-centeredness of the feeling, he tried to think of something else. But it was true that while his own marriage was deteriorating he had listened to the marriage troubles of countless others, had endured his own suffering all alone, going through each day with the weight of it on his heart. And Joan was discreet. No one had the slightest inkling. Life went on that way for the more than two years it took her to decide.

He turned the television on and flicked through the channels. Old shows, news, commercial broadcasts, movies. Everything in progress, nothing beginning. He felt locked away from the world where all this was happening. It was unnerving, and yet vaguely agreeable, like being proved right about something.

Ten minutes after 5:00 a.m.

He turned the television off, took a Xanax, and lay down to try going back to sleep. And sleep came, with stealth. He saw Natasha standing by the window, going on about the pretty water of the river. She said "river" and he corrected her. *It's not a river, darling.*

Yes, it is, she said with unfamiliar insistence.

No, it's the Mediterranean Sea, he told her, aware now that this was a dream, and yet feeling quite certain that what he had said made perfect sense. In the next instant, he experienced the suspicion that he was wrong and felt an unreasonable terror of the possibility. It was the *Life or Death* of dreams, and he was casting about in his mind for the answer, which kept eluding him. Finally he could only repeat helplessly "The Mediterranean Sea," like a prayer, the one explicable thing in the dream, and then that was obliterated, too, and he was not even dreaming anymore. Mysteriously, he was also aware of the blankness.

He woke shortly after nine with a sense of having worked his way up from an awful depth to consciousness. But the headache was gone. Rising, a bit groggy from the drug, he stumbled to the window and looked out. It was a perfect day for a wedding. "There it is," he said aloud, smiling at the infinite rinsed sky stretching away over the tall roofs of the city with the small cylindrical water tanks and thickets of antennas and wires. "The Mediterranean Sea."

It came to him that he did not feel like attending a wedding, even this one, with its happy couple and proud father. Just now, the thought oppressed him.

He made his way to the bathroom and cleaned his teeth, then moved to the closet and started to dress, thinking of calling Natasha, though it was well past the time. She would already have left for the beach. He decided to try anyway, wanting to tell her about the dream. A recorded voice said that the volume of calls was too much and to try the number later. He pushed the button for the front desk and waited. No answer. Finally he lay back down, hands behind his head, and drifted a little, intending to sit up and try again in a moment. He looked at his watch and remembered that she was an hour behind him.

2

Because it was the day of the wedding in New York, Natasha did not expect to hear from him. This was her last day in Jamaica. She and Constance went out to the beach and had an hour sunning themselves and reading. Natasha stepped into the clear shallows and looked down at her feet in the sand. The water was cold, clean, and lucid, with its lime green color as you looked across it, and you could almost see the place in the distance where it began turning to the deepest blue. The sand was smooth and perfectly consistent, as though it had been designed and produced for human feet to track in it. She turned and looked back at Constance, who lay on her multicolored blanket, one arm across her face, one leg bent at the knee. The picture of relaxation. Natasha wondered why people weren't strolling down to the beach, as on all the other mornings. "You suppose this is some kind of holy day?" she called to her friend. Constance raised her head and looked at her, then held both hands up, a shrugging motion, and went back to her sunbathing.

Natasha turned to look out at the waves coming toward her, and thought of Faulk. There was so much happiness to come, and now she made an effort not to allow it into her thoughts—as if to anticipate the fond future might render it precarious: her new life in Tennessee and her journey back to Europe in the spring. She saw herself painting in a sunlit room with the lovely countryside of Provence out the window and Michael Faulk somewhere close by, writing perhaps. Imagining this scene, she experienced suddenly a dark shift inside. She dipped her hands in the water and moved them back and forth, watching the swirls, concentrating on the traces running from the ends of her fingers. She saw the gulls gliding low across the iridescent surface and inwardly searched for the contentment she had just been feeling so strongly. Of course this propensity for the flow of her thoughts to shade into darkness was not new, and she had learned to accept it. But with Faulk she had come to believe she could grow out of it at last—that it would fade, becoming only an aspect of past life.

She had never known anything like this passion, and today's crossing shadow was only that he was so far away. With the thousands of miles between them, it was natural to fear that the world might take him from her.

Though the unease she felt, missing him, brought on other worries.

His experience of the world was indeed unlike her own, and occasionally his seriousness about religion concerned her. The way his eyes glittered as he uttered the phrases of his faith. His fervor sometimes produced in her an irksome displeasure, which she had labored to stifle. Occasionally, she had made light of it, teasing him with the intent of bringing him back to earth about sounding too priestly.

At times her teasing was received in a less-than-lighthearted manner. "There's stuff I'd rather not ponder," he said. "Or be too conscious of. Thoughts that lead nowhere and only end in pain."

"So you don't question?" she asked him.

"I don't expect an answer to the questions. So I try not to ask them."

"And you've succeeded in that?"

"Failure," he said with that sidelong smile, "is rampant where I live."

How he fascinated her! She was sure now that she had never been in love before, had never even gotten near it. And there was something else, too: in the last few days, watching Constance conduct business over the phone with contractors about the design of the Maine house, she had begun to receive intimations about how much she, Natasha, had let the job in Washington take over her life. She had accepted the position merely to make enough money to spend a year in France painting, and the very effort to make possible the hoped-for journey had somehow diluted the hope itself. Constance's focus was that house. She was continually rethinking everything about it, wanting the design to be in keeping with new ideas she had about the efficient use of energy and the least possible impact on the wildlife in the vicinity. It was her passion; it gave her definition and purpose.

Natasha stood in the cold water of the beach and thought about her own lack of some central resolve. She had dreamed of putting together a real body of work, a portfolio of paintings and drawings, too, and when actually painting she had always felt so fresh and glad. Yet she had let anything and everything, including her own wandering in the world, take precedence. And perhaps this had to do with her particular beginnings. After all, her earliest memories were of crisis, near and loving presences inexplicably taken away, first into distance and then into the limitless far quiet of the sky—something gravely wrong and her grandmother crying in the nights. Teachers had told her she was talented. Friends had marveled at what she could bring about with the stroke of a brush, and she had wasted so much time, so much of her young life chasing after some nameless inkling of happiness, as if she might come to a place, a physical *somewhere else*, where she would find whatever it was she had always missed, the right combination of nourishment for her soul, a sense of completion, and, at long last—she could admit it to herself now—relief. Solace.

Here, on this beach in Jamaica, remembering her plans with Faulk, she felt that very thing, that sighing release of the long pressure, and she murmured "My darling," as though he were standing at her side. She looked at the shimmering horizon with its small white triangle of a single sailboat crossing.

Constance called to her from the beach. "Let's go eat."

Walking up to the resort, they saw Ratzi standing in the entrance. Natasha greeted him with a little wave and then, seeing the strange look on his face, paused and waited for him to speak.

He walked up to her and took her by the arms. She thought something had happened to Iris. But then he turned to Constance, and now she thought of Constance's daughter. Ratzi stood back, almost bowing, wringing his small white hands. "Awful." His voice was shaky. "I'm so sorry. It's terrible. Terrible. You must come." He went along the walk, and they followed, hurrying. Now Natasha thought that something must have happened to Maria Ratzibungen.

They entered the lobby, with its slowly turning ceiling fan and its plush chairs and benches and all the shapes of civilized enjoyment and recreation, the paintings and the statuary and the lush green plants, leaves the size of capes, several of which now screened some of the people—an alarming number of people—gathered there. The television was on. Natasha heard the voice of a newswoman say the phrase "minutes past the hour." On the screen was a wide panorama of New York with smoke rising from it, a video taken from a distance, probably from a traffic helicopter. It did not quite register in her consciousness. It was something bad in the city. News. In the twelve days she had been here, she had not seen anyone watching this TV, which was hung from black wires on the side wall; only a few of the rooms had TVs in them. Now everyone crowded nearer the screen, and through the gathered others, Natasha saw the Twin Towers capped by the churning clouds of smoke. A little frame inside the larger picture showed the second plane cruising into its own shocking ball of flame.

"My God," Constance said.

"What happened?" said Natasha, feeling the helpless absurdity of the question. Then, under her breath: "Michael's there." No one spoke. They were all staring at the screen. The images were like elements of an awful dream, one that played out impersonally, "witness dreams," Natasha had always called them, where she saw things in the distance, as if she had just happened upon them in some series of events unwinding in general unconsciousness, a property of night, set to prey on anyone sleeping at that hour. On the television with its pixels and little strands of failed light, doubtless from a cameraman in a helicopter, she saw what she came to realize was a man and a woman standing in the open side of one of the buildings. They were holding hands; you could see that they were holding hands, flames licking up the widely spaced vertical steel ribs on either side of them. They seemed to falter, and then they leaped, and let go of each other, separating and disappearing into the smoke.

Everyone in the lobby of the hotel in far-off Jamaica screamed.

The newswoman went on talking, speaking carefully, slowly, in clipped phrases, inflectionless, concentrating on the smallest details, as a person might think of measurements and minutiae in order to preserve some hold on sanity. And now the camera caught another body hurtling down, that of a man, his suit jacket open to a white shirt and tie. The female newscaster tried to report it. "My God, are you seeing this," she got out in a tearful voice. A video cameraman from a helicopter hovering near one of the openings made by the planes focused on a woman in light orange slacks and a dark blue blouse standing in the ruin and smoke. She actually appeared calm, so small there in the wide gash with all the destruction behind and around her. She lifted her hand and waved. That simple, forlorn, graceful motion looked almost like a greeting. The mind wouldn't accept what it really was. She clung to the shattered place at the edge of the opening, leaning out slightly, and then turning, facing into the rubble edge of the wall. When smoke or steam began to come from her whole body, the image abruptly shifted, the cameraman evidently having turned the camera away from what was coming.

As the first tower began to collapse, another cry went up among the people in the lobby, and the young newscaster's voice carried above it. "I believe there's been some kind of further explosion. Are you seeing this?"

No one spoke. The crowd gathered in a tighter circle around the screen, another news voice talking about the Pentagon in Washington, D.C., and still the cameras in New York showed the churning ash and smoke, the street-level cameras capturing the panic, people running, the yellowish-brown dust covering everything.

"The whole of southern Manhattan's coated with this dust now," said a male voice on the TV.

And Natasha turned to Constance. "Michael's *there*. He was talking about going to the top of—he said he was—he was going up to the top of—he was—"

The other woman stared, beginning to comprehend.

Natasha, gasping for breath, felt all the strength go out of her legs. Constance gripped her by the arms. "We don't know anything definite," she said. "We don't know anything. He's probably not anywhere near it. Natasha, listen to me."

Crying, Natasha said, "I think he—I can't—no. No."

"He's probably still asleep in the hotel. There's always a long line down there. And—and listen. I was there a couple of years ago, and I don't think you can get up to the observation deck until something like ten o'clock. Now, really, honey. I remember that."

They were both quiet a moment, and they saw the second tower collapse.

"Oh my God," Constance said. "Those poor people. Those poor, poor people."

"I have to get home," Natasha told her, beginning to cry. "Oh, I have to go home. I want to go home."

3

Faulk rose from the bed and finished dressing, and as he was tying his shoes the phone rang. He thought it might be the hotel desk.

It was Aunt Clara. "You all right?"

"Hey," he said.

"Where are you?"

"My hotel room."

"Look out the window."

"I was just doing that."

"And you're all right."

"Clara?"

"Turn the TV on."

He reached behind him on the bed to get the remote. "What is it?"

"They've hit the World Trade Center."

The television came to light, and there were the towers, burning. He looked back out the window and saw the spotless sky. "*Who* hit them."

"Planes. Extremists. Airliners. *Some*body."

"Airliners?" he said. Then: "Airliners."

"Where are you?" Clara said.

"Fifty-Fourth Street."

"You tried calling Natasha?"

"They'll be out at the beach."

"Gotta try leaving a message for her."

"My God," Faulk said, watching the clip of the second plane hitting.

"They're saying another one hit the Pentagon."

He stared at the bloom of fire in the side of tower one being played over and over—the second plane. For a few moments, Aunt Clara just breathed into the phone, and he listened. "Are you okay?" he said.

"I'm all right. But oh, God, how many people—"

"These were *passenger* planes?"

"Are you looking at it? Planes. Yes."

As the first tower went down, the newswoman began breathlessly repeating the word *incredulous.* Faulk, watching it happen, said to Clara, "The building's collapsing."

Silence.

"Clara?"

When he understood that the line was dead, he tried once more. Nothing. And no answer at the front desk, either. Hurriedly, he packed his bag and then realized there was nowhere to go. He made another attempt to call Clara, with no success. He tried long distance to Jamaica, got the ring, but the phone simply went on ringing. Sitting at the end of the bed, he waited. No answer. He put the receiver back in its place and then picked it up and punched the number again. Nothing.

There wasn't anything else to do but watch. He saw the second tower collapse. He tried to pray. At last he made still another attempt to phone Jamaica. Now there was no signal at all. He hung up, and almost immediately it rang. It was his father. "You're okay," the old man said almost as though trying to reassure him. "I just talked to Clara."

"I'm way up on Fifty-Fourth Street. I lost her. The line went dead."

"That's what she said. You believe this shit?"

"No."

"I'd better call her back. She thinks the building you're in might've collapsed because the connection got broken and you were talking about the building collapsing. She was pretty upset. And I told her there wasn't anything about buildings collapsing uptown. But she couldn't get through."

"Tell her I'm okay."

"When're you getting out of there?"

"I don't know yet. Today for sure now if I can. I want to see if I can get hold of Theo."

"Get on out of there, Son. You don't know what else they might be planning."

"I'll let you know," Faulk told him.

"I'm gonna tell Clara you'll be in later today."

"Yes, do."

After he hung up, he tried to open the line, but it was dead again. He pushed the buttons down, and there was a dial tone. But nothing happened—nothing interrupted the dial tone.

Downstairs, the lobby was crowded and quiet. People were checking out and checking in as usual. He waited in line with his bag. No one appeared willing to look at anyone else. It was very quiet. He went out to Fifty-Fourth Street. There was a subdued something even in the normal traffic sounds. The sunny sky was unchanged. When he got over to Fifth Avenue, he heard the sirens, and looking south he saw the massive ash-colored cloud. The cloud was bizarrely contained, one spiral-shaped strand extending out from it to great height. He saw clear pale sky above it all.

He started down the avenue. Trinity Church, the planned site of the wedding ceremony, was in the vicinity of the World Trade Center. Yesterday, he had seen the towers from the window as the train neared the city, and seeing the two structures looming above everything, gleaming with reflected sunlight, he thought of being inside, high up, looking out.

Remembering this made him momentarily short of breath. He went to the curb, intending to flag down a cab. But none of the cabs were stopping. Most of them were coming from the opposite direction.

It occurred to him then that he was in fact headed to where the calamity was taking place. There would be no wedding today. He stopped. The entire morning remained. He had been wandering south. His headache had returned; his mouth was dry. The street now seemed nearly deserted. He saw some people sitting in a sandwich shop with a phone booth at the back. No one seemed to notice him. They were all talking quietly, huddled together, or simply staring with dread out at the sunlight and the buildings opposite. A woman sat crying while two others attempted to calm her.

In the phone booth he was absurdly elated to find that there was a dial tone and that the phone was working when he touched the numbers. He called the downtown Marriott, and to his surprise someone picked up, a woman, who sounded hurried but nothing like someone in the grip of panic. He asked for Theo Ruhm, and she immediately clicked off. He heard a buzzing, and Ruhm answered. "Hello." It was nearly a shout.

Faulk said, "This is Michael."

"It's awful," Theo Ruhm moaned. "Total confusion. Nobody can get ahold of anybody. But the wedding's off. They're setting up to do triage at the church. *Triage*, for Christ's sake. Oh, God—I saw it. I went over there and saw everything. It's awful. We're headed out. Back to the house. Can you get here?"

"I'm almost to Penn Station," Faulk said. "I'm going down to D.C."

"They hit D.C., too." Theo began to cry. "The sons of bitches."

"Is everybody all right?"

"We're all going home. If you can get to Brooklyn, you know you're welcome."

"I'm gonna try for D.C.," Faulk said. The other had hung up. He put another quarter in and tried to call Iris, Aunt Clara, and then Jamaica. Nothing was going through.

He went out and walked down the blocks, hearing the sirens, his head throbbing, the gritty air smelling of exhaust and drywall and plastic and, scarily, of jet fuel. All his training and all the years of practicing his vocation rose in him, and he looked for some way to help those he encountered on the street—but no one looked at him; they were all moving as if in a kind of severe blundering trance, northward.

4

It was impossible for Natasha to absorb what she saw as something really happening. She couldn't think past the images on the television.

In the crowded lobby, people were lined up at the row of public phones, waiting to try calling relatives in the States. She saw several people with cell phones, but no one was having any success. There were six wall phones. The sixth was broken, the wire hanging from the silver cabinet without a receiver.

The phone lines to the United States were overloaded. But people kept trying. They kept redialing and putting money into the phones while the crowd waited behind them.

There was a movement to drive the twenty miles to Kingston, to try calling from there. Several people stepped forward, Natasha and Constance among them. They climbed into a van with three older women in shorts and blouses who wore big straw hats and sunglasses, a very heavy middle-aged man in a flowered Jamaican shirt, and a thin, ascetic-looking man in his thirties, whom none of them had seen before. The three women were together. They muttered back and forth about where they would sit, getting settled, and then they were still. Natasha saw the strands of red hair coming down over the ears of the nearest one. No one spoke. Ratzi drove. Constance was in the passenger seat in front; Natasha was in the middle seat, next to the window, the two other men on her right. The three ladies had jammed together in the far back. They were sniffling and murmuring to one another, and it sounded like a kind of whisper argument. Constance kept chewing her cuticles and sighing, staring out at the narrow road. She looked back at Natasha and repeated, "It doesn't open until something like ten o'clock. I'm certain of it. He couldn't have been in either building yet unless he worked there."

One of the women in back, the one with the red hair, said, "I lived in New York for thirty-three years. Those buildings don't open to the public until nine-thirty."

"There," Constance said. "See?"

"You have someone in New York?" the woman said to Natasha. "Yes."

"My whole family's there. In Queens." She sniffled. "My whole family. I'm so afraid for them. What else is going to happen?"

Ratzi turned the radio on, but it was all static. He kept turning the dial. It had been mostly static before, Natasha remembered, though it was difficult not to think of it as part of the catastrophe. Palm trees shaded the road thinly on both sides. There were mountains to the left. Through the palms to the right was the sea with its repeating foamy waves tumbling across the green surface and crashing ashore. The sight seemed unreal, pitilessly immaculate in the clarity of the sun. She felt sick to her stomach, looking at it, so beautiful, and it occurred to her that there was something ruthlessly insensible, blank, heartless, about the exquisite beach and every natural wonder out the window of the Jeep she and Constance rode in with the six silent others. Absurdly, she thought of the senator's expansive back lawn and the little pleading statues.

Now the young man spoke. "It must have been the pilots. They must've infiltrated the pilot force."

"Force?" Constance said.

"The roster of pilots," said the heavy man in the flower-print shirt. He had his big hands folded across his belly. His eyes were red and shadowed, and the sclera were faintly yellow. The odor of alcohol came from him through strong cologne. He had a bulbous nose, with little red lines forking across the tip of it.

"Surely no one could force a pilot to do that to his own plane?" Ratzi said.

No one answered. The young man turned to Natasha. "My name is Nicholas Duego."

Constance glared back at him from the front seat.

He shrugged and then muttered low, dispiritedly, as if it weren't even worth saying, "We might as well know who we are."

"You an American?" Constance asked.

"Cuban American." His demeanor changed slightly. He was plainly buoyed by the question and felt the need to talk. "On my father's side. I lived in Cuba. We went to Canada for a vacation when I was nine years old, and my father got us to Detroit. We moved to Orlando, Florida, when I was twelve. My father was a horse trainer. I did not speak English until I was ten." Constance stared. There was a curious formality in his speech. No one else said anything, and after going on a little more he seemed to wind down, with a sort of sullen embarrassment. "We might as well know," he muttered into the silence of the others.

On the outskirts of Kingston, houses and huts and shacks lined the road, teeming with Jamaicans, all going about the business of life in their native city. Children ran and played under the spray of water hoses, and there were many roadside stands selling goods—coffee, exotic fruits, vegetables, barrel-cooked meat and fish. The proprietors stared after the crowded car as it moved by into the busy stream of traffic, but people on the streets scarcely glanced at them. On the side of one building was a big painting of an imperial-looking black face superimposed on the form of a lion, with the phrase JAH RASTAFARI below it.

"What's that?" said the heavy man.

"It's a religion," Ratzi said.

When they reached Kingston city center, they saw more roadside stands, including one built out of bamboo and containing bins of melting ice in which stood dozens of different kinds of bottled beer. They drove past a big crowded marketplace under a long bamboo roof. There were a lot of taxis—more than usual, it seemed. The Hilton was too crowded. Every American was trying to contact home. When Natasha finally got to a phone, the voice on the other end said all lines were busy. She tried her contact numbers for Faulk. His cell phone, the hotel. And she tried Iris, Aunt Clara.

Nothing was getting through. Every circuit into the United States was over capacity. She went to one of the four televisions in the big orange-carpeted, palm-shaded lounge and watched with the others. She had missed the news about the fourth plane—the one in Pennsylvania—and she saw the reporting about that, and when the TV showed the flames and smoke still erupting out of the side of the Pentagon, she thought of all her friends on Capitol Hill. Constance had gone into the English-style pub and was watching the television there. She had ordered a drink. Natasha sat across from her and buried her face in her hands. "I'm numb. I can't think."

"You have to know I'm right," Constance said. "He couldn't have been there."

"If I could just get through to him."

"You heard the lady in the car."

"I just want to talk to him and know he wasn't anywhere near it."

"I'll get you a drink," Constance said. "This is Campari and soda. You want one?"

"How can you drink?"

"Are you kidding? Look at this place."

It was true. Everyone was drinking. The room was crowded, and everyone had something in hand.

"It's sort of what we have instead of Valium," Constance said with a soft bitter laugh.

They watched the people out on the sidewalk. Many of them—doubtless Americans—hurrying aimlessly one way and then another, some clearly panic-stricken, unable to decide where to turn. An elderly couple in ridiculously unfitted clothes—bright white long-sleeve shirts and silly-looking bell-bottom red slacks, stopped on one corner, crossed the street, then turned and waited and crossed back, and went on. Natasha felt suddenly so tremendously sorry for them that she found herself weeping again. It was as if she had just awakened from a dream of crying to discover that she was indeed crying.

"Here, baby," Constance said, reaching to touch her cheek with a handkerchief. "It's gonna be fine. You'll see."

Many people dressed for holidays in the sun were gathering in front of the hotels and restaurants on that side. They all appeared confused and harried.

"The airlines are grounded," Constance said. "No flights. We're stuck here. *Stuck* here. You know that? Jesus Christ. We're stuck."

The news on the hotel televisions kept replaying the pictures: the planes slamming in, smoke towering skyward, clear sky beyond the city, devastation, the immense squat black toadstool of a cloud over its southern end—and the buildings collapsing in that terrifying straight-downward, floor-upon-floor, pancaking way, like thick gray powder.

The ride back from Kingston was completely silent. The three ladies had disappeared into the streets, so it was just Natasha and Constance and the three men. They filed out of the van and back into the lobby of the resort's central building, where others still watched the television with its inexhaustible voices and images, the pundits all weighing in, the discussions of the short presidential speech, and the fact that the president at first seemed to be running—or flying—away, Air Force One heading west for a thousand miles before turning around.

Natasha went up to her room and lay down. A fit of low, breathless crying came over her. The window was bright with sun, and the wind blew through. She turned, pulled the blanket over her shoulder, and lay there trembling. The chill persisted, and though she might have allowed herself to fall asleep, nothing like drowsiness came to her—she was as wide awake as she had ever been in her life. She wiped her eyes with the backs of her hands and finally pulled the blanket high over the side of her face and breathed into her palms.

A while later Constance came and knocked on the door and called to her. She got up and opened it and then walked back to the bed. Constance followed her into the room. "I'm sure he's fine. He's probably trying to call you."

The younger woman sat up and put her feet on the floor. "I can't stay here."

"Well, there's nowhere to go."

"I mean this room." She stood and looked at the open French doors leading to the balcony, showing the sea and the sunny sky and the broad pure beach, where, now, there was no one.

"Imagine," Constance said. "We'll always feel a kind of hatred for this place now. This is where it happened to *us*."

"I can't stand it here." Natasha moved toward the other window that looked out on the mountains to the east.

"You want to go down to the water? It's almost lunchtime."

"I can't eat."

"Then let's have more to drink. I'd like to get drunk if it's all right with you."

Natasha saw something broken and frightened in the other woman's round, double-chinned face, and she put her arms around her. They stood there embracing, hearing the sounds of others moving down the hallway and still others on the patio below. Someone laughed, a young boy—you could hear the edge of adolescence in the scratchy notes, that lean, pointless exuberance. It seemed excruciatingly out of place, incongruous, even ill spirited, an assault. In the next instant, a voice spoke harshly in Spanish, and the laughing stopped.

Downstairs, the lobby was still crowded, the television blaring. They went past it to the outside patio, where meals were served, a wide veranda in sunlight overlooking the beach. Several other people were already seated at the tables near the stone balustrade. At the farthest table sat the two men who had been with them in the van. They were not talking or looking at each other, but they were together, with the air of strangers clinging to the familiar, or near familiar. The younger one, Nicholas Duego, stood and waved at them.

"Well?" Constance said.

Natasha went with her to the table. It was better to be in company. They sat down, and the waitress came over. The waitress was a beautiful island woman named Grace, and they knew her. "What will it be for you?" Grace said to them with a note of solicitousness. There had existed a sardonic, teasing banter between her and her customers until this day. She had played a version of herself, a performance—an island character with no need of these tourists and interlopers—and now all her normal rosy, affectionate disrespect was gone, replaced by gentle concern. The difference was disheartening.

"Piña colada, Grace," Constance said. Her voice carried, and Natasha realized how unnaturally quiet it was, turning to look at the other tables, where people were alone or with others, not saying much, staring, some of them, or concentrating on their meals. At one table the three elderly ladies sat, with untouched glasses of beer before them.

"How did they get back?" Constance said, then turned to Grace. "Make it a double, will you?"

"Yes, mum. And the young miss?" Grace was not more than five years older than Natasha. Her eyes were midnight dark and full of mournful kindliness. She wore a floor-length wraparound skirt, and her wild brown hair was tied in an impossibly big tangle atop her head, dark tan dreadlocks trailing out of the knot of it. "Well?" she said.

Natasha pondered a moment. She had been drinking rum punch or white wine all week. "Whiskey," she said. "I'll have a whiskey."

"Bourbon?"

"Yes. Neat."

Grace nodded and walked off.

The heavy man held up his glass as if to offer a toast. "Whiskey sour," he said. "I haven't had one in ten years. This is the first one. Ten years. I'm an alcoholic."

Natasha remembered smelling alcohol through his heavy cologne in the morning. She almost said something; it seemed pointless now to keep any kind of pretense about things. But she saw the shadows under his eyes and the way his hands shook. He was just someone suffering this, like everyone else.

Duego was drinking water. He took a long swallow of it, set the glass down shakily, then rubbed his eyes. The muscles of his jaw tightened.

Natasha took the rolled napkin from its place on the table,

removed the heavy silverware from it, and put it to her eyes, trying to gain control of herself. Duego offered her some of his water.

"Where is Grace?" Constance said.

As if summoned by the question, the tall woman appeared in the doorway and started toward them. Constance reached up and took her drink off the tray and gulped it down. "Bring me another one, please," she said. "Make it two more. Doubles both. Please."

Grace nodded, setting Natasha's glass down, and turning to move off.

Natasha lifted her glass and sipped from it, but caught Grace's eye as Grace started away and nodded at her questioning look. "Yes. Me, too."

The heavy man also ordered more, and Duego, as if wanting merely to keep up with the others—there was something grudgingly acceding in the gesture—touched Grace's elbow and ordered a screwdriver. She moved off, seeming to glide away in the yellow wraparound skirt.

"I haven't had a drink in ten years," the heavy man said. "My name's Walt Skinner. I'm an alcoholic." This time, the meaning of the words seemed to arrive in his mind as he spoke. His eyes welled up, and he took the last of his drink. "My wife's here somewhere."

"I do not usually drink," Duego said. "I do not like the taste of it."

"I do," said Constance, "and I do. I do drink and I do like the taste. And I want to get very drunk today."

"Jesus," said Skinner, wiping his eyes with his fat fingers. "I can't find my wife. She's here somewhere. I can't feel a thing. This isn't touching a thing." He put the glass to his mouth and took what was left in the melting ice. His hands shook. He kept moving one leg, a nervous up-and-down motion, toe to the ground, heel raised, the movement of someone normally much thinner, so that the ticlike nature of it glared forth, the frenetic shaking of panic. "We're from New Orleans. You think they'll keep us from flying there?"

"Everything's grounded," Constance said.

"I guess I ought to go looking for her. This feels so helpless.

All those people and there's nothing we can do. My wife went off with some lady friends this morning. She might not even know." His face seemed to register this possibility. The mouth dropped slightly, the eyes widening, all the color leaving his round face.

Duego said, "I am from Orlando. I have no relatives in New York."

Both men seemed now to be waiting for Constance and Natasha to speak, to say where they were from. It was a peculiar moment: social expectation spun over appalling actuality. Natasha nearly laughed, and an odd braying sob rose from the bottom of her throat. "She's moving back to Tennessee," Constance said. And in the next moment Natasha did laugh, turning away from them. The laughter turned to tears.

Constance patted her shoulder. "It's all right, honey. I know it is. It's all right."

Natasha feared allowing herself to think so. Thinking so could bring on the thing through some terrible convergence of fate: Faulk deciding to go down there and stand on the street, looking up. And perhaps he was looking up when the plane hit. It was as if she could cause this to be true by accepting the probability that it was *not true*. And then something like premonition came to her that things were only beginning. There were other horrors to come.

Tall, stately Grace came back with another tray of drinks.

"That was fast," Constance said. "Just the way I like it."

Grace set the drinks down. For a few moments, they all drank and were silent. Natasha began to feel as though she were violating some kind of morality, greedily taking this form of analgesic help in the face of the unbearable visions of the morning. She finished her drink and excused herself, wanting solitude now, moving away from Constance's questioning expression across the wide lawn leading down to the beach.

She walked there through the hot sand. And when she reached the edge she felt a deep pang, centered in her chest, just below her neckline. For a moment she thought her heart might be stopping. She put her hands there and looked for a place to sit down. It came to her that she might never get up if she let herself sink to the ground in this moment. Unsteadily, slowly, she walked into the water, feeling the cold pull of it and then the slap of it as it came back, wetting her to the knees. The pain in her chest wall lessened. She waited, crying soundlessly, while the water sucked back, pulling sand along the sides of her feet, foaming there, and then rushing at her. Iris would be worried and trying to call. Iris would know where Michael was. Michael would call her. And why hadn't he called? The circuits, the overloaded circuits. She looked out at the horizon, that straight dark border under the moving sky, and it terrified her. The waves came in.

Finally she turned, and here was Constance, being helped along by Walt Skinner. They both had their drinks.

"I've switched to vodka," Constance said, holding up her glass. "For my fourth double." Then she stopped and seemed to consider. "Sounds like something from a tennis match. Fourth double."

Skinner held his drink up. "My second."

"That's your fourth," said Constance.

"Okay. I stand corrected. I must've miscounted."

"How many did you have this morning?"

"Nothing this morning. I'm goddamned certain of that."

"You're lying through your teeth."

"Madam, I have no teeth. I wear dentures." He laughed with a low snorting sound, enjoying his own humor, staggering, and she helped him stay on his feet. Together they splashed unsteadily into the water, holding on to each other. They were in almost to their knees when Skinner fell back into a sitting position, holding his drink up, spilling none of it. "Looka that," he said. "Didn't lose a drop." He seemed to be grasping at the fact. There was something hysterical about it: a moment of mastery over the physical world. "We're stuck in paradise. We're the lucky ones." He held the glass higher.

"Shut up," Constance said. "Don't talk like that. Jesus."

"You gonna stand there?"

"Cold." She sat down carefully. "I am never ready for it to feel so cold."

"It's warm as toast," Skinner said. Then he seemed to recall himself. "Goddamn. What're we doing, anyway? I don't know where my wife is." The water rushed away from them and then came back in foam.

"I'm beginning to believe you made her up," Constance said.

"I hope we bomb the living shit out of them all. Nuke the fuckers. Pardon my language."

Natasha started back up the beach.

"Don't leave," Constance called to her. "We came to get you."

"I can't find my wife," said Skinner, coughing. "I'm scared. I need another drink."

"Natasha," Constance yelled. "I can't get up."

Natasha went on, hearing their commotion. They were no longer aware of her, the two of them helping each other get up and laughing crazily. Before she reached the central building, she encountered a man and woman, roughly Constance's age, headed down to the water. The woman was distraught, and he was supporting her by the elbow. They were talking about how they had visited the World Trade Center only last week.

"You've been there?" Natasha said to them.

"Yes," said the man after the slight hesitation of his surprise at being spoken to. "We were just there, visiting with our son. And he took us to the top."

"He's safe?" Natasha said.

"He lives in Brooklyn."

"Can people get in to go to the top at nine o'clock?"

They looked at her.

"When is it open to tourists?"

"Oh, I don't remember," said the woman. She had a big brown mole on the side of her neck.

"It's nine-thirty," the man said. "I'm certain of it. I looked at the sign."

People could be so perfectly kind. Natasha thanked them and wished them a fast return to their home.

She went on into the lobby with its television still transmitting the foment of voices, repeating the images that now suddenly, somewhere beyond language—despite everything you knew and feared—were weirdly, distressingly thrilling, too. It was the awful majesty of the terrible. In the bar, she sat at one end and watched the crowd of people trying to find a way to occupy themselves. Duego walked over from somewhere beyond the patio and stood looking at her. He was holding a glass of what looked like orange juice.

"I cannot concentrate on anything," he said. He had been crying. She felt an urge to touch his wrist but held it back.

The bartender walked over and stood staring. He was a small man with a gray ponytail. When he smiled, a gold tooth showed.

"A whiskey," she told him. "Bourbon."

He looked at Duego.

"Another, yes," Duego said. "Screwdriver."

"I thought you didn't drink," Natasha said.

"I do not know what is in this. I knew the name of it as a drink. I do other things. But I have heard the name of this drink, and I know that it is made with orange juice. Orange juice is healthy."

"Yes. Orange juice is healthy."

"I drink orange juice every day."

"So do I."

"I do not usually like alcohol. But this tastes very amazingly good."

"Vodka is tasteless. So it's the orange juice. And we'll drink to orange juice." Looking past him into the lobby, she saw a group of people on their knees. A square-shouldered, balding man with angry red splotches from sunburn on his muscle-bound arms was leading them in prayer, thick hands folded under his chin, eyes closed.

Natasha went and stood in the entrance, watching for a few moments. The man was saying the Lord's Prayer. She could not see Faulk doing this if he were here. It seemed vaguely showy. She saw two of the women who had taken the journey to Kingston. In the flow of her thoughts, running through the bands of terror, was the fact that Michael Faulk was thousands of miles away.

"Your whiskey," Duego said. He had brought it over, with the little napkin at its base. "To orange juice."

She thanked him and repeated the phrase, and he clicked his glass against hers. They drank. She walked back to the bar and sat on the stool at the end. He followed and took the first stool, right angled from her. He put both elbows on the shiny surface, setting his drink down. "I have never liked orange juice. But this."

She didn't respond, looking around the room for Constance or Skinner.

"I am sorry," he said. "Forgive me. I am unable to be alone just now."

She gazed at him. "You said you do other things. What other things?"

"I can say nothing about that." He grinned.

There was that strange stiffness and overformality in the way he talked. "Did you come here alone?"

He nodded, his chin quivered, and she looked away.

"My wife left me," he said. "A dancer. And she—she fell in love with another dancer. Another woman dancer. Another *woman*. I came here to get away from all that. My wife the lesbian. I hope you are not a lesbian."

"I'm not a lesbian."

"I have nothing against it in principle. I am no rightist."

"To progress." She drank.

"My wife is a lesbian, and she did not tell me of this until one month ago and we were married five years."

"Maybe she didn't know it until one month ago."

"There are stories from her brother. It is painfully probable that she always knew. From when she was a girl in school. The brother did not tell me until it was too late."

The thought occurred to Natasha like a small autonomic impulse running along her nerves that in a crisis of this magnitude, people felt the need to confide.

"I'm sorry," she said to him. "You know, it's nobody's business."

"I wish I could put it into perspective." His voice broke. He took a long drink, then set his glass down. "I do not want to go home."

"Where's home?" she heard herself ask.

"I have lived a long time in Florida."

"That's right. You said that."

"Orlando."

"Never been there." She felt careless, reckless, the sensation stirring like a tic in the nerves of her face. It couldn't matter what she said.

Perhaps a minute went by.

"Yes," he said, with an air of acknowledging something, though she had said nothing.

She went shakily out to the bank of elevators and stood in a small group of people waiting to get on. Two young girls murmured and laughed, and the sound filled her with a powerful urge to tell them to shut their mouths. She saw one of the girls make an effort at another joke, some element of what they had been laughing at, but then she sobbed, suddenly, convulsively. Natasha touched her shoulder.

The girl said, "My dad's best friend—he's like an uncle to me—works in the Pentagon. I wish I knew he was all right. I wish I knew everyone was all right."

The doors of one elevator opened, and a lot of people, all older men and women, filed out, muttering low or being silent, with the dazed look that seemed to have settled into so many of the faces. Natasha waited until the elevator was empty, then stepped in, and the others who had been waiting followed. No one spoke. At her floor, two people exited with her, a man and a woman. They did not seem to be together, though they both went the opposite way from Natasha, nearly touching, the woman a step in front of the man. They were in their sixties or seventies, and she heard the man mutter something in Spanish. The woman laughed. Natasha made her way down the hall to her room. Inside, she went to the window and looked out at the beach. People down there stood at the water's edge, and some had gone into the water and were floundering in the wake of the slow waves. Nobody seemed to be swimming. She could not see Constance. The sun was sinking toward the mountains, behind towering dark-edged clouds. The wind had picked up, moving the palm fronds and riffling the cloth of the big umbrellas jutting from the picnic tables. She stepped to the bed and lay down, trying not to cry anymore and feeling what she'd had to drink. The gray light was warm. She heard the sea, voices rising, and wondered if she was imagining the distress embedded in each utterance, a panicky note in the cries, even those of apparent pleasure in the chill of the water, and the few bursts of laughter. She closed her eyes, intending, if she could, to sleep through until morning. But sleep wouldn't come.

She rose finally, steadied herself, then moved back to the window. Time wouldn't budge. There was the whole dreadful night to go through. Picking up the room phone, she called the front desk and asked for an outside line. The line was busy. "Will you ring my room when there's a line open?" Nothing. The desk clerk had simply punched the numbers for the outside line and gone on to something else or someone else. She waited a moment, still shivering, and when she repunched the number, this time she got the line. All cell-phone signals were still busy out of Jamaica or into New York; there was no telling which. She tried Iris at home.

And got her.

"Oh, I'm so relieved to talk to you, you poor thing," Iris said. "How will you get home? Are you all right?"

"Have you heard from Michael?"

"No."

"He's *there*, Iris, in the financial district—where the towers were. He's—I don't know if he's—"

"He's probably all right," Iris said in a shaking voice. "A *lot* of people were there. You saw it. He wasn't *in* one of the buildings, was he?"

"He talked about looking at the city from the top. Oh, God. I'm scared. Constance said they don't open that early, but I can't stop worrying and I know it's selfish."

"Honey," Iris said. "There's nothing selfish about worrying over someone you love."

"Will you call Aunt Clara for me? Can you do that?"

"Of course. And I'm sure he's fine."

As Natasha started to say the number, Iris interrupted her. "I already have the number, honey."

"Ask if she's heard from Michael."

"I'm sure he's all right. We'd have heard by now—"

"No, that's the thing," Natasha told her. "We don't know that. All the cell phones are down or too clogged to handle the calls. I can't get through to him." She sobbed. "Nobody can find out anything here. I feel so trapped."

"I'll call Aunt Clara. Honey, please, now. You have to stop letting your mind run away with you. I'll call Clara, and then I'll call you right back. Please try to calm down."

"I'm sorry," Natasha said. "I will." She pushed the button to end the call, then tried Faulk's cell number. Nothing but a jangle of electronic noise.

Lying back down on the bed, she stared at the ceiling and at the angles of wall and door and the entrance to the balcony. She looked out at the shining water. In an odd optical illusion it appeared to be a faintly shimmering black wall, until she raised her head and saw it clearly, stretching on to the horizon. The phone rang.

"Honey," Iris said. "I can't seem to get through. A voice keeps saying that all circuits are busy. The volume of calls. I'll keep trying. I just got through to you right away."

"That's because these are landlines."

"Yes, but Clara's phone is a landline."

"Will you keep trying for me? And if you don't get me when you call back, will you leave a message at the desk?"

"I will. And you come home as soon as you can, darling."

She got up and went out on the balcony and looked at the scene before her, a vacation beach, people moving through the fading shadows of the palms or playing in the shallows. She looked at the darkening sky and thought, for the first time in her life, of her country as a separate thing, a nation, harmed, at some kind of war, and unreachable.

5

Faulk reached Penn Station, limping from a catch in his knee, and stood in the center of the big space, holding his suitcase. People wandered aimlessly, many of them without luggage. A great roar of voices reverberated in the high vault of the ceiling, and yet no one appeared to be speaking to anyone. Everyone looked isolated and bewildered. In the waiting area, others were already lying down—preparing for a long wait. The board with the scheduled departures showed a list of cancellations. Faulk moved to a small space near the wall and set down his suitcase. His hand was stiff; his arm and shoulder ached from carrying the thing. His knee hurt. He sat on the suitcase for a while, feeling the fatigue of the long walk and waiting for some sign about what the trains were doing—he heard someone say that the authorities were calling for people to leave the city. But nothing changed. Absurdly, the sight of a small dark bird gliding and dipping in the upper reaches of the high ceiling saddened him beyond measure. Tears ran down his face. He attempted to lie down, but the floor hurt his hips, and then he thought of getting as close to the gates as he could. He had an intimation that something was coming, an announcement. The numbers and town names inside the slat-sized windows of the schedule board suddenly began revolving with a wild clicking sound, as though a whole new schedule were about to be revealed. But the clicking stopped, and the board was blank. He got to his feet, lifted his bag, and started to the nearest ticket counter, in the close, low-ceilinged far end of the station. Surprisingly, he did not have to wait long—the woman there was being very brief with each person. She looked bone weary, her round, dark face glossy with sweat. He stepped up to the window and asked when the next train to Washington would leave.

"Nothing from here right now, and not for several hours," she said. "One coming in soon, going to Newark. You can get on that one. There's one from Boston that stops in Newark. It's not an express. It'll end up in Washington."

"I have an express ticket to Washington from here."

"No tickets, sir. First come, first served. They just want everyone to get out. I don't know what it'll be like in Newark. The one from Boston's not an express."

A woman standing behind her, holding a stack of what looked like tickets of some kind, said, "The mayor just said everybody should stay. Guess to show 'em we ain't beat."

"Tell that to all these people here."

"Do you think there'll be seats on that train?" Faulk asked. "The one to Newark?"

"I can't say, sir."

He heard the announcement for track 9 as he started toward the stairwell down to the gates. In the crush, he got to track level and walked along the length of the just-arrived train, a long line of tall cars that were packed to the windows, though people were hurrying to board and being helped by the conductors. He took the entrance to one car and stepped up into the mass of others in the aisle, the thick odor of those tight quarters mingling with the smell of the tracks, the diesel- and ozone- and creosote-heavy air. He was carried on the tide of these others almost to the far end, where more people were entering or seeking to gain entrance. Seated next to one window was a woman holding a little boy. She was making an effort to entertain him by talking in an excited voice about all the people out there.

"Is everyone going home?" the boy said.

"Yes, they are," his mother answered with the brave fake cheer of a parent lying to a child.

Finally, the train jolted into motion. Holding on was difficult without touching someone else. Faulk, reaching to brace himself on one side of the two seat backs where he stood, felt the wrist bone of a gray-eyed old woman, who glanced at him and then looked away. There wasn't anything for it.

"How would they get pilots to fly their own planes into buildings?" a man said.

"Maybe the pilots were in on it," said someone else.

"I don't believe that. My brother's a pilot. This was some kind of hijacking, I guarantee it. Some suicide fucks. Excuse me for the language."

There was just the rocking motion of the car for a time, and the difficulty everyone was having staying in place with nothing really to hold on to. Faulk saw an elderly black man rise in the little space he had and offer his seat to a woman with an infant. She took it, and the infant began to whimper, and the man, whose dark face looked too slack to be healthy, had to use her shoulder to keep standing. He had large ears and thick gray hair, and he smiled at the baby.

The windows slowly gave way at last to brightness, the train leaving the confines of the station. Faulk saw other tracks, buildings and billboards, the tall blue shadows of the city, and, visible out the windows to the left, the smoke where the towers had been. The train picked up speed. The ash-and-smoke cloud was appallingly defined, a gigantic, ragged-edged, domelike shape, too strange a sight for belief. Bright, unblemished blue sky still shone far above its dissipating outline.

No one spoke to anyone.

Faulk watched until the cloud was no longer visible, and the many others watched, too, the harmed city behind them in the too-bright sun, and the silence felt almost supernatural, as if everyone here were already dead, spirits being carried away. Even the infant was completely quiet, staring at the faces. The ground on either side of the tracks gave way to tenements, yards with laundry on lines, and a view of the East River beyond, the factory silos and fortresslike walls of coal and metal, the auto junkyards, the cranes of the harbor lifting into the sun. It was all a confusion of commerce and waste, and the people in the packed car gazed at it out the windows, quietly taking in the vast industrial insignia of the country where they lived.

In Newark, there was more confusion and crowding, people hurrying to the escalators that would take them to the ticketing area. Faulk made his way up there and out of the building. The air was heavy and smelled strongly of gasoline and burning. He thought of the fires in New York. He saw a big barrel-shaped metal trash can with flames licking out of it. Someone had evidently thrown a lit cigarette into it. A man stood pouring a can of cola onto the fire. Faulk went on across the street, to the Hilton. In the lobby he saw men, women, and even some children lying on the furniture and on the floor along the walls. At the reception desk, which was surprisingly empty, he got the attention of a young man whose black string tie was hanging loose around his neck. The young man was bleary eyed, his reddish hair disarranged. He looked like someone recovering from a long night of overindulgence. He removed his coat, and Faulk understood that he was at the end of his shift. There was effectively no one behind the reception desk. The young man shook his head and gave him a commiserating look. "We don't have any more rooms, man. Absolutely nothing. We're letting people stay in the lobby." He indicated the others, one or two already sleeping on their bags.

"I guess there's nothing at any of the other hotels near here?"

"Everything's booked."

Faulk went to a side wall and set down his bag but a second later thought better of it and walked back to the station and to the ticketing area to wait along with the others. Hours went by, people moving incrementally closer, bending and picking up bags and setting them down, or simply standing with arms folded. The murmurous racket of the hall went on, and there was something nearly solemn about it. He thought of his training, the things he knew to say to shock and grief, but there was nothing to say, here, with everyone seeking only to go home. A priest came by him, hurrying somewhere, and Faulk saw his not-quite-looking-at-anyone face—he was just a man in a rush to get wherever he had to go, a little frightened and sick at heart.

Trains were leaving for Boston and points north. When he got to his window, he handed over his ticket for Washington and asked when the next train was. The clerk was a leathery-faced ruddy man with large green eyes and sandy hair. "There's one coming into the station in about fifteen minutes from Boston. But it's not an express."

"I don't care about that," Faulk said.

"This ticket'll work, then. Go right up those steps."

Faulk thanked him and started for the stairs, feeling the need to hurry and expecting many people to be rushing behind him. But no one followed. He went up the stairs and out on a platform, thinking that he must not have understood the directions properly. He believed the train he'd arrived on was below this floor, and he almost started back down. But here on the platform was another man, Asian, a boy, really, no more than twenty-five years old, sitting on the bench, leaning forward with his hands folded, his elbows resting on his knees. "The train from Boston," he said, simply. Faulk sat down next to him and adjusted his bag at his feet. The young man wore a business suit without the tie. His shirt was unbuttoned. It was very hot here. He turned and looked at Faulk and then looked away. He folded and unfolded his hands. Finally he looked over and said, "Were you there?"

Faulk nodded. "Up on Fifty-Fourth Street."

"I was in the second one, the south tower," the boy said, and took in a deep breath. It was as if something had struck him in the chest. He straightened, attempting to collect himself. "They—they told us—we were all going down the stairs—and they told us it was all right, we could go back up. But I didn't like it, and I kept going down." He gasped, trying to master himself. "They—all my friends—they—they went back." And with that he let go, crying quietly, hands over his mouth. Then he reached in the pocket of his coat for a handkerchief, opened it, and put it over his face. "I'm going home, to Baltimore. My parents live in Baltimore."

"Washington," Faulk said. He felt the uselessness of it. "I'm a priest. If there's anything I can do . . ." The words seemed false, and in the next moment he realized that they *were* false. "I was a priest," he said, low, wanting to be exact. It was ridiculous.

The boy's demeanor seemed to underscore the thought. He sat and stared off and waited for the train, and around them the noise of the station increased, a wave of distraught voices and sounds coming from the very walls. The train was coming in. The sound filled the hot little space where they sat, and it seemed strangely out of place, not something sensibly connected to this narrow room with its bench and its posters on the opposite wall advertising Broadway plays. They moved to the doorway leading out to the track. When the train stopped before them and the conductor jumped down and set the stool for them to step up, the boy hesitated. Faulk saw him wait to see which way he, Faulk, would go—into which car, the left or the right. He went left, took the first seat—the car was nearly empty—and glanced over his shoulder. The young man had gone the other way. The train pitched forward, rocking, and Faulk looked out the soiled window at the yellow lights, the empty platform, the vague shapes in the dimness beyond the wide expanse of other tracks, the cement abutments, switches, painted signs and symbols. The train was gathering speed, and once more, out of the tunnel, the light changed to daylight. But daylight was fading. Gazing at the burnished glow along the marshy fields south of Newark, he thought of how he had failed to be of help to anyone—how, until the minutes with the young man on the station platform, his one concern had been getting away from the city. He had spent most of his adult life performing the very tasks that were called for in this situation, yet he had only reacted, a numb, fearful refugee, like all the others, trying to get out.

6

It seemed to Natasha, looking out from her balcony, that the beach was less crowded. The part of the sky not barricaded by clouds had turned darker. It was almost black at its height.

Down in the lobby, she paused in front of the row of phones. People were still struggling to get through; others still waited to try. "Is anyone getting anyone in New York?" she said to a man who was holding a glass of something bright red with a little paper umbrella in it.

"Are you kidding?" the man said, drinking.

She felt the nausea returning and hurried into the ladies' room, which was crowded and deathly quiet. There was something about a room this small that made for silence. Everyone had a protective shell of self-concern. She couldn't breathe.

Back in the bar, Nicholas Duego was still there, with a fresh drink, leaning on the shiny surface with both elbows, head down, one hand making a swirling motion to move the ice and dregs of orange juice and vodka in his glass. The bar smelled of fear and the sweat of exertion, alcohol and tobacco—mixed with several kinds of fried food. She ordered a bourbon on ice from the small man with the gold tooth, and when he brought it she swallowed most of it, feeling it as a cold and then searing place at her middle. She grasped the glass with both hands, eyes fixed on the glossy water-spotted expanse of the bar.

"Are you all right?" Duego asked. "You have been gone a long time." His eyes were not quite focusing. He drank and then put his head back down.

She signaled the bartender, indicating her empty glass. He nodded at her but went on with what he was doing.

The bar was growing more crowded, the noise level increasing. Alcohol and crisis had loosened some tongues. She couldn't see clearly through the gathered faces, the crush of people pressing to the bar. She thought of Constance out by the beach somewhere, with Skinner, and the night coming on.

She kept replaying Constance saying Faulk could not have been in either building when the planes struck, and the old couple on the path, and the woman who knew exactly when the towers opened for tourists. Nine-thirty. Nine-thirty.

She went out onto the veranda, aware of herself now as being drunk, feeling nothing good in it, no release of tension or anxiety, but only the amplification of her fear, the need to hold on to it—as if to let it go would be to tempt God: it would be when she relaxed into the belief that Faulk was safe that she would discover something awful had happened.

But in fact something awful had already happened, and the images of it were still being broadcast, in little windows above the talking heads on the TV. She saw the irregular light at the entrance of the lobby, where an elderly man stood with a stricken expression on his face, staring in at the screen. She felt selfish, looking at this. She thought she might speak to him, but when she got to where he had been, he was gone.

It was like moving through a patchy, shifting dream.

She wanted another drink and remembered signaling the bartender. Looking into the bar, she saw the disorder there and decided not to go back in.

On the veranda, seated in one of the wicker chairs looking out toward the lowering red-daubed horizon, another woman sat quite still, with a handkerchief held tight in her fist. The backs of her hands looked bruised. There was nowhere to go—nowhere to escape these others and herself. She wanted sleep but feared being alone. The only empty chair was to this woman's right. The woman sniffled and opened the hand holding the handkerchief and commenced folding and unfolding the cloth. On the other side of her was Ratzi. He glanced over at Natasha, held up one hand, and moved the fingers in an almost-sheepish little halfhearted wave. Beyond Ratzi, a young man was kneeling in front of a young woman, arms around her middle, making soothing sounds. But the young woman seemed to be laughing.

Mrs. Ratzibungen walked out and stood speaking to Ratzi in German, not quite whispering, casting quick looks at the woman folding and unfolding the handkerchief. Then she stepped over to Natasha.

"You vent to Kingston," she said. "*Ja? Mit* Ratzi."

Natasha nodded, though the other didn't quite wait for a response, tilting her head slightly in the direction of the woman with the handkerchief. "This is Mr. Skinner's vife."

"Oh." Natasha started to offer her hand but then decided against it. Nothing in Mrs. Skinner's manner revealed any kind of tolerance for gestures.

She only glanced Natasha's way, sniffled, and then said, "Do you know where my husband is?"

"He was looking for you," Natasha told her. "Earlier. I mean this morning. He was with my friend Constance. You haven't seen him since this morning?"

The woman's expression was incredulous. "He has a drinking problem."

Natasha kept still. Mrs. Ratzibungen shook her head and looked out toward the beach.

"And a heart problem," Mrs. Skinner continued. "And liver trouble."

"I'm sorry."

"And psoriasis."

Natasha was silent.

"And asthma."

"Oh."

"And kidney and prostate trouble."

"Really."

"You don't believe me?"

"Yes."

Mrs. Ratzibungen moved off, saying something about having other guests who were scheduled to arrive and who were either stranded somewhere on the way or, worse, had canceled their plans altogether.

"He had a stroke last year," Mrs. Skinner continued, sniffling. "He's in terrible shape. Well, you saw him. The doctors have told him over and over."

"I don't know where anyone is," Natasha said. "My fiancé—"

The other cut her off. "What kind of person is your friend."

"Excuse me?"

"Is your friend a moral person." Mrs. Skinner's tone was devoid of the slightest hint of a question. "I'm asking you. Is your friend a moral person."

"Well—she's my friend. And of course—of course, a nice person."

Mrs. Skinner clutched the handkerchief tight in her fist again and, looking at Natasha with an expression very close to rage, said "What?" as if the younger woman had said something so preposterous that it caused offense.

Natasha gathered herself. "I said she's a nice person. A good person."

"Where are they, then? Where *are* they? Where is my husband. And where is your friend."

Natasha said, "They came down to the beach." She heard the grief in her own voice. "I was down there and they came down, they said, to get me. But that was earlier. And that's the last time I saw them. I'm sorry. They came down and got in the water. My friend and—and Mr.—and your husband. She's not that sort of person, really. Not at all. And he was looking for you. He said—he kept saying he couldn't find you."

"I was right here. *Right* here in this—in our room. I told him he was definitely and certainly on his way to hell. He had four—four, mind you—four of those little airline bottles of whiskey in the room. This morning—right after it happened. Eight o'clock in the morning. Right after the planes hit. And I told him. And he got sad like he does. Do you believe in God?"

Natasha was thinking now only of finding a way to extricate herself.

"Well, *do* you?"

"Perhaps it's just a misunderstanding," Ratzi said from his chair on the other side, leaning forward, glancing at Natasha and nodding as if to show his good intentions. "No one knows where anyone is at a time like this. I haven't seen my brother all day. I think he's in Kingston. We haven't seen him."

"Do *you* believe in God?" Now it seemed crucial for Mrs. Skinner to know whether or not they were believers.

"I do believe in God, yes," Ratzi said, taking one of her hands into both of his.

She pulled away as if he had scalded her. "Don't touch me."

"I'm so very sorry, madam."

"I'm looking for my husband."

"We're sure he'll turn up."

"He's a cheater. Walter is. He cheats."

"Misunderstanding," Ratzi said hopelessly.

"Cheats at everything—everything. Cards, games—Parcheesi. He cheats at Parcheesi. A game like Parcheesi. Can you imagine.

The man cheats at Par*chees*i. And in an argument—you know what he does in an argument? He makes up statistics. Makes them up. He *cheats*. There's no honesty in him at all. And physically he's at death's door and where *is* he?"

"Could he have gone into the city?" Natasha asked her.

"Do *you* believe in God?"

"Yes—you've already asked us that."

"But *what*. What do you believe? Do you believe in a God who forgives everything the man does no matter what? No matter who he hurts?"

They were both looking at her.

"Well?" Mrs. Skinner said, turning her gaze from one to the other.

"Yes," Ratzi said, a little too loudly. "I believe in a merciful God."

"You?" she demanded of Natasha.

"I believe in God," Natasha said.

"Well, *I* believe that if you're not good—if you *cheat*—then God will *get* you. I believe there's a price to pay. And good people pay it along with the bad people. It's in the Bible. You can find it in the Bible in plain English straight from God. And look at those people in New York and Washington, and the other place, too. They were all paying the price. And you can bet that a lot of them went straight to hell. You know it's very probable that most of them were in a state of sin. And where are they now?"

"What are you saying?" Natasha asked her. "Are you—" She couldn't speak.

"I'm saying I never did a thing in my life that was intentionally a sin. I have practiced my faith to the letter. And I don't know where my husband went with that woman."

"They were both in the water," said Natasha. She came very close to saying she hoped with all her heart that at this very moment on God's earth they were fucking their eyes out. It occurred to her to say this as she rose, shivering with quiet fury, starting off in the direction of the beach, having to stop to gain her balance. She heard Skinner's appalling wife say something about talking to drunks.

"I'm very sober," Ratzi said.

Mrs. Skinner put the handkerchief to her mouth, but got out, "I'll kill the little son of a—"

He held his hands up, a shrugging motion. "Horrible time," he said, though he now had a silly smile on his face. And then he was laughing. The woman had not meant to be funny, and she stood to walk away from him but ended up collapsing in Natasha's vacated chair.

"I'm very frightened," she said. "Aren't you very frightened?"

Natasha walked on toward the beach. People were sitting on blankets in the sand, some with coolers and wine, as though nothing at all had happened and this was just the fine weather of cloudy twilight by the sea. One small circle had lit a hibachi. They were speaking Spanish and what sounded like German. It could not matter as much to those for whom America was not home. That was just life on earth. Two girls tossed a beach ball back and forth, and another was trying to make a figure in the sand. Still another walked among the patrons with a little tray of beer. Natasha stood at the water's edge and looked toward the hills, then toward the open sea. People splashed and moved with the water a few hundred paces up that way. They were all shadows in the failing light.

Someone was playing a guitar back toward the entrance of the resort. Someone else was hitting bongos. She heard the sound of a metal drum, too. It was almost full dark.

She made her way back to the wide veranda, and standing there, staring out, was Constance.

"Where have you been?" Constance wanted to know.

"I was just looking for you."

"Is this your friend?" Mrs. Skinner asked from her chair. Ratzi was still sitting in his own chair, hands on his knees, his gaze darting from one to the other of them.

Natasha addressed Constance under her breath. "Where's Skinner?" To her surprise, she had to resist a manic urge to laugh.

"Who?"

"Mr. Skinner. Mr. Skinner—the one you walked down to the beach with."

"Why, hon-eh love," Constance said, running the syllables together. "I been down th' beach with two 'r three types this terrible day. Getting in the water and trying to get sober."

Mr. Skinner's wife got out of the chair and moved to face her. "You listen. His name is Skinner. He's an alcoholic, he *cheats*, and he can't have anything to drink."

"Don't you know what's happ'nin', hon-eh?" Constance said. "Ev'body's drinkin' t'day, sweetie. Ev'body. Whole world came down on us like a ton today. We don' even know how many's lost their lives today."

"His name happens to be Walter B. Skinner. He's in need of help."

"Walt. Oh, yeah—okay. Him. Skinner. Walt. How could I not remember Walt." She laughed into her fist. "You know—seriously, if yer innerested I—I ran into him jus' now. Jus' left'm in the bar. I swear he's in there. Good man, ol' Walt. He got a lil' sunburned. And, hon-eh, I gotta tell ya, he's been drinking."

Mrs. Skinner turned and hurried into the building, through the crowd that was still in the lobby.

"Guy's three sheets," Constance said. "Very in-ee-briated man. She's gonna be mad as hell when she gets to him."

Natasha said nothing, trying to keep from collapsing with laughter or crying—it felt like a form of psychosis—and she leaned into Constance, bracing herself against the pressure of the whole day.

"Hey," Constance said. "You look like you're about to fall down."

"No," Natasha told her. "I want another whiskey."

"I do believe in God," Ratzi said. "But not like that."

"I don' think God cares about us at all," Constance muttered, mostly to herself. "All we do ev'ry goddamned day is kill 'n' maim 'n' starve 'n' butcher 'n' fillet 'n' cook each other."

"Where were you all day?" Natasha asked.

Constance seemed not to have heard. But then she said, tearfully, "Been tryin' t'contact my daughter." She rubbed her eyes vigorously and seemed to let down with a sigh, her hands dropping to her sides. "Well—ev'body's unhappy. I'm gon' go t'bed. You go too."

"Do you need help?" Natasha asked.

But the other didn't answer, pausing long enough to stare at Ratzi, half wave at him, and then move toward the entrance. Natasha saw sand on her back.

"Nice lady," Ratzi said. "It's so sad for everyone today."

She nodded, then turned and followed her friend into the lobby. Constance had paused. There was commotion in the bar, several people standing around someone on the floor near the waiters' station. Skinner. A group of men had crouched side by side around him. They lifted him—it took four of them—and moved falteringly to the long couch against the wall. Mrs. Skinner stood by with her hands clasped over her middle, muttering to herself. And here was Ratzi hurrying in, with two members of the waitstaff. Skinner's head moved, but his eyes were nearly shut, and you could see he was only half conscious. Someone said an ambulance was on the way, and in a little while they all heard the siren. People were coming in from the veranda and the beach, and the paramedics moved through without looking to the left or right. They got to Skinner and started working over him while his wife stood closer, sniffling and saying to anyone who would listen that she had warned him, she had told him what was going to happen if he kept on. Now God had given his sign.

"Hope he'll be all right," Constance said. She fixed Natasha with a stony look. "I'm not as drunk as you think."

"Oh, what can it matter?" Natasha said to her.

"Well, I'm quite drunk enough, though. But look at 'm. He's just passed out. Pissed, as they say."

The medics got Skinner onto a stretcher and took him out of the place. He was more alert now, eyes open, taking people in as he was carried past them. Natasha looked around for Mrs. Skinner but could no longer see her. "Where did the wife go?" she asked Constance, who was moving unsteadily toward the elevators.

"Got on her broom and rode away, I guess."

They stood by the elevators, Constance leaning on the wall there, head down, pale and clearly tired. The elevator door opened, and she got on, put her hands on the small faux-wooden railing inside, then turned and looked bleakly out. There was no recognition in her face, no sense that she saw anything or anyone.

"Remember," she said gravely. "They don't allow tourists in th' place b'fore nine-thirty." The doors closed on her.

7

Natasha returned to the beach. The moon shining through a hole in the clouds made shadows of the palms. There were no planes in the sky, and though the palm fronds clicked when the breezes moved them, the quiet seemed deeper. The sea shimmered under the silver light, and she saw the silhouette of a passing ship out on the horizon, making its way east, probably with cargo. There was a faintly glimmering flash of movement in the water. Something jumped, and jumped again. A school of porpoises was swimming by, phosphorescence flickering in their wake. She had a moment of knowing that Faulk was safe wherever he was. Near the water she sat down on the damp, packed sand, supporting herself with both hands. So many people were suffering across the miles of darkness. The thought of her dead parents came to her, gone before she could have any memory of them, two young people in love, planning to have several children—according to Iris, they had wanted a large family—and the world had taken them. And now she could not unthink the possibility that this feeling of relief about Faulk was a great irony, and that the world had already taken him as well. She began to entreat the sea and sky, murmuring the words, "Please let it be all right." And the loss of her parents seemed mingled with this badness, all part of the same pitiless chance. Everything was exaggerated by the fact that she could not find out, could not know for certain. And even as she recognized the morbid indulgence of the fear, it raked through her. She could not change it or make it stop. Because what if he really was gone? All that fire and falling debris, and why could she not get through to him?

In her peripheral sight she saw a stirring nearby, a startling sudden movement that turned out to be a shape stumbling in the uneven pockets of sand toward the water.

Nicholas Duego.

And he had just seen her, veering in her direction. He stopped and fumbled with something in his shirt pocket. A cigarette. She watched him light it and then come on. "Hello," he said. "I wondered where you went."

"If you don't mind I'd rather be alone."

He seemed not to have heard. He sat down about three feet from her, elbows resting on knees, saying nothing, and not looking at her but at the moonlight on the water. After drawing on the cigarette, he offered it.

"I don't smoke."

"It is not tobacco."

She stared at him a moment, then took it, drew deeply on it, and handed it back.

"It is the only thing that relaxes me," he said. "When I want to relax. Sometimes I would rather not relax. For that I have other things."

She blew the smoke out and briefly had to fight the need to cough. Sitting back and looking at him, she said, "Really."

He smiled. "You are not used to the smoke."

She had the feeling that he was trying to impress her. She almost laughed. "I guess you're a bad character."

He offered the joint.

"Right," she said.

"I am not bad, no. I am a good man."

"That's nice to know."

They smoked for a few minutes in silence, passing the roach back and forth. She wasn't thinking about anything but relief from the whiskey-dimmed funk she was in, and it came to her that in its way this was similar to those passes in the bars and clubs of Washington when there was just the blankness of herself in the instant, just the time and place, no history or thought of a future, either, but only the counterfeit brightness of the exact present. The sky shifted before them, the clouds moving, and she could not think of the clouds as anything but emptily pretty things that did not apply to her. There was only this very minute itself: a squall out at sea, water lifting and settling, night with its terrors beyond the line of the horizon, far away.

"I have more," Duego said, holding out a little plastic bag. "Should I roll us another one?"

She watched him do it, saying nothing, and kept the one he'd given her, taking another hit from it, holding it between her thumb and forefinger, the coal burning very close to her flesh now. It was almost gone.

During

Islands

I

He offered her more, and she took it, gazing at the slowly vanishing lunar radiance on the water. You could still see small glimmering traces of it on the shifting surface, thousands of white wings. Marijuana after alcohol made her woozy, as if she had just awakened from a long sleep. But her vision seemed sharper, and her senses, her nerve endings, were tingling. She thought idly of the phrase *having a buzz on*.

He was talking, going on about something.

Food, she realized.

"I like things cooked dark. Crisp and brown."

She looked at the side of his face, a handsome Latin face, with a sharp nose and high cheekbones, and coal-black hair. She felt nothing. Yet when she handed him back the joint, and he rested his other hand on her shoulder, she did not remove herself. The moonlight was dying, shrouded in folds of cloud. She put her knees up and rested her head on them.

The other took a hit and said, "I did not speak English until I was ten years old."

She sniffled. "You told us that. Please leave me alone."

"I think if you talk to me you will feel better."

She did not speak.

He went on smoking, holding it in, then letting go, blowing the smoke. He held the joint out to her. "I am a dancer."

"You told us."

"I never liked it as a child."

"Dancing." She took another toke and handed it back.

"I did not like America. In my country there was a very strong official hatred of it. But my father felt differently. He worked for Americans before the revolution. My mother was Canadian. He wanted to go be an American or a Canadian. But I was a boy and I had friends. I did not want to leave my friends. In the house, when I was small, as long as I can remember, he talked about going to North America, and I have memories of them fighting about it. And then my mother died. I did not know when we went to Canada to visit her family that it was to go to America to live. A friend in America helped him."

She could think of nothing in response. And then she simply dismissed the worry about it. Mentally, she dismissed *him*. "Do you still hate America?" Her voice was flatly automatic.

He appeared momentarily affronted. "I am a citizen."

"Ever heard the phrase *America, love it or leave it*?"

He laughed. "I could have made that up. It could have been me. Because I love America. It gave me the chance to be a dancer."

"What kind of dance? Ballet?"

He shook his head. "Modern dance."

"Yes, well, I had ballet in school."

"Did you like it?"

"Not especially, I'm sorry to say. I wasn't any good at it."

They were quiet.

Presently, he said, "It's hard to be good at something you do not like."

"Well, I wasn't very good."

"I was not good in school. My wife helped me study and do better and now she is gone. The woman she is with—I thought this woman was my friend."

"I'm sorry." The dope was not making her feel anything. She had no sense of well-being or of the jollity it usually occasioned and, looking out at the seascape before her, she wished for solitude while lacking the will to do anything to achieve it. She sat quite still, her distress having shaded into this drowsy gloom, this sour observing.

"Where are you from?" he asked. "Your voice is different."

She told him.

"That is in Shelby County."

"How did you know that?"

"I had a friend I visited in Memphis. The second day terrible thunderstorms came and they kept saying the counties and we listened because it was a tornado and the storm hit Bartlett in Shelby County. I remember that. Because I thought of pears. We watched it on the television. It knocked down trees. I went to Graceland."

"Almost everyone who visits Memphis goes there. A lot go there *because* of Graceland."

He wrote in the sand. "That is my address in Orlando, Florida."

"Please. I'm really not up for talking."

"It feels good to carve it in the sand, after today. My place on earth. And I mark it here. Like a sign for everyone to see."

"People will walk on it." The idea struck her as funny. She laughed softly.

"Here." He offered her another hit.

"Okay."

They smoked. Somewhere behind them was the sound of a steel drum. It went on awhile and then died away. A girl laughed, and a man laughed, too. They spoke in German, and after a few moments you couldn't hear them anymore.

"Write yours," he said.

"At present, I have no address."

He stared.

"All right. Here's where my grandmother lives." And as she scrawled the number and the name of the street, she did feel strangely as if she were claiming something in defiance. The idea made her pause. Then she swept her hand across all of it. "This is what happens, isn't it."

"Why did you do that?"

"Because I'm not superstitious."

He wrote his name and wiped it away. "Neither am I."

A moment later, he said, "Why do you have no home?"

She told him about leaving the job in Washington and was surprised to find that she felt friendly toward him; something in her nerves, below the level of thinking, was actually responding to the cool night breezes and the quiet talk.

"I have never been to Washington and I would love to see it," he said.

"You should go."

"But you are leaving it."

"I've left it. When I get out of here, I'm going back to Memphis. A small truck with all my belongings in it is headed there as we speak. To Twenty-Three Bilders Street, Memphis."

"It sounds like a number of workers. Twenty-three builders."

"It does. We have twenty-three builders waiting to build this building on this street lined with buildings."

He laughed, and it went on. It was the reasonless laughter of dope.

"Lot of buildings," she said. "Count them."

"Twenty-three," he said, and his laugh went off at the night sky.

"It doesn't have a *u* in it. Bilders. It's a man's name." She sputtered, nearly choking with her own laugh. "I think he was a banker. So my belongings are headed to this street with a little house on it built by builders, and the whole street has buildings on it now, probably built by this banker named Building. No, Bilders. Off High Point Terrace."

He paused, wiping his eyes and his mouth with a handkerchief, which he crushed in his fist and jammed into his shirt pocket. "Do you believe in fate?"

It seemed that she couldn't move the muscles around her mouth. "Explain."

"That everything was leading to this."

"And what is *this*, exactly?"

"We two, here, on this beach."

"I don't believe in fate," she said to him. "So, no. But hey, thanks anyway."

"I feel something led me here. Something in a past life."

She flicked the roach off into the sand, and he got to his knees to retrieve it. "It's done," she told him. "There's just the ash left. We're done. All the fun's gone out of it."

He sat back and rolled another and lit it while she watched. The little residue of pleasant feeling had dissolved inside her.

"Do you feel it, too?" he said.

She sighed. "I feel dizzy and full of anxiety. And I don't want to be with anyone. Please."

"I only want to help you. And be helped."

"Let's talk about something other than 'fate' then."

Behind them someone was crying, and someone else was singing. It struck her all over and yet as if for the first time that she was thousands of miles from home. "Your wife is a dancer, you said."

"Yes." He looked absurd sitting there hugging his knees, talking about fate, his dancer wife gone off with another woman. "I cannot help this feeling that I have," he told her. "That the universe brought you to me."

She had to suppress an urge to laugh again. She watched him breathe out the smoke. When he offered her still another hit, she accepted.

"I guess it is stupid," he said.

She took the hit, handed the roach to him, and leaned back on her hands. The clouds over the moon were darker but still quite thin, moving faster than she thought clouds ever moved. The world was spinning. Everything was dissolving, going off.

"I believe the universe intends changes for us all," he said.

"All us builders?" She giggled, and it took hold and grew deeper.

"I am serious now," he said. "Hey, I am. I am serious."

"Sorry. Strikes me funny."

"I do believe the universe intends changes." And now he laughed, too.

"This isn't the best time to talk about the universe, is it. Or maybe it's the *only* time to talk about it. Right? Isn't that it? You get stoned and you talk about the universe? Only I don't want to talk about the universe, man. Truthfully, I am so fucking averse to talking about the fucking universe." This brought still another laugh out of her, and she looked at the fact of it, like marking the date.

"I am only trying to divert you," he said. "I do not like such language."

"Oh, God. Forgive me. I fucking didn't mean to say *averse*. That was very fuckingly rude and vulgar of me. Pure fuckery and I do apologize."

"I am not prudish."

"Oh—well, thank you for the smoke."

"That is helping?"

She saw the anxiety in his face. He was quite good to look at. "Listen, I don't want to hurt your feelings. Really. I'm sorry, okay? I'm drunk and stoned and sick and panicky and I hope you don't take it personally but I really don't want company anymore. So why don't you leave."

"You cannot even bring yourself to say my name."

"Oh, shut *up!*" She kept laughing.

"Say it, then."

"Please leave me alone."

He took another pull, inhaled it deeply, held it in, then sighed it out, offering her yet another hit. She took it. "Okay. Now. Please leave me alone. Nicholas."

"You were not enjoying this?"

"Yes, thank you."

"It is only a little kindness between friends."

"I'm sorry. You're right."

"We were laughing beautifully."

"Right. Okay, sure. And I fuckishly said *averse*. And you forgave me."

"I do not know what you mean, now. I wish you would not use that language. It is impolite and unladylike. Not worthy of you."

"Hey, fuck you, sarge."

"Sarge."

"Forget it."

He leaned over and lightly kissed the side of her face, then moved a little farther away. "I mean nothing unfriendly. I have some other things to take."

"No," she said.

"Do you know about Special K?"

"The cereal?"

He smiled. "It is called that. Is there a cereal? I have it in pill form."

"The *cereal*?"

"Ketamine. It makes things happen."

"No," she said.

They went on smoking. She felt the drug moving through her, numbness running along the nerves of her face. Time seemed to grow elongated and strange. She let him talk, and he was very willing to describe for her everything he was going through. It occurred to her that he was just an insecure, nervous boy.

In a little while they were talking about the day, the trauma of it, and the way everyone seemed to tumble off some private deep end. "I do not even drink," he said. "I like other things. But now I think I am drunk."

"You keep talking about your big drug habits. Are you trying to impress me? Because it's not working."

"I was not trying to impress you. Only to help relieve your worry."

"That's sweet. Thank you for it. But I really just want to sit here by myself."

He was silent. Perhaps a full minute went by.

"It *has* felt a little less awful," she told him.

"I'm glad."

Another pause.

"Suppose we are on a deserted island," he said. "From a shipwreck."

This seemed very amusing. There was a bleak something in the laughter now, and the fact that the laughter itself felt so mirthless made it all that much deeper. "Deserted desert island, right?" she said. "Oh, that's perfect. That's rich."

"Not a desert, no."

"That's hilarious. Not a deserted desert island?"

"The dope is making you hysterical," he said.

"Yeah, perfect. Hysterical." She saw moving light on the water. The clouds were opening again.

"I think we should be as if no one else will ever come here. This is the first place. Adam and Eve's garden."

"Adam and Eve's deserted desert island."

"I am drawn to you. Very much. You are very beautiful. May I simply touch your face?"

She watched his hand come up to her cheek. The touch was tentative and gentle, and she felt a little sorry for him. He let his fingers move carefully, slowly down to her chin, and under her chin. He turned her face up and leaned down to kiss her. She let him and then watched him sit back and regard her. The world was coming to an end. And then once more everything shifted: there was not the sense of this being anything but a small, desolate pass, one of the nights of her life before. She had no sense of a self, of herself, as more than a set of floating impressions. She wanted sleep. The effects of the alcohol and dope she had ingested seemed to be growing more profound. She lay back, and he was leaning over her, supporting himself on one elbow. *I am not the type*, she thought. *What type. Why is it a type?* The words went through her mind. *You are*, she thought. *You are, now. You were, then. What were you?* She thought of Faulk. She saw him riding home on the train. He was probably all right. All her irrational fear was leaching out of her as the night cooled.

"Michael," she murmured.

"What?" the other said.

"They don't let people in before nine-thirty. That's the hours. You wouldn't stay and wait for an hour. Not in New York."

"I do not understand you," Duego said, gazing down at her.

"Please leave me alone now."

"One kiss?"

She let him, opened her mouth with the tactile pleasure of it. "There," she told him. It was as though Faulk, so far away, were a child, and she belonged to the world of adults.

Duego put his mouth on hers, caressing her breasts, and then her lower abdomen, moving his hand down. His touch was insistent, and there was something hurried about it, as though he expected to be stopped or was afraid he would be. She was dizzy, eyes wide open, looking at him. His breath smelled of the dope and what he'd had to drink, and there was the thinnest displeasing red-olence of fruit in it, too. She had a sensation of sudden clarity: this was actually happening. It was as though what had begun to unfold had just now become visible to her. She pushed on his shoulders as he got over on top of her.

"No," she said. "Get off."

His weight was stopping her breath. She protested with as much force as she could muster, and he rolled off, making a sound she thought at first was more laughter. He was crying.

"Don't cry," she said, and patted his arm. The little smoldering roach lay between them. She threw it off into the night, then leaned down and kissed him. The kiss lasted a long time, and he put his hands on her lower back, pulling her closer. She was falling through some field of being that was far from herself, spiraling down, a darkness born of the waste of everything that this day had been. Some part of her—off in space, despairing—watched it all, believing that she was alone, that Michael Faulk was gone, that everything was gone.

They stopped for a moment, lying there out of breath, and for a while that was the only sound—their breathing, mixed with the low roar of the surf.

When he bent to her, she put her hands on his shoulders and pushed and made the word *no* out of the movement of his tongue in her mouth. She pushed hard. Repeatedly. And at last he lay over on his back, making the sound she now knew was crying.

"Please go away from me," she heard herself say. "I'm sorry to hurt your feelings, but I don't want this. I do not want this. I've told you. Please. Please leave me alone."

He didn't answer. He was passed out, mouth open, eyes squeezed shut as if he were facing into high winds. He looked to be suffering some kind of pressure inside, the veins of his neck showing.

Getting shakily to her feet, she stumbled to the water, splashed in, and pushed out to where it was up to her thighs. Then she dove under, suffering the shock of it like a slap to her face. She swam for what seemed a long time, away from shore, into the rising and sinking surf, feeling the pull of the tide and the weight of her jeans and blouse. Suddenly the tide gripped her. The thought rose to the front of her mind that she was going to drown. She swam parallel to the beach, working it, near exhaustion, keeping on, until the ocean began to let go.

At last, turning, going under, and coming up to gasp for air, she made her way back in and reached the shallow water, where she could get to her feet, standing while the waves pulled and pushed at her knees. She coughed and sputtered, shaking, then got down in the water and urinated, looking around at the sand, the sea and sky. The water jostled her. She finished and rose and walked, splashing and reeling, out of the waves and on up toward the line of palm trees bordering the wide half circle of the beach. Lying down in the sand, still out of breath, she looked up at the moonlit clouds in the sky, the sparkle of the stars across which they sailed. It felt as though the beach were moving. She lay there shivering. In a moment, she would get up and go back to the resort, to her room, and lock the door. In a moment. But it was good here, too, being alone. The waves came in with their shuddering, murmurous whoosh, and the sound lulled her. She felt a strange, empty kind of deliverance; that nothing, finally, had taken place. She looked down the beach in the direction of where she had left Duego but couldn't see him. Lying back, staring at the shapes in the silvery mists over the moon, she began to feel almost pleasantly sleepy.

2

The train made every stop heading south. At the Thirtieth Street Station in Philadelphia, it sat for more than an hour without any apparent cause. When Faulk asked one of the porters what was going on, the porter said, "Got me, sir."

"Is there something wrong with the train? Has something else happened?"

"Don't know, sir. I think maybe they waitin' for son'thin' down in the District." He was very dark and had a wide mouth that looked like a cut in his lower jaw.

"Thanks—if you hear anything, I wish you'd let me know."

"I doubt I'll hear anything, sir. But I sure will if I do."

"Which way is the dining car?"

"Both ways," the porter said. "Equidistant, too." He smiled.

"Thanks."

"Food ain't much good, though, I gotta tell yeh. Sammitches mostly. Process meat."

"Well."

The young man shook his head, wringing his hands. "Before today, I don't know that I would've felt the need to tell you that."

"I know."

"That boggles my mind, man. You feel how different it is now?"

"Yes."

"Maybe something good can come of this misery."

Faulk decided to take the opposite direction from where the Asian boy had gone, believing that an encounter would produce pressure in the other for some kind of response and be a source of further unease. He stepped out into the cool vestibule and pushed the panel that would open the door into the next car. This one smelled heavily of perfume, mingled with some kind of cleanser. A man was sleeping in the first row, legs draped over the arm of the seat next to him. Two elderly women were at the far end, talking quietly, and they studied him as he passed them. The dining car was empty. At the food counter in the little vending area a middle-aged woman sat, reading a thick paperback. Her tight-curled hair was red, and many freckles dotted the light brown skin of her cheeks. There was something puffy about her face. "Hello," she said, putting the book down.

Faulk sat at the counter. "Hello."

"Slow trip."

"Do you know why the delay?"

She shrugged. "Something about D.C. They got hit there, too, you know."

"I heard."

"You coming from Boston?"

"I got on this one in Newark. I was in New York."

"Oh, Lord."

"Didn't hear a thing. I was uptown. My aunt called me about

it from Washington." He gazed toward the small window into the next car, which looked empty. "There were so many people on the train out of New York."

"I don't think I ever seen it this empty on this one."

"How long have you worked here?"

"Eight years. Got the job when my husband passed. Raised four kids and never worked outside the house."

"I'm sorry to hear about your husband."

"Well." She gave him a forbearing look. "Eight years ago. You notice how this kind of trouble makes you want to tell people—" She stopped and seemed to have reminded herself of something. "Well, it does *me*, anyway."

"I know what you mean." He gazed at the menu card.

"You married?" she asked.

He looked at her.

"Sorry to pry. I just feel this need today to know everybody I meet."

"It's fine. We're all going through it."

"Right. You got that one right for sure."

"I'm divorced."

"There's a lot of that, I guess."

"Fifty percent of the time, I believe."

"Guess I read that somewhere."

Presently she said, "They all begin in hope, though."

"That's true."

"All that happiness and celebrating."

"Right."

"Nobody does it *planning* to get miserable."

"No." He liked her. He felt a surge of grief for her troubles, whatever they were. "Actually, I'm getting married for a second time. If she can get home from Jamaica."

"Jamaica."

"She was vacationing with an old friend. Now since all the planes are grounded—well, today I was stuck on one island, and she was stuck on another. She was supposed to fly home tomorrow."

"Well, I hope you can get together and be happy."

"Fifty percent chance." He smiled at her.

"I wonder what gets into people," she said. "My husband and me, we were happy as kids together right up to the end."

"You were lucky."

She nodded emphatically. "We were that. We *felt* that."

The door of the car on the other side opened, and a man entered, carrying a small brown briefcase. He sat at the far end of the counter and placed the briefcase in front of him. He looked to be in his late fifties or early sixties, with a drooping, pale face and light blue eyes that had shadows under them. His hair was dark gray with white streaks, and it was disarranged, as if someone had ruffled it. He smoothed the hair down with one hand, leaning forward to look over the varieties of snack foods in the baskets on the wall behind the counter.

"Hello," the woman said to him.

"You have fresh coffee?"

"Sure."

The man turned his attention to Faulk. "You live in Washington?"

"No, but that's where I'm headed."

He seemed satisfied with this.

"You?" Faulk said.

"I live there."

When the woman put the coffee in front of him, he took her hand. "I wonder what you think of all this."

"Oh—well. I—I can't—I don't know what to think. I was just telling this gentleman I feel like I have to get to know everybody I meet."

"Yeah." He let go of her.

"You got a family?" she asked.

"Four grown kids. Three girls and a boy. A nice friendly wife. Like that." He smiled. "They're all waiting for me to get home and try to explain this day to them, you know? They've all gathered at the house."

"I think the Lord works in mysterious ways."

"Yeah. His wonders to perform, right?"

"Mysterious."

"Okay."

"I think maybe it's like this," she said. She appeared to be trying to formulate the idea as she went on, hesitating. "It's like we all—flowers, and—and the Lord is like the gardener. Right. We all flowers in his garden. And sometimes he needs one flower, or maybe two or three, and then sometimes, you know, he needs a whole bouquet of them."

"You believe that."

"I hope so."

"And you're happy."

She stared at him. "Yes, sir."

"And today was just a gardening day for God."

"Will there be anything else, sir?"

"You know the suicide bombers over in Jerusalem. They believe that when they blow themselves up and a lot of innocent men, women, and children die, they themselves are going straight to paradise for it."

She took up a rag and began to wipe the counter. She lifted his cup and wiped under it and then set the cup down with a little force.

"They believe deep in their hearts that they're going straight to paradise where they will be greeted by virgins. Virgins. Think of it."

She said nothing.

"And for us it's gardening."

"Excuse me," Faulk said. "There's really nothing to be gained by haranguing someone at this time of night and in this situation, is there?"

The man did not answer but opened the briefcase. For the moment his head was obscured by the open lid of the case. Both Faulk and the woman watched him. Then she turned to Faulk and said, low, "You want anything to eat or drink?"

"Thought I was hungry," Faulk said. "Feeling's gone."

She said, "Terrible day."

The man closed the lid with a snap and lifted his coffee cup. He sipped from it. "I was in Boston at a funeral," he said. "Business associate of mine. We were in 'Nam. He got wounded, and I pulled him onto a chopper in a firefight. Bullets ripping the air all around us and pinging on the metal. All hell breaking loose. I pulled him in. Nice guy. Another war altogether. Jungle rot and little people hiding in the leaves, some of them just kids. Kill you quick as look at you. I'll tell you, lot of gardening going on in that war. And it's one goddamned war after another, isn't it."

The woman did not respond, standing by the cash register looking at him.

"Wish I could see the world like you do, ma'am."

"Excuse me, but you don't know how I see the world, sir. You don't know the first thing about me."

He raised the cup as if to toast her. "To gardening."

"Maybe I said that to make *you* feel better."

"Well, it did that, all right."

"What's your point, anyway?" Faulk said.

"Pardon?"

"What're you getting at? What's the point of bothering to be so unpleasant tonight?"

"And what are you, a lawyer?"

"I happen to be a priest."

Both of them stared.

"Now, you want to start in on me?"

"I didn't know I was starting in on anybody. I was just talking. Seemed odd, that's all—that business about God the gardener. I don't know how anybody can think anything positive after today." His voice broke. "I'm sorry."

After a little pause, the woman, in a soft, ameliorative voice, said to him, "You want more coffee?"

"Yes, thank you." He held out the cup.

Faulk said good night to them and went back through the vestibule and the door, the mostly empty car, to the next vestibule and his own car and along the aisle to his seat. The train rattled and tossed, and then it entered a tunnel, the dark at the windows becoming blackness with intermittent rushing lights. He sat down and saw his own reflection in the glass. *So,* he thought. *I happen to be a priest.*

3

She woke in bright moonlight, wrapped uncomfortably in the wet clothes. She sat up and had a shaken realization of the whole long day. It played across her memory in an instant. She saw the couple, looking so small, leaping from the hole in the massive burning side of the building. She saw the slight, brave, doomed, waving woman with the smoke coming from her hair and back. And she thought of Michael Faulk. "Oh, Jesus God."

The sea made its steady rushing. She could not see the resort nor anything but empty beach with the blackness beyond it and the moving whitecapped waves. She sat up, shivering, the residue of the dream playing across her nerves.

Suddenly, with a strange forceful slow assuredness, someone was upon her from behind, hands on her breasts.

She yelled and tried to turn, swung her elbows back to strike. Reaching over her head, she got ahold of hair and pulled and was pushed forward until her face was in the sand. The other was heavy on top of her, knee in her upper back, one hand pressing her head down. The sand was in her nose and mouth, and this was going to be her death. But then he let go enough for her to turn over, and she saw Duego and kicked at him, attempting to rise, the sand choking her. "Stop it! Get off me! Are you—get *off*!"

"You—are—beautiful," he groaned, moving back on top of her. "We both—want this. You—know we both want this."

The force of it amazed and bewildered her. He was very strong. She kicked twice more at him, gagging, coughing, and when she reached for his eyes, he took her wrists and forced her over and held her, so that once more the sand was in her mouth. She had to use her hands to keep her head out of it, to breathe, and now he was pulling at her jeans, the sand choking her. She lost consciousness, her mind buckling. She was elsewhere, her hurting body separate from her, something not hers, and his hands were at her hips, pulling her up and toward him. "You know you—want this," he breathed. "Come on." She was sick, coughing deep, spitting, trying to scream and gagging, crying. He was ramming himself at her, thrusting at her and then into her with what felt like a tearing. He held her there, by her hips, rigid, pressing tightly and then moving, murmuring something about fate, their fate. It went on, hurting, wounding, until she lost consciousness for another moment, drifting off in a terrible asphyxiating fog, her face down in the sand. Everything was blank, gone, nowhere, and suddenly she was awake, him pushing in and pulling out and pushing in, gripping her at her hips. "Oh," he said. "God." Then there were the little spasms. He held her even tighter to himself, shuddering, moaning.

Finally he moved away from her, lying once more on his back, making the crying sound of before, arms flung out, looking like someone who had been knocked down.

Struggling to her feet, she kicked him in the side of his chest. It hurt her foot, and she shouted in pain and rage and then couldn't get sound out anymore, still choking on sand and blood where she had bitten her tongue and her lip. She kicked at his groin and fell back. He did not seem conscious. But then he was up and upon her. "You should not have done that," he said, holding her down with one hand on her chest and with the other taking hold of her jaw. She flailed, and gagged, and his knee came down on her middle, both hands at her head. He took a fist full of sand and thrust it down in her face, then took more and held her jaw tight, squeezing, jamming the sand at her mouth, packing it in, and pressing it, and grabbing more and pushing it at her, while she tried to bite at the fingers and coughed and the knee was pressing her chest, the one hand pulling her jaw down, the sand going in. He rolled with her, was back on top, ranged across her lower spine, his palms on the base of her skull, forcing her face down into the wet sand. Her vision blurred and ended, was all black. She was gone and nothing, no sound and no sensation but the choking and no air at all, and the heaviness on her chest, and this was death. This was the last of life.

But she rose from the dark, awake, still choking. He had fallen from her. She got to her knees, gouged at his eyes, spitting, the sand coming up in a clod with the contents of her stomach. He pushed her aside and stood up, taller than she could believe, as if he had undergone some elemental transformation and had become more than human, taller than anything. He would surely kill her now, and now all she wanted was to keep breathing, to be alive, away, and quiet. She watched him stagger away with his long shadow in the moonlight, on down the beach, crying that he was sorry and that it was something meant to be. Apologizing. *Apologizing!* She tried to scream but was too woozy and sick. The sickness kept coming and coming, mixed awfully with the sand. "Oh, God!" she screamed, choking. "Help me."

She managed to get briefly to her feet, sought to bring forth another scream, nothing coming but more heaving. She was on her knees again and then on all fours, head down, sputtering, gagging. The sand burned in her eyes, the grains of it scraping the iris, stinging, and she couldn't get it out of her nose and mouth. It came rushing out of her with the whiskey she had drunk. She could not breathe in, kept trying to, hearing the whooping sound that came from her.

At last, slowly, with great difficulty, as if having to break through something heavy and solid in the air around her, she rose and moved to the shore, tottering into the surf, falling to her knees, the waves crashing over her. She put her face down in the water and ran her hands over the grit of sand in her hair and along her hairline. The water seemed colder than it had been earlier. There was so much moonlight now. She got down, so that the water was just below her shoulders. It jostled her, but she remained crouched there, shoved by the motion of the waves, looking at the clean white moon surrounded by shadowy clouds.

The moon of any night on earth.

She kept her arms wrapped tightly around herself, sobbing, coughing, hacking. The tide seemed to be rising, the waves growing stronger. She let the waves come over her. The beach was empty, and she could see her clothes lying there—the jeans, with the panties tangled in them.

She did not know how long she stayed there, afraid that he might return. The moon went away and then came back again.

She could not stop the crying or the gasping for air. A few hundred yards up the beach, a couple walked to the water's edge and in. She knew the tide would carry them this way. And she felt fear of them. Gathering all her strength, she rose and left the water and made her way to the little sad pile of clothes. She managed to get into her jeans, still feeling where he had pushed into her, the pain there and across her lower back and along her jaw. She kept looking down the beach where he had gone, but there were only the looming palms.

Faltering in the loose sand, she walked, tottering, back to the resort, and in, toward the elevators. A few people still lingered in the bar. At the elevators, she pressed the button and waited. Smoothing her hair, she kept back a scream, looking to one side and then the other, fearing the sight of anyone, wanting more than she had ever wanted anything to get to her room and be quiet there, safe, door locked, all the lights on. She heard a man shouting in one of the first-floor rooms. The words were not distinguishable, but the tone could not be mistaken: someone was being mocked and belittled. She thought of men beating up their wives.

The elevator door opened, and she stepped in, and as it began to close, the fingers of a brown hand grasped the door and pulled it back. Nicholas Duego got on, looking soiled and ill, his shirt open, his hair wild and full of sand. He simply looked at her, where she had backed to the corner away from him, arms crossed over her chest. He would kill her here. Yet she wanted to fly at him, too, wanted to find the force within herself to obliterate him. She was crying. "Please," she said. "Don't. Don't."

"I am a nice man," he said. "You will know that about me."

"I'll scream. I swear I'll fucking scream."

"I have never—" He stopped. There were actually tears in his eyes.

Suddenly she felt power, unreasoning strength. Some part of her knew that it was the last thing she would do or say. "Keep away from me, you *fuck*."

"My unhappiness and anger made me cruel." He lifted one hand.

She pressed against the railing, turning from him. "No."

"I am not unkind. I would not take what was not given."

The elevator door opened. He had pushed no button. "Keep away," she managed, backing out. "I swear to God I'll scream."

He followed. There was an aluminum trash can with an ashtray full of sand by the elevator door. She picked it up—it was surprisingly light—and backed away from him, down the hall. He kept coming, but he was holding his hands out in a pleading way. When she got to her door she held the thing up level with her shoulders, as if to throw it. "I'll hit you with this," she said. "Get the fuck away from me. God*damn* you."

"I did not mean to hurt you." He seemed incredulous. "It made me mad when you kicked me. We were together on the beautiful beach, you and me." He turned and looked behind him and then moved to the next door down—Constance's room.

Natasha got her door open, scrabbled inside, and closed it. She set the ashtray trash can down with a loud metallic thud, and fumbled with the chain lock. She couldn't get it, couldn't make it work, but a moment later, just in time it seemed, she got the dead bolt to click into its socket.

His voice came, too loud, from the other side. "I do not take what is not given. It was ours."

She put her ear to the wood, listening for a moment, and when she peered through the peephole she saw that he was still there, head down, one hand out leaning on the frame of the door. "Oh, please go," she said, with a loud whimpering cry. "Please. I won't say anything. Just please. Please leave me alone."

Nothing. She waited, afraid to look. The nausea was returning. She went to the window and looked out at the light on the water. Back at the door, she put her eye to the peephole, and, seeing the long prospect of the empty hallway, turned around and sank slowly to a sitting position, knees up, crying and retching drily while the night breezes came in. The air itself felt dirty, stained. Time went away while she half lay there. It might have been hours. The hands of the clock were dead. Finally she made her way into the bathroom and ran the water, all the water—hot and cold, in the sink and in the bathtub. She tore the clothes off herself and threw them to the floor, shuddering, but then gathered them and put them in a plastic bag and stuffed the bag into the trash can that was still by the door. In the bathroom, avoiding the sight of herself in the mirror, she got into the tub and plugged it with the shiny metal lever, then sat down in the hot water and watched the swirls of it, blood streaked, at her ankles. When the water was near the middle of her calves, she turned the spigot off and unplugged the tub and let it all run out. Then she reseated the plug, adjusting the water so that it was even hotter. She soaked a washrag and put soap on it and went over herself, crying and scrubbing, hurting.

All this time the spigot in the sink was running, too. The room was steaming up. She stood up in the soapy water of the tub and turned the shower on. The shower water was losing its heat, but she remained under it, letting the stream of it run down her body. There was so much sand in her hair. She washed it, stood, head back, under the flow. The mirror and the window were a blank fog. The steam rose and curled about her. She turned the water off, thinking of fire and death. The attacks in the far-off cities of home.

Oh, yes. That.

She could not get clean. There was not enough water in the world.

After

Natasha and Michael

I

He might've slept. He had a moment of believing himself to be home, then realized that this trip was not taking him home. It had felt like mind wandering, but he understood now that it had been dreaming and that he had been asleep. He sat forward and looked out into the moving-by of the houses and streets and fields. The train was coming into what he thought was Washington, but it was Baltimore. It slowed and rocked and clanked, and now the platform came into view, the light there making a wide white bell shape in the dark. When the train stopped, through the rising steam and dust from the wheels, he saw the Asian boy get off. The boy went by the window and glanced at him and hesitated, then tentatively held up one hand for a few seconds. All his heartbreak was in the gesture, and he was someone moving through the most terrible hours of his young life, being determinedly decent, going on away.

Michael Faulk looked at the station platform. The light sputtered, threatened to go out, some momentary drain of power. A lone figure, a man in a hooded sweatshirt, wandered out of the dimness and took a seat on a bench by the wall, arms folded, face in the deep gloom of the hood he wore. The man's shadow went out from him. Faulk thought of the people of his country, personified in the Asian boy's last gesture and in this image of a man sitting alone in unsteady light. The train had come, as trains do, into the station. Things would go on. And yet it all felt broken. He had left the priesthood.

Finally the train rocked into motion. He sat back in the seat and tried to sleep, and couldn't. He thought of Natasha, so young and so far away. He hoped that somehow she had got in touch with Aunt Clara. He did not want to think of her worrying about him.

Washington looked unchanged. He tried to peer into it as the train neared Union Station. He did not know what he might find, but it felt important to watch for some essential difference, whatever that might be: cordoned-off streets or police flashes, more light in the neighborhoods. But there wasn't much to see except the other rails with their dull strand of sheen, paralleling the track he was on, and, beyond that, the city's businesses and the monuments, the neighborhoods, flickers of brightness in many windows, and then small vistas of avenues and the darker shadows of trees in the streetlamps. The angle wasn't right to see the Washington Monument, but the Capitol dome was visible, glowing somehow with greater dignity in soft white light. When the train stopped it seemed to give a last shudder, as though sighing with weariness. He hurried out of the car and up the stairs to the main level. All the lights were on, and a few passengers walked behind and in front of him. It was very quiet. No one was saying anything to anyone else. Every sound carried hollowly—footsteps, baggage being pulled along, the small clatter of the cleaning and restocking of shelves by quiet workers. It all reverberated in the cavernous height of the ceiling. A few men and women were lined up at the ticket counter. No one seemed to be *with* anyone. Most of the restaurants and shops were barred and closed. Several people—it looked like a family—were ranged among the benches at one gate, amid suitcases and cartons of food and blankets they'd obviously retrieved from their bags. The man and his wife and a young boy were asleep. A girl in her early teens slouched on the shoulder of the sleeping woman, reading a book. She stared glumly, almost warily, at Faulk as he crossed in front of her, headed for the front entrance.

Out in the circular road at the front, the flags were at half-staff. He had never really looked at them before. A warm breeze blew. It was a humid night. Cabs were parked along the curb. He got into the first one and gave the driver Aunt Clara's address.

The driver was a young man with large black eyes under thick black brows in a narrow, bony face—he looked like someone who had spent all day studying and whose mind was elsewhere.

He pulled out in traffic, and for a little space Faulk gazed at the back of his head, watching him negotiate the crowded lanes with a measure of aggressiveness, muttering low at other cars, attending to everything as if he were alone. At length, Faulk sat back, determined to ignore him. He saw the shifting views of the street and the other people in the cars they passed. Massachusetts Avenue. A couple in one car was laughing at something, the woman gesturing and nodding, the man holding up one hand as if in surrender.

How could anyone find a way back to lightheartedness?

This abysmal day had brought everything of normal life into question. What could be left of banter, jokes, silliness? He knew that this thought was irrational and that people would go on being people. Long ago he had learned to cultivate a healthy distrust of his own thinking when he was in the grip of anxiety.

He endeavored to concentrate on the ride, the streets and sporadic lights sweeping across the windows. He thought of Natasha in Jamaica. He looked at the night outside the car window, trying to picture her warm and asleep. And there her image was, clear and true, and his heart ached.

"Washington is your home?" the young man said suddenly.

Startled by the sound of the voice, Faulk took a few seconds, then said, "No."

"You're visiting."

"Yes."

"I have lived here twelve years."

He searched his mind for something neutral to say.

The other spoke first. "Twelve years. I love America."

"Me, too."

"I'm a citizen, and some men wanted to beat me up today. Me. An American. They wanted to take my life."

"Sorry to hear that."

The young man seemed about to cry. "I'm not a Muslim." He was looking in the rearview mirror, waiting for Faulk to respond.

"Well, in any case you're not a terrorist—"

"My family—they—we're Palestinian Christians, and I've lived twelve years in this city, and I'm an American citizen."

"It's been a bad day for everybody. Some people don't know how to handle it."

"They wanted to do me harm. For the way I look. An American citizen."

"Hysteria." Faulk shook his head at the inadequacy of his own expression, staring out at the city in the sparkling dark, the houses set back from the street with their warm lights and open windows. He saw some people sitting on a porch in the light from a doorway.

"My driver friends, they helped. They protected me."

He did not want to talk now. He let a moment pass, watched the traffic coming the other way. Out the window to his left was Dupont Circle, with its little knots of people smoking and talking and drinking. He saw litter on the grass under a tree with a broken branch drooping onto the sidewalk. The streets feeding into the circle were full of glittery light. All the cafés and bars were closed, but there were people on the sidewalks, standing in the false brightness, talking. He saw two women embracing. The cabbie had grown quiet, and now Faulk worried that there was something hurtful about not taking the man's part more.

He said, "People get scared and it makes them stupid."

But the cabbie drove on quietly, having expressed his outrage. Someone called on the dispatch, and he spoke in another language into the little microphone. Then he turned his music up.

The rest of the ride was silent, but for the low music and the occasional sputter on the dispatch speaker. Faulk looked at the streets of his second home, and at the back of the cabbie's head.

When they pulled up in front of Aunt Clara's house, the cabbie tipped his cap back on his forehead and said, "You're a kind person." Then he smiled—there was something dimly hangdog about it.

Faulk paid him, smiling, and nodded. "Yeah," he said. "You, too. Keep the change." He got out of the car, pulling his bag, and pushed the door shut with his hip. It didn't close all the way. Putting the bag down, he opened the door and slammed it, then leaned

down and waved. The taxi pulled away. Michael Faulk watched it
go down to the end of the street and turn, on out of sight. The
bag had never felt heavier. He strode across to the porch and up
the steps to the door. Aunt Clara opened it and pushed the screen
toward him. She was in her nightgown. "God," she said. "You
scared me to death."

"I've never been on a longer ride."

"It's three-thirty in the morning."

He put the bag down in the living room. She came to him and
put her hands on his shoulders. "You all right?"

"Have you spoken to Natasha?"

"The lines are all jammed from here out of the country. I tried.
Believe me."

"I've got to call Iris."

"I spoke to her. She knows you're all right. She had another
little fall. But she's all right, she says. The hurt knee was unscathed.
That's how she put it."

"She wouldn't say anything if it *wasn't* unscathed."

"Well, she says she's fine. She doesn't sound fine, I have to say.
But she says she is. And who can be fine after a day like this. What
am I talking about?"

"I'm not thinking straight, either," Faulk said to her.

"Greta's upstairs in her old room. Her hubby's in meetings or
something with Congress and Senate people."

Faulk nodded and sighed, and felt his exhaustion like a form of
failure.

"Somebody said the Pennsylvania one was headed for the Capitol Building or the White House."

"Jesus."

"Can I fix you something to eat or drink?"

"I think I just want a glass of water."

They went together into the kitchen, and she put ice in a glass
and poured the water. "Jack went to bed at nine. He hasn't been
feeling all that well. He's been fighting the first cold of the year.
And then this business has really upset him."

"Still can't quite believe it," he told her. "The whole thing."

"Nobody can believe it. Everybody's in shock."

Then Jack was there, leaning on the frame of the doorway. "I'm feeling all right," he said. You could hear the congestion in his voice. "Don't get up, son," he said as Faulk started to rise. He shuffled over to the refrigerator and got a beer. "Do you believe this shit?"

"That's exactly what my father said," Faulk told him.

"We were just saying—" said Clara.

"I heard you." Jack opened the beer. "And I still end up saying: do you believe this shit?"

"I remember being so appalled at the bombing there in '93. At what they were *trying* to do."

"The cabbie who brought me here got attacked this morning," Faulk told them. "Poor guy only looks the part. A Palestinian Christian, for God's sake."

"What will happen next, I wonder," Clara said. "I mean we're at war with *somebody*. Maybe the whole rest of the world."

Greta came to the doorway now, wrapped in a light blue robe, looking at each of them. She walked over and hugged Faulk. "Hello, Cuz."

"Hi."

She looked at Jack. "Can I have a little of that in a glass?"

Jack got a glass out of the cabinet and poured some of the beer. Greta sat down across from Faulk. "I can't do this at home unless there's a big gathering." She shook her head and smiled, turning to Faulk. "Have you got in touch with Natasha? And congratulations, by the way."

"Thanks. And no."

"Imagine. Stranded in paradise."

"How are you?"

"We were sitting outside eating breakfast and watching the rowing crews on the river. We heard the explosion. It shook the water glasses on the table. And then we saw the smoke. Tom knew immediately it was a plane."

Jack stood leaning on the stove and drank the beer. He said, "I heard tonight on the news that the bastard who did it, the mastermind, is a guest of the Taliban. In Afghanistan."

"I can't remember the name," Faulk said.

Greta said the name. "Tom's been talking about him for years."

"Clinton tried to get him," Jack put in. "A goddamned rich kid from Saudi Arabia. Big oil family."

"So we're gonna be at war with Afghanistan?"

"Looks like it."

They were silent for a few moments.

"I'd like to see us rebuild both towers even taller than before," Jack said. "And with both buildings culminating in the shape of a fist with the middle finger raised, facing east."

"Jack," Clara said. But she smiled.

"Tom's afraid they might use this as an excuse to go after Iraq."

"That's alarmist," said Clara. "Isn't it?"

"Well, there's a lot of worry about the nuclear thing, and the chemicals. Biological weapons. That pig is importing uranium, they say. And we know he's used chemicals and gas on his own people."

"Have to see about the train to Memphis," said Faulk. "Sorry."

"Stay with us," Clara urged.

"Gotta set out finding us a house. Natasha's furniture's due to arrive—well, the first day it might arrive is tomorrow, I think. They get a window of ten days. But God I hope it's sooner." He sighed, briefly contemplating the new life. "We should've settled on something before she left Washington, but it just wasn't possible."

"She'll want to look with you, don't you think?"

"You'll stay with Iris," Jack said. "Wasn't that the plan?"

"I guess." Faulk looked into the water and ice in his glass, and rattled it a little. He drank. The water tasted faintly metallic. He held the glass toward his aunt, remembering that he had awakened in the morning of this terrible long day with a hangover. "Do you think I could have a little whiskey in this?"

2

"Oh, Jesus God." The words coming from her own mouth awakened her, and she lay crying silently for many minutes. Here, in her mind's eye, was Duego standing over her. She had the realization that this had played and replayed in her fitful dozing the whole night.

A moment later, the idea of Michael Faulk inside the squat cloud in New York, among the dead and dying, flickered across her consciousness with the picture of herself lying in the sand, drunk and stoned, kissing Duego on the beach in Jamaica, before Duego showed himself to be what he was. Putting her hands over her eyes, she attempted to erase all the images, sobbing.

In the night, after the long time in the bathroom, she had come out and wrapped herself in a robe and simply collapsed across the bed.

Now, trying to be quiet, not wanting Constance to hear her, she reached for the room phone and rang the front desk. No answer. She pulled the robe tight around herself and went into the bathroom. There was pain where he had pushed into her, and she took the little mirror attached to the sink and tried to examine herself. Her inner thighs were red, and it felt as though there might be a little tear just inside the opening. Moving her finger gently there, she felt only the slight sting of it but no abrasion.

There was no more blood, either. Her foot hurt, where she had kicked him, and her middle toe was bruised.

She took another long warm bath, trembling and washing herself gingerly with the soft rag. The muscles of her hips ached and were also tender to the touch. Probably there would be bruises there, too. She would need time for that to fade. She wanted desperately to find a way to make it so nothing had happened. Nothing. It would be something not done, not lived through. It would be something that had not ever been.

She heard herself breathing and then realized, slow, that the breathing was a low scream. She stood there in the steam of the bath, dripping wet, turning in a small circle in the light.

Finally she applied a towel to her body and willed herself to clean her teeth, nearly retching when she spit the water.

After managing with her trembling hands to put her hair back in a ponytail, she dressed and went out into the hall and to the elevators. This took all the courage she could muster. She saw no one.

Down in the lobby, there were people on the phones. She went to the front desk, where Mrs. Ratzibungen stood writing in a notepad. "I want to call my fiancé," Natasha said to her in a shaky voice—oddly, painfully aware of the frightful ordinariness of the words. She pressed on: "They usually put a call through to my room from him about this time."

"I vill make zuh call for you. Vill you vrite zuh number here?"

She wrote the number. Mrs. Ratzibungen stared at the shakiness of her fingers with the pen. Twice she dropped it and had to pick it up.

"I vill put it through to you upstairs," she said, softly.

"Thank you." Natasha hurried back around to the elevators and up to her room. The hall was empty and quiet, no one stirring. Certainly there would be open phone lines now. Certainly she could know for sure, for good and all, that Michael was safe. Alive. Himself, as she could learn all over again to be herself.

Sitting on the bed waiting, she kept shivering and trying not to let her mind run. But it was running. Not about Faulk, now, but about possible pregnancy, the varieties of venereal disease, the ways people were deformed or scarred by such calamities, or died from them. And each thought was woven over the image of Nicholas Duego towering above her.

Could one report a rape the next day? Whom would she report it to, here? No, she had decided definitely not to do that.

She had never consistently taken the pill. There had been the others, and after Mackenzie there were those strangers, and of course there was Mackenzie, too. And Faulk. And nothing had happened, and her last period had ended more than a week before she left for Jamaica. "Oh, God. Please. Help."

The call would not come. She felt certain now. She believed that the news, whenever it should reach her, would be bad. A punishment. More of this hell that had enveloped her. A voice from her life in the world came to her, accusing, judging: *You deserve it. It's you.* She shook her head and closed her fists in her lap.

"No," she said aloud. "It is not. It is *not*."

She heard Constance moving around next door.

At last, startlingly, the phone rang, and she dropped the receiver trying to bring it to her ear. "Hello?"

"Baby." His voice went over her like air for someone suffocating.

"Oh, Michael—oh. Oh, my God. Michael. Michael."

"I'm all right. I didn't even know it was happening. Clara called me with it. I was up on Fifty-Fourth Street in the hotel room. A long way away."

"I've been lost, Michael. I'm lost." She sobbed.

"I'm so sorry, honey." He went on to tell her about how he woke up and it had already happened and how clean the sky looked out his hotel window. As she listened, she experienced again the sense of him as being innocent, less worldly than she.

"Have you been able to get through to Iris?" he asked.

She could not stop crying. A part of her wanted to tell him what had happened, blurt it out—but then the breath for speech itself was gone. Wouldn't it mean that he would come to know more than he would understand? He would have to know everything.

"Natasha," he said. "I'm all right, honey. We're fine. You'll be back here in no time, and we'll be together."

"Oh, yes," she got out, sniffling. It occurred to her that the anxiety regarding what he would come to know of her past must stem from something existing between them as a couple. The disorienting sense that she was the one who was older came rushing back, and the lightness of his voice—that boyish unaware brutal confidence—frightened and depressed her. She felt this in a second, and it was obscurely some failure on her part.

"Enjoy the water," he said. "And the sun and fresh air and try to put it out of your mind. It's over. I'm safe. We're safe. If we let it make us less than we are, then they win. Nothing good can come from dwelling on it, right? We're okay. Call Iris."

"It's hell," she said to him. "I want to come home. Can't you or Senator Norland do something to bring people who got stuck overseas home? I was important to him. He tried to discourage me from leaving. I was important to him. Can't he do something?"

"I'm sure if he could, he would."

"I want to come home, Michael."

He said, "I know. But, honey—stop that. Stop talking like that."

"I can't help it."

Perhaps thirty seconds went by with only the small sound of static through the line.

"You there?" he said.

"Do you—do you want me to call you back after I talk to Iris?" she asked.

"I've gotta go to the train station in an hour or so."

"Okay."

He murmured, "We're okay, darling."

"I miss you," she said, and felt it, a physical pang, like something molten being poured into her bones. It stopped her breath. She would never love anyone so much. "Michael!" she burst forth in a moment's terror that he would hang up before she could tell him that. But she had said the words. There were no other words. "I love you," she told him. The tears kept coming.

"It'll be all right, sweetheart. I'm out of there. And soon we'll be together in Memphis."

"Yes," she got out. "Yes, darling."

He was gone. She put the handset back in its cradle and lay over on her side, facing the window and the French doors leading out onto the balcony, still seeking to compose herself, working to beat back the images that kept repeating in her thoughts. Constance had come out on her own balcony next door. The older woman's shadow was on the green tiles there. A silhouette that held a glass up and drank. "Is Michael all right?" Constance called.

"Yes," Natasha said loudly, and then she repeated the word in a near whisper. "Yes." She sighed, feeling momentarily released, the first real sense of things working out all right moving through her with a surge of near elation, until she stirred on the bed and felt the discomfort in her hips and between her legs.

After a few seconds, Constance's voice: "I myself never thought otherwise. But we're grounded, you know. Stuck here."

Natasha did not answer.

"Want some orange juice?"

She watched the shadow-shape drink; the head back, tilted to the sky. She got up from the bed and stepped out. You could tell it to a friend. You could say it to a friend. The other woman was in her Japanese robe, holding the glass at her hip and gazing off into the measureless distance. The sea was ablaze with morning, and in the brightness it was difficult to see her face.

Constance looked at her. "How do we feel?"

"Fine." Now Natasha would say it.

"You look awful. You been crying?"

"Yes, hasn't everyone?"

"This has done something to you. Michael is safe, right?"

"I just talked to him."

"Hey," Constance said. "So it's over. Everyone *we* know is safe." She leaned on the rail with the nearly empty glass in her hand and stared. "I mean, *right?*"

"Yes."

"Right." Constance gave forth a small derisive laugh.

"Constance?"

"I saw you on the beach," she said evenly. "I came looking for you. And I saw you."

Natasha waited, a freezing at her heart. Then: "You—what?"

The older woman nodded and with a furious motion tossed what remained of the orange juice over the railing. "That's right. I saw you. I saw you and that Cuban guy, whatever the fuck his name is. Lying on the sand going at it."

Abruptly, Natasha felt the chill under her heart as a kind of strength. She looked directly back into the other's eyes. "Why don't you tell me *exactly* what you think you saw."

"Are we really going to do this?"

"Yes, why don't we go ahead and do this, as you put it. Let's *do* it, Constance."

"Well, I saw you."

"You said that."

"He was on his back and you were leaning over him, kissing him. Deep."

"Nothing happened, Constance."

"It was serious tonguing. I'm not naïve."

"I—yes, I—I kissed him. I *kissed* him. I felt sorry for him. But that was the end of it."

"You expect me to believe that."

She turned to go back inside. "You can believe whatever the fuck you want to believe. Or whatever your ideas about me tell you to believe. This conversation is over."

In her room, she muffled her own sobs in the pillows of the bed, trying to stop. When she looked at the window, expecting to see Constance's shadow, the shadow was gone.

She took time to collect herself and then tried the front desk. No answer. She went out and along the hall to the elevators. The middle-aged couple she had seen the night before, who did not seem together, were waiting there. They had been murmuring animatedly in Spanish but stopped when she came up to them. The elevator opened, with a young Jamaican man and two little dark girls already on it. They all rode the four floors down in silence.

The lobby was nearly empty. At the front desk it was Ratzi now, looking beset and worried. "My brother," he said to her as she approached. "No one can find him."

"Sorry to hear that," she said. And couldn't ask him to put a call through to her grandmother. She walked to the entrance of the bar and asked a woman who stood there, a member of the restaurant staff. The woman went to the desk and spoke to Ratzi, who looked past her at Natasha.

"I'm sorry," Natasha mouthed.

Back in her room, she sat on the bed and waited. There were voices outside, shouts, children playing. The call came through. Once more, the ring startled her. "Hello?"

"Oh, my dear girl."

"I'm okay. I am." But her voice was all tears.

"You're not okay, I'm not deaf."

"No. I am. I'm all right." She would not. Not anyone. She waited.

"Father Mi—," Iris began but then stopped herself. "I mean, Michael is on his way home. He took the train, if you can believe it. He'll get here tomorrow morning."

"The first day the truck can get there is the day after tomorrow." Her voice began to leave her. She cleared her throat and made an unsuccessful attempt not to cough.

"You sound awful," her grandmother said.

"It's just a little—a little cough."

Iris sighed. "How long will the planes be grounded, I wonder. They're not charging you for the extra days, are they?"

"No."

The line crackled. Iris said something about the truck with Natasha's belongings.

"It's mostly books," Natasha said. "My bed. A table and some chairs and pictures."

Silence.

"Iris?"

Again, the old woman's voice, faint in the static distance: "Don't worry about me. But I did have another little fall getting out of bed. I'm fine. I called a cab and got myself to Dr. Rayford's office for X-rays, and it's fine. The original injury is healing fine. They gave me a cane."

How simple: you were injured and you went to see some people and they made sure you were all right and then they gave you something to help you keep going.

"God's sakes," Iris said. "Here I am talking about *my* little trouble. I'm sorry. When do you think you'll be able to come home?"

"I'll call you when I know more," Natasha got out.

"Okay, hon—"

And the connection was lost. She went into the bathroom and tried to put on a little more makeup. Her hands were shaking too much, and anyway makeup was something you did to look sexy.

Sexy.

She washed the makeup off, pat-dried her face, gathered herself, and went downstairs. Several people she didn't recognize were in the dining area. One couple had their bags around them. Jutting out of one bag was a small pennant advertising a cruise ship. The woman was writing furiously on a card, her face unnaturally pale.

The sun was pouring through the windows along the right side of the room and through the silk curtains over the French doors there. The patio outside was bathed in brightness and looked empty. The chairs were still upside down on the tables. All but one. At that table Constance sat reading a newspaper. Natasha crossed to another table, one that looked out onto the grassy hill leading to the mountain behind the resort.

Grace, the tall waitress with the dreads, approached. "Hello, young miss."

"Hello, just coffee, please. Strong."

"I remember how you like it." There was the faintest trace of a smile on her face and then heavy concentration as she moved away.

Ratzi came in from the lobby and looked around. When he saw Natasha, he walked over and took the chair opposite her. Feeling his proximity as obscurely invasive, she made an attempt not to show her aversion, holding herself erect, hands clasped in her lap. For a moment he sat there, pushing the hair back from his forehead, adjusting his shirtfront. "My brother was with an old girlfriend," he said. "All day and all night."

"I'm glad you found him." It was autonomic speech. She did not even hear herself.

"He didn't know about the disaster. The whole time. *Ficken*."

She said nothing.

"Sex crazy. Sorry for the vulgarity."

"I don't care about it."

"My mother is lying down in a terrible state from worrying."

"Sorry to hear it."

"That man, Mr. Skinner, he almost died. His wife is with him."

"Sorry to hear that, too." She felt the impulse to ask him what he wanted from her.

"Mr. Duego checked out of his room this morning and went into Kingston."

She felt something give way in her chest.

"He left a letter for you."

"Why would he write a letter to me," she managed.

Ratzi sat back and reached into the front pocket of his shorts and brought it out. It was in an envelope that was folded tightly in thirds. "I don't ask questions. I have to say that he did seem upset, though. Worried about something. I don't know—do you want it or not?"

She took it and put it in her purse. "Did you read it?" she asked.

"Of course not. And in case you don't believe me, you'll see that it's sealed." He stood. "Good day."

"I didn't mean anything by that," she told him. "I might've asked you to tell me what's in it. I don't want to look at it."

"It has nothing to do with me. If you don't want to read it, simply throw it away." He bowed, smiled emptily, and moved off.

> *Dear Lady,*
> *You will have to believe me that I am a gentleman. I have decided to remove myself from your vicinity as it is clear that something is between us now that you are very conflicted and still enraging about. I must not allow us further contact for this reason. As you know, I have just ended my relationship with my wife. I am not ready for the society of others and I have a great anger in me that you saw last night, and for which I am deeply apologizing now. I am sorry if in any way I made you uncomfortable and I do admit that I had more to drink after our first pleasant moments on the beach smoking and I did some other things and I was so mixed up I must say that there is much that I do not remember. It was very good for me to spend our time together, and I am sorry if I blacked out, as I must have done. I do wish you well. Podría haber amado.*
>
> *Nicholas Duego*

Podría haber amado. She wrote it down on a corner of the envelope and then with shaking hands tore the rest of the envelope and the note into many pieces and dropped them into her purse. Grace brought her coffee.

"Do you speak Spanish?" she asked Grace.

"Yes."

"What does this mean?" She held the piece of the envelope toward her.

Grace stared at it for a few seconds and then looked at her. "Who wrote this? It looks like a note in school."

"Tell me what it says," Natasha demanded.

"It says, 'I could have loved you.' "

She crumpled the piece of paper and dropped it in her purse, then picked up her coffee and blew across the surface of it, feeling the tremor under her heart of the wrath that had seized her. *I do not take what has not been given.* "Thank you," she said to Grace, who gave a little shrug and walked away.

Outside, Constance had stood and was stretching her arms into the sun. Constance. The reason for being here at all. Natasha finished the coffee quickly and went out, across the lobby, heading back up to her room. She saw as she passed that the television was on, playing to no one. Talking heads. She stopped, absorbed in spite of herself. The details of the attack were being discussed and analyzed and argued over. There was a scroll now at the bottom of the screen with further information. One of the hijackers had evidently lost heart and gotten on a train to the Midwest, no doubt meaning to lose himself in the vastness of the country. The discussion went on. The airlines losing tremendous amounts of money. The economic damage. Still many people missing, the search going on in the rubble. She couldn't watch it anymore.

In her room, she took the pieces of the letter and envelope out of her purse and put them in the trash can. Then she went out into the hall to the ice-and-vending space and emptied the trash can into a larger bin there. She returned the can with its sand-filled ashtray to its place, next to the elevator. Back in the room, she lay down with her hands folded over her chest and waited in vain for sleep. She heard Constance in the next room, and then saw the other woman's shadow out on the balcony.

"You asleep?" Constance called to her.

"No."

"Want to talk?"

"No."

"Not even a little?"

"What would we talk about?"

Constance sighed. "Anything."

Natasha sat around on the edge of the bed facing the window.

"Maybe go down to the beach," Constance said.

"I don't want to."

"We could swim and cool off."

"You go."

She came to the opening and looked in. "I'm sorry about before."

Natasha waited a little. "Forget it."

"It's none of my business what you do."

"Nothing happened, Constance."

The older woman came into the room and sat at the dressing table opposite the bed. Her gaze trailed down the wall, to the spatter of sand on the rug near the door, where the ashtray trash can had been. "Is that from the beach?"

Natasha hadn't seen it. "I don't know," she said.

"Well," said her friend. "It's nothing."

"Nothing is right."

"But you can't blame me for thinking it. I mean you *were* lying there on the sand together and he was on his back and you were leaning over him with your mouth on his. You were going at it like a couple of teenagers."

She could barely find the breath to speak. "I kissed him, and then he passed out. You should've stayed and spied a little more."

"I wasn't spying."

"And what exactly were *you* doing on the beach all day *drunk*?"

"Okay, let's just drop it."

"Well, I'm sure it's your business entirely, of course. But you *were* out there with the notorious Mr. Skinner. The cheater with all the health problems. Did you cheat with Mr. Skinner? You said you'd been down to the beach with several men. What went on,

Constance? Or is it that you're the grown-up and don't have to explain yourself?"

"Stop this. Right now. Before we say things we can't take back. And you know nothing happened with that poor browbeaten toad. Or anyone else, either."

"Well, you say that, but what *about* those others? The way you told us about going down to the beach with several men was pretty suggestive. So, really, what *happened* with them?"

"Now you cut this out. Nothing happened."

"Okay," Natasha said. "Right. Are we really going to do this?"

"Look. I wasn't—I wasn't spying."

"What was it, then? What do *you* call it?"

"Okay. I believe you. All right? I'm sorry."

She was close to screaming at the other, close to saying at the top of her voice what had happened later. She felt the hot urge to do so in the nerves of her throat.

"Really," Constance said. "It's none of my business anyway, like I said."

"You had sand on your back," said Natasha. "I saw it."

"Okay, okay. Really. Let's just stop this, now. Please."

They were quiet for a long time.

Presently, Constance said, "What will we do today?"

"I don't want to do anything but sleep. And be away from you."

"No, now, come on, sweetie."

Natasha said nothing.

"I said I'm sorry. I *am* sorry."

"I'm staying here."

"All day? You have an extra day. Maybe more."

"I don't feel like doing anything else. You do what *you* want."

There was another pause. At last, Constance rose and went around into her own room. Natasha drifted on the edge of sleep and woke with a start and then drifted some more. She wanted very badly to be down in sleep. When she stirred, there was silence, no sound from the other side of the wall.

She got out of the bed and moved to the entrance of the balcony, pausing there. She saw the different nuances of blue at the horizon. There were no clouds, no hint of them anywhere. People were sunning themselves and playing in the shallows or sitting in the pockets of shade, picnicking, talking quietly. Two dark men were standing over a lit barbecue, waiting for the flames to die down. The life of the island was proceeding. Life elsewhere was going on. Her native country would honor the dead. The president would make another speech, visiting the ruins, the wreckage of so many assumptions about the world. It was too far away to imagine. She stepped out into the peace of this afternoon in Jamaica, with the sun shining in jade light through the palm fronds, and the air stirring softly, warm tropical breezes that carried the low repeating roar of the sea.

3

During the long train ride to Memphis, Faulk tried to sleep. There was no comfort to be had. Late in the night he made his way to the dining car and asked for a brandy. They had nothing but beer. He drank three beers in iced glasses, though the good clear taste disappeared after the first. He ordered a fourth but didn't finish it. A young couple entered and took seats at the bar, nodding at him. He paid for the beer and wobbled slowly back to his compartment and lay down. The bed was narrow as a plank, the mattress so thin that he could feel the bands of metal supporting it.

He slept fitfully, the whole compartment pitching back and forth with the motion of the train, town lights gliding past the windows, other trains, seeming impossibly near, flashing by in a speeding instant, bells and blinking red lights at the crossings. The windows were black for a long time. And then they were full of sun, which made it stifling hot in that tight space. He'd lost track of time. He got up and went out and down to the dining car. There were no empty seats. A porter approached him and asked if he wanted to wait. But looking at the packed car with its faces showing the strain of the last two days, he decided that he wasn't hungry.

To be here felt too much like the bad journey down to Washington from New York. A quality of exhaustion hung in the air, the other passengers looking out at the rushing countryside. As he started out of the car a seat opened up near the door. He took it, realizing how tired he was. It was almost as if he collapsed into it. No, he told the porter, he had not decided what he wanted to eat. He asked for black coffee. Gazing out the windows at the countryside south of Cincinnati, he reflected on the fact that he had spent more time on trains now, just in the last two days, than he had spent on any other form of public transportation in his life. And he did not feel safe. And he wanted company. Something of the shock of those burning and collapsing buildings was only now beginning to weigh on him. He looked over at the thickset man across the aisle from him.

"We had the Renaissance," the man said to him, "and then we had the Enlightenment, and they've always hated us for that."

Faulk did not want to talk about it. "Awful," he said to the man, hoping to leave it there.

The man was traveling with two young girls, the taller of whom pushed past his heavy knees and out into the aisle. She stood before Faulk. "My name is Sheila."

"Sheila," the man said. "Come here."

"That's all right," Faulk told him. "Hello, Sheila."

"How old are you?" Sheila asked him. Her eyes were the color of clear water in sunlight.

"I'm very old. How about you?"

"I'm going to be seven. We saw a catastrophe. We were on vacation in Washington, D.C., and we saw a catastrophe. Have you ever seen one of those?"

"Sheila, don't bother the gentleman."

"No, it's fine," Faulk said. "Really."

"Have you ever seen a catastrophe?" the girl persisted.

"Well, yes."

"Did you see what we saw?"

"No, ma'am. I wasn't there."

"Don't you think it's elegant that I know the word *catastrophe*?"

"It certainly is." Faulk smiled at her and then at her father. "I think it's elegant that you know the word *elegant*."

"I know a lot of words."

"That's wonderful. You can never know too many words."

"I know the word *fanatical*, too. And *theocracy*. Do you know those words?"

"I do. But I'm so old. It's excellent that you know them."

"I just learned those two. My father said them and I learned them."

"Sheila," the girl's father said.

"We were there at the catastrophe," Sheila said. "We were going to the airport, and we saw a building on fire and smoke going way up in the sky. Way, way up. Way farther than anything we ever saw. So far. Smoke can be a catastrophe, can't it."

Faulk nodded at her and kept the smile.

"It scared me. Are you scared?" Sheila looked like she might begin to cry now.

"Sheila," her father said. "Come here, honey."

Faulk looked at him. "I was in New York."

"Our flight home was canceled."

"We live in Chicago," Sheila said, sniffling. "We're taking the train from Memphis."

"Come up," the man said, and pulled her onto his knee. The girl on the other side of him, probably four or five, said, "Daddy, I'm hungry."

The girl named Sheila said, "You always whine when you have nothing to whine about."

"Sheila."

"She has nothing to whine about. We didn't get a catastrophe."

"Be still." The man looked over at Faulk. "Tough to explain."

"Yes."

"You live in Memphis?"

"Yes."

"New York on business?"

"A wedding that got canceled."

"Yeah. Cancellations."

The girls went on arguing, and the man murmured to them.

Faulk got up from his seat and nodded at the man, then went to the entrance of the car and out, to the vestibule. Another man was standing there smoking a cigarette. The man wore a uniform—a dark blue coat and pants. Faulk pushed open the door into the next car and strode carefully in the rocking motion of the train to his compartment. Out the window there was a farmhouse and wide fields, rows of corn. He sat on the thin fold-up bed thinking about his country as he never had before. His own sighs came back to him from the walls, even with the rush and roar of the train, and he let the tears come.

4

Most of the day, Natasha kept to the room, and in the night she made herself walk out alone, along the shoreline. Just at the edge of the bath of light from the resort, she found a piece of driftwood a little smaller than a baseball bat lying in the sand and dry weeds. She carried it with her, tight in her fist. The night was peaceful and clear, and she watched the lights of a passing ship at the farthest line of the horizon. When she returned to the resort, she sat for a little while in one of the chairs on the veranda while the night breezes went over her. The susurration and clicking of the palms soothed her a little, though the whole scene also seemed to increase her sense of the uselessness of everything.

No one spoke to her.

Back in the room, she tried to sleep and couldn't. She wrote a few lines to Iris, and more to Faulk, but then crumpled the pages and threw them away. The phrases were fraught with complaining, and the complaints were colored by what was really the matter. It looked absurd, *was* absurd and selfish to be lamenting about being stuck in paradise, and if she kept the real situation to herself while complaining about being here, that was how it would seem.

The night wore on. Toward dawn, she woke sitting in her chair, her neck sore and stiff, both her hands asleep. She paced and swung her arms and rubbed her own numb fingers along her thighs and finally got into the bed under the sheets and lay staring at the white ceiling or at the flicker of lights out in the dark reaches over the sea. At last, sleep came, a dream that she was home, and there was nothing slightly nightmarish about it, yet when she woke, fear roiled in her stomach. Turning over on her side in the softly rising light, she thought about how far she had come from where she had just dreamed she was. There would be no more sleep in this dawn.

She went into the bathroom and looked at herself in the light. Amazingly, the sore places were not bruising. She saw herself, tanned, slim, no sign of violence showing. Her jaw was sore.

The hours of the morning were rainy with a slight chill in the air, though by early afternoon the temperature had risen. The waves thundered continually on the beach. She had gone back to bed, and she lay listening to the sounds. She did not even get up to eat.

She slept more, not aware of it as sleep until she opened her eyes and saw that the light was different. She turned and looked at the entrance of the balcony, the railing, and the ocean. She closed her eyes, dozed, and awoke to the rhythmic pounding of the surf and the fading light.

The day passed like this, and Constance stayed away. Constance was leaving her alone.

Natasha couldn't think now what they might find to talk about. And then of course she knew. They would talk about the attacks, the planes, the killings, and the backdrop of it all would be what Constance had seen of her and Nicholas Duego on the beach. It would be there, unspoken, the mud on the floor, as Iris used to say. Constance would never be able to accept that nothing had happened; and what she *did* believe about it was too far from the actuality to contemplate without anger.

There were little bottles of liquor inside the minibar. Constance had opened the one in her room on the first night. Natasha opened hers now and drank four of the bottles, two whiskeys, a brandy, and a rum, sitting up in the bed with the blankets over her knees. When she was finished with the rum, she stood, a little shakily, moved to the window, and closed the curtain across the entrance to the balcony, and then got back in bed.

It was night when she woke, still woozy from the drinks and with the beginning of a headache. Her lower back hurt, but she was sure this was from lying down so long. She lay there in the dark, suffering it, too near sleep to rise, and waiting for the drifting off that she thought would come. She could still feel the ghost-pressure of Nicholas Duego between her legs and along her hips, and she thought of finding some way to be insensible until that was gone, until it would stop. She got up and drank the last two little bottles, a gin and a vodka.

Faulk called in the morning. He was back in Memphis and would be looking at houses. "I'm just checking out places we can go see together," he said.

She felt nothing. "You choose," she said. "Really, I mean it, honey. I'm sure it'll be wonderful. I just want to be with you. You decide."

"Well, I'm not going to do that. If I see something I think you'll like I'll ask them to hold it until you get here. Baby, are you all right?"

She lost composure for a few seconds.

"Natasha?"

"No, I'm not all right. I want to be home. I hate this."

"I know," he said. "I know."

Later, she called Iris, who said that she wanted them to have a place of their own, nearby. She was healing fast from her fall. She sounded harried and stressed and worried about making everything perfect for Natasha's return.

"But I'm really feeling stronger every day," she went on. There was a quaver in her voice. "I'm worried about you. You don't sound right."

"I'm so tired of being here," Natasha got out.

She did not leave the room on this day, either. The hours passed. She bathed and cared for herself but did not eat. She could not read anything in the books she had brought, because her powers of concentration were broken. And when she could concentrate, she worried about being ambushed by something in the words. She felt this as a kind of fracturing of her deepest self.

Late that night she went on another walk, this time far along the beach, believing herself to be facing down the fear, heading straight at it, toward the lights that shone there. She wondered if it was Kingston, and then thought of Duego somewhere in that low sparkle far off. She went into the brush and picked up a heavy stone the size of a baseball. The walk back was hurried and aching, the muscles of her legs cramping, and there was a raggedness to every breath, a rasping that caught and seemed about to choke her. Near the resort, a man stepped out from the path leading there. She stopped and held the stone as if setting herself to throw it. "Keep away from me," she said.

He was gaunt, wasted looking, all bone, and his eyes looked too big for his head. He stared at her, standing very still. "Not moving, as you see."

"Stay back."

His movement was shaky, and she saw that he was very drunk. He staggered slowly by, as if meaning to circle her, but then went on to the water and in, where he simply waited as if expecting to be knocked over by the waves. Mrs. Ratzibungen came down the path and went past her. "Harmless," she said. "Poor creatuh. It is Lawton. My former friend. You remember. Please. He is drunk. He vill not hurt you."

Natasha dropped the stone in the sand and started toward the resort. Nothing would change, and this was now the way life would be. Full of unreasonable fear all the time. She went on, pushing through the sand, stumbling in it. The night was as hot as the day had been.

Constance was sitting in one of the chairs on the porch. She had a large flower in her lap. "Ratzi just went in to get us a rum collins. We saw Mrs. Ratzibungen's old boyfriend. The one who's been drinking himself to death the last twenty-five years. When we saw you coming, Ratzi had the idea of the rum collinses."

Natasha looked toward the entrance to the lobby.

"Sit," Constance said. "Come on."

Ratzi approached, carrying the drinks. "On the house," he said.

IIis mother came back up from the beach, looking tired and beset, strands of hair loose on her forehead. "He vent home. I vill check on him later."

"Does he know what's happened?" Constance asked.

Mrs. Ratzibungen said, "I vill be ruined. Kaput. But I feel zo bad for you Americans."

"Sit," Constance repeated to Natasha.

Natasha, feeling the obligation, sat down.

"Here's your drink." Ratzi said. "On the house."

"No, thank you."

"Vee are ruined. Lawton just here drunk, sick. *Und* you buy drinks."

"My mother is an alarmist."

"Look at zuh books, you think I am alarmist. You don't look at zuh books. Zuh Gleister people vill close me down."

Ratzi said something harsh sounding to her in German, sipping the drink Natasha had refused. Then he looked over at Constance. "The Gleister Corporation owns the buildings and the grounds. We own the franchise. And we also have another place, a restaurant in Kingston. Doing very well. Quite well. Even now. I do look at those books." He turned and said something else in the other language.

"Maybe I can loan you some money for the short term," said Constance

Natasha stood. "I have to go to bed. Good night."

"Sit down. I want to ask you something. Sit."

She did so.

"Are we still friends?" Constance had tears starting in her eyes.

"We're still friends."

"Where have you been?" She wiped them with the table napkin and folded it tightly in her fist. "I haven't seen you since yesterday morning."

"I haven't felt well." Natasha sniffled.

"Zummer colds are zuh bad vons."

"This thing happened to *all* of us," Constance said. "And people behave differently in this kind of extremity."

Natasha nodded but said nothing.

"My daughter isn't answering her phone. We've talked once. That's it."

"Maybe she's out with people. You wanted to go be with people, remember?"

Ratzi said, "Maybe there's still—you know, the volume of calls."

"Volume of calls at two in the morning," said Constance. "*Her* time."

Natasha simply waited to be released.

"Zometimes I unplug my phone ven I go to bed at night."

"Natasha, how many times have you talked to Iris?"

"I don't know."

"I heard you talking to somebody."

"Ruined," Mrs. Ratzibungen said.

Two young women came from the other end of the beach, laughing and talking. One, Natasha realized, was the girl she had seen crying in the lobby two days ago. The girl seemed wildly happy now and, seeing Natasha, walked over to her. "Guess what?" she said. "My father's friend, they found him. He was in Washington having breakfast with some people. He wasn't even there."

"Oh, how happy," Mrs. Ratzibungen said.

Natasha smiled at the girl and nodded, watching her go off with her friend, and she thought of all the people for whom this had not ended happily. When she came down for her walk, she had seen on television an image of people putting pictures of the missing on a wall near the rubble of what was left.

"Natasha's fiancé was in New York."

"But he is safe," Mrs. Ratzibungen said. "*Ja?*"

"Safe," Natasha said. "Yes." She excused herself. This time Constance did not try to stop her. In the room, she lay down and closed her eyes, and a humming sounded in her ears. She got up and took some aspirin, swallowing it with a little water she got bending over the spigot, then went to the bed and lay down and pulled the blanket over herself as if to hide. *I will not let it do this to me. I will not let it do this to me.*

The humming in her ears went on.

5

He took a cab from the station to his apartment in Chickasaw Gardens. The cabbie and he traded remarks about the surprisingly cool, dry air for mid-September in Memphis, and it felt refreshing to be talking about something other than the attacks and the coming war in Afghanistan. Except that he knew the cabbie was carefully avoiding all of it, and so the overall feeling was of complicity in a kind of ruse. At his apartment, he dropped off his bags, then called the hotel in Jamaica. "You choose," she had said about a place for them to live, and he heard the note of apathy in her voice, wondering at it, almost as though he were admiring a quality of hers. He thought of her there, alone, marooned, and felt all the more powerfully the will to protect her. Finally he got in his car and drove straight to Iris's house. She opened the door as he came up onto the stoop. "I'm so glad to see you safe," she said.

He followed her into the kitchen. She moved well with the cane.

"I've been sleepless this whole awful time," she told him. "I close my eyes and dream I'm sleeping and then I wake up."

"I guess nobody's sleeping very well."

"You too?"

"Me too."

Sun shown through the white-curtained windows of the patio door. She had made coffee, and she poured him a cup without asking if he wanted it, supporting herself with one hand on the countertop. Her knee was in a brace, and he thought it must be difficult to maneuver with it. But it didn't seem to bother her at all. She came over to sit across from him with her own cup of coffee.

"I know I've fallen asleep for little spells, but it sure doesn't feel like it."

He looked at her thick fingers with their chewed nails and the slight arthritic curvature of them.

"How did you fall?"

"Which time?"

"The most recent one." Faulk knew of the original injury.

"I'd thrown my bedspread off in my sleep, and it was bunched on the floor. I caught my foot in it getting up. If it had happened ten years ago and if I wasn't already hurting from this other one, it wouldn't even have been noticeable."

They drank the coffee in silence for a few moments. It struck him that, apart from the fact that in the normal outward way she had been his parishioner, there wasn't really very much they knew about each other.

"I've got several houses to look at," he said. "I've been research-ing it. But there's not much I can do really until Natasha gets back."

"No."

"You're sure you don't need us to stay here. Because we will, you know. I'm perfectly all right with that."

She smiled. "It's the word *perfectly* in that sentence that gives you away."

"No," he said, and he repeated it while she laughed quietly. Her laugh was that of a much-younger woman.

"I *am* perfectly all right with it."

"I don't need you to stay here."

He sipped the coffee. She looked out the window at her small flower-bordered lawn and sighed. "I don't like the way our girl sounds on the phone."

"She just wants to be out of there. And home."

"Something's different."

He had felt it, too. But he did not show this to Iris. He desired to reassure her, and he took some of the reassurance for himself as he spoke: "Coming back home will help her get back to herself. Must've been awful being that far away and not knowing, not being able to get through."

"Best medicine," Iris said. "People you love around you."

"Everybody safe."

"Nothing feels that way, though, now, does it?"

"No."

"I haven't felt this apprehensive in a long time."

"It's all of us."

When he left Iris's he drove to Chickasaw Gardens, intending to arrange his move from the apartment. He had taken the apartment less than six months ago, and there was the problem of the lease. Also, his landlord knew about him and had let it be known that he considered him some sort of renegade. The landlord, Mr. Donald Baines, was by his own conception of himself a devout Christian. The lease was for one year.

"One year," Mr. Baines said. "Not five and a half months." He was fifty-something, balding, with an outsized, eerily corrugated beer belly. He wore knit shirts that made the heavy, dimpled, drooping shape of the belly all the more noticeable. There were thick pouches under his small eyes, like emblems of his general flabbiness. Everything about him suggested immobility. He did not drink much, he had told Faulk, but he liked food. He was, he said, addicted to food. It didn't really matter what it was. He had continually to resist the urge to satisfy not his hunger but his taste buds. It was that simple. Many things, to Mr. Baines, were "that simple," and anything that wasn't, he let alone. He had a habit of talking about himself in the third person.

"Of course, I'll be looking for someone to sublet," Faulk told him. "But we don't have much time."

"You can bring your lovely bride to the apartment and live with her there until the lease is up. Then you'd have time to find a nice place for yourselves. Donald Baines isn't that much of a stickler about the fine points of the lease."

"Well," Faulk said. "I'll work something out."

"A person has to keep his agreements. But as long as Mr. Baines gets his rent payments—you know."

"Yes, I do know."

The apartment was in a box-shaped brick row of them across the street from Donald Baines's cottage-sized house. Faulk crossed and let himself in. He looked at the rooms—the barren place where he had lived through these months. How Natasha would hate living here. Cracks lined the ceiling, and a sheen had developed in places over the old paint, as if the humidity of the town had begun some process of melting in the walls. He cleaned the floors and the fixtures in the sinks and dusted the surfaces, then packed laundry in a bag and spent time on the telephone, calling in the ad about subletting. The inheritance from his mother paid nine thousand dollars a month. It was enough for them to live on. He could, if he had to, afford two rent payments for a while. Natasha would want to find something to do, to support her painting, until they could have their spring in France. This was a vague fancy at the edge of his consciousness. He was not thinking practically, since there would be a lot of matters to address if indeed they were to decide to live in France for a few months. He put details aside and told himself that things would be all right. And he felt a wave of excitement, thinking of her walking the beach in Jamaica and wanting to come home.

In the morning he tried to call her, but the line was busy. He tried four times and then left a message on the room phone. "I bet you're on the phone with Iris, or with the airlines. I can't wait, babe."

6

She was indeed on the phone with the airlines, getting her flights rescheduled. It took an hour. The woman who helped her was very kind but spoke with a slight indistinguishable accent that made certain words hard to understand. Natasha guessed, using context, but felt the frustration of it. Now, certainly, you had to bring forth all the generosity you could muster. But she couldn't shake the annoyance. She could hear Constance talking on the phone in her room, the voice strangely antic, as though she were addressing a small child. This was the third day of slow time.

Mrs. Ratzibungen had let everyone stay the extra days without charge, even as she was losing money steadily. People sat in the lobby and watched the news reports of the aftermath and the investigation. Natasha wanted none of it. She took another walk, this time on a path leading toward the mountains, the path rising steadily to a level nearly at the height of the palm trees, where she paused and looked at the country and the shoreline. In her travels in Europe she had never felt the slightest hint of the alienation and isolation that gripped her now. She wanted to be home. She wanted Memphis, the house where she had grown up—though that house was now occupied by others, and she had not been near it in almost ten years. But far more than anything now—oh, more than breathing—she wanted the affair with the photographer never to have been, those nights in Adams Morgan, and the beach, here. She wanted the whole of it obliterated, erased, rubbed out. Gone. The drinking and the unhappiness and the not caring what happened, the throwing away of hours, the sinking, all the weeks of deadening intoxication and self-loathing. These last three days.

She felt it now, returning down the path. Wiping her eyes with the backs of her hands, and her nose with her forearms, she slowly made her way to the entrance of the resort, muttering low under her breath.

Stop it. Stop it.

Lunch was being served. She took a sandwich and went to her room hoping for sleep. But sleep was fitful and tormented, so she simply lay in the bed, staring. And later she ate dinner in the restaurant, alone. She saw Constance out on the patio with Ratzi, a bottle of rum and a pitcher of orange juice on the table between them. A little later, near the end of the meal, the older woman came in and sat across from her, one hand fisted under her chin. Natasha had ordered a vermouth on ice and now held it, looking into the facets of color reflecting in the ice cubes.

"Mind if I join you?" Constance said.

Remembering once more, with a pang of guilt, that the other had paid for her stay here, she said, "No, I don't mind."

"I don't seem to know anymore whether or not I'd be welcome."

"You're welcome. And stop it."

Constance ordered a beer from the waiter, whom they hadn't seen before. He was tall and olive hued, with small round black eyes. He brought her beer and walked away, saying nothing, and she held it up. "Well, here's to our trip. Neither of us will ever forget where we were when all hell broke loose."

Natasha raised her glass and drank.

"So you're still going back to Memphis."

"Still?"

"You're going back. You haven't changed your mind."

"Why would I change my mind, Constance?"

"A lot of people are changing plans because of this, dear. That's all I'm saying."

"I'm *still* going to Memphis."

They said nothing for a few seconds.

"It's nobody's business, anyway," Constance said. "Where we're going from here."

Natasha decided to leave it alone. She nodded and drank.

"I think I've ruined our friendship."

She could think of nothing to tell her.

"I know I got under your skin about that business—but I thought I'd apologized."

"Forget it," she said.

"But you're different. Something's changed."

"I said forget it. So forget it. Please."

"I'm going to California, though I'd rather go to Maine."

She did not respond.

"I'm going to see my daughter. Who I'm pretty sure doesn't want to see me."

"I bet she does, actually. Given what's happened."

"She says she's upset because I didn't try harder to call her."

Natasha nearly spoke the words aloud: *Sounds like something you'd say.* Instead, she drank the last of her vermouth.

"I don't think anybody wants to go to New York," Constance said. "And then, in a way, I think everybody does."

"I just want to go home."

"I don't really know where home is." This was the first time the older woman had ever made this kind of confession.

"You've got the house."

Constance smirked. "Actually I'm not liking how it's turning out. I feel selfish." Swallowing the rest of the beer, she signaled the bartender. Before he reached the table, she called out, "Another one."

"Yes, ma'am."

"And could you bring me a shot of Mount Gay, too? Neat."

He nodded and went off. Both women watched him go.

Natasha said, "I'm going upstairs."

"Our last night, sweetie. You—you don't want to sit and talk on our last night?"

"I want to sleep, Constance. That's all I want to do right now. And I'm having trouble doing it."

"You're depressed."

She gave no answer.

"Well, me too."

"Can we not talk about it?"

"I think you're depressed because things have changed for you, and you don't know what to do about it."

Natasha looked at her.

"You've hardly been out of bed the last two days."

She drew in a breath and then managed to speak, with only the slightest tremor in her voice. "I want to be home, that's all."

"I really don't mean anything, you know."

They sat there without speaking for perhaps a full minute. Anyone walking through would have thought they were simply enjoying the evening light, looking at the other people in the big high-ceilinged room and at the scenes out the window—the several little tableaux of people eating and drinking and being together. Finally, Constance said, "Why don't you have another vermouth. We could go out on the patio."

"I don't want anything else."

"Okay."

"I'm grateful to you for the time here."

"Well, for some of the time here."

The waiter brought the drinks on a small tray. Constance took the Mount Gay with one swallow, then wiped the back of her hand across her mouth. "I swear I've never drunk this much."

"I promise I won't tell anyone about your drinking," Natasha said.

Sipping her beer, the other woman looked over the lip of the glass at her, then set the glass down, smiling.

"Good night," said Natasha.

"You probably won't see me tomorrow." Constance picked up her glass of beer again, drank from it, and set it down. "My flight's at seven o'clock in the morning." She stood as Natasha stood. They embraced. "I'll miss you, you know."

"I'll miss you, too," Natasha told her, feeling empty and wanting to be shut of her.

"When you make the wedding plans, let me know?"

"Early next month. I know that."

"Maybe I'll come? If asked."

"We both want it small."

"Let me know? I'd love to be there. I want to be there."

"I'll let you know."

Constance looked at her.

"I will."

She sighed. "I'll be in Maine over the Christmas holidays. You and Michael are welcome."

"I think we're leaving for France pretty soon after that. Lots of planning to do. But thank you." Natasha went on up to her room and closed the door and saw that there was a message on the phone. She punched the button and then lay down and let it play, and cried softly, hearing him say, "I can't wait, babe."

She replayed it twice, then called the front desk and asked the female voice to put in the return call. There was no answer, and she left her own message. "I'm coming home. Soon, my love." She heard the frail sound of her own voice.

7

Faulk spent the morning looking at houses and apartments in Midtown. He played the radio, driving from property to property—air conditioner turned up full blast—following a kindly, quiet, elderly gentleman named Rainey, whose thick shoulders, long face, and protruding lengthy ears put him in mind of his father. Rainey stood by while the younger man went through rooms that were being lived in and contained intimations of the lives their occupants led, or toured houses that were vacant, standing in musty, old-wood-smelling parlors, looking down hallways and into closets and walking out onto back lawns in the scorching brightness, moving through the peculiarly depressing silence of abandoned dwellings. All the forenoon they were at it, getting into their respective cars and heading on to the next property. The air had already grown sultry by nine o'clock, laden with dampness and the smell of exhaust—late summer in the city. The ends of tree branches drooped, and the scattered wide shady patches on the lawns made Faulk think of something spilled. He listened to the different voices on the radio talking about the cataclysm, the developing crisis, the new face of war, and all the victims who were missing. Finally he turned it off, unable to bear it anymore.

He felt empty. Rainey caught his mood. "Not liking much of what you see," he said.

Faulk shook his head and sighed.

"This is not a good time, is it," the older man went on. "A bad time for all of us."

"Yeah."

"And of course you have to go with your gut when it comes to picking a place to live."

"You remind me of my father," Faulk told him. He hadn't known he would say it.

"Hope that's a good thing. Is he still with us?"

"Yes. Very healthy. A little touch of gout now and then and some trouble with peripheral vision. He lives in Little Rock."

"My mother's got trouble with that. The peripheral vision thing. Still going strong, though. Ninety-two and sharp as a tack. She said something to me this week—stopped me. We'd been talking about it all, you know, and she said—I mean she was smiling, but I think she was half serious—said things get so bad and ugly all around you, everything changing for the worse as you age, that you don't hate so much the idea of going."

They were standing in the center of a large square living room with freshly polished hardwood flooring. An arched entrance opened into a freshly remodeled kitchen.

"Good light here with these windows," said Rainey.

"I should probably have waited until my fiancée could be with me," Faulk told him. "I'm sorry."

"Well, but it'll be good to have an idea, anyway."

"This *is* very nice."

"I had a place just like this once. Raised three girls in it. Theresa, Coleen, and Marilyn."

"My mother's name was Marilyn."

"Good name. I picked that one."

Faulk imagined him as a young man. "Do they live close?"

"Not too far away." Rainey sighed. "One's in Chicago, and two're in Nashville. I get to see them pretty often. Them and the grandkids. I've got nine grandkids. Each of my girls has three boys." He smiled. "I tell them it's a baseball team."

"That's wonderful."

"I'm afraid they'll all end up as part of a platoon, now."

Faulk nodded. "Bad," he said.

"Should we take a look at the upstairs?"

"I'll keep it in mind. Might be a little big for just two. Can we look at the ones in High Point?"

They walked out and got into their separate cars. Faulk looked back at the house, with its porch and the forsythia lining the left side of the front yard. Mr. Rainey pulled away slowly, and they went on down to the end of the street, toward Poplar Avenue.

Following the real-estate agent, Faulk thought of his father. He did not put the radio on. It was hard to feel himself in his own age, almost fifty. The road ahead was blue, baking in the sunlight, an end-of-summer day in Memphis, Tennessee, in the United States, and a war had begun. He had seen in the news that religious fanaticism was the one motive being advanced most by observers (there were already acts of violence against mosques and shrines), and it came to him that just now he felt detached from it all. He was driving around Memphis looking for a house and a neighborhood, anticipating life with a new, young wife, and when he thought of her he felt excitement, even gladness. Yet there was something faintly reflexive about that, too.

At High Point Terrace, Mr. Rainey showed him a couple of houses, and then they came to one on Swan Ridge, where the key in the lockbox was the wrong one. Faulk liked the look of the house and the yard, and Mr. Rainey tried calling his office. But he had to leave for another appointment. The two men arranged to meet later in the morning.

Faulk drove back to his apartment, opened a can of ravioli, heated it, and ate, and then called his father.

"Glad you're home," the old man said. "I talked to Clara and she said you were on your way."

"I'd have called when I got here, but it's been crazy."

"Your girlfriend get home okay?" This was simply his way of speaking.

"I pick her up late this afternoon."

"You find a place yet?"

"I think maybe I have."

"You figured out what you're gonna do, now that the church thing is over?"

"Dad."

"Just curious. I don't mean anything by it."

"You make it sound like some phase I was going through."

"Well," the old man grumbled. "No sense giving all your money to the phone company."

"Right," Faulk answered with an old sense of being held at an emotional remove.

"Make a trip out here, why don't you, now that you're not a priest anymore."

"That sounds like now you'll be able to tolerate me, since I'm a layman."

The old man sighed. "I meant now that you're more free to travel. Come on, boy. Quit *inter*preting everything I say. I'd like you to drive over to see us."

"We'll do that. You coming to our wedding?"

"If we can. When is it?"

"Early next month."

"Give me some notice."

"This is it."

"You want to give me a definite date, Son?"

"I will. Of course. Promise."

Faulk sat with the phone at his ear, picturing the old man in his television room leaning back in the easy chair amid all the law books he never looked in anymore, with a movie paused on the VCR, anxious to get off the line.

"Not everything I say is intended as a criticism," Leander said.

Faulk apologized, meaning it.

"Just sometimes," said the old man with a cheerless little snickering sound.

"Right," Faulk said. "Well, I'm home."

"Good."

"I'll call you when it's set."

As long as he could remember, a barrier had existed between them. Periodic conflict about religion kept flaring up in the house, and according to the old man, Faulk was more his mother's child. Marilyn Dealey Faulk was quite austere in observance, while Leander had, as she said of him, no covenant with anything but the hours of the day. From Faulk's earliest memories they quarreled about the discrepancy. The old man would say that Marilyn's pietistic attitudes and habits never kept her from feeling murderous resentment over some real or imagined slight. According to him, she was only interested in those superficial elements of Christian living that permitted the slaughters and terrors of the world to continue, all in the name of God. *Onward, Christian soldiers.* He would whistle the old hymn, just to needle her.

Marilyn never flagged in espousing the age-old, Bible-haunted tenets that had traveled down the generations from culture to culture; she was very strong in her belief.

They were, then, in fundamental disagreement about the whole human journey.

Even so, they generally went for periods looking like a settled couple in the calming waters of habit. If you paid attention, you might observe that there wasn't much affection between them—not much of that kind of warmth emanating from intimacy when intimacy is easy and relaxed—but only a form of detached consideration. To others, they seemed normal. But Faulk always had the feeling that something was brooding under the surface kindness and the usual staid rituals of family life. He had no way to express this at the time, but it was a feeling strong enough and steady enough to last until he did have language for it. The boy, precocious, unsure and uneasy and watchful of every little fault line between them, was full of anxiety all the time that they might fly apart, like shards from a shattered window. This was when he learned to fear the insubstantial stirrings that lurked in the dark of what people refused to look at: the ways in which thought could injure you. He watched his parents go through their days, rarely affected and seemingly oblivious to the damages resulting from the passions that arose when they did fight. And any fight, invariably, was about religion. Always, the religion. In one of those conflicts, the old man said forcefully, at the top of his thin voice, that he wanted something from his son to shore up what he called the puny remnants of sanity in the house. His house. Faulk sided with his mother, because he feared his father, and he had nowhere else to go.

He took to retreating into himself whenever Leander was near. By the time he was in his teens, Christianity, with its rituals, and more important its literature, had become a sort of haven for him, and he spent hours reading through Hooker, Bonhoeffer, Duns Scotus, Tillich, Kierkegaard, the mystics, and, finally, especially, Aquinas—*The Summa Theologica*—that massive intellectual construction explaining all the knotty inconsistencies and the shadowy grottoes and crevices of faith in the world. All that, and of course he never thought of any of it as refuge, not back then; he never perceived it as any kind of withdrawal from the realities of the house where he lived. Yet he was perpetually a boy in hiding, buried, separated—even from himself.

Later, during his journey away, through the years of study and absorption in college and then at seminary, there were days and sometimes weeks when he experienced the same emotional detachment that he believed came from his parents—a malaise, even a form of paralysis, doing things automatically: a pair of eyes, two hands, a creature sleeping and feeding, someone absorbed in reading and study, feeling nothing. And recalling Sartre's comment about hell being other people, he thought he understood the feeling; hell was being aware of one's separation from other people—who looked discouragingly like specimens, so far from him as to seem somehow not of his kind.

How he had hated it.

After his ordination, he took on the busy life of his first assigned parish, and that element of his being seemed to have gone the way of other youthful troubles. He grew out of it, probably by the simple pressure of what there was to do. When he met Joan, shortly after coming to Memphis, he was already far past that time; it was an old memory then.

Except that of course it was what had led him to leaving the priesthood. And it was with him now, this disquiet: he could not bring himself to care about much of *anything*, not in the way that you normally associated feeling. Things happened to you and around you and what you felt stayed; it was almost a kind of sustenance. But when that failed, what you were left with was the waiting for the next thing. Even the terrors of the catastrophe, all that, even that, left him strangely anesthetized. Suddenly, it seemed, he was someone only reacting, an onlooker, attending to his own discomforts, and in a sort of suspension about all the rest, waiting to see an outcome that did not exist.

Natasha was the answer to all that. The bright center of everything.

And now he realized that the apartment smelled of the cleansers he had used, so he made another trip out to find some scented candles and to get some coffee. She liked the smell of coffee. Back in the apartment, he lit the candles, brewed coffee, and then sat by the window, drinking it.

8

She woke before first light after a static interval of half sleep, and for a little while she tried to go back. When the sound reached her of Constance struggling out into the hall with her luggage, she thought of getting up to go thank her and to say something else—perhaps even to apologize, complicated as that would be. A moment later, she rose and went to the door, opened it, and called out the name. Constance was gone. The sun had risen and the day was heating up. Some people were already out on the beach.

She was packed. She had the clothes that she would wear—jeans and a white blouse—on the chair next to the bed. A wave of panic came over her as she put them on, and she sat back down on the bed, arms wrapped tightly around her middle, rocking back and forth and trying to breathe slowly. Finally she opened the minibar, took one of the bottles of whiskey out, and drained it in two stinging gulps. Then she was in the bathroom, coughing and spitting into the sink.

When she had gathered herself and patted cold water on her cheeks, she stood out on the balcony and breathed the humid air with its fragrance of cooked sausage and bacon. She was not remotely hungry. At last she moved to the door and into the hall. There was a note taped just below the room number.

> *I'll miss you. Really sorry about everything. Please call when you get to Memphis?*
>
> *Love, Constance*

Downstairs, the lobby was nearly empty. A van waited to take people to the airport. In the van already, in the far back, was Skinner, with his wife. Skinner looked very pale and tired. He had a bandage on one heavy arm and another above his left eye. He nodded at Natasha but did not speak. Mrs. Skinner stared straight ahead, hands clenched tightly in her lap. Ratzi drove, and he, too, was silent, even sullen, watching the road with an air of overfamiliarity and boredom, and seemingly far away in his thoughts. Natasha looked out at the sea and sky through the placid stillness of the palms.

At the airport in Montego Bay, Ratzi asked in a flat tone what airlines they were flying. Natasha got out first, and again Skinner nodded at her. She tried to smile but felt only a sense of having looked foolish. Ratzi hauled her bag out of the back of the van, set it down, and then shook hands—no grip, not even quite fully making contact. Then he got back in behind the wheel and pulled out and away with his cargo of unhappiness and recrimination: Mrs. Skinner glaring out the back side window.

There was a very long line leading to the check-in counter. It took an hour to get to where you checked your bags. Natasha checked hers, then made her way through the muddle and noise of others. A garbled voice announced a gate change for another flight. She heard a loud beeping from somewhere. Reaching the gate with nearly an hour to spare, she sat down to wait. The whiskey she had drunk was making the beginnings of a headache, so she went and ordered a Bloody Mary at one of the little kiosk bars. *This is what I'll do*, she thought bitterly, swallowing the drink. *I'll just stay crocked all the time.*

The airline had overbooked the plane, and the gate clerks kept asking for volunteers to take another flight. An apparently unmanageable number of people were waiting, the backup of four days without flights. It looked like the whole island wanted out. Through the tall windows opposite where she sat, you could see, beyond the tarmac and a span of grass and low-roofed buildings and skinny palms, Montego Bay.

She sat quite still, fighting sleep, with her purse and a newspaper in her lap. The newspaper was full of images of the destruction, but she could not concentrate on it. She saw the plane taxiing slowly into its place at the gate. It looked like the same kind of plane that had been flown into the towers. Near her, a heavy man—nearly Skinner's size—was talking to a small woman, worrying aloud about fitting into a coach seat. "I usually always fly first class because of my girth," he said. "Even though I'm not wealthy."

"I'm sure it'll be all right," the woman muttered. Then: "Where are you seated?"

"Way back. Twenty-three A. The only one I could get. First class was completely booked *before* the shutdown."

"Twenty-three A. Is that a window seat?"

Natasha tried to read. The flight had already been delayed an hour out of Dallas. There were so many other people trying to get somewhere, and for most of them, of course, somewhere was home. *Home.* She felt a blankness for an instant. What *was* home? Not a dwelling, not even the place of one's blood relatives, finally. That was not home, not really; that was, in its way, without denying the love that might be there, where you belonged before you went out in the world. Just now, she felt nothing like the settled sense of one place where she belonged. Then she turned in herself and looked directly at what she did feel. Home was Michael Faulk. And she was home for him.

Now a sparse stream of people came from the gate and headed toward customs. They did not appear to be vacationers. Most of them looked Jamaican. It was not long before the last of them had exited. Natasha saw herself arriving fifteen days ago, remembering it like a brief waking dream, how happy she had been, anticipating a good time. Now it felt like remembering some sort of failure. Presently, a slender woman with dark green eyes and a tight blond bun tied at the top of her head took the little microphone from the console at the gate, called the number and destination of the flight, and said people could begin boarding. Natasha stood. Her back hurt. She could not imagine that the plane would fly safely to its destination: Miami. In line in front of her the large man stood, looking tired and worried. They were moving slowly, past the attendant and down a long corridor toward the jetway. As she got close to the entryway, she looked back into the busy high-ceilinged, white-lighted gate area with its blue seats and low tables, the crowd there. It looked like an exodus, people seeking refuge. Yet they seemed calm enough, preoccupied with their bags and their tickets. It was all completely ordinary looking. And then, as two elderly women moved to get into line and a small nattily dressed black man moved to stand where they had been, through the little open space created by their movements, she saw Nicholas Duego. He looked right at her with a surprised expression of intense concentration, a frown tinged with fright. Something dropped inside her. The bones of her legs felt as if they were turning to liquid, and she had to put her hand out to the wall. Evidently he had just seen her. But he did not look away.

She turned, hefted her purse, held it at her middle, feeling the shudder come, the trembling. There was no movement in the line. She thought she might be sick.

The big man in front of her coughed, then moved to the side a little and bent down to reach into his bag, apologizing. Whatever he was looking for was not there. He straightened and looked at her. "I'm sorry, would you happen to have any Kleenex?"

She opened her purse and found a little packet at the bottom. She handed it to him and watched him open it, and she saw the little spiral shapes of white, like facets in marbles, inside the buttons down the front of his shirt. There were two more buttons holding his collar down. She noted them and noted the same spiral shapes. Little details that were solid and dependable. She looked down the line toward the left turn into the jet and saw the others. The heavy man used three Kleenexes out of the packet and then tried to hand the packet back to her.

"You keep it," she told him, or thought she told him. He stood there holding it out. Finally she pushed his hand away.

"Are you all right?" he said.

"Thank you," she said, still not certain that the words had actually left her lips.

He pushed the packet into the top of her purse, smiled reassuringly, then went on. She followed in a kind of daze. She did not look back, and when she came to the doorway she put one hand out and held on to the steel frame of it. Waiting there was a square-faced, middle-aged blond woman, the flight attendant, who smiled and greeted her and then caught her as she tumbled forward. It was only a second, but in that second she had lost consciousness. The flight attendant's grip was strong, and she held her.

"I'm okay," Natasha said, low. "Please."

"Looks like you went out for a second, honey. You all right?"

"Fine, yes."

"Want help to your seat? I think we'll help you to your seat."

"I'm *fine*. No." She moved into the cabin, past the people staring at her in first class, on down the narrow aisle, stopping to wait while others put bags in the overhead bin. Her own seat was 25C. An aisle seat. A young woman and a child were in the middle and window seats. The child, white as paste and too thin, was at the window. His mother was already reading a book. Natasha took the seat, and the woman turned to smile at her. Natasha saw her brown eyes and the little blemish on her right cheek.

"Hi. At last, we can fly out of here," the woman said.

Natasha thought she nodded.

"Where're you from?"

"Wa—," she began. "I'm sorry. Memphis."

The woman offered her hand. "Durham, North Carolina."

Natasha took it, felt the warmth of it, the roughness of the underside of the fingers.

"I'm a sculptor. I work in wood." It was as though this were an explanation.

Natasha nodded.

"You?"

"I used to work in D.C. Assistant to Senator Norland."

"That must be wonderful. A senator's assistant."

"Well, I've quit that." She was surprised that she could hear her own voice. She thought she might've smiled. It was difficult to tell because everything seemed to be taking place in a suspension—somehow the part of her that was watchful and aware was a half second behind everything. She felt light-headed and dizzy just as the woman leaned close and murmured, "Are you as scared as I am?"

Natasha looked at her and couldn't draw the breath to answer.

"What if somebody decides to take this one and fly it into something, you know what I mean? Oh, God—I'm so sorry, I shouldn't talk like that."

She could only nod, fearing the next second—the little distressing increments of time. Now. And now. People were moving past her, and several hit her elbow or rubbed against her shoulder. She turned to the woman, who was now talking to the little boy. "Teddy, you have to wear the seat belt. It's the rules."

Natasha touched her wrist. "Excuse me," she murmured. "Can we talk? I have to—there's a man coming and I have to be talking to someone."

The woman seemed faintly alarmed. "Excuse me?"

"Please," Natasha said. But then she saw that Duego was waiting at a seat just past the demarcation of first class and coach. He put his bag in the overhead bin and said something to the elderly woman sitting in the aisle seat there. His manner was deferential. The woman stood to let him take the middle seat. He turned and spoke to the adolescent boy there, who was wearing a blue bandanna over long brown hair.

"I don't understand," the young woman beside Natasha began, and abruptly she appeared to come to herself, and began talking. "My name's Priscilla, and my family calls me Priss. We're from Durham, but we moved there from Houston. I couldn't get the flight to Durham, so Miami it is. My dad was an engineer in the space program." She went on, nervously trying to supply what Natasha had asked for, chattering about the space shuttle program and the people she knew because her husband had worked at Mission Control.

"Thank you," Natasha said, and squeezed her wrist. "Thank you. So much. It's—it's all right now."

"Mama," the boy said. "I want to sit in the middle. I'm afraid."

"We have to put your seat belt on, Teddy. We'll move you to the middle after we take off. You want to see out the window, don't you?"

Natasha watched him pout, folding his thin arms, his lower lip sticking out. His mother sighed. Natasha sat quite still, eyes fixed on the boy's pinched face. Her heart was running, the air beginning to feel thick, and all of life seemed to bend toward the one moment, nothing else having any reality at all, not her life in Memphis or France or Washington, not the first good days on the island, not her future plans or hopes, not Constance or the bad winter, or even Michael Faulk. It was wiped out, everything, annulled by the criminal act she had suffered, and she looked at the little boy, thinking of him grown, thinking of him forcing someone to the ground, seeing it like part of the coloration in the downy flesh of his skinny freckled white arms; and the shaking commenced deep inside, her hands tight on the ends of the armrests, the freeze expanding behind her heart, and this was how it felt to go insane. The flight attendant went through the routine about the exit doors and the floor lighting, the seat belt and the oxygen masks and the cushions that, in the unlikely event of a water landing, could be used as flotation devices. The words knifed through her. *Unlikely event. Unlikely event.*

When the plane started down the runway, she gave a little cry, and the woman, Priscilla, leaned over and said, "It's fine, honey. Really. You'll see."

9

The house on Swan Ridge was a small two-bedroom bungalow, with a good yard and a shed in the back that could be converted into a work space. Faulk gave Mr. Rainey a small deposit for it, an amount he could afford to lose if Natasha decided that she didn't like it. But he felt sure she would. It was very close to Iris's house on Bilders. Mr. Rainey let him have a key to the place and took the lockbox. The two men shook hands and agreed on a time to meet and finalize things. Mr. Rainey drove away, and Faulk took one more look around, moving through the rooms and imagining life there.

This was the one he would take her to.

After lunch he drove to East Memphis to see a friend in the employment services department of the parole board. The friend had left him a message to come see him. His office was in a small windowless annex behind the main building. Faulk had a little trouble finding the place, walking around in the hot sunlight for long minutes. The door was unmarked. It looked like a warehouse entrance. His friend, the supervisor, was a short, squat good-humored man named Lawrence Watson, who smelled of the unlit cigar he kept like a lollipop in the corner of his mouth and always wore a starched white shirt with the sleeves rolled up. The cigar would be smoked in short breaks all day and then patted out and, as Watson cheerfully expressed it, worn for reassurance indoors. A man with a cigar in his mouth was a more confident, forward-going man, he would say. For him the phrase *forward going* was synonymous with phrases or words like *strong willed, resolute, tough minded, progressive, confident,* even *stubborn.* The shades of meaning in it were there in context when you listened to him holding forth. He liked Faulk, and the two men had spent time over the years working together, Faulk having served as a volunteer for some of the programs the board sponsored, including several halfway houses for paroled prisoners or mental patients, or for people who needed medical rehabilitation. Faulk had also been chaplain at the community center in Midtown. Lawrence Watson was a man whose working life had been spent attempting to have a direct effect doing beneficial things for individual people. His goodwill was both boundless and practical. He possessed an unspoken passionate concern for the less fortunate and the troubled, and about this concern he often made jokes, always undercutting the obvious fact that he was a good and loving man. You could not pin him down or get him to speak earnestly about any of it. It was just his work, the thing he was happy doing, and he had been doing it for thirty years.

A job had opened up in corrections, a position in employment counseling for men on parole. "It's yours if you want it," he said to Faulk, chewing on the dead cigar.

"I want it."

"Doesn't pay much."

"I don't need it to."

"Can you start Monday?"

"If you want. My fiancée's coming in from being stuck in Jamaica—"

Wilson gave him a look, grinning crookedly.

"I know. Stuck in Jamaica. Sounds crazy. Anyway, she's arriving later today, and I was thinking we should take a little time."

"When's the wedding?"

"First week in October. That first Saturday. So, three weeks. You're welcome to come."

"Never met a wedding I didn't want to miss."

"You can miss this one, too—it's going to be very quick and very small."

"And Jamaica was where she was when the flights stopped?"

"Yes, and all she talked about was wanting to come home."

"Well, under the circumstances."

"I know."

"Way I feel right now, they can nuke the whole goddamm region," Watson said.

"Is this *you* talking?"

He smiled the crooked smile. "Don't tell anybody I said that. Maybe just hoping for another flood in the general area. How would that be? Another forty days and forty nights of rain to cool them all off."

"You need me to start Monday?"

"How 'bout Wednesday?"

"Wednesday, sure."

"You know the drill. Look at the history and try to match it up with whatever's available."

"See you Wednesday," Faulk told him.

He went back to his apartment and saw Mr. Baines sitting out on his front stoop. Mr. Baines waved him over.

"I don't want to be unkind," he said. "I think I was unkind earlier."

"No," Faulk said. "Not really."

The other man had a beer and a plate of chicken wings on a small portable table. He held out a wing. "Want one?"

"No, thank you."

"Settled on a place?"

"I think I've found something, yes."

"Donald Baines never gets in the way of anybody's happiness if he can help it. And you're about to be *married*."

Faulk thought he heard a note of sarcasm in the voice. Baines, chewing on a wing, gazed at him with a jovial expression and asked, through his chewing, if the younger man would like a cold beer. Barbecue sauce was smeared all over the wide mouth. He looked like a big kid in need of his mother to wipe his face.

"No, thanks anyway," Faulk said, wanting to feel kindly toward him. "Of course I'll pay the rent on the place until I can find someone to sublet."

"Well," said Baines, noisily slurping the beer. "Of course I'll have to insist on that. Will you bring your bride here this evening?"

"That depends on how she feels."

Baines seemed to urge him with a look, as if to say, *Go on, there's more to tell.*

"Probably tomorrow," Faulk said.

"Ah," said Baines, leaning back. "Tomorrow your life begins."

10

She had put her head back and closed her eyes, still feeling nearly choked with fright and rage, and her exhaustion took over. Briefly she was in a blankness that, when there was a touch on her arm, she relinquished almost with grief, sitting forward a little and opening her eyes.

Duego was standing over her with that pleading look, the eyes sorrowful, wider and darker than she remembered them.

"No," she said, shaking her head and pushing herself against the seat back. "Get away. Get away from me or I'll scream."

"I cannot bear this," he said, taking a step away. "This trouble between us."

Natasha shouted. "Get *away* from me!"

"Is he bothering you, honey?" Priscilla said, rising out of her own sleep. Others had looked up from what they were doing.

The blond flight attendant approached. "Go back to your seat, sir."

Duego returned quickly to his row. He looked back at Natasha before stepping into his seat. The expression on his face was distressed and full of entreaty. She kept her gaze on him, glaring, as full of hatred and fury as she could make it.

The flight attendant said, "You okay?"

Natasha nodded.

"What's *his* story," Priscilla murmured after the attendant had gone.

"He thinks I'm someone else," Natasha told her. She had begun to cry, and the other woman reached over and took her hand.

"Anything I can do?"

"He was bothering me in the airport. He—he wouldn't leave me alone."

"I think we should get them to do something about him."

Natasha touched the wrist of the hand that held hers and pulled away softly. "Thanks, you're so kind." She sniffled. "I just want him to stay away from me." Reaching into her purse, she brought out the packet of Kleenex, took one, and held it over her eyes.

"Well, it's good the flight attendants are aware of the situation," Priscilla said.

"Can you stay close to me when we get off the plane?"

"Where am I gonna go, right? I'm here."

When the plane landed in Miami, he rose, pulled his bag down from the overhead bin, faced front, and waited for the door to open, without looking back. And when the people around and before him moved, he followed and was gone. Natasha walked behind Priscilla and her son to the opening and out, and along the tunnel to the gate area. Priscilla made a show of being wary. They entered the open area, and she stopped, and Natasha stood at her side. Others moved past them.

There was no sign of him during the wait in the long lines at customs.

"I have to get to my connection," Priscilla said after they had passed through.

Natasha hugged her, fighting tears. "Thank you."

"I hope you make it okay."

"You've been so kind. I can't tell you—"

"Hey, if we can't protect each other."

After another quick embrace, Natasha watched her hurry on, pulling her boy along with her. In the other direction was her own gate. She went there, keeping to the wall, and took her seat. The flight for Memphis would board in an hour.

She looked around her and was abruptly aware of a bizarre, painful sense of loss, almost of yearning—a perverse wish, like something floating loose in her soul, that he would be there, that he would make another effort to speak to her. It filled her with shame. She rose and moved to where she could see the long prospect of the row of gates, going back to the exit from customs. Where could he have gone? He would have had to go through customs.

Finally, she went back to her seat. People moved by, and the sounds of the place rattled in the walls, and she sensed the eerie longing for him, the wanting—yes, that was it, that must be it—to finish things somehow. To have it answered and done with. Over. But there was something else, too, that pulled and nagged, and she looked at it inside, this cowering element of her being, while she kept still, watching the others cross and recross in their clamor and hurry, their insular worlds of will and worry, around her.

These Two

I

Late that afternoon, in a stifling swale of heat, he drove to the airport to pick her up. He wasn't allowed to go to the gate. A security guard stopped him. He waited beside the escalator leading down to baggage claim. Watching the people come one by one into the narrow hall, he kept thinking she would be the next person and felt new disappointment each time it was someone else. When she came into view, he felt a thrill and realized again how lovely she was. He could not quite believe in this happiness, his own.

For her part, there was the shock of seeing him unchanged. She experienced as a kind of release the calming familiarity of his features, as though being able at last, after many confined hours, to spread out her arms; and, wanting the feeling to stay, she hurried into his embrace. "I've missed you so, so much." She brushed the tears from her eyes and smiled, and stood back to gaze at him. "Oh, you don't know," she went on. "My darling." Her whole body was trembling.

He said, "It's over, now. It's done. We're home."

They made their way down to baggage claim, holding hands. He was aware that they were both in some zone of fragility.

When they reached the baggage carousel, she came close again and put her arms around his neck. She saw herself on the beach in the early moonlight with the other, and she held tighter, eyes squeezed shut against the uneasiness that was rising like a cold chemical in her blood. She held on to the first good feeling of release at the sight of him, sensing his consternation but unable to let go.

He had to take her forearms and gently break her hold to look at her. "You okay?"

"Now, yes."

"You made it home," he said. "You're home, darling. We're home."

She saw his hands, the bones of his wrists, the sinews of his forearms, as the flesh of a man, separate from her as that of any other man. And her shaking resumed.

He said, as tenderly as he could, "I was never in any danger," and it was as if he were talking to a child. Gripping her arms soothingly above the elbows, he made an effort to strike a less condescending note. "You look so wonderful."

"I feel beaten up," she got out, but smiled back.

When they had the bags, three of them, he put them on a cart, and they started out of the building, to the parking lot. Outside it was even hotter than before. To her, the air seemed cooked. She kept her hand on his, where he held the cart handle. They got to the car, and he put the bags in the trunk while she watched, and then she walked into his arms again. "Oh, Michael," she said. But his name on her lips was just noise to her. She repeated it: "Michael." And felt the simple goodness of this moment. He was her love; she was home.

"We're all right," he kept saying. "We're okay. It's okay."

They got into the car. "I want to spend the night with you," she told him, flying in the face of the anxiety that she had beaten back. "In your apartment. Tonight. I don't want to visit with Iris for very long."

"I think she's planned to make dinner for us."

"Can't we get out of it?"

"Babe—she's been as worried about you as I have."

"I wasn't the one in danger," she said with an edge of impatience. "I just want to get started with things. Get past all this and be together and not have to think about it or talk about it."

The fretful rush of her speech troubled him. Something else was in her downcast eyes. "Iris already suggested that we spend some time alone. Hey, sweetie, we're *okay*."

"I've missed you so terribly, Michael. I want you."

He decided to go past any more talk about what they had separately been through. "I think I found us a house to rent."

"Oh, that's wonderful. Take me to it."

"It's just two blocks from Iris's."

"I love it. Take me there."

He started the car and drove out of the lot and on, down Airways Boulevard. She gazed out at the trees, still as pictures in the windless heat. As he pulled onto 240 and headed east, she caught herself trying to imagine how it would look to her in a year. The road was full of speeding traffic. Everyone seemed to be in a careless hurry to arrive somewhere. At Getwell, he pulled off and went north to Walnut Grove. He turned left there, and above the distant horizon a big thunderhead was moving across the sun. Light poured out of the complex folds of the cloud in lovely lines, and the pelagic blue spaces beyond were bordered with tender fingers of gold. As the beauty of the scene struck through her, she received the unbidden thought that she would have no more free enjoyment of sights like this, and in the next instant the dread of the darkness she felt, the fear of losing forever her very ability to love, and the pure terror of what she had been through, combined in her to form a single, breathless spasm of sickening agitation.

When they pulled onto Mimosa, he said, "It's the fourth one on the right."

She looked at the house fronts, the lawns. Each of the entrances had an iron screened door. She had known them all her life, and now they made her think of jails. He saw her pale hand fly up to her face and then drop into her lap.

He parked in front, and for a moment they sat there looking at it. "Here we are," he said.

The house was the color of coffee with cream. The light changed on it as the lowering sun came through another opening in the clouds, and she saw the small square windows across the top of the front door. "I used to walk by here," she said, low. "Going for walks in good weather."

"Does it feel strange to think you'll be living here?"

"I guess it does. I never even really looked at it. It's nice."

A thin sidewalk led up to the front stoop. She got out and stood waiting while he came around the car and took her hand.

"I always thought it was a pretty neighborhood," she said.

In the front yard, to the right of the walkway, a small tulip poplar stood. Crepe myrtles lined the street, making oblong ponds of shade on the grass going up to the crossing road. There was a tall, leaning river oak behind the house. It looked as though it had been arrested in the process of falling.

They went up the walk to the stoop, climbed the seven steps, and he opened the iron-framed screen door and put the key in the lock. It didn't want to turn. Remembering Mr. Rainey's trouble with the wrong keys in the lockbox, he wondered if somehow he'd got the bad set. He felt the need for things to go smoothly, pressing a little, aware of her standing there watching him. Finally he got the key to work and, pushing the door open, stepped back for her to enter. She went slowly, as if in wonder or disbelief, looking around. Her manner was that of someone still in a far place, alone. "We'll paint this room, of course," he said about the living room, which was a deep brown, with a large picture window at the back, looking into the yard. "Something bright. The real-estate agent said we could treat it like we own it where that's concerned."

"I like the window," she said.

Their voices echoed slightly. She couldn't shake her unease, moving through the rooms, the tight spaces inside the walls of the house. He was obviously proud of his choice, though now he murmured, as though the two of them were in church, that she did not have to like it at all; they could look for something else. It was quite small. She walked out the back door, to the patchy green yard with its shed and koi pond. Beyond the pond was a separated area, like a dog run, but whoever had lived here before had not used it for that purpose; it showed signs of a garden gone to seed. To the right of this was a rose arbor in the shape of a domed gazebo, with a wooden swing in the middle of it. The rosebushes were all overgrown, and some of the longer branches lay across the entrance. The petals were scattered everywhere on the ground.

"Needs work back here, too," he said. "I can do some things. I should've looked closer at everything, I guess."

She broke forth suddenly with a sob. "I shouldn't have gone to Jamaica!"

It startled him. "Hey—we're fine, honey. We don't have to take this."

So much stood in her mind: what she was going to have to do, the distance she would have to travel, and—she could not shake the feeling—everything for which she would have to atone. It seemed wholly out of her reach, past her strength.

Standing there, hearing the rasping breath of her distress, he was filled with a queasy kind of wonder. He stood back. "Baby," he said, low. "It's all right now. We're all *right* now. Come on. We can look for somewhere else."

"I should've come here with you," she said through her tears. "I should've been here. I should've been here."

"It's okay if you want something else," he said. "We don't have to *take* this one."

"No." She turned to him. "No, I *want* it. I do. I want us in it. We could be moving into it by now." Wiping her eyes with the backs of her hands, she started toward the rose arbor, feeling his proximity as oppression: if she could just walk out into the open space of the yard, where there was still a pocket of sunlight, to breathe a little and get command of herself. By herself.

"I'm okay with whatever you want to do," he said, following her. "Really, honey."

"I know. I love it. I wish we lived in it right now."

"We'll fix it up together."

"Yes."

"There's a lot we can do." He longed to take her arm and pull her back to him, but, sensing that it wouldn't be what she needed or wanted, he refrained. There was something inaccessible about her now. "The two of us," he went on helplessly. "It'll be fun."

She was still sniffling, still shying away from him.

"We can be like a couple of graduate students. Like we talked about." It was as if he were pleading with her. "Remember? Going to antiques stores and shopping together for our house in Memphis. Here it is, if you want it. Our house in Memphis." Now he felt garrulous.

"Yes, our house in Memphis," she said.

They said nothing for a space, walking to one side of the house, and then around to the other, trying the gate there and looking briefly out at the street. Without expressing it to himself, he determined that the distance between them could for some obscure reason be a thing she required in order to come fully to him. He reassured himself with this notion, watching her walk back out past the river oak and then on to the center of the yard. Undeniably, something else was weighing on her mind. He decided it was the house and the fact that he had chosen it without her.

"I should've waited until we could look together," he said.

She faced him. "No, I'm glad. I didn't want to have to do that. You did it for us. I'm glad. I am. Really. I *love* it." Seeing the concern in his features, she believed she knew what he was thinking. She stepped toward him, indicating the house. Through tears, she said, "Home."

He understood it as a gift she was offering him.

"Perfect." She went on, "I'm so happy."

"You're sure." He felt wrong. He rested his hands on her shoulders and gathered her to him. In that moment something shrieked high in the branches of the river oak, a crow or a blackbird. She jumped and looked up. "Honey, we're *fine* now," he said.

"Has Iris seen it?"

He sighed. "Not yet."

She took his arm at the elbow. "I just need a little time. Everything was so awful when I couldn't reach you."

"I know."

"I think Iris'll like this house."

"You can do physical therapy with her every morning for her knee, or just visit with her in the rose arbor and have coffee, and then spend the mornings painting."

"That sounds lovely." She reached out and touched the soft petals of one of the roses. "I've been hoping to get started again."

"There you go. And, you know, I could keep my little apart-

ment and you could use it as a studio, so you won't be interrupted.
I hadn't thought of that until just now. Whatever you want to do,
babe."

"I like it when you call me that." She thought horribly of his
innocence. "You're so sweet."

"Babe," he said.

Any moment, he would be able to read what was rushing
through her mind. The tips of her fingers came to her lips, touched
softly there. Then she dropped her hands to her sides and offered
herself for another kiss.

He put his arms tight around her.

She made herself smile, looking up into his eyes, and she forced
the light tone. "And what will you be doing while I'm painting?"

"A friend of mine named Lawrence Watson runs a service for
the parole board. I start Wednesday. Job counseling."

"That'll be helping people in trouble. Working with people."

"Exactly. One at a time, you know."

"But what about France?" She could not help bringing it up.

"It's not permanent. Just helping out."

"Isn't that really what you were doing anyway? Helping people
one at a time?"

He noted the tone of feigned interest in her voice and once
more received the urge to soothe her. "I've been thinking. I don't
know how to put it. I can't seem to get my bearings after what's
happened."

All the color went out of her face. "Me, too." She reached
for him. "Oh, baby. I feel so sad for everything and everyone." It
seemed to her that this was the first completely honest thing she
had said to him since her arrival.

"You should've seen the cabbie that drove me to Clara's in D.C.
A Palestinian Christian. He had quite a story to tell about *his* day."

"It's all so hideous."

He began telling her about the poor cabbie and the near violence that had come at him solely for his appearance.

She interrupted him. "Let's not talk about it now. Please?"

"Well, but you know we're all supposed to go on with our lives
and shop up a storm. You've been hearing that, right?"

"No."

"It's true. If we change anything they win." He took her hand, felt the thin bones there. "You think the truck will arrive on time at Iris's?"

"How are we supposed to just 'go on' with our lives?" she said. "It's all changed, hasn't it?"

"They're playing football games this weekend. And the baseball teams are going on with things. We're supposed to not become paranoid. Not show any fear."

"And what about rage?" Her eyes shone.

"I know."

"Let's go," she murmured. She put her arms around him again.

He stood there hugging her while she cried a little more, and some part of him stirred with annoyance, like a breath of air at a window. It passed through him and was gone.

As they went back out to the car, she asked what he had to do to secure the house and close the deal, and as he explained it his gladness in seeing her returned. He marveled at the little creases in the corner of her mouth, the perfect dark shine of her hair in the sunlight. They were together, and the fact of her physical presence lifted him. He felt suddenly quite strong and resilient and free of doubt. The disquiet he had felt earlier, the apathy—that had been caused by having to be away from her. He was almost proud of it. "I'm so happy," he said.

She smiled, and her eyes welled up again. "Yes—happy."

She wanted to drive to Iris's. So much time had gone by since she had driven a car. It felt good to get in behind the wheel, with him at her side. On the little two-block jaunt over to Bilders Street, they talked about Iris's most recent fall, and he remembered the first time he had ever seen the old lady coming into his church, asking to talk to him. He described how it was to see Iris yesterday, none the worse for wear, constant as ocean waves.

Iris was in front of her small house, watering the flowers in the wooden box that ran along the window. She had her cane with her, and when she saw the car pull up, she put the watering can down and started toward them across the lawn.

Natasha got out and said, "Stay there," but lost her voice on the second word. She ran to her, and there was Iris, arms spread wide to greet her.

2

The truck with her belongings had been delayed by traffic on Interstate 70 and by bad storms in the mountains near Knoxville. It would not arrive until tomorrow morning. Most of what was on it would be moved into storage for the time being anyway, since they could not occupy the house until the end of the month. Late that evening, they drove back over there with Iris, to show it to her. Once again, Faulk saw the beset look in his future wife's face and heard notes of a kind of hectic, feigned cheer in her speech—something dark coursing under the timbre of her voice, the slightest tremor there, giving her away. He wondered if Iris heard it as the two women went through the rooms and out to the back, Iris moving quite well with her cane, actually going in under the drooping branches of the rose arbor to sit in the little wooden swing there. Natasha joined her, and Faulk watched as they swung back and forth, Iris talking about how nice this would be when the first real fall weather arrived.

It was full dark now. The smell of the roses was in the air, and of the leaves that kept dropping with the light wind that stirred. Faulk studied Natasha's face in the glow from the kitchen window of the house. She saw him watching her and tried to ignore it, turning to her grandmother and saying that she would plant a garden in the little dog-run area, as someone else obviously had. But whereas it looked from the tilted tomato stakes as though it had been a vegetable garden, she would make hers all flowers, wholly for the color. "It's a perfect spot, don't you think?" she said, and heard the infinitesimal quaver in her own voice, aware of him attending to it, standing there, a shadow in the light from the window. He had his hands clenched down in the pockets of his white slacks, and though she couldn't see his face, he seemed calm and glad to be where he was.

This, she knew, was for Iris's sake. Inside the house, she saw the inquisitiveness in his eyes, the wish to know more, to question her, because clearly he had seen the turmoil she had concealed so poorly. She found the strength to remark placidly to Iris that she, Iris, would have to make it a practice to have her morning coffee here, perhaps in the rose arbor. "After you're fully healed, of course. It's just a two-block walk for you. And you're already so much better now."

"I thought I was going to need more surgery," Iris said. "At my age." She turned to Faulk. "You picked a very nice little place. Are you sure it's enough for you?"

"Oh, yes. I like it a lot." He addressed Natasha. "You sure about it, darling?"

"I adore it," Natasha said, smiling but not looking at him.

Back at Iris's house, the old woman put the lights on and then lit candles, too, insisting on making coffee. They sat in the kitchen and breathed the aroma of the coffee and of the candles, and they talked to her, also by her insistence, about the last four days—their separate journeys home. In the paper there was a report that the plane that went down in Pennsylvania might have been shot down. Several witnesses reported two fighter jets flying near it. The deputy secretary of defense was denying that any planes had been in the vicinity. And the first intimations were surfacing that the passengers of the hijacked airliner had caused the crash. Faulk read this aloud from the paper while they sipped the coffee. And then he told Iris about his Palestinian cabdriver. "I couldn't really say anything, and I guess I felt the smallest bit chary of him—the way I bet a lot of people will feel for a while about everybody from that part of the world."

Iris said, "They should have a government-required course in all the schools on earth where people are asked to meet people from distant places and get to know them as individual people."

"In the best of worlds," Faulk said. "But these killers knew people personally. It didn't matter to them. They lived here. God. They made friends and went to parties."

"What is the name of the one they say did this? I've been hearing about him for years. But I can't keep it in my mind. The names are so scary sounding, anyway, don't you think?"

Faulk said the name. She sipped her coffee and pondered it. "I never dreamed I'd ever see anything like this. It's like science fiction."

Natasha looked at them both, her grandmother and her husband-to-be. They were going on about it—the subject, she knew, of most conversations now. She rose and excused herself, claiming tiredness, and wanting to get cleaned up. She took the bag with her toiletries in it and went up the dark stairs to her bedroom. When Iris and she had made the move into this house, Iris had tried to make the bedroom exactly like the one in the old house, painting it the same off-white and hanging all the same pictures on the wall: a framed photo of her parents standing in rainy light on a street in London; drawings and early watercolors that she had done of Iris and of people she knew and singers—Phil Collins, Sting, Bob Dylan, and Joni Mitchell. Folded in the dresser to the left of the door were clothes she had worn back then or clothes she had left here on visits through the years. She opened the top drawer of the dresser and looked at the tight folds of cloth. It felt like being given a vision of the earlier life. Finally, she closed it and in the thrown light from the hall, put the case on the chair by her bed and opened it. She could hear their voices below, but no words—Faulk laughing briefly at something. Stepping to the window, she looked out at the street, the lights in the houses that lined the other side. There was so much suffering in the country now, so much grief. And fear. She took a deep breath and resolved to stop letting her own predicament block her vision of the general calamity.

She felt like crying again and caught herself. She went into the bathroom and put some fresh makeup on.

Downstairs, Faulk heard her cross the hall into the bathroom, heard the door close quietly. He had been reading another part of the paper to Iris, who sighed now and told him she liked how the president, a man she never thought much of, handled the speech at the site of the destruction. "They're calling it ground zero," she said.

"I know." Faulk glanced at the stairs.

"She was pretty sure you were hurt or killed," Iris murmured. "I know how her mind works. She has a catastrophic imagination in the best circumstances. She's always been that way."

"Yes."

"She thought for sure you were in one of the towers. Or on the street below. I must say that crossed my mind, too."

"I talked about going down there and going up in one of them for breakfast. The wedding was supposed to be in that neighborhood, by the way. I don't know if she mentioned that to you. That church is where they took some of the injured."

"God, it just hasn't really sunk in yet, for her, that we're all okay."

"I think there's something else bothering her, though."

The old woman waited.

"I'd like to talk to her friend Constance."

"What could it be other than this? She was certain she'd lost you."

"Maybe I'm just reading into things."

"But *what*. What would—what could you be reading into it?"

"I don't know. Maybe something's changed for her."

"I don't think we know how to *be* anymore," Iris said. "That's the thing. It's all completely unthinkable and awful."

"In New York," Faulk said, "on Fifty-Fourth Street, unless you were looking south, you would not have known anything was wrong—except for the sirens. I didn't know about it until Clara called me."

"I was listening to *Morning Edition*." Iris stood and opened the refrigerator. "I've got a roast ready to go. I put it in earlier today."

"Can I help?"

She smiled. "You can mash the potatoes."

Natasha, coming down the stairs, heard this and felt a twinge of nausea at the idea of the three of them sitting at that table with dinner before them. Dinner. A task requiring energy she did not have. She took a breath and strode into the room and leaned down to kiss Faulk on his cheek. His hand came gently to the middle of her lower back.

"What can I do?" she asked.

Faulk saw the bones of her jaw. "You've lost a little weight," he said, casually, wanting to be talking about anything else, realizing almost immediately that this was the wrong thing to say.

She removed herself from him and went to the other side of the table. "I don't think so."

Iris stared. "You do look a little drawn, honey."

"I'm fine," Natasha said, and sat down.

There were red blotches on her cheeks. "I didn't mean to embarrass you," Faulk said.

She waved this away, aware of him looking into her. She presented him with a smile, then rose to go stand next to Iris, who was preparing to slice the pot roast.

"Tell us," Iris said. "What people did, stuck like that? I mean the ones who weren't affected—Europeans and such."

"It seemed to me that everybody got drunk and stayed that way."

"And you?" Faulk said.

"The first night, I did. And as a matter of fact I'd like something to drink right now."

"I have some wine," said Iris, opening the cabinet and bringing out a bottle of Bordeaux. Faulk uncorked it, and Iris put three glasses down on the counter. For a moment the only sound was the wine pouring.

"Love that sound," Faulk said. Then he held up his glass. "Nice dark color." He drank and smiled at them and set the glass down. "Delicious."

"Very good," said Iris.

"I like that word for describing it," Natasha said to Faulk. "*Delicious.*"

He stood and reached for the bowl of potatoes. Iris had set a milk carton out. He poured a little milk over the steaming potatoes and then put a big dollop of butter on them and began mashing them. Natasha and Iris went on sipping the wine.

"*Delicious* is the word," Iris said.

Natasha saw out the window the little moving flickers of fire-flies rising on the lawn, just past the light from the porch, as if the very light itself were breaking up and flying off. The grass was overgrown, and tall weeds stood in it. At the far end of the lawn, she knew, was a swing set, one swing dangling by a strand of rope; another, on chains, still intact. It had been there when they moved in. She remembered the Collierville house and thought of herself as a girl there, the calm of an afternoon in summer, sitting on the porch swing and looking at the empty field across the way. How strange that she never regarded herself, then, as having lost anything; and now, thinking of her long-dead parents, she felt their absence with an unexpected stab of heartache. She drank more of the wine.

"Slow down, babe," Faulk said warmly to her. "We've got the whole rest of the evening."

Iris set the plate of cut beef on the table and took another sip from her glass. She held it up. "To having everybody home safe and sound."

Natasha drank her glass down, then poured more. She took some of the beef and potatoes, a few of the green beans. "I'm afraid I don't have much appetite."

"It's all very good," Faulk said, smiling at Iris.

"Oh, good, yes," Natasha said. But she couldn't eat much of it. She swallowed more of the wine, which had begun to taste thick and filmy.

Iris and Faulk went over the arrangements for tomorrow—the signing of the lease and the arrival of the truck. They could stay here a couple of days, if they needed to, Iris told them. To avoid having to drive back and forth to Faulk's apartment in Midtown.

"We'll have to put the stuff in storage for a few days," Faulk said. "Until the place is ready for us. But we can stay at either place."

"It's not much stuff," Natasha said. "Really. I didn't keep much."

Faulk noticed the moistness in her dark eyes and thought she might cry. But she had more of the wine and smiled at him and took another forkful of the potatoes.

"Think you'll miss Washington, honey?" Iris asked.

"I'm so glad to be home."

"Well, I'm not going to argue for you being anywhere else."

"Southern France?" Faulk said as though he were offering it.

"Just now, I'm going upstairs to sleep," Natasha said. "If that's all right."

"Why wouldn't it be all right?" Faulk said.

She stood up, walked around to him, bent down, and kissed him on the mouth. He held her for a moment.

In the tone of a statement, he said, "Are you okay."

"I'm just spent." It was true. With the slight calming the wine had provided, she felt that this was what was really happening to her. The waves of fright and despair were all the product of being exhausted. "Do you mind if we just stay here tonight?"

"Not a bit," he said. "Really, babe."

She gave him another kiss, turned and hugged her grandmother, then went quietly upstairs. The dark of the hallway was inexplicably inviting. She went along it to the room, entered without turning the light on, and lay across the bed in her clothes. Closing her eyes, she saw an image of Iris standing in the yard with that welcoming smile.

3

Sleep came without dreams. She woke briefly three times and listened for their voices. The second time she realized that Faulk was at her side, snoring lightly, one hand resting on her hip. The third time she heard Iris moving around in the hall and then there was silence, and she settled back with the sense of being secure and warm in a sleeping house.

Faulk woke her, gently, kissing the side of her face. "Time to wake up."

"I'm awake," she said, stirring, sitting up, and putting her arms around him. Looking into his eyes, she said, "Good morning."

"Iris's making breakfast."

"It smells wonderful."

They went downstairs together. In the kitchen, the old woman had put bacon on and was tossing eggs in a bowl. The smell of the bacon mixed with the aroma of the coffee was wonderful. Natasha sat at the table and looked at the newspaper there, but did not pick it up.

Faulk stood at the counter buttering slices of toast.

"I have leftover beef, too," Iris said.

"This will be fine," said Natasha, watching them work.

She was surprised to find that this morning she did have an appetite. And she could look across the table and appreciate her future husband. Her grandmother appeared ruddy and healthy and glad of everything. Bright sun poured in at the window. They ate quietly for a little while.

"What did you have to eat in Jamaica," Iris said, looking down, concentrating on her eggs.

"Ackee and salt fish."

"Ackee."

"It looks like scrambled eggs with fish in it."

"What *is* in it? Can we make it here?"

"Salt fish—dried cod," Natasha said. "Ackee is a fruit. And there's onion and different peppers and butter. Actually I didn't—I didn't like it that much." She remembered that she *had* liked it and knew in the same instant that she never wanted to taste it again.

Faulk saw that she was holding something back, and it came to him that he was a little tired of all the unspoken emotion. "Well," he said. "It's over. Let's just enjoy what we have."

Having finished the eggs, she looked down at her hands on either side of her plate. "We saw it on TV when we came in from the beach," she said. "It was such a beautiful morning, too, and we came in and it was happening. The television in the lobby." She shook her head.

"Okay, darling," Faulk said to her, touching her shoulder. "Come on. It's okay now. We're okay. Look at us."

"You must've felt so isolated," Iris said. "Well, I know you did."

"I haven't been through anything like—" She gestured, as if to indicate something at the windows.

"No," Faulk said. "Of course."

After the meal, he and Natasha did the dishes together, and he tried to find joking things to say but couldn't. They worked silently for a time, cooperating, she washing and he drying.

"I can't believe my own good luck," he told her, taking her by the upper arms when they had put away the last dish. "I've found someone I like drying dishes for."

"That's lucky, all right."

He kissed her, a light touch on her lips, and then put the palm of his hand gently on the side of her face. "Beautiful kitchen help."

"Thank you, kind sir."

She felt almost lighthearted, pushing all the bad thoughts back, shaking them from her as the hour passed, drinking more coffee and then sitting with Iris and Faulk on the porch, watching the light change, the day heating up.

They had so much to talk about, and yet they said little. Faulk described more of what happened on his way south, the crowded train station in New York with its scores of people simply trying to leave, the young Asian man on the station platform in Newark.

"What do you think you'll do now?" Iris asked him.

He told her.

"I thought you made a good priest."

"I was miserable."

"No one could see that."

"That's kind of you to say."

"Maybe we *can* spend spring in the south of France," Natasha said.

He thought of the job he had just taken as if it were an appointment that had slipped his mind. Spring was months away. He reached over and patted her wrist. "We'll do whatever you want."

When, a little later, they got up to go, Natasha felt as if they were leaving for good. "Therapy on your knee?" she asked Iris, who smiled, shaking her head.

"Acclimate yourself a little, dear. There's plenty of time."

They went out to the car and got in. The old woman stood in the sunlight on the porch with her cane.

Faulk thought, as he pulled the car away from the curb, that perhaps he had been imagining things. Natasha appeared fine now, staring out at the sunny, humid morning, arms folded across her chest. She had merely been feeling the strain of the journey home.

As they pulled up to his apartment building on Cooper, and he was helping her with her bags from the car, he heard a small polite clearing of a throat and turned to see that Mr. Baines was waddling over from his cottage. He came up to them and bowed slightly. "Happy to make your acquaintance," he said to Natasha before Faulk could introduce her.

"Hello," Natasha said to him.

He turned to Faulk. "I congratulate you on your choice of a young wife."

Faulk heard the slight emphasis on the word *young*. "Thank you," he said.

The other man stood close, offering his hand. He smelled of the cigarette he was smoking. "I was just sitting out on my porch over there, you know, and I saw you pull in. Can I interest either of you in a glass of something cold? Orange or grapefruit juice?"

"We're fine." Natasha saw the aggravation in Faulk's face.

"You had some luck, didn't you," Baines said to her. "Stuck in paradise for three days like that. I wish somebody would stick me in Jamaica for three days and tell me I can't leave." He seemed about to laugh and in the same moment to realize the inappropriateness of the joke. He went on: "Of course it's just a terrible thing."

Natasha said nothing.

"Yes," Faulk said quickly. "Well, excuse us."

Baines cleared his throat again. "If I could speak with you for just a few seconds."

"I'll come back out," Faulk said. "Let me get Natasha inside."

"I should have an extra key made?"

"We'll talk."

Natasha followed him into the building. When he had gotten the door to the apartment open and turned on the light, she saw the front room—no paintings, no pictures on the walls, books crammed into a makeshift cinder-block-and-pine-plank bookcase. He sensed that she was discouraged by it and moved quickly to get her bags into the bedroom, where there were pictures—photos of him in college, of his mother and Aunt Clara, of Natasha and himself from his summer visits to Washington, and also some prints of famous paintings—Sargent's *Carnation, Lily, Lily, Rose* with the girls in their pure white dresses and the lovely lit paper lanterns and Vermeer's *Milkmaid* and *The Music Lesson*. They had discovered in their trips to the galleries in Washington that they both prized the way the two artists created the sensation of luminescence, Sargent's sharp flashes as opposed to Vermeer's muted glow. Faulk had admired how she accomplished similar effects with her watercolors. Now she walked to the Sargent print and appreciated it while Faulk went into the bathroom. He decided that things weren't clean enough and ran more water in the sink, making another effort to lessen the rust stain on the porcelain under the faucet. The room smelled like the Ajax he had used to go over it. He opened the window and fanned the air.

She undressed and lay down. On the wall next to the window was a cross, the only sign of his former life. She considered it in that context and then tried to dismiss the idea. It was—emotionally, anyway—the same life.

When he came out of the bathroom, she got up and moved gingerly around him to go in. He stopped her for a moment. "I'm so happy."

"Me, too," she told him. "We're going to be so good together." She wanted it to be true; she would make it true. In the little room, she saw the open window and breathed in and then out slowly, fully, working to imagine that all the badness of the past few days was being expelled. The white curtain blew inward with a stirring of air from the outside. She heard a train, near sounding. The breeze died, then came back. He had put her makeup bag on the space next to the sink.

"I'm going to take a shower," she said.

From the other room, he called, "Want me to join you?"

"Not this time, honey. I kind of need to have this one alone." She waited. "Okay?"

"Sure," he called. He was sitting on the bed, looking at the door, which she had closed. Her shadow moved in the strand of light at the bottom. He heard the water running and lay back on the bed, hands behind his head. He felt good. Rested. They could begin their lives together, with this warm-feeling domesticity, her calling him *honey* from the other room, ministering to herself, preparing for this day with him, the first in what seemed such a long time.

There was a knock at the front door. Baines. "I was coming down," Faulk told him.

"Uh, no need," the other said, looking past him.

Faulk stepped out and closed the door. "Well?"

"I wondered if you'd met with any progress about subletting."

"Not yet, no. And I think I might just keep it, for a studio."

"Oh, well, then," Baines said, and cleared his throat. "That's— well, anyway, I wanted to make sure you knew that I could forgive the rest of the lease if it would help." He gave a small smile. There was something almost pleading about it.

Faulk reached over and patted the side of his arm near the shoulder. Baines made his way back down to the street. When he waved, Faulk waved back.

On her side of the bathroom door, Natasha stood with her back facing the mirror and looked over her shoulder to see if there was any bruising. She could see none. She kept the water running, cleaned her teeth. Then she turned the shower on and got into the hot stream, thinking of Jamaica and the long night there, the hour of running water over herself trying to get clean.

Here, the stream was soft, without much pressure, but it was very hot. In her mind's eye she saw the crowded veranda at the Ratzibungens' resort and Mrs. Skinner with that fanatical judgment of poor Mr. Skinner. She saw Constance and Skinner dropping down into the cold water on the beach. And then she saw Duego as he stumbled toward her in the sand under the moon, with his dope and his perfectly enunciated English.

Her hands shook as she turned the water off and reached for a towel. She heard Faulk moving around in the room. She rubbed her hips and felt the slight soreness and searched once more for any sign of a bruise. "Stop it," she whispered to herself, looking at the face in the mirror, which she did not quite recognize with its glittering eyes and beset look, seeking not to let thoughts come, since thoughts flowed inexorably into all the bad possibilities.

He had come back in and taken his clothes off, and he lay in the bed and watched the little moving shadow at the base of the door. Finally the door opened, and she emerged, wrapped in the towel. She let it drop and got in with him. "Oh," he said, "you are so beautiful." He put his mouth on hers. The light was coming in the window, and she recalled that they had both liked making love in the light. But the brightness of it now seemed vulgar to her.

"Can we close the curtain?" she said.

"What?"

"Please?"

"Sure, babe. I'm sorry."

"No, it's nothing. I just want it to be a little more romantic."

He got up and went to the window.

"Just—this time," she told him.

He pulled the curtain shut, and they were in dimness. "Well, this is a *little* like candlelight."

She held the soft blanket open for him as he came back to her. Again he was kissing her, and when he moved over onto her, she couldn't breathe. She waited for him to let up, lift his head to take a breath himself, but he exhaled into her mouth, and now she thought she might choke. She pushed on his shoulders, and he quickly moved off her, lying on his back at her side. "Is something wrong? Was I too heavy?"

"No, I want to come over and be on top."

"Darling."

She turned, got herself to her knees, and then straddled him. She was sore; it hurt, and he thrust up into her. "Easy, honey."

"You're a little—dry." Her apparent rush troubled him faintly, but he made himself savor the wealth of her being so close, with her smell of scented soap from the shower. The ends of her hair were wet. "Maybe let's kiss some more."

"No, I want you. I want you inside me. Please."

"Baby, are we all right?" he asked, hearing the boylike plea in it. He felt like an adolescent, nervous now and worried about himself.

She touched his face. "It's just that—it's been such a long terrible time."

He reached for her shoulders to bring her down close and put his arms around her. They lay very still. He was inside her and flexed slightly. "That okay?"

"Good," she murmured. "I wanted to be close. Yes."

He thought she might be crying, felt something like a shiver go through her. "Babe, is it all right?"

She couldn't lie about this. The dryness was hurting, and she could tell that it was making him tender. "I'm just still adjusting," she murmured.

He gently disengaged, turning so that she lay down at his side, and he kissed her cheek, her neck, her breasts. The whole thing felt labored now, forced. Her nipples were soft, and when he licked them she moved to bring him up to her lips. He stopped. "Maybe we should just go get a few things for the house." Irritation sounded in his voice despite his resolve not to show it.

"No," she said. "Come on. I'm sorry."

So he rose and came over, and she lifted her legs and felt him push against all the sore places along the backs of her thighs and inside her, too. She said his name and moved to help him, and he came.

"I can keep going," he said, still moving, though it stung him, too, now, a little.

"No, darling. It's fine. I think it's just that it's getting near my period."

He pulled out of her and turned over, and took her hand, sighing. "It was beautiful. Beautiful." He seemed happy, lying there.

They spent the day buying things for the house—a few pictures, some tableware, place mats, wineglasses, two chairs and a sofa that would be delivered, a duvet and comforter, sheets and pillowcases and towels, four one-gallon cans of off-white paint.

They stopped at the Michaels store, and she bought watercolors in tubes and some new paper and brushes. Together they visited two antiques stores, and she picked a group of photos from one bin. There was one face in particular—that of a woman with soft rounded features, lovely skin, from 1921, and she looked to be in her late thirties or early forties. She had the saddest eyes. It was an old color photograph, and the color had faded to a yellowish tinge, and Natasha wanted to capture it exactly. The image had sunk into her as she picked it out of the others in the bin, most of which were sepia photographs of the many occupants of a large house. A group portrait showed them all on some sunny summer day, ranged across the veranda and the steps in front of the house, a place that, from the note on the back of the photograph, was no longer there. The woman of the color photograph that Natasha wanted to paint was at the very end of the veranda, younger, holding a child. Faulk, looking at that picture, pointed to the child and said, "Think of it. That baby, if it's still alive, is more than eighty years old, now."

"This is the same woman." Natasha held up the color photo.

"Wonder what's broken her."

"Don't be glib."

"I mean that entirely, from my heart."

She kissed him and felt as though she had harmed him somehow. "I'm sorry. Of course you do, my love." She was near crying.

He saw this and busied himself gathering all the photographs from the bin and putting them in a manila envelope. "Riches," he told her.

"Yes." She brushed the hair back from her forehead and took the envelope from him, forcing a smile.

They put everything in the house, and in midafternoon they met with Mr. Rainey to sign the lease. They sat talking with him about his daughters. Natasha felt warm and glad of him, this quiet and benevolent old man with his watery eyes and stern-looking eyebrows and his obvious loneliness. He wanted to extend the appointment, insisted on walking through the house with them one more time.

When he had driven away, they stood in the mostly empty living room with the boxes stacked haphazardly around them and looked at everything.

"Now what," said Faulk.

"I guess let's put away what we can."

They had dinner with Iris—the leftover beef—and then went back to his apartment for the night. He waited for some sign from her about lovemaking, and when she gave none, he let it go. She sensed this but could not bring herself to do anything about it. She was still very tired, and sore, and she wanted sleep, and anyway it was true that her period would start soon enough. They lay talking softly about the day, and about Mr. Rainey and his nine grandsons. It was just the sort of back-and-forth observing that people do in circumstances where there are certain subjects that cannot be brought up. To Faulk, it felt false; but he was certain that he would be bullying her if he mentioned it. So he went along, craving contact with her, aching with desire, but wanting, too, not to think so much of his needs. She grew drowsy, trusting him, nestling close. They went to sleep like this.

4

In the middle of the night she woke with a start and thought she was still in Jamaica. The realization that she wasn't filled her with relief so great that she shuddered pleasurably, pulling the blanket tight over her shoulder. He stirred, then settled back. She moved closer and had the sensation of trying to live down a betrayal of him. She knew rationally that this was not so, that even in those few despairing, drunken, exhausted moments on the beach in Jamaica, feeling afraid and sorry for herself and for the other, too, and allowing him to kiss her—even then there was no real betrayal. It was a thing born of the anxiety and distraction of the moment and it had ended there; she had ended it, stopped it. Stopped *that*. What happened later was ruthless force, nothing she could help

because finally it wasn't within the bounds of ordinary human relations to think anyone would do such a thing. Yet lying wakeful in
the dark, hearing another train haul its moan across the night, she
felt it all as something guilty to hide from him, and once more it
was as though he were the one who was so much younger.

No sleep.

The train was gone, and she heard the continual high-pitched
ruckus of the insects in the trees, a sound so constant that you
almost ceased to notice it. And then you did. It was such a noisy
place at night, Memphis. You did not hear the thrum of the city;
you heard the insects, and the train in the night, fading, giving way
again to the insects.

She turned onto her other side, facing away from him, and
attempted not to allow anything into her mind but the calming
hours of the day before with Iris, the being together again with her
husband-to-be. She was back in the world. She had come home
and could have a life now and be happy. She told herself that she
was happy. He mumbled something unintelligible, and then said,
clearly, "No."

It startled her. "Honey?"

He turned, put his arm over her hip, said "Darling," fidgeted
for a moment, and grew still. She heard only the soft breathing of
sleep. She lay there and drifted, dreaming that everything was fine,
and *she* was fine and she could let her mind wander, like a person
without anything to hide and no distressing memories.

In the morning he was up first. She heard him moving around
in the small kitchen, and the aroma of coffee came to her. She got
out of the bed and into a pair of jeans and a T-shirt and strode to
him across the spare, monklike cell of the living room.

The kitchen was very small: refrigerator at one end, small sink
and counter across from an oven and a stove, and a table not much
bigger than a TV tray, with two hard-back chairs. One window
above the sink looked out on leafy shade. The sun was bright
beyond the leaves. He was sitting at the small table, reading the
newspaper and drinking coffee. His night had been a blankness,
restful and deep, and when he woke, and got carefully out of the

bed so as not to wake her, he received a sweet intimation of how it would be when they had already been married for months or years, and the chaos and terror, the war, whatever this was, had receded into the past.

"Didn't want to wake you," he said now. "You were sleeping so well."

"What time is it."

"After ten."

"I *did* sleep. But I woke up and thought I was still in Jamaica. Then I was awake for a long time."

"What happened in Jamaica?" he said suddenly.

She could say nothing for a moment. "I—you know. I was stranded, and I couldn't get through to you. I thought you were dead." The tears came to her eyes.

"I'm sorry," he told her. "But we're safe. It's over now. We're home. Together."

"Yes." She ran the back of one hand across her cheek.

"Let's just concentrate on each other," he said. "Let's try to forget it a little, and stop dwelling on it all the time."

"I'm not dwelling on it."

"I am, a little. Let's not. I wasn't—I didn't mean just you." As he spoke the words, he believed them, even as part of him recoiled at the falsity of it: he had indeed been talking only about her.

"I want to never talk about it or think about it ever again," she said.

"All right."

He stood to pour her some coffee and saw out of the corner of his eye that she had picked up the paper. Something in him wanted her not to look at it, not to see the horrors there. But then he decided to stop worrying so much about her reactions; she was a grown woman.

"They think it might be as many as six thousand people," she said, settling into the chair.

"God."

He set the coffeepot back in its place on the stove.

"You talked in your sleep," she said.

"What did I say?"

"You said 'No.' It was like you were giving orders to someone."

"I can't imagine who."

"You do that. Talk in your sleep."

"Yeah."

"It felt like the sweetest discovery the first time I noticed it."

"You're so sweet." He put the cup of coffee down for her and sat across the table. They said nothing for a moment. She sipped the coffee. He saw the frown of concentration in her features. "The fires are still burning," he said. "And—and apparently one Saudi didn't get on board one of the flights and took a train west."

She did not look up.

"Imagine," he said. "Nineteen men committing suicide. Planning it and then carrying it out. For murder. Twenty people committed to it, and one decided it wasn't something he would do."

"They haven't found him? The other one?"

"Guess not. And there may be others. If you can get nineteen, I guess you can get others."

"Oh, I really don't want to think about it." She put the paper down. "I'm sorry."

"No." He took part of the rest of it. "Right."

She watched him turn the pages. Here were his wrists, the muscles of his forearms, and she felt, with the same shock of those first moments at the airport, the sense of his physical presence as unnerving, even threatening—the solidness of him, the size of him. His very maleness. A part of her marked the reaction as if it were a separate thing, a phenomenon to be studied: why should this about the man she loved, the curve of his wrists and the rippling tendons and musculature of his forearms, make her feel so queasy? He was the gentlest man, the kindest and most considerate person. She *liked* him, along with being in love with him.

Having realized that she was staring at him, he put the paper down and said, "Want to try again?"

She did not want to, and the fact struck through her. Against the rush of it, she leaned forward a little. "Oh," she said. "Let's."

He rose and took her hand, and they crossed into the bedroom and lay down. She kissed him, moving with him, the worry about everything lodged at the back of her mind like the knowledge of death.

For him, it was exquisite, uncomplicated. He lay on top of her, breathing the faint honey odor of her hair, kissing her neck, murmuring the words of his love.

"Oh, darling," she said, feeling as though she were performing, as she experienced again the pain of him inside her. Wrapping her arms tightly around him, she moved her hips with him.

"I'm going to come," he said, breathless.

"Do, baby." She felt the small spasms and was far away from him, turning in her soul to look at the thing itself, this ludicrous animal act, this grossness, all flesh and need; and those other spasms, the ones she had felt inside her on that Jamaican beach, after the ripping and hurting and the sand blinding her, and the choking—the quivering that let her know the awful thing was ending at last—that was all part of the same brute thing. The same helpless little stutter of being. It appalled her.

He lay back and sighed, looking at the ceiling, and felt the rushing of his blood slowing down. She was quiet. He put his hand on her thigh. "God."

"So good," she murmured.

"You okay?"

"Yes."

"You sure?"

"Why?"

"You seemed—well, you—I felt you being a little, I don't know—" he said.

"What? Tell me."

"Elsewhere?"

She said nothing. She had an impulse to be sharp with him, tell him to stop thinking of himself so much. But here he was, with his sad eyes, wanting so badly for the two of them to be as they had been before all this. It wasn't such a selfish thing, wanting love back. She reached over and touched his cheek.

"Are you all right?" he said.

"I—I can't get those images out of my head. I wish I hadn't looked at the paper. I'll do better, I promise."

"No, no," he told her. "It was wonderful. Don't get me wrong. I just want it to be as good for you, you know."

"But it was. Really. I only want to be close to you now. I need it so much now. I thought you were—you'd been—I couldn't believe you were all right."

He kissed her cheek, putting his arm across her middle, deciding not to press it. Something was not right, and he could not persuade himself it was solely the attacks on the cities. How could that affect a thing like their intimacy? He murmured the word "sweetheart," attempting to clear his mind of everything but this moment's warmth, all a man had the right to hope for in a world where people killed themselves in order to murder thousands of others. This tenderness was the only thing anyone really possessed in order to defeat that hatred. He believed this, even as he recognized it as being at the level of a homily he might write. A second later, he remembered that he was no longer required to think that way. He gave another sigh and sat up. "I've got to find a place for storage before the truck gets here. I never seem to get organized."

"You're beautiful," she said, and looking back at her he saw tears in her eyes.

"Baby, what *is* it."

"I'm just happy to be here. Glad, and relieved and scared to believe it." As she spoke these words, she felt the truth of them slip away in a self-accusatory surge of doubt, the sense of having deceived him. *It is not. I did. I did think so. I did think I'd lost him.*

He lay down and wanted to begin again, kissing her. It went on for a few moments, but she couldn't do it, finally. She stiffened and pulled back. "Iris might walk over."

"Iris won't do that."

"No, honey. Please. Later, okay?"

"Okay," he said, "I'm sorry," and got out of the bed, keeping his back to her because he was aroused. He felt a measure of humiliation and strove to put it down in himself, moving into the bathroom and turning the shower on. *I am not a selfish man.* He attempted to put that away, too, stepping into the stream.

He heard her come in. "Have to pee," she said, just loud enough for him to hear.

She saw the shape of him behind the shower curtain and caught herself feeling sorry for him. Back in the bedroom, she opened one of her suitcases and started picking through what she would wear. The shower water stopped.

"I'm already your wife," she called. "Do you feel that?"

Toweling off, he called back to her. "I do." And then laughed. "I do," he repeated. "Do you?"

"I do," she said.

But he felt walled off from her in some subtle yet lacerating way, and he could not shake the suspicion that this was the beginning of something, that some nameless trouble was near.

5

The truck arrived, with two young men in it who looked like brothers—big, round shouldered, heavy in the belly, and with longish blond hair. The driver introduced himself as Bud and pointed to the other. "That's Joel. We got hung up in Pennsylvania first. All the traffic going up to see that field where the plane went down. At least I guess that's what it was."

"There was construction, too," the one named Joel said. "And then the storms near Knoxville."

They worked together putting the most important of Natasha's things into the space in the house that wasn't to be painted or worked on, and then what she would immediately need—the rest of her clothes and a few books—in Faulk's apartment. Mr. Baines sat on his porch with a plate of spaghetti and watched. Iris worked with Natasha going through the books to choose the ones Natasha wanted to keep within reach—volumes of poems, an anthology of

Russian short stories, several novels. There were overlaps between her books and Faulk's, and all of those she wanted to leave in storage, even after the house was ready.

"I'm going over tonight and start on it," Faulk said. "I want to get some wood and more paint. Build some bookcases."

He followed the men in the truck to a storage place on Summer Avenue, across from the wide parking lot of a closed-down motel, the Washington, the end of its sign broken down so that what you saw as you approached was THE WASHINGT. There was a lot of traffic, and the young woman behind the desk at the storage place seemed worried about it.

She was talking on the phone as she worked, taking Faulk's credit card and handing him a form to fill out. "I don't know what it is," she said into the phone. "But I'm not going home that way. You see something and right away you think—you know. Is this another attack?"

Faulk filled out the form and signed it, and signed the credit card slip, and the woman handed him a key with a number on it. "Wait a minute," she said into the phone and then in an apologetic tone directed him around to the back of the building. He mouthed the words *Thank you*, and went back out to the truck. Joel and Bud were standing there smoking and talking about someone they knew who had been in New York.

"I was in New York," Faulk told them.

"Really?" Bud, the heavier of the two, said without interest.

Faulk helped them unload the truck. It wasn't much. Among several boxes of knickknacks and keepsakes, he came upon a large square metal camera case full of photographs and papers. Seeing the corner of a photograph, he unlatched and opened the case. The photograph was of Natasha, smiling, standing in a living room with a Christmas tree behind her. The tree had no decorations on it yet; boxes of glossy bulbs were open at her feet. She looked to be about fourteen or fifteen. Her hair was cut very short, and she wore a scotch-plaid skirt and white loose-fitting blouse. He smiled, looking through the other photos. He did not allow himself more than a minute. He looked through pictures of her with friends, other women, Senator Norland and cousin Greta, school friends, several from her time in Provence. Many of them were dated. A more recent one showed her standing bundled in a black coat outside a restaurant on some snowy city street. He looked at the back of it and saw that it was dated January 2000, and *Chicago* was written under the date. Below the name of the city, in other hand writing, were the words: *Love of my life. On Our State Street.*

He put it back in its place. He put everything back and closed the box, taking another brief moment to look at her face in the one photograph. *State Street.* She appeared very happy and, he decided, she also looked full of love. It was in the eyes and around the sensuous mouth with its small, shy smile. January 2000. He thought of the April day of this year that he had met her and then counted to there from the date of the Chicago picture. Thirteen months. And when exactly had it ended?

"Memories?" Joel startled him, standing at the entrance of the cubicle with part of the frame of her bed.

"Yeah," Faulk said, straightening quickly. "Memories."

They followed him back to his apartment, and he paid them. Joel said, "So. Did you see the whole thing?"

"Excuse me?" Faulk looked at him.

"The towers."

"Oh—I didn't even know it was happening until I turned the TV on. I watched it on TV."

"Man, that is weird."

"My brother lives in Brooklyn," Bud said, "'cross the river. You know. *He* saw it from his living room window. He saw the whole thing. Couldn't believe his own eyes. Said, you know, it was like looking at movie special effects."

"I've heard other people talk about that," Faulk said. "You can't get your mind around the fact that people are dying right in front of your eyes."

"I can get *my* mind around it," said Joel. "All the way around it. And I'd like to kill me some Islamers."

Bud said, "My brother wants to come home, you know. Can't stand living up there now."

"Well, thanks, sir." They shook hands. It was odd, how close he felt to them in that moment.

"You guys be careful," he told them.

They climbed into the truck, waved at him, and drove away.

In the apartment, he found a note.

Gone to the store with Iris

Love you.

He sat in the chair by the window that overlooked the shady lawn. Less than two years ago she was in love with someone else, happy, smiling into a camera, standing on State Street in Chicago. *Our State Street.* He knew there had been unhappiness in the months before he met her, and he knew that it had something to do with the end of a love affair. He did know this. She had even spoken about it in an oblique way. But why had she kept the photograph with the handwriting, not her handwriting, on the back of it?

Just now, feeling this way, he did not want to be in her company. He looked at the note and had an uneasy moment's vision that in Jamaica she had run into whoever it was that had taken the picture in Chicago. It felt true, as if he already had proof. He could not unthink it.

On the street below, two young women came by, one pushing a stroller with a sleeping baby in it, the other walking a small dog. He had seen them before. They lived nearby. They ambled along, laughing and talking, and the one with the stroller stopped to adjust the shade screen on it. The other tossed her pretty brown hair and looked at the sky. It struck him that people made some kind of peace with their country's troubles and somehow never lost the ability to laugh and chatter or to enjoy good weather and the smell of flowers, the smiles of friendly company on a walk in the city. Why, then, could Natasha not go on a little, as these two were, coming down a dappled street talking, appreciating the late-summer light, the softly swaying shade and the breezes?

6

She sat with Iris on the stone patio of a small coffee shop off Poplar Avenue. They were in the shade of the building, but it was hot, and Iris kept fanning herself with the menu card.

"There's something else going on, isn't there," Iris said in a flat tone.

"Stress is going on," Natasha told her. "Okay? I've been through hell. I thought my fiancé was dead or hurt, and I couldn't get through."

"But he wasn't." Iris's face took on a ruminative look, as though she were dealing with some pain or cramp behind her eyes, a thought that hurt. It was an expression Natasha knew well. And just now she felt a sort of wondering disorientation, realizing the fact. "And, sweetie," Iris went on, "this feels like more than having a scare about Michael."

Natasha was silent. The server was a slight, dark brown young man wearing thick glasses. He brought the tea Iris had ordered.

Iris said, "Thanks, Philip."

"You know him?"

"I've been coming here."

Natasha smiled, shaking her head. "The things I don't know about you."

"Well."

A moment later, Iris said, "Could it be that you're having second thoughts?"

"Don't be silly."

"That's not silly. It's a legitimate question. It happens all the time. I had them before I married your grandfather."

"I'm not having second thoughts."

"Okay."

They sipped the tea and watched the cars go by on the street.

"You really had second thoughts?"

Iris nodded. "They were the silly nervous thoughts of a girl. And given what happened I guess I should've had them. But remember, I was only twenty-four years old. And he was fifty-eight."

"Everybody was married by then when you were a girl, right?"

"Yes, they were. Silly girls rushing into everything."

"Do you have any regrets?"

"A little late for that, don't you think?" Iris's smile was tolerant, but it went away quickly. "Did something happen with Constance?"

"Constance got very drunk that first night after it happened." Natasha saw a mental image of her friend, drink in hand, settling into the chilly water of the beach, and Mr. Skinner complaining about how cold it was. She found herself shaking a little, deep in the bone, and she sat forward slightly, both hands cradling the cup of warm tea.

"What just went through you." For a second time, her grandmother's question had the flat inflection of a statement.

"Nothing."

"You just had a chill."

"I did not—will you stop?"

"All right. So Constance got drunk that first night. Did she do something to you, or say something that upset you? Was it that she got drunk? I thought you said you got drunk, too."

"No. Everyone—it seemed like everyone got drunk. I'm just saying—"

"Well, I need some sense of what's still going through you."

"*Nothing's* going through me. I'm putting my life together. I left a job I had for six years and I've moved home and this awful disaster has happened and the whole country's reeling. What do you want me to do? I mean how do you want me to behave?"

"There's no need to get upset."

"Well, Michael said something this morning, too. I can't seem to process all this the way I need to without everybody questioning me."

"I wasn't questioning you," Iris said. "I want you to be all right. I was a little worried."

"Can we go soon?"

"You haven't touched your tea."

They drank without looking at each other. Natasha was thinking about how little she actually knew of this woman who had raised her—a person of unvarying consistency in the way she went through her days. Everything precise and orderly as the notes in a Mozart concerto. Now and then she would have friends over from her work in the mayor's office, women and men who knew her in her professional life and treated her with a deference. Sometimes, after Natasha was old enough to be on her own, Iris would go out with them to concerts or to one official occasion or another. Iris's job was to organize such things, to be a kind of public relations maven for the city. But because there was always reluctance on the part of people from downtown or Midtown to go "all the way out" to Collierville, Iris and Natasha were alone together a lot. In the evenings they talked, grandmother and little girl, and then grandmother and young woman. Iris read to her from books, and they watched television; sometimes they went to movies. They were like girlfriends and, as Natasha had once started to say to Faulk, this was probably one reason she had been comfortable forming the friendship with Constance. Yet through all that time together in the house, they had never really talked about Iris herself, Iris's life in the world before she was Natasha's grandmother. Natasha knew that at the birthday party of a friend, she met a middle-aged man, William Mara, a colonel in the army, getting ready to retire. Pearl Harbor was a year away. They dated for two years while he was stationed in Anacostia, Virginia, and Iris went there and lived in a small apartment in D.C., near Catholic University.

There were romantic stories of him coming in the middle of the night to the street outside her apartment, standing down there whistling tunes from Glenn Miller and Benny Goodman for her. But on those occasions he was drunk, and the stories stopped there. She and William were married in 1942; he went away to the war in January 1943. She had Natasha's mother, Laura, while he was in the Pacific.

He came home from the war and was changed, as a lot of men were. Iris would say only that she hadn't remembered him as being that much older and that things were very different with him. His age had caught up with him, and also he had wounds in the bones of his legs that gave him trouble. He had caught malaria during the ordeal of island hopping in the tropics. And there really wasn't anything for his kind of trouble in those days—men were expected to get on with their lives, and for a time William Mara did just that. But he had walked out when Natasha's mother was five years old.

Natasha knew all this.

But of the life her grandmother led with him in those four and a half years, she knew almost nothing at all. It was something Iris simply never talked about because in fact she did not want to talk about Laura, did not want the memory of that loss in her thoughts. Natasha had come to the knowledge of this without actually having it expressed to her. Their talk was usually pleasant and affectionate, but it seldom became personal. This left Natasha feeling at times starved for something other than chatter.

Yet at that age, too, it was good not having so strongly inquisitive a guardian as others she knew.

Now she took a ten-dollar bill out of her purse and put it on the table.

"So," her grandmother said. "About the wedding. You said you wanted it small. His father and stepmother, his aunt and uncle. Me. Your friend Constance?"

"I said I'd let her know the date. I guess I should."

"Well, it's your ceremony, isn't it."

"I will. I'll call her. She probably won't come."

"Other friends?"

"Marsha Trunan. Who also might not come. But I really do want to keep it small. As small as possible."

"Justice of the peace? That sort of thing?"

"It'll be a civil ceremony, but performed by a priest."

Iris shrugged. "Well, since Michael's not preaching anymore, I didn't think going secular was such an outlandish idea."

"We sent the marriage notification into the church a while ago," said Natasha. "Before I left for Jamaica."

7

That afternoon and evening Faulk spent painting the living room of the house. Natasha and Iris bought some art for the walls—prints mostly, though Iris did choose an original that she found in a local gallery, done by an artist she knew when she worked for the mayor's office. The artist had gone on to New York and was doing very well for herself there. Iris mentioned this and said that Natasha would have her own work to hang, of course, but the idea was to sell it. The painting was of a girl in a white dress holding a guitar and gazing off into shadows. The light in it was very Sargent-like. Natasha liked it, without feeling that anything of its quality was beyond her.

After they bought the art, they went into a little shop to buy something to wear for the wedding. Iris helped her choose a simple pink dress with small white ruffling across the low neckline and a slender, darker pink ribbon slanting from the waist to the hem.

The two women went to a Thai place for dinner, and Faulk joined them there, splotches of the off-white paint on his jeans. He sat across from Natasha and was full of hope and anticipation as Iris went on about the artist friend and the original she had bought. She brought the prints and the painting out of the protective plastic to show him. He admired it all, especially the original. "It's perfect," he said. "But not as good as the work of my future wife."

Natasha waved this off and made a fuss about showing him the dress. He folded his arms on the table and grinned at her. "It's glorious."

"We got it for a song," said Iris.

They did not talk about the impending war with Afghanistan or what was still going on in New York and Washington. They were preoccupied with the house. It would need more furniture, a dining room set, and another bed for the guest room. He had bought the wood for the bookshelves, and he hadn't done that sort of thing for a long time, so he was looking forward to it. He would spend all day tomorrow on it.

After dinner, they all went to Iris's house and drank two bottles of Bordeaux. Natasha lay on the couch, drifting in and out of a soft slumber while her grandmother and her fiancé talked. Iris began telling him about raising Natasha, and Natasha, listening, imagined her mother, Laura, also raised by Iris. Laura, the woman in the photographs. Natasha made an effort to picture her in motion, and soon she was having another dream about Jamaica. She was alone on the bright beach, and behind her was the big shadow of a building, one of the imposing temples of democracy in the city where she had lived, though she could not have said which of them it was. There was something threatening and at the same time sad about the vast shadow of the thing, and then she turned into wakefulness, hearing Faulk's voice, softly saying it was time to go. He stood there, smiling, waiting. She sat up, feeling the wine she had drunk.

"I didn't mean to fall asleep."

"You're so tired," Iris said.

In the car, with the cool night air coming in the window, she was fully awake, and she looked over at him, at the features she loved in the light from the street. It had been a good day, and she could sense that the trouble was fading, though the memory of it was still fresh, and, maddeningly, thinking about having it behind her had brought it forward again. A little wave of anxiety rushed over her, and she reached and put her hand on his thigh.

"Want to go in and look at what I've got done?" he asked.

They were pulling by the street.

"Yes," she said. "Let's."

He made the turn and parked in front. There was a big rose-bush along the fence across the street. She hadn't noticed it before.

"Look," she said. "Roses."

"Wait here," he told her, and crossed the street. He picked one of the largest of the blossoms, white and cup-shaped and fragrant. Crossing toward her, he stopped and did a slow turn, as though dancing a waltz, and bowed grandly, holding the rose toward her.

She laughed softly, taking it and holding it to her nose. "Thank you, kind sir," she said.

They went into the house—again, he had trouble with the key—and he turned the light on to show her the difference the off-white paint had made in the front room. He had draped plastic sheeting over the furniture and the piles of books and on the hardwood floor.

"It's a different room," she said. "I love it." She put her arms around him. "Perfect."

At his apartment, he helped her undress and then gave her a chaste kiss on the cheek and pulled the blanket up to her chin. She was warm, and sleepy again, and she had a small unhappy feeling of relief that he was apparently not expecting to make love. She experienced the mixture of emotion as a kind of sinking at her abdomen.

He got into the bed with her and turned to put his arm across her middle. "See you in the morning."

"Yes. My love."

He turned off the light and lay there at her side, thinking about the picture of her on that street in Chicago. *Our State Street.* Soon her breathing told him that she was asleep. He moved gingerly a little away from her and tried unsuccessfully to drift off. His mind presented him with images of the last four days, and now and then he would doze, only to be jolted awake, as if he were standing on a high ledge and to let go would mean falling from it. He thought of the people who had jumped from the towers.

Finally he got up and went into the kitchen and poured himself a little whiskey. He turned the small television on with the sound set low and watched the news without really taking it in.

She woke to find him gone and saw the light in the other room. Because she loved him, she rose, put a robe on, and went out there. "Honey?"

"Oh."

She saw that she'd startled him. "Do you mind if I have a little?"

"Sit," he said. "I'll get it."

She sat on the sofa and looked at the spareness of the room. He came back with the drink and sat next to her. "To us."

They clinked the glasses. The whiskey was scotch, and it heated her from inside; it was very good. He also felt the warmth of it and enjoyed the peaty finish.

"Couldn't sleep," he said.

"I was gone. I don't think I've slept that deeply in a while."

"I kept starting to drift off and *that* woke me." He remembered similar nights when he was in the seminary, after hours of study. He would be near sleep and then come bolt upright. Pure dread. He started to tell her about it but then stopped himself. That kind of night was always the product of anxiety.

"I didn't dream this time," she said. "I was just out and then I was awake and I saw the light in here. I didn't want to be in there alone."

"Didn't wake you, did I?"

"No." She noted the concern in his face, the slight crease in his brow. It made her heart ache. "You're my considerate darling."

He wanted to make love but decided that it should be her decision. And indeed now he did feel his own consideration of her like a virtue.

They sat staring at the shifting images on the television and sipped the whiskey.

She said, "I have to find something to do to make money."

"But you don't have to do any such thing. You paint. I'll take care of you."

"You're sweet."

"No, it's what you've wanted for a long time."

"All that time I thought I was saving to go back to France, and I didn't save a penny."

He thought of the picture of her on State Street in Chicago.

"Young and dreamy and foolish," she said.

"And beautiful," he got out.

A moment later, she said, "Do you think your father and Trixie will come?"

"Probably."

"I'll ask Constance, though I bet she won't. And Marsha Trunan is coming back to Memphis anyway, I think. And then there's Aunt Clara and Uncle Jack. Which means the senator and Greta."

"Couple of my old friends, too, maybe. It'll be large enough."

This time there was a lengthy pause. It created in them both a pressure to speak.

"I think I'll have another one," he said. He got up and brought the bottle back. He was deciding that he might get drunk, since she clearly had no intention of seeking him. Pouring more for himself, he said, "Want another touch?"

"No, thanks, I'm gonna go back to bed when I finish this."

"It's so good to know that we don't have to go away from each other."

"I know."

He felt himself bending inside toward initiating things. "Guess that's why I don't feel pressed."

"How 'pressed'?"

"Oh, you know—that sense that we have to use the time. For instance—just for instance, you know, that we don't—we don't have to make love tonight. We can wait until tomorrow, or the next day. There's no time pressure because we don't have to go away from each other the way it always was before."

She understood what he wanted her to do, and couldn't produce the will to make the gesture. She took the rest of the whiskey, put the glass down on the table, leaned over and kissed him on the cheek, and went back into the bedroom. In the dark there, she wrapped herself in the blankets, curled into a ball, eyes closed, listening for movement from him. She heard the bottle clink against the lip of the shot glass. Off in the Memphis night, a train sounded. Her hands smelled of the whiskey, and she realized it was her own breath on her fingers.

Later, when he came in to lie down, he was careful not to wake her. He told himself things would be all right. It was true that they did not have to hurry or force things. He lay there thinking about the days ahead, when they could take the time to learn all over how to be at ease with each other.

Do You Take This Woman

I

She'd had four relationships. The first lasted almost five years and was generally supposed by everyone, including Iris and the young man's rather large Italian American family, to be an engagement. His name was Constantine, and everyone called him Connie. She had met him in Provence, at the end of her first week there. He was a tall, blond, serious boy who loved the beach and had beautiful light blue eyes. He had come to France from his home in California to spend part of the summer with his older sister, who was studying in Provence. Natasha was with him almost continually after their first meeting. When he left to return home, he gave her a ring he had bought in a little store on a visit to Paris. They were together. He was going to get a degree in history. She would finish college and join him. Before he left, they spent time planning things, and one afternoon it occurred to her that she wasn't having any fun. He could be so somber about things, and all of the history he knew—or, more accurately, what fascinated him most about it—concerned the depredations, the atrocities. He knew about these things in great detail, was nearly fetishistic about them. And of course there was no playfulness in him. They fought all the time. The long-distance relationship they ended up having—he in San Francisco, and then in Chicago, and she in France and in travels through Europe and finally in Washington—seemed better and less stressful than being with him every day, and far easier than the stratagems and antic posing she got from the other young men with whom she occasionally found herself socializing. After college, she wanted to explore and see things and live in other cities, and so when she broke off the "understanding"—as her grandmother called it, probably taking her cue from Constantine's family—she felt relieved.

There were two other relationships, both full of exhausting emotional storms.

When she met Mackenzie she was several months past the fourth one—poor Constantine again, who showed up from a stint as a history teacher in an American school in Spain. He was seeking her as a wife, and she almost went with him. But over the years she had seldom given thought to marriage. Friends accused her of supposing snobbishly that it was an estate for young women of a certain sociological type. But that was far from true. She was too suspicious of abstractions to take such notions very seriously. It was just that finding a husband had never been a concern, had never been something she sought in and of itself, not even with Constantine. She enjoyed her freedom and the progress she was making with her painting, though she hadn't sold enough to come near supporting herself. In fact, it was his desire to support her that pulled her toward him that second time. But she refused him again and went on with life. And did not give it much thought. She was adventurous and smart, and the milestones, whatever they would be, would come whenever they would come.

She had embarked on her own study of the great watercolorists, had discovered Xie He, the art historian who lived in fifth-century China; his *Six Principles of Art* described ideas about modes of expression that had been passed down from master to student since antiquity: The first part of the sixth principle essentially was to know and emulate what preceded you as an artist; the second part was *directly copying nature*. But she was impatient with nature, with still lifes and landscapes and paintings of barns and lakes and fields and even city streets. She had discovered a feeling for the faces in photographs that did not seem posed so much as staring out, as if the frame of the photograph, its border, were the border of a window someone had simply glanced out on the way by. So many of the pictures she found in the bins in the antiques stores *were* posed, family members smiling into other sunlight, and the sunlight, of course, looked like a rainy day. But there were also very many—more than she expected to find when she first began to think of them as windows—people who did not really know how to be in front of the new invention. And so the best subjects for her paintings were the old daguerreotypes and sepia plates from the first few decades of the existence of the camera as a means of recording things. And the challenge was giving them color without cheapening the expression.

Once, in Rome with Marsha Trunan on one of their journeys from Provence, they had walked a long hallway inside the Vatican Museums where many sculpted heads were displayed, hundreds of them, human countenances, a lot of them showing the effects of age and excess, rendered with such exactness that you felt the urge to reach out and touch them. It was almost as if your fingertips required tactile evidence that these features were made of stone and not flesh. All the faces looked blind, the pupils and irises the same stone color, and the guide said this was because the paint had worn off centuries ago, and these were the faces of nameless well-to-do citizens of Rome. Marsha spoke about not being able to stop looking at the blind-seeming eyes, but Natasha kept staring at the ears, the jawbones, the pouches under the eyes and the sagging chins, the lips and nostrils and brows. Even the hairlines.

It was the ordinariness of the faces themselves, the people as they were, from antiquity, that fascinated her.

Faces. And in those years she had painted so many, miniatures and full-size ones, and she dreamed about faces and watched them and believed she had begun to discover in her portrayals something she might express about the thousand nuances of human feeling. She kept the work in a big portfolio that she took with her through various au pair jobs, and the year and a half she spent as assistant to a travel writer named Ben Eldridge, who treated her as a student and hit on her and said cruel things to her about her "little works of art." She even took photographs for him of chapels and doorways and country towns in Provence and in Italy and Turkey and North Africa. And when his wife joined them for the trip to Morocco, Natasha endured his overweening benevolence, like a kind of hopeless bribe for her silence, which she did keep. At the end, she even listened to his wife complain about his general slovenly ways and his uncleanliness.

This was on the journey to Morocco—the last one, because his commission was over. And it was on this last trip, somewhere between Istanbul and Rabat, that she lost the portfolio. Three different airlines, and none of them ever located the large canvas bag it was in.

She spent two grieving months back home in Memphis, and finally Iris got her the job in Washington. It would be temporary, Iris said, and only for the purpose of saving money to return to the south of France. But, withal, it was also an answer to what Iris believed was an unhealthy stasis, since she was no longer painting very much and did not like much of what she did paint.

So she went to Washington and started working for the senator and found that in fact aspects of the work absorbed her. Life grew pleasantly full, and after a few months she began searching out the faces in the old family photographs again, looking in antiques stores up and down the Shenandoah Valley, and painting the series of smaller portraits, actually framing them for herself and putting them on the wall in her apartment. They were like company on some nights; they gave her a warm feeling of involvement in her own becoming. She spent weekends quite happily working on them. But the job and her life in the city began to get in the way, and more and more weekend evenings were spent going out and being with people, much of it stemming from her responsibilities in the senator's office. On some weekend mornings she went to flea markets in the valley and set up a little station to sell her work. One weekend an older lady bought five paintings at fifty dollars apiece. And on others she sold one or two. She always put the money in savings. But then it was winter again. And the mornings were free. She was young, and perhaps she had grown a little lonesome. The cost of living in the city made saving very hard to do, and though she kept her goal in mind, the difficulty of saving enough to make the leap and leave the job eroded her will to do the small things necessary to approach the possibility.

The affair with Mackenzie had begun on a campaign trip to Gulfport. They sat up late sipping bourbon in the hotel bar, and he began telling her what was happening at home: heartbreak and borderline lunacy, his wife's fanaticism, the delusions—the woman's belief that she possessed a form of second sight and was having visions of past lives. The visions were becoming more frequent and more bizarre. He said they were sleeping in separate rooms, staying together only for the boy. Natasha was just twenty-nine, in her third year of work in the senator's office.

Mackenzie was uncomplicatedly fun because he was married and appeared to think of her as a friend. She felt the same. She spent time with him at various functions of the senator's in the state. They made each other laugh.

But then that evening in Gulfport, there he was, telling her all those too-personal details about himself.

"We were so young," he said about his wife. "We didn't really know each other."

Natasha listened with an increasing sense that a line had been crossed. It had been crossed when she remained behind with him at that late hour in the hotel bar. But he was such a good friend. And with the whiskey blurring her thoughts, she was moving beyond the line anyway, looking into his mournful eyes and beginning to be in love.

An hour later they were in his room, and they spent the rest of the night there. She woke with a little start and felt a rush of guilty remembering, the bedsheets clinging to her body, his legs touching hers, too warm, too close. She had the sense that she must find a way to make things right and then swooned toward sleep, half aware of him stirring next to her. He sighed and coughed and moaned and came to, obviously upset and anxious, claiming disbelief that he could ever have let it happen. But he also held her, and they saw the sunrise from the window across from his bed. The quiet and their soft breathing plainly were calming for him, and he spoke of their life together as if the night had been a source of some overwhelming discovery and truth. Breaking off with his wife would take time. There was his son to think about, and the boy was already emotionally confused, already spending too much time with video games, computer gadgets, fantasy, and goth. The responsibilities of a father were so complicated in these times of collapsing values. He went on in this vein, and Natasha believed that he meant what he said.

As the weeks and months went by, she fell more deeply in love with him, and before long she was spending her nights alone, writing him long letters and poems and admonitions that she never sent, pleading with him to do what he kept saying he would do and what he kept putting off because of the pain it would cause. She threw the letters away in the mornings. It was humiliating to look at them.

And she had completely stopped doing the watercolors.

Once, she told him she did not want to see him anymore, and he began calling and begging, swearing that he would make it so they could be together like any other couple. He sent her little cards and flowers and left phone messages, and after more than a month of this, they returned to the pattern as it had been: seeing each other as his schedule permitted, she often spending her own money to fly wherever he was on assignment.

All that ended with the phone call from the wife.

And what followed, she believed back then, was the worst year of her life, the thing she had found respite from with Faulk.

Michael Faulk, the man with whom she felt she had at last discovered what love really was—that happy inner blaze, the passion that let her breathe fully, and gave a shimmer to each hour. She would never have believed that she could love like this, where the whole world seemed divided in two: on the one side, away from him, the tiresome and gloomy city; on the other, where he was, all intensity and life, vividness and humor, and fascination in the littlest things.

2

They had set the date of the wedding for the first Saturday in October, the sixth. Natasha made calls instead of sending invitations. There wasn't time for anything else. Constance Waverly and

Marsha Trunan were coming, as were Aunt Clara and Uncle Jack. As Faulk had expected, Senator Norland and his wife said they were bound by other, long-standing commitments. They sent a large bouquet of flowers and a five-hundred-dollar gift certificate from Pier 1 Imports.

Iris placed the flowers in the middle of her dining room table.

They watched the president's speech to a joint session of Congress that Thursday, the twentieth, where the president demanded that the government of Afghanistan hand over all the terrorists and declared the war on terror. The newscasters talked about the sense of a threat inside our borders, and how people were dealing with it.

Iris said, "Maybe we should all move to Jamaica and just stay there."

The mention of the island turned something over under Natasha's heart. She said, "Can we turn the TV off? Let's do something fun."

"Any ideas?" said Faulk.

He put off starting the job at Social Services and worked all the following week on the house, painting, building bookshelves, working outside on the rose arbor and the lawn, planting flowers in the dog run, a surprise for Natasha, he thought, until she saw what he was doing and joined in. The work calmed them both. They went on with daily tasks, and even so their trouble was always there, unspoken. For Natasha, the toil was beautiful, and she would look at her own hands patting down the earth around the stem of a plant and realize that she felt none of the fear. Such moments would unvaryingly cause it to come rushing back at her, and she went on working until slowly it would begin once again to subside.

She also went with Iris to the Pier 1 on Walnut Grove and used some of the senator's gift certificate on flatware, dishes, place mats, tablecloths, linens, bath towels, and soaps. And she spent the mornings helping Iris with exercises for her injured knee. The two women avoided the subject of the news, though both of them were paying attention to it.

Work on the house was so involving that Faulk would periodically lose track of the noise on the TV. He was displeasingly reminded each day when he emerged from the house, and there would be a plane coming over toward the airport, nine miles to the south. But he saw that Natasha seemed better. In the nights, in the apartment, they held each other. She was having her period—the beginning of it had come with a feeling of inexpressible relief—and it was a heavy one, causing the usual headaches and cramping, but the headaches were more severe. He read Aquinas into the nights, and she would lie trying to sleep, hearing the little shuffle of the tissue-thin pages turning. It was the thinness of the sound that told her what the book was. "Honey," she said, "what are you looking for in Aquinas?"

He said, "Remember, I talked about rereading it."

"You don't find it a little dry?"

"Have you been reading it?"

She had only looked at the first page of it. "I've browsed through it some."

"Why would I be looking for anything?"

"I don't know. Come be with me."

"In a little while. Go on to sleep."

He brought her coffee in the mornings and gave her time alone to rest. She lay with her head burning, having drunk the coffee, and listened to him moving in the other room, preparing a breakfast for them. It was always something new: French toast stuffed with blueberries; a one-egg omelet thin as a soufflé, with cheese and spinach in it, on two toasted English muffins topped by Canadian bacon, with hollandaise sauce poured over the whole thing; or an egg cooked on a slice of provolone cheese and sprinkled with lemon juice. It was always arranged so elegantly on the plates, and he would bring it all in on a tray, with fruit and glasses of orange juice and, twice, a little half bottle of champagne, to make mimosas.

"You're spoiling me," Natasha said to him.

"It makes me happy," he told her. And it did. He spent some of his reading time looking up the recipes each evening after she was asleep, and when he went out to get things for the house he stopped and bought what he would need for the next morning's feast.

The following Wednesday, he went to the new job at Social Services. Lawrence Watson showed him around the place and introduced him to the other man who worked in that office—a young man on whose desk were two heavy books, like account books, and a lot of typing paper. "This is Pete," Watson said. "Pete's condensing the state regulations to a manageable size for field workers. Been on it since the beginning of the summer."

"Pleased to meet you," Pete said.

"Hello, Pete."

Pete had little round dark eyes and a very long nose, a pleasant gentle smile. They shook hands, and then Pete stood by while Watson demonstrated the use of the computer files, data banks concerning jobs in the area and within a twenty-five-mile radius of the city. Parolees were not allowed to travel farther.

"That's basically it," Watson said. "Your clients will come through here." He pointed to another doorway. "There'll be a steady stream of them on some days, not so many on others. They all have their referrals, from the various officers. They line up out there to sign in, and then they'll be funneled this way to see you, or Pete if there's a long wait. Any questions?"

"None that I can think of," Faulk said.

"Okay." Watson left them alone.

For a few seconds they just stood as if waiting for him to come back. Then Faulk went around and sat at his new desk. Pete stayed where he was, watching him.

"Like some coffee?"

Having had a mimosa that morning with Natasha, Faulk said, "Sure. Black. And strong."

"That's the way I like it, too."

When the younger man returned, he pulled his chair around to sit at Faulk's desk. They sipped their coffee. "I'm in your church," he said suddenly. "I mean I've seen you preach."

"Oh," Faulk said, dismayed and trying not to show it. "I hope you weren't disappointed."

"I liked what you had to say."

"Well, the gospels, you know."

"So, you're not a priest anymore. Is it because of the attacks?"

"It predates all that." Something about this earnest young man made him feel stiff, almost pompous.

"I would bet it got a lot of religious people thinking."

"It probably got everybody thinking, wouldn't you say?"

"The Taliban kind of tears it for me."

Faulk left a pause.

"I mean if people can really believe they're going straight to heaven if they kill themselves along with a lot of other people, and that for this the reward in heaven is a bunch of virgins, I mean Jesus, that kind of—that kind of carnal idea of reward—well, I don't know . . . that's a pretty venal thing for us run-of-the-mill believers to deal with."

"Run-of-the-mill believers," Faulk repeated.

"But—the martyrs, then. You—you see what I'm getting at?"

Faulk nodded at him.

The other stared, head tilted slightly. "Anyway—your sermons were very eloquent. You could be a writer."

He was faintly chagrined by the pleasure he took in the remark. "I'm sure whatever you heard came from some other source."

"Yeah, but the thing itself." The younger man smiled. "You have a nice way with words."

Faulk smiled back. "You're very kind."

"Well. Thank you." The other seemed abruptly embarrassed and moved his chair back across the space to his own desk, with its tomes and the strewn paper.

"Is that what you want to do," Faulk asked him. "Write?"

The younger man seemed baffled. "No."

It was a long morning. One man after another with a bad history, each of them hoping for work. Yet they seemed cheerful, determined, even brave. He saw very little discouragement; and everyone wanted to talk about the attacks—where they were when it happened and how they learned of it.

Regarding jobs, most of the time there was nothing at all available anywhere. Each man appeared more unemployable than the last, as if the computer were cutting away possibilities by the minute. He could have sworn he saw openings for one thing while looking for another, and yet when he tried to return to the listing, it wasn't there. At lunchtime, he drove over to the house to find

Natasha in the second bedroom, painting, wearing one of his old shirts over a pair of faded denims. He had never seen anyone so beautiful.

She was working on the faded color photograph of the sad-eyed lady as he had called her. She had spent most of the morning painting, after helping Iris exercise her sore knee. Seeing him coming up the walk startled her in a troubling way, as if it would be an unwanted intrusion, but she suppressed the feeling as best she could and waited for him to come to her. He kept his arms around her for some time, she with the wet paintbrush in one hand and patting his shoulder with the other.

"I missed you all morning," he said. "I feel like a kid. I don't like this going to a job."

"I missed you, too." She put her cheek against his. "But it's only a little while, and then we can have a nice dinner."

"Come with me now. I've got forty-five minutes left. We can get something quick at Pei Wei or someplace like that."

"I've got paint all over me," she said. "You just came here for a kiss."

"I wish it was more than that."

"Soon," she said. "My darling."

They went on through the weekend. In the evening they watched the news and ate dinner with Iris, who insisted on doing the cooking. She made brisket one night, and lamb chops the next. And on Monday she and Natasha brought home a container of pulled pork and ribs from Corky's. They all had a little too much to drink, and Faulk put his arm around his wife-to-be and told her he loved her. Resting her head on his shoulder, she had to ward off the sense that everything was a kind of forgery. She resorted to carefully constructed, tenaciously *resolute* thoughts of being in the new house, all the things she would do to make it her place, make that poor little place her own. That was how it seemed to her when she looked at it on its small street, with the big tree looming over it. When she was in those warm rooms, painting the trim and putting up wallpaper and waxing the floors, or when she was trying to get the watercolor of the sad lady so it showed the depth of what was in that face, she was happily almost clear of mind. There were few bad images, few intimations of jarring memory.

3

They rented a U-Haul trailer and moved into the house the following Saturday. It took most of the morning, Faulk moving the furniture and setting the bed up and organizing the books in the new shelves he had built. His back ached. He was pleasurably weary, and he made jokes about feeling like a college kid moving into a dorm. But he was proud of the bookcases, and very meticulous about setting the titles in alphabetical order. The day was hot and muggy, and even in the air-conditioning his white shirt was soaked. She would come past him and stop to kiss his cheek, and it was their little house, he said, their home with its big picture window and fresh wood- and paint-smelling rooms, and its leaky kitchen sink. Iris put dishes away while the other two arranged the furniture and hung pictures.

She surprised them by taking the kitchen faucet apart at the base and rubbing soap into the threads of the pipe, stopping the leak. "Old trick," she said.

She made a lunch of boiled eggs and English muffins, and they sat in the little dining area off the kitchen while she talked about moving from Collierville into the city, to this neighborhood, and walking past this house so many times with Natasha before Natasha went off to Europe. Faulk had bought a half bottle of champagne to make mimosas, but nobody else wanted a mimosa, so he put the bottle in the refrigerator, which was mostly empty.

He spent the early afternoon hooking up the television and the computer while the women went shopping for groceries. When he had done everything he could to make the place comfortable, he sat out in the shade of the rose arbor and tried to read, waiting for them to come back. Birds sang in the branches of the river oak, and a breeze had come up; but it was finally too warm and buggy to stay out there, and he went back inside. He felt hopeful, walking through the rooms of the little house and looking at things.

That night, after they drove Iris home, they made love in the dimness, in the quiet, new-paint-smelling bedroom. He lay on his back while she straddled him and moved slowly, looking down at him. "My love," he said.

"Oh," she murmured. "Yes." Resting her elbows on either side of his head, she let her hair come around his face. She kissed him and then nuzzled at his neck. For a long space she simply stayed that way, with him inside her. She felt relaxed, and easy, and wanted it to go on. After a soft few moments, she lifted herself very slightly, and then let down.

"Oh, that's so lovely," he said. "Yes. Do that."

It was as things had once been between them. She moved her hips, her face in the pillow at his ear, and she wept soundlessly for the relief of it.

He gave a slow thrust upward and she murmured, "Oh." And he began to thrust quickly, his hands tight on her shoulders.

"Wait," she said. "Oh. Wait."

He held very still, and she felt herself fall through, moving quickly now, and kissing his forehead, his cheeks.

"It's us," he said. "Oh, babe. It's us."

A little later, they lay still. She straightened, and gazed down at him. "So good."

"Beautiful," he said.

"We have our house and our place," she murmured.

"Are you crying?"

"I'm happy," she told him.

"Yes," he said. "Yes, me, too."

"I don't ever want to leave this room. Let's stay here forever."

"Oh, baby, I want that."

"We can make it our own little crypt."

"But I'll want to walk through the rooms and savor everything, too. Our house. Ours. We're in our house."

"We are. Let's brick up the doors and windows."

They lay side by side, looking at the slightly shifting light on the ceiling from the passage of a car in the street. They went to sleep like this, and they slept deeply. She dreamed they were on an island somewhere, not Jamaica. It was like the *idea* of an island, sunny and with the smell of the ocean and, oddly, cooking meat. The odor of the meat became too thick, and the rest of the dream was of looking for a place on the beautiful island where you couldn't smell it. She woke feeling physically spent and struggled to go back to sleep, concentrating as best she could on the perfection of the night before. But its very exquisiteness seemed now unreachable in its contrast to what she had been suffering. She got out of the bed and put on a robe, and sat shivering in the predawn at the window. After a few moments, she made coffee and went back and watched the sun come up. The panic had returned, the freeze at her abdomen. It was worse now, utterly and only itself, unalloyed, connected to no thought or idea, a separate thing coiled under the flow of her thoughts and wired to all the nerves of her body. She sat very still as if trying to hide, watching color come to the sky, a fair sunrise, full of gentle shades of gold, and how it shone through the membranous leaves, some of them even beginning to turn.

He had busy dreams, too fleeting to take hold or reach even the level of consciousness nightmares have, or good dreams. It was nonbeing for a space, and when he woke he saw that she had already left the bed. He rose and went in to her and saw her sitting on the couch in the light from the picture window. She was staring out at the backyard, holding a cup of coffee.

"Morning," he said.

She spilled the coffee.

"I'm sorry." He moved to the kitchen to get a paper towel. "Who did you think it would be? It's just us. At home in our house. Remember?"

"I didn't know you were up," she said, laughing too loud. He saw tears in her eyes.

Drinking the coffee had warmed her from the inside as the sunlight warmed her skin, the sun rising over the treetops beyond the end of the yard and shining on her through the glass. She stood and wrapped her arms around him, feeling the solidness of him, the bone and sinew, and breathing the sleep odor of him.

"Tears of happiness," he said. "I hope."

"Oh, yes, my love."

They cleaned up what she had spilled and then had another cup each, and then he had to go to work. She stood with him in the doorway and embraced him.

"Iris coming here today?" he asked.

"I'll go over there."

"You okay?"

"Go," she said, forcing the smile.

4

The Thursday before the wedding, Leander and Trixie arrived. Trixie was a tall, very mild woman with an oval face and slightly crossed brown eyes. This made her inexplicably more attractive. She looked much younger than sixty. The old man called her Trix and was attentive to her in ways that were surprising to his son.

There was nothing at the apartment in town but a folding cot and two folded easels, leaning against the living room wall, so it was decided that Natasha and Faulk would stay with Iris, while Leander and Trix stayed at the house on Swan Ridge.

That first evening, they all went in Faulk's car to Rendezvous for dinner. Trixie was so deferential to Leander that Faulk found it awkward to be around her, and her conversation seemed stilted, as if by some inner conviction that no one would listen to her. It was clear, though, that coming to Memphis for the wedding was her idea and that she had insisted on it. Faulk was grateful to her for the effort, and he tried hard to draw her out, but reticence was clearly in her nature.

The old man would begin to talk, or tell a story, and she would sit watching him, rapt, eyes wide.

Natasha stayed close to Iris, who had her cane with her and complained that the bad knee was giving her a little trouble. They all ate ribs and corn on the cob and drank cold beer in tall iced mugs, and when they walked out of the place, the foyer was packed with people waiting to be seated. They stood at a traffic light on the corner of Union and Third, and they could hear the uproar of Beale Street, three blocks north. It was a warm, cloudy night, and the various strains of music—drums and bass and wailing guitars and brass, and from somewhere an electric piano—went up to the low sky. It felt as though the whole block were a vast echo chamber.

"Do you want to go over there and have a look at it?" Faulk asked his father. "It's really something, truly. Every warm night in Memphis."

"Not tonight, Son. I'm tired. My foot hurts. This gout."

They got into the car and drove back to High Point. Iris and Natasha got out at Iris's, and Faulk drove the other two around to the Swan Ridge house.

"Let's have a nightcap," the old man said.

They went in and sat in the small newly painted living room with the dark picture window and had whiskey in shot glasses. Trixie threw hers back and then asked for a glass of water. "I wish I liked that stuff more," she said. Faulk got the water for her, and she drank it down and lay on her side on the couch, head resting on one folded arm.

"Let me get you a pillow," he said.

"I'm fine."

Leander said, "She'll be asleep in two minutes."

"I'm listening," she said.

"I should go on back to Iris's."

"Have another drink."

Faulk poured more. They sat there quietly sipping it while Trixie began to snore. "Told you," Leander said, smiling.

"Well, it's a long drive from Little Rock."

"Clara and Jack coming in the morning?"

Faulk nodded. "They're driving, too. They stopped in Knoxville tonight."

"You don't mind if we sleep in tomorrow?"

"Of course not."

"I miss your mother."

Faulk looked over at the sleeping woman not ten feet away and then took a little more of the whiskey and said nothing.

"Funny thing," Leander went on. "She wasn't at all religious when I first met her. She'd thrown off the Catholic thing before we met, you know. She came from all of that and was in rebellion against it. Wild as hell. Parents were furious at her, of course. And she hardly spoke to them. Wild and beautiful. Nobody would've believed she would become so—churchy."

Faulk sipped the whiskey and waited.

"Meaning no offense, there, bud."

"No offense taken," Faulk told him. "Bud."

A moment later, the other said, "A man's gotta do what a man's gotta do."

Faulk filled the little glasses, not looking at him. "I don't have any idea what you're talking about."

"Talking about you."

"Okay. I guess."

"What do you think she'd say about you leaving the church?"

"I'm not leaving the church."

"You know what I mean."

"I don't think it's useful to guess such a thing."

"She was a strange lady, that woman. And I do miss her."

"Dad."

"Well, I do. It wasn't always misery and strife."

"What did you think of the barbecue tonight?"

The old man looked at him. "This bothering you?"

"I don't know what good it does."

"What good is talking about a barbecue?"

"It's refreshing to speak of pleasurable things. The barbecue was good. I like it dry, and I noticed you asked for it wet. How did you like the wet?"

"The barbecue was delicious. Wet and dry. I tasted both. Now, do you want to talk about the damn coleslaw?"

Faulk sipped the whiskey, and kept silent, watching him sip his.

"Or leaving the priesthood."

"Neither, really."

"You know Theo Ruhm was talking about coming out here for this."

"That would be a happy thing. I felt so bad for him when everything came down in New York."

"Ah, he's a tough bird. He actually helped with some of the triage, early."

"I spoke to him on the phone. What a thing—the church where his son was supposed to get married."

"Well, they got it done anyway, two blocks from his house in Brooklyn. That weekend. Should've planned it there in the first place."

Faulk poured still more of the whiskey.

"I gotta say, I do miss your mother."

He took another sip. There was no sting from it now.

"I started cheating on her pretty soon after she went with that church you're in. Your particular church. You might as well know that."

"She's *gone*," Faulk told him. "It's all over now. Please. Can we talk about something else?"

"Might as well have some truth."

"Please stop it. There's no reason to say any of it. I've left the priesthood."

"But you've still got that old-time religion, don't you."

"I'm gonna go."

"Wait. Finish your whiskey."

Faulk took it in one gulp and set the glass down on the coffee table. His father reached for the bottle and poured another shot into it.

"Let's change the subject," he said. "Okay?"

"Good idea," said Faulk.

"Well, boy, I hated feeling like an apostate in my own house."

"Look. I really don't want to talk about this. It's none of my business."

"What if I tell you as a priest?"

"Please cut it out, will you?"

"You know what I think? I think we all come from blankness

and we all go back there. Back to the way it was before we were born. The great null and void. No darkness at all. We'd have to be able to perceive that. Just blank."

"I think it's safe to say I know how you see things, Dad. And nothingness isn't a particularly original idea, is it."

"Nor is the idea of a merciful God."

"Oh, but that's actually pretty radical. People believed it back when painkillers were unknown. When the world was a savage place full of unmitigated suffering."

"You mean it's not that *now*?"

"You know what I mean."

"Tell it to those people in New York and Washington and Pennsylvania."

"You *know* what I mean, Dad."

The old man sipped the whiskey and looked off. "Well, we do seek comfort."

Faulk sipped the last of the whiskey in his own glass and poured a little more. He could feel it now, on top of the beer he'd had earlier.

"I guess I just didn't like it when you started sounding like her," his father said.

"Did you hector her this way?"

"Hell, after a while it wasn't worth talking about."

"I heard plenty of the talk, Dad. From my earliest memory."

"Really. It was all that bad, was it?"

"Let's drop it," Faulk said. "It was what it was. Sometimes it was fine."

"Sometimes."

He took another swallow.

"Well. I don't think *she* believed in a merciful God. Her God was more of a—a celestial cop, I'd say. When he wasn't an invisible concierge."

"Well, I believe in a God of mercy."

"No wrath of God, then?"

"I said. Mercy. You know the story. Christ comes and dies. You remember."

"That's one story."

"Well. The point is that an average life used to be somewhere around thirty-five years. It was full of misery, and someone discovered a sense in all that of one loving God."

"And you think that's some kind of proof."

They said nothing for a disagreeable few moments. The old man drank his whiskey in a gulp and then added still more. "I've always been a bourbon man."

The whiskey was Glenlivet, single-malt scotch.

He tipped the shot glass a little and looked into it. "Don't know why you like this stuff."

"I don't know why I like it, either."

"She didn't even know who she was, did she—at the end. She was already almost there, almost to nothing—to the blank again."

"It was a coma."

"Yeah, but I mean the dementia."

Faulk kept silent.

"Wonder what the hell it's all for."

"I'm going," Faulk said, controlling his voice. "Lot of getting ready still to do."

"You got any experience talking to people suffering from depression?"

"I'm trained to do some psychological work, if that's what you mean."

"Let's say that's what I mean."

"Okay," said Faulk. "And?"

His father took a small sip this time, as if testing the flavor on his tongue. Then he swallowed and frowned. "What about despair?"

"I said I'm trained to do some psychological work."

"You got medicines?"

"I'm not a doctor, no. But I can send you to one."

"Oh, this isn't for *me*." With the hand that held the shot glass, Leander indicated Trixie.

Faulk knew without having to think about it that this was not the truth. Trixie, lying on her side, sleeping peacefully, with her placid mouth half open, was not the type. "Does she want to talk to somebody?"

"Probably not. Probably couldn't get her to."

"Well, I can suggest a doctor, if you'd like." Faulk wanted to press him a little. "Shouldn't we ask her if she'd like to speak to somebody?"

"Nah." The old man drank.

"I'll talk to her about it."

"Let's leave it."

After a pause, Leander tilted his head slightly, staring at him. "It doesn't bother you that I cheated on your mother?"

"I said it's none of my business. Not that it doesn't bother me."

"You don't show it."

"Are you trying to rile me?" Faulk asked him. "Because it's working."

"Nah, hell."

They were quiet for a long time, then, drinking. They had drunk more than half the bottle.

"Just trying to have a real father-and-son talk," Leander said.

"It's a little late for that, wouldn't you say?"

"Never too late, I believe, is what you hear."

"Well, we can talk about anything you want except my mother and my religion. How's that?"

"You drunk?"

"Getting there."

"Yeah, well, I'm already there. Thought I'd tell you a few things, Son." The voice trailed off, almost as if he had run out of breath. "Get to know you a little better."

They endured another long silence.

"Well," Leander said at last. "I'm glad I came." He tried to rise and then sat back down quickly. "Damn."

His son stood and took him by the arm and helped him stand. They looked down at Trixie where she slept.

"I don't want to wake her," he said.

"She'll be sore," Faulk told him. "That couch is new but it's hard."

The old man leaned down and shook her shoulder. "Trix."

She lay over on her back and then hurried to her feet. "I'm sorry."

"What're you sorry for?"

She looked from one to the other of them. "I didn't mean to be rude."

"Come on, girl."

She moved to help her husband toward the bedroom.

Faulk let himself out, got in the car, and drove the short block and a half to Iris's house, windows open, breathing the odor of the crepe myrtle that lined the street. It was a clear cool windless night, and he heard the traffic far off. He saw the glow in the sky from over there. Night in the world. He felt what he'd had to drink. The lights were on at Iris's, and he got out and made his slow way up to the door and entered.

The women had left the living room lamps on and also the ceiling light in the kitchen. He went in there and looked for something else to drink. Why not? There was white wine in the refrigerator and a can of beer. In the cabinet above the stove he found a tall bottle of vermouth. He put ice in a glass and poured himself a little of the vermouth, then sat at the kitchen table and drank it, looking through the newspaper that had been set there unopened earlier in the day. He caught himself drifting far away from what was on the page, to Natasha in Jamaica. He had what was now the familiar and unwanted image of her walking the beach with the one who had taken the picture of her in Chicago. He shook his head, as if to come fully awake. He returned to the paper. One article was about a man in Florida who had contracted inhalation anthrax, and the secretary of health and human services claiming that the disease does occur in nature and that there was no reason to connect this case to the terrorist attacks. Inhalation anthrax. And they felt it necessary to announce that it was not terror. There was an article citing comments from scientists about efforts to produce the germ in laboratories for use as a weapon, how the Russians and the Americans had worked on it. The article went on to say that according to scientists, two hundred pounds of the germ sprayed over Washington could kill three million people. Bioterror.

The world was changing terribly.

Suddenly Natasha was at the door in her white nightgown. "It's late," she murmured. "I thought I heard you come in at least three times."

"The old man wanted to talk."

She crossed to the sink and poured herself a glass of water.

"I have a headache," he said. "Do you know where she keeps the aspirin?"

She opened a cabinet above the stove, took a bottle of Aleve out, and held it toward him. "There's prescription strength in here, too, for her knee, if you want it."

"This'll do. Can I have some of that water?"

She refilled the glass and gave it to him. "What did he want to talk about?"

"Cheating on my mother."

"Oh, God."

"Yeah." He took three of the pills, swallowed them with the water, and then handed her the glass. "I think I'm a little drunk. Good thing I didn't get pulled over."

She put the glass and the bottle of Aleve back.

"I think I'm a *lot* drunk, now. After this vermouth."

"Constance called and left a message. She's staying at the Holiday Inn on Central. Clara and Jack are going to stay there, too, but I guess you know that. My friend Marsha Trunan hasn't called. She could already be here, staying with her parents."

"I haven't heard from a soul. My old warden of the vestry— that's it."

"Did you call anyone else?"

"Couple old college pals who were living together in Nashville. Must've moved. Nobody else. I've left that life."

"Well. Neither of us wanted much to-do."

"I guess." He looked at her and had the unexpected notion that she was about to tell him what had taken place all those miles away. This was the moment when she would confess. His own hysterical musing sickened him. He poured more of the vermouth.

Seeing this, she walked over and kissed him on the side of the head and then started out of the room. He muttered something behind her, and she turned, and saw him lift the glass of vermouth to his lips.

"Pardon?" she said.

"Wondered if you wanted to have a drink with me."

"I'm beat. I'm going back to bed."

"I should go to bed, too. But I seem unable to let go of the day."

"It doesn't sound like it was all that special for you."

"No." He raised the glass. "Very. Very special. I learned about cheating on someone you supposedly love."

She studied his face as he drank. He was watching her, staring. "Honey, come to bed," she urged.

"I wonder why he wanted me to know about it now."

"No offense," Natasha said. "But he strikes me as strange."

"He *is that*," Faulk said. "But then, so am I." He gave her a peculiarly conspiratorial look, almost a leer, out of that sidelong smile she had always liked; now it unnerved her and seemed to be eliciting something from her.

He saw the small step back she took, putting one hand on the frame of the doorway, and he wanted to say more, draw her out concerning unfaithfulness. He thought he saw the guilty pall of it in her face. The color had left her cheeks, he was certain of it; she was hiding something. "Talk to me," he said.

"I'm so tired, Michael. It's late. He's your father. He'll go back to Little Rock, and you won't have to see him if you don't want to."

"Just wondered what you thought about it." He poured still more of the vermouth.

"Honey, please come to bed."

"I'll be there in minutes. So fast you'll be astonished."

She went and sat down across from him. "Do you want to talk? It must've upset you so much. I should be here for you."

"It didn't upset me."

"But you're—you had—you said you had drinks with him and—"

"Whiskey. We drank it slow."

"It's no good to sit here getting drunk. We're getting married day after tomorrow."

"You're absolutely right."

She patted his wrist and then tried to take the glass. He held it tight.

"This one more."

"Okay. And you'll come right to bed?"

"Promise."

He muttered something else as she stood. "What?" she said.

"I was thinking—your present state of mind."

She waited.

"You—you're—how you are now. It's just the way you were when we met. You were grieving the lost—the end of the—whatever it was . . . "

"No, honey. Please."

"I was just wondering what happened in Jamaica to change everything between us."

She said, "Oh, baby. Nothing's changed between *us*, has it?"

He swallowed the dregs of the vermouth.

"I've just been so nervous about getting everything done," she told him. "It's a—it's a big step for a girl." She felt the falsity of her own voice and sought to cover it by moving to his side and bending down to kiss him. She meant it as a passionate kiss, but he kept his mouth shut tight. He did not close his eyes but looked at her with that bleary-eyed expression of someone with too much to drink.

"My God," he said, meaning it. "You are so beautiful."

"I'm a mess." She moved to the door and turned and made herself smile into his disturbing, suspicious, glittering gaze. "I love you."

He held up the empty glass. "Here's to love."

5

Early in the morning, her grandmother came to the doorway of the room to say that Constance was on the phone and wanted to talk to her. The night had been long, full of dreams that woke her, and near fallings-off that shook her into fearful listening to the house, Faulk sleeping heavily at her side. The sound of Iris in the hall outside the door startled her, and as she left the bed, carefully, her heart was pounding, knocking against her breastbone. She dressed hurriedly in jeans and a sweatshirt and went downstairs to the phone in the hall.

"Hello," Constance said. There was an evenness, almost a guardedness, in the voice.

"I'll come get you," Natasha said. "I'll take you out for brunch."

"I just want something light."

"I'll pick you up in five minutes."

Iris was sitting in the kitchen with her coffee. "I had a long night," she said, as Natasha entered the room. "Not much sleep."

"Tell me about it."

"It's just nerves, honey."

"What're *you* nervous about?" Natasha asked her.

"I'm an old woman. And my knee hurts."

Natasha kissed her forehead.

"I've got to take it easier on it," Iris said.

Natasha poured herself a little of the coffee and stood there sipping it while the other watched her. She put the cup down in the sink with a small clatter.

"I'll shut up," Iris said.

"I have to go. I won't be long."

"Take my car," she said with the air of someone deciding to let something pass.

"Okay."

At the Holiday Inn, Constance was sitting under the canopy in front. She wore a light scarf and white slacks with a blue puffy-sleeved blouse, and she looked rested. The sight of her brought everything back in another bad interior rush, and the effort of the past days to find a way beyond things, the little victories of will, all seemed to collapse again as her friend got into the car and leaned over to hug her. The awkwardness of it made Constance frown. "You look frazzled," she said, with her customary bluntness. "Do you wish I hadn't come?"

"Stop it," Natasha said, and flashed a brittle smile.

"I almost didn't. Now I don't know what to say."

"Did you go to California?"

"Briefly. I came from there."

"And?"

Constance sighed. "It's a nice little shop. I still want her to use her degree."

"Does she seem happy?"

"We're fine. I'm wondering what *you've* got planned."

"A small wedding. So we can start our lives." Natasha drove down Central to Cooper Street, and over to Otherlands Coffee Bar café. They went in and ordered, and stood waiting, and Constance wanted to know about the café and about some of the other places in Memphis that she remembered with fondness. When they had their food, they went out on the open patio and took a table overlooking the cars in the lot with the sun on them. Constance remarked about the leaves not having begun to take on color yet. "In Maine, some of the trees were already bare when I left for California."

Natasha had ordered granola with orange juice, and she was surprised at her own appetite for it. Constance sat there tearing up a bran muffin and washing bites of it down with sips of black coffee. "So—how are you—"

"Fine."

"You've let go of being mad at me."

Natasha stared at her.

"Okay. Okay."

They ate quietly for another few moments.

"You know I thought I saw him at the airport yesterday."

Natasha paused only slightly, concentrating on her food. The blood was hurtling through the veins of her neck.

"Unpleasant, to say the least. Reminded me of my stupidity."

"Are you going back to Maine or to California when you leave here?" she asked, hearing the tremor in her own voice and feeling the coldness rising at her abdomen. She had put her spoon down and sipped her water.

"Maine. Until the end of the month, anyway. I'm gonna sell that house."

Others came up onto the patio and entered the café. They were talking animatedly, interrupting one another and laughing, and they seemed perfectly happy and at peace with things as they were.

"Well," Constance said. "It was a strange moment, anyway."

"But it—you know it—but it wasn't him."

She shrugged. "Not much chance of him being here unless you invited him to the wedding. No. Not him. He looked right at me because I guess I was staring, and I have to say it looked enough like him for me to stare. He must've thought I was somebody crazy, eyeing him like that. And I'm sure I looked as stupid as I felt."

"But it *wasn't* him?"

"No. I said. It wasn't."

A moment later, Constance went on: "I shouldn't have mentioned it. It reminded me how stupid I was in Jamaica, that's all. And even if it *had* been him it would just be one of those weird coincidences you see in novels. Because I know nothing happened between you except a harmless kiss under the moon on a beach, being a little drunk. I know all that and I was so stupid to assume anything."

"But it *wasn't him*," Natasha said. She thought of him saying he had been to Memphis.

"Hey. Honey. Calm down. You're white as the salt in that shaker."

She stood and looked around her and then moved to the stairs and held on to the wooden railing. The ground before her, the gravel with the front of a car in it and the grass growing through the stones and the little fragment of a candy wrapper, all seemed to tumble away from her. She put one hand to her eyes, thumb and forefinger clamping the bridge of her nose. Constance breathed at her side. "Hey, I said it wasn't him. It *wasn't him.* God, I'm so stupid."

Natasha turned and saw her and then for an instant couldn't quite remember what she was doing there or where they both were. When she looked out over the tops of the cars, she saw the beach, and blinked, and then saw the street, the sun on it through the leafy trees.

"Honey, what is this?" Constance said.

"Nothing. Forget it. I don't want to think about Jamaica. Can we please, please, please not talk or think about Jamaica."

"I didn't mean to upset you. I only wanted to get past my stupidity about it all."

"I have to go," Natasha said.

She went out to the car and got in, and Constance followed, muttering to herself all the way, and then apologizing. "I'm so sorry I mentioned it. Honey, I've messed up again, haven't I."

Natasha was crying, and only dimly aware of the fact. She put the car in gear and backed out into the street and pulled up to Cooper. There was a lot of traffic. Constance stared at her. "I'm so sorry. I should've kept my mouth shut. I was just making conversation. I wanted to reassure myself we were past it and could even talk about how stupid I was, and maybe even joke about it."

"I have to go home," Natasha said.

"Honey. You *are* home."

She couldn't speak.

"I'm so sorry. Can you please forgive me? I'm sure it wasn't him."

She shook her head and drove. And her friend sat there looking at the side of her face, and then out at the road, and then at the side of her face.

"Honey, it wasn't him. I told you I only thought I saw him. I really am sorry I mentioned him. You're not still thinking about him."

"Oh, God. *Please.*"

At the Holiday Inn, she pulled under the canopy and waited for Constance to get out. "I'll see you later today?" Constance said in a weak little voice, looking as if she might cry.

"Yes."

"People make mistakes, honey. I wanted to think we could talk about it."

Natasha said nothing.

The other got out of the car and looked in at the window. "I don't know what this *is* for you, and I was only trying to say how stupid I was and I really—whatever pain I've caused, I am so, so sorry."

Natasha may have nodded.

Constance went on quickly, as if wanting to get it said before Natasha could interrupt or protest, "And I don't think you should go through with this wedding in the shape you're in."

"*Stop* it."

The other went on, hurrying, "If you're in love with someone else you can't—"

Natasha pressed on the gas, pulling away so fast that the tires squealed.

6

She drove to Iris's, parked the car, and went into the house, through the living room to the kitchen. Leander and Trixie were there. She said good morning to them, and to Iris, who was making bacon and eggs, standing in her leg brace at the stove. The whole house smelled of bacon and coffee. The light coming in the windows was blinding and showed every blemish on the old man's face. He looked grotesque.

Iris said, "Marsha Trunan called. She's in town. She'll be here for the party this evening."

"Did she want me to call her?"

"You okay? You look pale."

"She's nervous about tomorrow," said Leander, raising his cup.

"Want some coffee?" Iris asked her.

"I'm going upstairs and take a shower."

"Tell your husband he shouldn't sleep so late," Leander said.

His wife playfully slapped the back of his hand. "*You* just woke up yourself."

"I'll convey the message," Natasha said. Her stomach hurt. Climbing the stairs, she thought of Nicholas Duego coming to Memphis and remembered writing the address of this house in the sand and then wiping it away. But Constance had said it was a mistake; she'd mistaken someone for him. It was a mistake. It might even have been some kind of ploy on the older woman's part in order to gauge Natasha's reaction to it. That would be like her. Yet the possibility had entered Natasha's mind. She felt it like a weight on her chest.

She found Faulk sitting in the sunlight at the bedroom window. He had on a pair of brown slacks and a white T-shirt. He rose as she entered and put one hand to his eyes, as if to rub sleep out of them. "It's bright out there."

"You were looking right into it," she said, trying to sound cheerful. "Your father said to tell you you're a lazy bum for sleeping late."

"That's me." He moved to kiss her good morning, looking into her eyes and seeking to find the something he believed now was simply not there anymore. Her smile was strange. It was always strange now. There was something *willed* about it.

"I think he's trying to be funny."

"Yeah, well. His kind of being funny can drive you nuts."

"I'm sorry."

"That man in Florida—Stevens—the one with inhalation anthrax. He died today. It's the first case in twenty-five years."

She said, "Hold me? Please?"

They stood in the light from the window for what seemed a long time. He removed himself finally and, taking her hand, started to lead her downstairs.

"I'm gonna take a shower," she told him.

"Okay."

"It's all so awful." She held her hands clasped at her middle.

He thought she looked years older. Something petty in him wanted to feed her anxiety. "Anthrax. My God. Eerie. Twenty-five years—and now . . ." He reached to touch her hip, sorry for the little cruel impulse, and aghast at the level of his own discontent.

"How's your headache?" she asked.

He looked down. "It's better."

"Good."

"I'm sorry about last night," he said.

"Nothing to be sorry about. You were talking to your father."

"Well, that—but I meant—" He stopped, realizing that there were no words to express it short of standing there and accusing her. "Nothing. I had too much. And I shouldn't have."

"But you meant what?" She studied his face.

It was calm, the expression flat. "I don't know. I'm hungover. I'm like you, honey. I want *us* again. Like the other night. I want all this to be just a bad memory."

"It's our wedding," she said, fighting tears.

"I'd just like to get on with things." His tone was nearly that of a little boy, distressed and wanting a thing fixed that could not be fixed. He turned and went on down, head slightly bowed. She wanted to call him back, take him into the bedroom, and close the door and tell him what had happened to her.

But in that case she would have to tell him everything. She thought of trying to explain what it was like there, on that beach, and on those wasted nights in Adams Morgan, all that. For the first time, he looked sixteen years older, going on down the stairs, and she had a moment of knowing his age difference as *difference*: his different life, and all the years he had as a priest, and his young years and the seminary.

Turning as he went out of sight, she stopped and held on to the wall for a moment.

No. The thing was to live it down, live past it, find a way to forget it ever happened. Her first decision had been right. She told herself that things were slowly getting better, and she must only keep struggling to recover in this incremental way the ease and loveliness she had known with him. Except that now there was this new worry, of what Constance had told her. All the anxiety kept folding in and out of itself, and she wished with all her heart that Constance had not come.

She took a fast shower, dressed, and returned to the kitchen. Faulk was sitting in the living room drinking coffee and reading the newspaper. Iris had gone out to cut flowers. On the table in the kitchen were two bundles of chrysanthemums that she had already cut, along with the bouquet from the Norlands.

"Dad and Trixie went shopping," Faulk said. "I think he was just looking for an excuse to get away."

She sat next to him and took his hand. "Were things okay this morning?" she said.

"No mention of anything. Pure joviality like nothing was said at all."

"Maybe he's embarrassed."

"He's not blessed with that capacity, believe me."

She kissed him. "You smell like lemons."

"Probably the flowers," he said. "It looks like a funeral parlor in here." He put the paper aside and turned to kiss her. It was a long kiss, and she worked to empty her mind of everything else.

For him, as they broke apart and she went about tidying the room, things were freighted with what he feared and suspected about her. He watched the frenetic way she moved getting the room ready, and he saw the pale cast of her skin and the way she seemed to be glancing at him, as if to gauge his mood.

7

Iris had planned the party as soon as she knew the date of the wedding. She hired a catering service that sent two young Mexican men who were very efficient and very quiet. They went about their business, setting out plates of vegetables and cheese and chicken wings, and they sliced a big ham. Iris had ordered five bottles of red wine and three bottles of white and a case of beer, which, along with the white wine, they put into a galvanized tub of ice. They placed all the food on a long folding table with a white linen cloth over it. Iris had them put the tub of white wine and beer on the back porch and the red wine in the kitchen, with a corkscrew and a bottle opener.

"We'll let people help themselves," she said to the two caterers, who had marginal understanding of English. Natasha drank coffee, watching her grandmother get everything ready. Iris would not let her help.

"Done," she said to the two young men. "Good. Now you can relax."

The darker of the two looked at her with comical puzzlement, half smiling. The other touched his shoulder and repeated the word: "Done." Then: "*Relájete*."

Iris went on into the other room using her cane and moving with obvious discomfort. When Natasha offered to help with the final touches, she smiled and waved away the thought, and she was working on the room right up until time for the party, fussing and rearranging things—she had Faulk begin putting chairs around from the kitchen and then moved a couple of them herself, using the backs as braces. Then she took more flowers she had cut from the garden in front of the house and trimmed the ends of them and placed them in vases around the room. Faulk went upstairs and changed clothes, and Natasha followed.

They said very little, moving around in the room and being quietly considerate of each other. "Should I put on a tie?" he said.

"No."

"Sure? Leander'll wear one, I can guarantee it."

Clara and Jack arrived first, bringing Constance. They had just met at the Holiday Inn, and they were already in animated discussion of the news, mostly about the anthrax, Jack expressing worries about biological agents and the new terrorism of mass suicide. Most doctors, he was saying, wouldn't even recognize the symptoms of exposure to anthrax early enough to help. He brought up the use of mustard gas in World War I. "Everybody's been working on that kind of thing," he said. "Chemical agents and biological agents like anthrax. Germs and chemicals. All the big boys: *us*, the Russians, the British, the Chinese. We're gonna see that kind of thing again. Refined and more efficient than it was back in the trenches. It'll be in grocery stores and subways and schools. Count on it."

Iris offered her hand to Constance. "I don't think we've met."

Natasha hurried to introduce everyone while Jack apologized about his choice of subject matter. Marsha Trunan drove up shortly afterward, as did Leander and Trixie. Leander had bought a bottle of George Dickel. Natasha performed the introductions, and everyone gathered in the living room. There were remarks on the food and the fine weather and the promise of a sunny day for the wedding, and Constance made friendly observations about the art on the walls, Iris's nice house. Faulk stood in the entrance of the kitchen with a glass of cold beer. Leander and Trixie were drinking the bourbon, and the old man asked Natasha if she wanted some of it. Without thinking, she said, "Sure."

Iris talked about plans for the ceremony, set for three o'clock tomorrow at a little place called Lucy Wedding Chapel, in Millington. A simple civil ceremony, though it would be presided over by a priest. Faulk explained that this was a matter of principle for him, and Natasha, squeezing his arm above the elbow, said, "It's me. I'm the one who doesn't want the wedding in a church."

Faulk looked at the faces and resisted the urge—simply for the sake of clarity—to launch into an explanation about having left the priesthood.

But then, almost as if by some inevitable shift in mood, the talk returned to the war and the attacks. People began trading stories about how it was for them. Clara told of finding out about the Pentagon while taking a walk through her neighborhood. She got to the top of the hill near Wisconsin Avenue and saw the smoke rising over in the direction of the river. The smoke went high into the sky, and she heard the sirens and knew that something awful had happened.

She asked Faulk to tell about his journey, and he obliged, watching Natasha gaze at him as he did so and feeling as though he ought to apologize for the fact that she had to hear it all repeated.

She nodded at him, as if to encourage him to continue, and took a sip of the bourbon. It tasted sweeter than she liked just now. Remembering the turmoil of the crowded bar in Jamaica, she put the glass down on the coffee table. Faulk went on about the terrible look of the skyline in New York as the train headed away from it, and she stepped past him into the kitchen, got a wineglass, and poured red wine. Marsha Trunan, having followed her, poured more for herself. The caterers were there apparently having some sort of argument, muttering hotly in Spanish, the one leaning on the frame of the back door and the other standing out on the stoop. The one on the stoop had lit a cigarette and was blowing the smoke into the dimness.

Natasha had a long slow sip of the wine.

"Wonder what those two are talking about," Marsha said. "Only subject of the day, right?"

"Did you drive out?" Natasha asked. "That looked like your car you pulled up in."

"I did. I've moved back for good. You knew that, right? I'm middle-of-the-country from now on. You know where I worked back there. Imagine. I come up out of the metro station at Crystal City on my way to the office like every day of the last five years, and there's the fucking Pentagon burning. And I smelled jet fuel. I'm sure of it."

"You knew right away, then?"

"Well, the airport's so close, right. So yeah, I smelled the fuel and knew instantly it was a plane. I mean what could it be but a plane? Remember the one back in '81 that crashed into the Fourteenth Street Bridge?"

"I was twelve and thought the world was going to end every day anyway because Reagan had just taken office—nuclear cowboy, Iris and her friends called him. So, yes. Yes, I remember it. Iris and I watched it on television."

"Didn't everybody."

Presently, Marsha said, "So tell me about Jamaica."

Natasha turned quickly to her. "What do you mean?"

"Excuse me?"

They stood there.

"It's a pretty straightforward question, Natasha. I ask it and then you answer, you know, *Great.* Or *Okay,* or *Really shitty.* Right?"

"Well, but you knew we were stranded—what did Constance say about it?"

The other's voice took on the tone of another question. "Um, well, she said you were stranded?" Then: "Jesus, kid. You want to tell me what's going on with you? I just asked how it was in Jamaica. You were there almost two weeks before you got stranded, right?"

"It was good for the two weeks. There's nothing else to tell. I mean, I—we got stuck there. We were having a really good time until it happened." She swallowed; it was a gulp. And with a rush of buried wrath at her continuing disquiet, she took another long drink of the wine.

"You turned green when you sipped that bourbon, and just now you turned the same color when I asked you about Jamaica."

She managed a shrug. "I had too much bourbon in Jamaica the day it happened, okay? It made me sick. All of it. The whole thing, and the whiskey."

"You liked bourbon so much. Is the love affair over?"

Natasha stared.

"You and bourbon are done with each other."

"Okay. Yes."

"Did you think I was talking about Mackenzie?"

"I knew what you were talking about. Mackenzie. For God's sake, Marsha."

"Well, why're you so fucking nervous?"

She said nothing.

"I was talking to Constance, and she said you were really nervous. Scared, I think is what she said. Scared. I mean you're living a dream, right? What's to be afraid of?"

"Oh, well, Marsha, you know—obviously I'm in a panic. And it's so sweet having a person like Constance worrying about me and putting her own interpretation on everything and then reporting it to the whole fucking civilized world like Reuters news service."

"Hey, honey. Hey. *Hey.*"

She swallowed more of the wine.

"You didn't actually have much fun together on that trip, did you."

She took another long drink.

"Go easy, kiddo. You don't want to be hungover on your wedding day."

"Oh, you too? You're going to worry about me, too?"

Marsha took her own long sip. "I'm glad I didn't go with you guys. I think I'd've gone batshit stuck like that. Even in a place like Jamaica."

Faulk saw them talking, and even as he himself continued with his story, the fact registered at the back of his mind that there were a large number of associations and incidents in Natasha's life of which he had little or no knowledge. He went on telling about the little girl on the train who was going home with her father and who had seen the disaster close up from a highway in Virginia, but he wanted to go stand with Natasha. He looked at Constance, who was sipping a beer and listening to Leander talk about the role of religion in the world's violence. Constance had been there, in Jamaica. Faulk determined that he would speak to her about it. He stood and moved across the room in her direction, but then Andrew Clenon arrived.

Because Clenon was a priest, the others assumed he was the one who would perform the ceremony, and so Faulk took him around the room introducing him as the best man. "We were in seminary together."

Leander shook Clenon's hand and smiled at him warmly. "Another priest," he said, having his own little joke.

"Our numbers seem to be dwindling in some quarters," Clenon said.

Faulk guided him across the room to the kitchen, where Natasha and Marsha Trunan were still standing. Constance had joined them, with Clara and Jack. They were pouring more wine—Saint-Estèphe—which Jack had bought for them and which Natasha had opened. Faulk stood with Constance in the entrance of the room, while Clenon exchanged pleasantries with Jack about the wine, and they watched Aunt Clara swirl it in her glass, making a sardonic show of being about to taste it. Everyone seemed lighthearted now, and Natasha's smile was broad and lovely as she lifted her own glass to her lips.

Faulk leaned slightly toward Constance, as if to confide something. "You flew in from Maine?" he said, feigning interest.

"California," she told him. "I have a house in Maine."

"Natasha mentioned that. Guess that's why I thought—"

"I may be selling it."

"It was kind of you to give her that trip to Jamaica. Even if it worked out so badly."

"Well, she was good company for me. You know."

He saw the narrowing of her eyes, the color in her face. Her

cheeks were blotchy now, and she sipped her wine without returning his gaze. "I can't get her to talk about it much," he said. "It's
still got some kind of hold on her emotions."

"Well, *wouldn't* it? It was so terrible being—being stranded like
that. And—and thinking *you'd* been in one of the towers, you know.
An awful time for her. I'm still having nightmares about it myself."

"Were you together when you found out?"

"On the beach together, yes, like every morning. The two of
us. Every morning we would go down to the beach. But you knew
that. Anyway, we came in, and it was already going on."

"She must've—you both must've felt so alone."

A small silence followed. She glanced down at the wine in her
glass. Then: "Yes. Exactly. All the Americans felt that. Being alone.
I know I did. It was very strange."

"Even when you were with someone."

She stared.

"I mean you and Natasha were together and—and alone at the
same time."

"Yes."

"The feeling of being alone."

"I didn't know where anyone was for a while. I'm afraid I got
pretty drunk. A lot of people just went off the deep end. There was
a man there—" She stopped, having apparently seen the change in
his features.

"You were saying."

"A man there with his wife who said he hadn't had a drink in
something like ten years. He announced that he was an alcoholic,
and—and, well, he already smelled of it when he said it and he
went on and drank himself silly. He fell off the wagon in a big way,
and I'm afraid I helped him do it."

Faulk waited, thinking there was more.

Her head tilted slightly to one side. "How does it feel to leave
the priesthood after so many years?"

"I'd been wanting to leave for quite a while."

She nodded, without quite seeming to take it in.

"So you lost track of Natasha, too, that day?"

"Everybody lost track of everybody that day."

"And this man . . ." Faulk saw the glimmer of relief in her features as she realized what he had meant.

"Yes," she said. "Stinking of it when I first saw him and he was claiming he hadn't touched it in years."

Natasha walked up to them and took Constance by the upper arm. "Please, let's not have any talk about all that tonight. This is the night before my wedding."

"I was telling him about Skinner," said Constance as if to explain herself. Faulk considered her expression, the uneven color in her cheeks. "Poor Skinner," she went on. "Married to the most awful woman. A harpy."

Natasha shook her head, looking pleadingly at Faulk. "I don't want to think about any of that now. Please?"

He gave her a light kiss on the cheek. "You're absolutely right, my darling." He smiled at Marsha Trunan, who had walked over and put one hand on Natasha's back. The two of them chatted with Constance about Memphis, Natasha and Marsha the returning natives, and laughter and gaiety rose all around them. Faulk kept the smile, but he was full of darkness inside. He stood there while the three women went on to speak of Natasha's and Marsha's travels in Italy. He had lost the thread.

"Where was it," Marsha was saying.

"That little gallery behind the Duomo," said Natasha.

"Oh, that's right. I never saw such a statue."

"Which is that?" Faulk asked.

"Donatello's *Magdalen*."

"That, to my mind, is the greatest statue in the world," he told them. "Did you notice how quiet it is around it? That statue shuts *up* everyone who walks into that room." He felt pompous and stiff. But he couldn't stop himself. "I think it's much more impressive than the *David*."

As the others took up the subject, Natasha moved closer to his side and put her arm around his middle. He took it as a signal that she wished for him to stop. But she nodded and smiled at him and seemed proud. Over the next few moments they were separately aware of the appearance they made: the center of attention; the happy couple. They did not acknowledge this, even to themselves.

He struggled each moment to forget his suspicions while at the same time seeking to have them answered once and for all. She kept trying to wipe the shadows from her heart, drinking more of the wine and staying close to him.

The party went on, and Leander insisted that Trixie dance with him. Iris put music on, and they danced, and soon Marsha and Clenon were dancing, too, then Aunt Clara and Uncle Jack. The song was "Knock on Wood," and Iris played it three times, loud. She was the only one who did not take a turn; she stood clapping her hands.

It looked like an effortlessly happy occasion.

But as things went on, Natasha could scarcely hold on to herself inside, for the way Faulk kept watching her, and she was growing panicky about what Constance might have said, or would say. She was afraid about Marsha Trunan, too, for that matter. They knew too much about her, even being ignorant of the one thing, details about her involvement with Mackenzie; and Constance unmistakably still believed what she believed.

The wine wasn't helping. Natasha went into the kitchen and out the back door for some cooler air, standing on the stoop, taking deep slow breaths. It was a star-bright night, and the lawn was rich with the smell of honeysuckle and crepe myrtle. She heard the whoosh of far-off cars and trucks on the highway. The two Mexican caterers were out by the back fence, smoking and talking and laughing. Natasha stood gazing at them. Aunt Clara came out and took her hand, smiling, then patted her shoulder and let go.

"Hi," Natasha managed.

"It's a beautiful night." Aunt Clara sighed. "I always like to think that if I can only savor something enough, it won't go so fast. I'm savoring this night."

"Yes."

"Are you all right, sweetie?"

"Oh, just—tired. I had too much wine."

"Wine gives me a headache. It's Jack's passion, though. He drinks enough of it for both of us." She laughed softly. It occurred to Natasha that Aunt Clara had such a charming laugh. And oh, why couldn't life give Natasha back herself as she had been? She wanted to tell Clara how much she loved her, but the breath wasn't there for speech, and she turned, crying silently, pretending to be interested in the starry light.

In the kitchen, Faulk was leaning against the counter, listening to Clenon tell his own story about discovering something was wrong the morning of the attacks—he'd gone for a run and noticed that the streets were empty. "Suddenly, it seemed to me that Midtown just emptied out. Midtown—no cars moving, nothing."

Nearby, Marsha Trunan and Constance Waverly were in a conversation that Faulk caught the tail of. He heard the phrase "that photographer" come from Constance's mouth, and the tone was defensive. He realized they were arguing and tried to listen through the confusion of other voices. The photographer Constance mentioned certainly must be Mackenzie. He went over to the two women, and immediately they changed the subject.

"Anyway," Marsha said. "A lot of people don't know it, but vanilla extract is thirty-five percent alcohol. And like I said, I took to stealing it out of the grocery stores—those little bottles. There I was in the afternoons, smelling like vanilla ice cream and drunk as a skunk."

He could not think of a way simply to ask them about the photographer, so he smiled at Constance and moved off, feeling thwarted and wronged at the same time. He wanted no more wine, though Clenon walked up with a bottle and poured some into his glass. Clenon was drinking Diet Coke. "This is so you can relax a little. I swear you look like you're waiting for a firing squad."

Natasha came in from the outside and went up to him, looking teary eyed, and took his arm. Leander had announced that he wanted to offer a toast to the new couple. Everyone gathered around in the room, and all eyes were on them. Natasha gripped Faulk's arm as Leander spoke.

"Here's to the happiness that surprises us when we least expect it," Leander said, wavering a little as he stood. He'd had too much of the whiskey. "And I would like to congratulate my son on his choice of a second wife." He nodded at Natasha. "Who's jus' as lovely as the night." Then he smiled at her with an amiably lubricious expression, obviously meaning it as a compliment; but the following silence, as the others waited for him to say more, was awkward.

Natasha nodded back at him and held her glass up.

"Oh," Leander said. "Right." He drank.

The laugh that came was exaggerated by the relief it expressed. Everyone followed suit.

Faulk removed himself from Natasha and went into the kitchen, where Constance had gone. He stood near her as she poured more wine for herself.

"Something happened in Jamaica," he said, looking directly into her eyes. "Didn't it?"

She seemed momentarily stricken and actually took a step back from him.

"Tell me. Please. I think I have a right to know."

Her cheeks looked bruised. "I—I told you what happened. What is this? We were stranded there. People have been talking about it all night. It was terrible. I—I don't understand you." But he could see that indeed she had understood, and that there was something she was taking pains to conceal. "Nothing else happened," she insisted, looking away from him.

Natasha, who had come over to them, heard this, and she took him by the elbow. "Baby," she said. "What's wrong?" Her voice shook.

"Nothing," he said. "Forget it." Suddenly he felt heavy and sodden with what he'd had to drink, and with his own suspicions. He put his wineglass down and reached into the cabinet for a glass to pour himself some water.

"Honey?" Natasha said.

"Really. Forget it." He managed the smile, then turned and went to the back door and out onto the little porch, where the two caterers were sitting with arms folded across their knees. He asked for a cigarette.

Natasha saw him light it, saw the features of his face illuminated by the match, and in that moment she wanted everyone to be gone. She watched him talking to the two Mexicans, trying to make himself understood, gesturing at the night. She saw the look of hopelessness on his face when they did not understand him.

He took a deep draw of the cigarette and walked out of the light toward the end of the yard. When he looked back he saw the two caterers watching him, two shadowy figures under the porch light. Beyond them was the lit kitchen, and Natasha staring out, Constance at her side with a look of concern and vigilance on her face. Something was between the two women and, whatever it was, it had to do with the stranded days in Jamaica. He smoked the cigarette and walked to the side yard, the only light now the coal of the cigarette as he drew on it. You could hear the chatter going on inside the house, but he did not look at the curtained windows. He was alone, and beginning to think that this was as it should be. The wedding tomorrow seemed absurd, and he was being made a fool of by these women. They knew something that he did not know, that it was his right to know. He could simply call everything off, refuse to tie himself to this young woman and her complicated life. He took a few shaky steps toward the front lawn, the streetlight there in its cloud of insects. Why? Why!

Remember who you are, he muttered aloud to himself. *God forgive me.*

Why would she go through with things if her feelings had changed? What had he done to deserve such treatment if it was true? But then, he told himself, trying to be philosophical, what did anyone deserve, after all, when love rode through the soul? He was in love. He knew the force of that. He was in love—completely in love with this young woman, Natasha, who no longer felt that way about him and was trying to hide it, with the help of the two friends who knew how she really felt.

Suddenly he broke out crying and moved deeper into the dark, to the hedge along that side, wiping his face with his forearm and seeking to gain control of himself.

God, please help me to be the man I want to be.

For some reason he saw himself lapsing into that pretentious talk about the Donatello statue, and he repeated his own line about it, like a sort of ridicule: *That statue shuts up everyone who walks into that room.* Seeing himself, so earnest and stupid, talking like that into what the women knew, he drew deeply on the cigarette and threw it down, and sobbed quietly. At last he straightened, took a breath, and murmured aloud: "Stop it. Stop it. For Christ's sake." Even with what he'd had to drink, he found that he could look coldly at his own panic. He was afraid of losing her, afraid the process had already begun. But everyone had suffered through the calamity, and he understood that he must stop imagining things. "You're pushing fifty," he said aloud, off into the dark. "Quit acting like a kid."

Help me, I'm drowning.

He took a deep, slow breath, trying to get calm. He was quiet, standing there in the dark.

In the house, Natasha stared at the place where he had stood lighting the cigarette and saying whatever he had said to the caterers. She thought of going out there to find him.

Constance touched her elbow and murmured, "Does he know?"

"About what?"

"Come on."

"Oh, Jesus *Christ.*"

"Have you said something to him?"

"There isn't anything to say, Constance. For God's sake."

"Well, he challenged me. He knows something."

"There's nothing for him to know. Oh, God. Can you please— why did you come here? Was it to ruin everything? Do you know how guilty you looked just now?"

"I'm sorry," Constance said. "I was trying to protect you. I was stupid before and I was—I've been trying to make it up to you."

"We have to leave, sweetie," said Aunt Clara, reaching to embrace Natasha. Jack stood behind her. "Where'd Michael get off to?"

Natasha looked out the back-door screen again and saw only the two caterers. "He was out there."

"Well, tell him we'll see him tomorrow."

"I will." Tears blurred her vision. Aunt Clara evidently thought they were tears of happiness.

8

The morning was long but filled with preparations. Faulk set things in order and washed all the dirty dishes from the night before and then made breakfast for them, and for Leander and Trixie, who drove over just before noon. It felt good to be busy. All his darkness of the night before stood in the back of his mind like a fever dream. He would not let it ruin things. He told himself he did not know anything for certain except that the horrors of their mutual experience had left everyone unsettled and changed. But change did not have to mean unhappiness.

Standing at the sink washing dishes, he concentrated on the life they had planned. They would go to the south of France next spring. They would find the means to rediscover each other out of the disaster that had befallen the whole country. He would win her back to him, and she would be as she had been before.

Natasha wanted nothing to eat. She took a bath, washed and dried her hair, and put on makeup. People were arriving downstairs. They were going to make a caravan of cars to Millington. Faulk seemed calm, almost resigned, and he had been very drunk and sorrowful when he came to bed. Fretful and distressed with himself for getting so bad. He remembered putting his arms around her and asking her to forgive him when she came to lie down at his side, and then, waking in the middle of the night, he wasn't sure of it. She was not there next to him. After some time of drifting in and out of sleep, he got up, went downstairs and stood in bright light that made it impossible to see, and then realized that he had dreamed this; that he was still in the bed. And she was there. She had either come back or had never left. He turned from her and went back to sleep, and slept so deeply and snored so loudly that for a couple of hours, and for the second time, she had to try sleeping on the couch downstairs. She was sober in spite of all the wine.

One cup of coffee, sitting and talking with Iris before going up to
bed, and she was wakeful all night.

But everyone said she was beautiful when she walked downstairs in the new dress. Faulk had put a dark suit on, and an electric-
blue tie. He looked wonderful. He took her hands in his own and
kissed her.

They all went out into the bright sun, got into four cars, and
headed to Millington, with Faulk and Natasha leading the way.

"I feel like we're at the head of a parade," Natasha said.

"So we are."

The Lucy Wedding Chapel was a small A-frame cottage with
white tulips in a flower box along its front and rosebushes bordering the lawn. The little pockets of shade from the bushes looked
painted on the lustrous fresh-cut grass. The priest who was commis-
sioned to perform the ceremony was the one who had taken Faulk's
place at Grace Episcopal. This was suggested by Andrew Clenon.
The new priest was a slight, round-faced, nervous man named Lee
Wuhan, who was, he said, of Asian descent, and who, in his celebra-
tory remarks, made a metaphor of the World Trade Center, talking about how it represented power and worldly pursuits and how
love flourishes best when coming from the individual spirit: the
recent catastrophe was a message from on high about what is most
essential in life. As he spoke, Natasha lowered her gaze, feeling the
inappropriateness of bringing this sort of topical homilic remark-
ing into her marriage ceremony. It angered her. When she stole a
glance at Faulk, she saw nothing of what she felt. Faulk stared at the
man almost blandly. Natasha gave his hand a little squeeze and kept
her eyes down, listening to the notes of providential import.

Aunt Clara, Uncle Jack, Leander, and Trixie sat on one side of
the aisle. On the other side were Iris and Constance. Father Clenon stood with Faulk and Marsha Trunan stood with Natasha.

Father Wuhan seemed ill at ease, and the more he spoke the
worse things got. He let go of the attacks and went on strangely
about a calamity of his own, gathering assurance as he spoke,
speaking in an almost prideful voice of something that happened
nineteen years ago: he had killed a boy in an accident, in traffic,

in the streets of Johannesburg, South Africa. He described himself, a young man in a hurry, not paying as much attention as he
should have to the road he was on. That accident was why he had
entered the priesthood, he said, and then as if compelled by some
moral imperative to refer to his predecessor's decision, he avowed
that he would never leave it, no matter how complicated the life
became for him. He paused significantly before saying he was so
very happy about being asked to perform today's holy ceremony.
Then he attempted to connect all the cataclysmic history by citing
the blessings of love and forgiveness as a hedge against it, and he
asked everyone to learn first to forgive oneself, to see the enor-
mous effect we have upon one another, and to acknowledge the
undeniable significance of changing one's moral compass.

Iris and Aunt Clara began clearing their throats and looking
at each other. Leander coughed loudly twice and then blew his
nose with a high flatulent sound and took a long time putting his
handkerchief away. Then he yawned. Natasha saw Trixie touch
his forearm. He leaned back, stretching his legs under the pew in
front of him. Soon they were all shifting on the benches, coughing,
crossing and uncrossing their legs. At last, Father Wuhan finished
with his homily and commenced with the actual ceremony. Natasha looked into his dark eyes and thought of the judgments he had
already made. There was something too starchy about him for all
his studied humility about an accident he reported like a kind of
accomplishment.

When the ceremony was over and Faulk spoke about asking
him to come to dinner with everyone, she looked into her new
husband's eyes and murmured, "You're such a good man. No."

He nodded. He understood. He had in fact decided that he
would speak to Father Clenon about him. He gave Wuhan an envelope with fifty dollars in it and thanked him. Father Clenon, giving
Faulk a look of commiseration, begged off going to the dinner and
walked out of the chapel with Father Wuhan. Faulk saw him talking, gesturing at the other as they went on down the sidewalk.

"Jesus Christ," Leander said.

Uncle Jack, walking over to congratulate Faulk, said, "That was
certainly bizarre, wasn't it?"

"I've heard some weird things," Leander began.

Faulk said, "Well, we're married. We got it done. And we don't ever have to see him anymore."

"Sounds like an inconvenience you had to go through," said Jack, smiling. "It's always a little like that with the men, isn't it."

"You see the look on the other one's face?" Leander asked him.

Faulk said, "That's my friend, Dad. His name is Andrew. I think I introduced you to him last night."

"No offense, there, Son. But did you guys see the look."

"I saw it," Jack said. "I think he was embarrassed."

"I think he was enraged," Leander said. "And I was bored."

"No trouble for any of us recognizing that," Faulk said. And then, seeing the look of embarrassment on his father's face, patted the old man's back and said, "Me, too."

They all went to the River Café on West Poplar for dinner. Natasha admired the way her new husband handled everything, getting Iris situated with her cane and making sure everyone was comfortable. Leander offered another toast and then told a story about his son making a dive off a forty-five-foot cliff into the bottomless water of a reservoir in Maryland. According to Leander, Michael Faulk had been a marvelous athlete as a boy, good at everything. He had played football and baseball and basketball. "A wonder in all three," Leander said. "But you know, he was also a complete mystery to us all."

"Dad," Faulk said.

"I always had the feeling he was hiding inside his own skin."

"I was," Faulk said.

Jack and Constance began talking about the invasion of Afghanistan, which was imminent. The president had turned down an offer from the Taliban to put the master terrorist on trial there. They had all heard the news about the poor man, Stevens, in Florida, and the anthrax. There was news that the spores had been discovered as powder on computer keyboards in the tabloid newspaper office where he worked. The suspicion was that the powder had been in something mailed to the paper.

"It's not contagious," Iris said. "I read that. I mean you can't get it from someone coughing on you."

"Spittle, though," said Jack. "I think you can get it from the spittle—the—the mucus of the victim?"

"They're saying *inhalation* anthrax," said Clara. "That means it's inhaled, doesn't it?"

"But what in the world do you suppose the delivery system was?" Leander asked.

They all talked about the possibilities they had been reading about, the horror of a microbe being rendered into a form that made it potent even through the mail, the technology and skill required to refine it for such a thing.

"Hey," Faulk said suddenly. "Let's quit this talk right now."

"Yes," said Aunt Clara. "This is our happy occasion."

"To our happy occasion." Natasha raised her glass.

After their dinner, they drove in the same caravan downtown to Beale Street and the Rum Boogie Cafe for drinks and music. Aunt Clara and Uncle Jack danced beautifully together, alone in the middle of the small space for it, and then Leander pulled Trixie out there. The four of them looked splendid. Natasha took her new husband by the hand and led him into the gathering crowd of dancers. Faulk claimed that he did not like to dance and was no good at it, but he was very smooth. She told him so, and this made him self-conscious. He moved with her, breathing the perfumed tangle of her hair and looking through the crowd at his father and Trixie. They looked happy. He said into Natasha's ear: "My dear wife."

She leaned back slightly to look into his eyes and smiled and then kissed him.

"I'm so happy," he told her. And for that moment, he found that he was.

"Yes, happy," she said, resting her head on his chest. The room was spinning slightly, though she'd had nothing to drink. She saw Iris watching them, sitting with the others. Faulk seemed to want to perform for the old woman, turning toward her with Natasha in his arms, and grinning at her applause. Iris wore her brace and held her cane, and even so she stood for a while and moved her upper body rhythmically to the music.

"Let's sit down after this one," Natasha said, breathlessly.

He clung to the happy feeling, thinking of the house and all his work on it and the job and the night ahead, the days coming when they would be together, just the two of them.

Natasha, with her ear pressed to his chest, closed her eyes and swayed with him, the loud voices and music all around her. She sighed happily and raised her eyes to his and offered her mouth. He stopped dancing and kissed her, and a cheer went up around them, husband and wife. Then they separated and went on dancing because the band, which was called the Boogie Blues Band, had switched to a fast song. The lead singer started throwing strings of beads from the stage, and now some of the waitresses were doing a choreographed dance together. People stood and clapped their hands and watched and caught the long strands of colorful beads—everyone except Aunt Clara and Uncle Jack, who kept dancing. Constance shouted over the music that it all looked like a dance number from a Broadway show. People clapped in rhythm, standing on the edge of the space where the dancers moved. They were excellent, every step perfectly timed.

"I want this night to go on and on," Natasha said to Faulk, having to shout. Iris, standing now, smiled and nodded, and then reached down and got her tall glass of beer and had a long drink from it. She sat back down, already having drunk two glasses and she seemed almost playful, beating time on the table with the flat of her hand.

When the song finally ended and everyone was seated, Faulk stood and said, "It's been a lovely evening. Thank you all for coming."

"Can't hear you, priest," Leander shouted from the other end of the table.

Faulk nodded at him, giving him the thumbs-up sign. "A lovely time. Thank you."

"Yes, my son."

"Wonderful," said Trixie. Then she stood and pulled Leander up to embrace Faulk and Natasha. "We're leaving early in the morning," Leander said. "You two'll come visit us, okay? Remember I've got this damn macular thing. My old eyes."

"We'll come."

"Make him keep his word," Leander said to Natasha, putting his arms around her and kissing her on the cheek. He smelled of talcum and cigars and whiskey. As Trixie pulled him toward their side of the table, Faulk looked across the room at Marsha and Constance, returning from the restroom in the noise, talking seriously to each other, pausing, staying where they were for the moment it took to finish what they were saying.

Natasha leaned into him. "Let's do go now."

He bent down to kiss Iris, then walked around to kiss Clara. Iris beamed at him, and Natasha wanted to tell him what kind of a smile that was for Iris Mara to give anyone. The others rose to wish them happiness one final time for the evening. At last, they went out onto Beale Street.

Arm in arm they walked up Third, toward Madison, to the newly remodeled boutique hotel of the same name, at which he had reserved the honeymoon suite. It was growing cooler now. Natasha pointed to a horse-drawn carriage with a woman driving it and a big Labrador retriever sitting up next to her, ears cocked as if to listen for something in the street ahead of them. Faulk stopped to appreciate it, watching it go on. The street was crowded with tourists, and you could hear the music rising to the sky over the buildings from all the cafés and bars back on Beale, rising like the light that shone there when she looked back. More carriages went by with their sparkle and shine, the horses prancing, hooves sounding on the asphalt. Each driver was accompanied by a dog.

"I love that tradition," Faulk told her. "Every driver with a dog that rides along."

"You forget I grew up here," she said.

"Sorry."

"No need to apologize, my darling." She held his arm as they came to Union Avenue, where the light was red. To their right was AutoZone Park, the baseball stadium. For some reason the lights were on there. Two women stood at the crossing dressed in white ball gowns with identical-looking dark denim jackets on over all that soft finery. One of them was smoking a cigarette. They had just come from the Peabody Hotel and were drunk. The one with the cigarette seemed about to topple over and was being held up by the other. Natasha turned to Faulk, and he winked at her while the two women kept tottering at the curb.

"Do you believe Wuhan's remarks?" she asked him.

"I thought Father Wuhan was a little pompous."

"But I mean about what he said."

"He was trying to be profound, and he ended up sounding like a dull Sunday. No—worse than that. He could've been a party hack spouting the line."

The light changed, and they crossed with the others, who walked up Union toward the parking garage. Natasha and her new husband went on along Third, toward Madison.

"I'm so relieved," she said. "I was afraid you weren't horrified."

"I felt sorry for him, to tell you the truth. I was hoping he'd get to the end of it without realizing what effect it was having on us. I mean it wasn't harmful or rude or anything. It was just—well—way, way off-key."

"And revealing."

"Very revealing. So a poor little boy died—mostly to be a character in a story about when this priest, the hero of his own story, was an impatient, inattentive young man. And the dead boy earns status as some kind of exemplar? And I don't think the guy had any idea what an act of naked self-regard it was, telling it that way, this thing that was all about him and his own moral life, a paradigm of sins remembered and forgiven—and—and somehow all of it a comment about my leaving the priesthood—and there we were, waiting to get married."

"You're a gentle and good man, sir."

"That's a lovely thing to say. Thank you."

They stopped and embraced, and kissed.

"At this rate, we'll never get there."

"I'm enjoying every second," she said.

He kissed her once more, and they went on. "Anyway, Wuhan was a mistake."

"You really didn't like him," Natasha said. "Did you."

He laughed softly. "Not very Christian of me, is it."

"I've been a little worried about the religion." She hadn't known she would say this.

"Hey, did we just meet?"

"Well, it does worry me a little. It worries me that I don't feel it the way you do."

"Everybody's different," he said, hearing the inadequacy of it. "We'll find our way, you know?"

"But does it upset you?"

"No." He smiled tolerantly.

She stopped and stood on her toes to kiss him still again. It was a long, tender kiss. They held hands and went on up the street. She looked at the restaurants and bars, and the hill beyond where the river shone with the perfect reflection of the lights outlining the bridge to Arkansas.

Under the marquee of the hotel was bright light. The doorman spoke to them pleasantly about the winter air coming down from the north. He missed the cold nights in Minneapolis, he told them, opening the big, ornate brass-handled door and holding it for them. Faulk thanked him and handed over three dollars. He had deposited their bags earlier in the day, before the wedding, and had struck up a conversation with the doorman. They were already friends.

"You're so good with people," she said as they entered the lobby.

"Well, one learns to care for one's own kind." He grinned sardonically and rolled his eyes to the ornate ceiling with its carved baroque look of the decorations on a wedding cake. "You're good for my old ego."

"Don't say old."

"It *is* old."

"Come on, Michael—"

"Well. It's old*er.*"

She patted the side of his face. "Poor man."

They went to the roof and had a glass of sweet vermouth on ice. The waiter was a man close to Faulk's age. They talked about how beautiful the city was at night. Natasha noticed that the waiter was missing the little finger on his left hand. This upset her unreasonably, and when he brought the vermouth she drank it quickly and thought of ordering another. She watched Faulk sip his and reached over to touch his knee. The air was growing cooler. They looked out at the rooftops and saw the faint twinkle of the river through the mist settling everywhere, as if spilling out of the stars, which shone dazzlingly through broken fragments of moving clouds. He drank his vermouth. There were two other couples nearby drinking beer, and an elderly pair on the other end with a pot of coffee between them and two snifters of cognac.

"I think I'd like a cognac," Faulk said. "That looks good." He got the waiter's attention. The waiter walked over, a white towel draped on his forearm exactly as if he were someone imitating a waiter. Natasha cast her gaze into the night sky, thinking of the missing finger. Such an odd thing for her mind to fix on, and it was this kind of inward plunge toward revulsion that kept happening to her; how easy it was for things to turn nightmarish. She had the thought and then sought to reject it.

"Can we have two glasses of Hine VSOP?" Faulk said.

"Coming right up, sir." The waiter walked away.

"We'll have a real honeymoon in France, for the whole spring. If that's what you want."

"Yes." She was disinclined to think about it now but wanted to please him. And then the full import of what he had said came to her. "Isn't it what *you* want?"

He watched the old couple sip their cognac.

"Michael. Isn't it what *we* want?"

"Sure."

The waiter brought the two snifters of cognac. Faulk picked his up and swirled the liquid and breathed the sting of it into his nostrils.

"Why did you say it that way? If that's what I want?"

"I don't know. I just want you happy. If you're happy, then I'll be happy."

"I am happy."

He sipped the cognac, and she took a little of hers, watching him. He seemed to be pondering something, looking at the other people, and then out at the river, tapping his fingers lightly on the table, not even quite aware of it.

"So, then—you're happy?" She waited.

"The world doesn't feel all that safe a place to travel right now." He signaled the waiter.

"You're going to have another?"

"Just one more. I'm nervous."

"So am I."

The waiter came over, and Faulk held up two fingers. "The same."

She finished hers and handed the empty glass to the waiter.

"I'm happy, too," Faulk said. "Let's keep to that."

"Are you getting drunk? Are *we* getting drunk? On our wedding night?"

He smiled. "It's been a great night. I'm drunk on that."

The waiter came with two more cognacs and set them down.

They watched him move off.

"Because we're nervous?" she said.

"I'm getting calm." And in fact, he felt suddenly quite calm. Bizarrely, gratifyingly superior to her. The realization of this obliterated the calm. He couldn't believe the turns of his own mind.

"I'm shaking," she said. "I think it's getting too chilly to be up here."

"You look so beautiful, sitting there." There was only the surge of anxiety now.

"After this, can we go down to the room?" she asked.

"Should I carry you across the threshold?"

"That won't be necessary."

"At the house, then."

"Michael, really."

He watched her for a moment, sipping the cognac. She had been loving and charming tonight and had even seemed calm, as he was now far from it. He touched her glass with his and drank the cognac and held the complex taste of it on his palate. It occurred to him that he was drunk, and that this explained his sudden panicky mood. He had been needling her about the threshold in order to break out of the cloud of fright.

"I'm worried about my drinking," she said. "I had a vermouth and now the brandy. And I had a beer at the café. And wine with the dinner."

He gave her his gentlest smile. "If you're worried about it, I think that's a sign that you're healthy about it, too."

She shook her head. "I'm gonna finish this brandy and then stop."

They were quiet for a few moments. They had both become watchful inside, aware of the silence as being somehow like a pause in some struggle they were engaged in together. He drank the rest of his cognac, and then the rest of hers, and felt the easing inside as it warmed him.

Others came to the roof, though the night was indeed growing chilly. A waiter lit the gas lanterns above the tables. Faulk ordered one more cognac because she seemed to enjoy the heat coming from the gas lanterns. They listened to the chatter that went on around them. A man kept looking over at them, and she noticed it.

"Probably one of my old parishioners," Faulk said. "Though he doesn't look vaguely familiar."

"Can we go to our room now?" she said. "The lamp feels good, but I'm getting cold."

"Oh," he said. "Darling. We're going to be so happy." He drank the rest of the cognac and, after signaling the waiter, reached into his jacket pocket.

Tomorrow they would spend the first part of the day here, downtown. They would have coffee at the hotel and then take a walk in the old part of the city. They would eat breakfast in the penthouse restaurant at the Peabody.

"I've never been so glad," he told her. "I can't explain it, but that's the feeling." A nagging little mote in his soul rebuked him with the fact that much of what he felt now had been produced by the brandy. "I am," he said, against that knowledge. "I'm very glad."

She wanted so to believe him. And to believe it was true for her, as well. She told herself that she had done nothing wrong, and she was not going to give in to the idea that she must spend any amount of time atoning for something she did not do. As they went into the light of the hallway to the elevator, she kept her hand in his. There was nothing to fear anymore. She was safe. Back in America. Back in Memphis. Home. Nothing wrong anymore.

As they got onto the elevator, she took a deep breath and tried to settle her own nerves, feeling this happy moment and the unease of the past days like warring parts of her soul.

For him, it was exactly the same.

9

In the room, he undressed her, and she stood and let him. It was unlike the lovemaking they had done before. There was an element of the staged about it—a compensation for something on both sides, as if without being fully aware of it as such, they were performing some ritual to exorcise ghosts. She lay in his arms looking into the dark beyond his shoulder and murmured his name, but she could not quite feel it as pleasure; it was work. She moved to help him finish, feeling ashamed and wanting more but finding herself unable to shake free of the thoughts and images that troubled her.

When it was over they lay side by side in the quiet, hearing only each other's breathing and the low hum of the heater vent.

"Well, Wife?" he said.

"So lovely," she told him.

"Did you come?"

"Too much brandy."

"Cognac."

"I thought they were the same."

"Technically. There's something about how they do it in Cognac, though. Double pot stilled."

"Explain."

"Next time." He smiled.

"You don't know, do you."

They laughed together. And nothing about what they had just done in the bed mattered beyond the fact that they were together, and close.

"Shall we have a little 'next time' tonight?" he said.

"If you want to, of course. It's honeymoon night."

"But we know each other so well already."

"What a thing to say."

"Well. A little truth can't hurt. Truth's good, don't you think?"

She was conscious of another specific way he could have meant this. She got out of the bed and went into the bathroom, where she washed herself and brushed her hair. The silence in the room behind her was not calming. When she returned to the bed he was lying there with his hands clasped over his chest, regarding her.

She touched his wrist. "Kind sir."

"Better clean up myself." He rose, yawned, and stretched.

"If you want to make love again . . ." she began.

He coughed and cleared his throat, going into the bathroom. He had heard her, of course, but he felt obscurely that somehow his dignity was involved. He looked at himself in the mirror and uttered the word "Please," like a whispered prayer. He cleaned his teeth and urinated into the bowl, and then went back to stand over the bed. She lay there, eyes closed, on one side, hands together under the side of her face.

"You awake?"

She opened her eyes and looked at him. "I thought I was. But I was talking to Iris so I must've drifted."

"Want to watch television?"

Her smile was sardonic.

He turned the bathroom light off, got back into bed, and put his arms around her.

"You sleepy?"

"Yes, I guess so. Sorry. All that double-pot-stilled stuff."

"I'm not sleepy."

"We could do it again."

"You're tired."

"I said I was sleepy."

"But you *are* tired."

"Oh, baby—maybe I am, a little. Aren't you? It's been a long day."

He sighed and lay over on his back. "It has been that."

"Want to talk?"

"Sure."

They were quiet. Perhaps a full minute went by. It felt to them both like a long time.

At last, he said, "I wonder when I'm going to find out more about Jamaica."

This struck through her. "Oh, God."

"It's all right, whatever it was. You're my wife now."

"Michael."

"Well?"

"What do you think might have happened? Tell me that."

He leaned up on one elbow and was a darker shadow in that dim space, looming over her. "I don't have any idea. And I'm sorry. But when I asked that—when I asked your friend Constance about it, why you're still so much—she looked for all the world like she was hiding something."

"Constance looks that way no matter what the subject is."

"But you *are* different."

"Tell me what you think it is. Do that. What is it that you think happened in Jamaica."

He took in a breath to say the words and then held them back. A part of him quailed at the thought of having it spoken, told out, whatever it was. This was their honeymoon night. He saw himself as being unreasonable and like an adolescent boy. Then, in an instant, he felt sober and awake, and very, very old. "I guess I'm jealous," he said. "It's stupid."

"*Jealous.*"

"I said—it's stupid. I think—maybe it's—you're so much younger. It's natural for you to desire life. I know there's something about me that makes—there was something about my—way of being that made Joan want to leave me."

"Do you hear yourself?"

"I know," he told her. "Forget it."

"I've left a job and moved back here," she said. "And I'm in the stages of recovering from the fright of my life, the fear that something"—she began to cry and tried very hard not to, wanting to speak definitely and clearly and to control her voice—"that something happened to you and we—we wouldn't have this. Look, it's all new to me and I'm sorry but I can't help being nervous—and—and anyone would be and why can't everybody stop reading into everything I do or say."

"By everyone, do you mean Constance?"

"No," she said, too loud. "Iris. *You.* I don't know how to do this, Michael. I don't know how to recover from thinking my life is over and my love is dead in a collapsing building in New York. I don't know how to go on from all this we've been through."

"I'm sorry," he said into her sobs. "I'm sorry. Baby, please forget it. Forget I said anything."

It was a while before she could speak. And when she could, the force of her own will surprised her. "Can we just go on with our lives together now? I don't ever want to talk about Jamaica anymore. Please? Not ever. It was awful and it's over and you're safe and we're here."

While she spoke, crying, he put his arms around her and murmured through it, "Of course, my darling. Of course. We'll never mention it."

They lay there for a long time, both awake and both silent, while the city made its clamor out in the night—the heater had cut off, and they could hear everything—sirens and car horns and trucks going by and steadily, like a reminder of where they were, the far-off strains of music from Beale Street.

Mr. and Mrs. Faulk

I

ARTICLE 1. *Whether, putting aside her simple kindness, any evidence exists of my wife's former passion for me?*

We proceed thus to the First Article: It seems that, putting aside her simple kindness, we have no evidence of my wife's former passion for me.

> *Objection 1.*
> It is true that there have been stresses beyond the norm, therefore something external to her is affecting her behavior and her moods. The whole country is in panic now about the anthrax attacks. And of course the war is under way in Afghanistan.

> *Objection 2.*
> It is true that people in courtship are different than they are in marriage, and this is Marriage. My wife is loving and considerate and seems happy, and she spends most mornings doing physical therapy with her grandmother, and they laugh together and tell each other stories and my wife looks like any other young woman glad of her circumstances, and glad to see me. But there are panic attacks in the night and when we are intimate I can feel her unhappiness in it and have tried talking to her gently about it and striven to be more what she needs, being as circumspect as possible and then by turns seeking to be more passionate, as passionate as we were. Yet something is in the way, something is displacing us, something is on her mind. She is not here, and it is hard not to fear that someone else may be in her deepest thoughts.

On the contrary, she has always shown in her relations with everyone a direct and honest bearing and a truthful nature. Her every gesture shows forth a strong-minded and gentle spirit, and she seems as troubled about our secret problem as I am. She still seems as loving to me as she always was and *in other things* pays generously careful attention to me. But there is an undeniable sense that something happened that she is hiding from me, and it seems that this which she feels she must hide can only have to do with the something in Jamaica, with the *someone* in Jamaica, that her friends evidently know about as women sometimes are supposed to know about these matters among themselves.

I answer that, there seems no evidence of involvement with anyone else, and I further admit that I have been watching her, and attending very carefully to her movements and her communications with others. Though there have been several calls from her friend Constance, and she has been going on afternoon walks with her friend Marsha. She seems vaguely unhappy to hear from Constance. Several times the calls have further upset her, though from what I can hear they are only talking about Constance's decision to sell the house she spent so much of herself on and move permanently to New York; but there has seemed more distance between us after these conversations.

Reply Obj. 1.
Although there have been stresses in the daily round of news and in the country as a whole, people seem to be making their way along in their lives without noticeable effects on mood or bearing.

Reply Obj. 2.
Intimacy, of course, involves trust. And the trouble now is there seems an undeniable lessening of trust, on both sides. It would seem that, even if what happened in Jamaica was a momentary fling with an old flame—this person who by her own account she was willing to lie and cheat for and her affair with him was less than a year old when I first met her—even if this was the thing hidden, I cannot but conclude that whatever has existed between us is now made false, and it is the falseness of it that is causing all the quiet suffering.

ARTICLE 2. *Whether it is feasible to believe that love can exist in an atmosphere of suspicion and the sense of having been betrayed?*

We proceed thus to the Second Article: It seems that it is not feasible to believe that love can exist in an atmosphere of suspicion and betrayal. For every instance of such distrust and anxiety about faithfulness requires that the two people believe each other and believe *in* each other and believe that what they feel for each other is grounded in truth.

Objection 1.

Suspicion does not mean or imply that grounds for it are real. It is possible to imagine things in a state of anxiety especially if the person afflicted with the suspicion is already struggling to overcome the effects of a general calamity.

Objection 2.

There can be no denial that love exists because there is such pain at the arrival of all suspicious thoughts, and there is a concerted effort to put suspicions down. There is also much effort on her part to be what she believes I need her to be and to put down all those things that trouble her about us.

On the contrary, suspicion may arise without there being a tendency toward suspicion and that has not been my nature, and I would never have felt the suspicion if there were not these signs of an unforgettable event in Jamaica having to do with my wife's feelings toward me. And I fear an erosion in my love for her out of these growing suspicions. I want to know what she and Marsha Trunan talk about, and why it is that Marsha seldom comes here when I am home, and I do not really feel included in this friendship. I want to know why she never talks to Constance on the telephone with me near, as if she is afraid something will be said, some reference to something will slip out.

I answer that, love can only exist as itself in an atmosphere of mutual trust and acceptance, and that if one truly loved one's partner, one would confide in him, not turn from him, trying to hide the fact by pretending nothing is wrong.

Reply Obj. 1.

Because I am not normally of a suspicious nature—and Joan was in fact thinking of leaving me long before I was aware of it—and am in fact rather slow to judge anyone's actions, it cannot be said that my suspicions are produced by something other than the circumstances in which we find ourselves.

Reply Obj. 2

There must be some demarcation between love as *possession* and love as it is or was between us at the start. It was beautiful and we shone with it and people saw it and felt happy when they saw us because we were so happy. They were made happier or for a time they forgot their unhappiness or they turned away in envy because they saw how happy we were. I believe that. We glowed with it. We were so utterly glad of each other.

2

Nights while she slept, and he couldn't, he sat up reading or writing in a spiral notebook that he kept locked in his desk drawer. It was for the mechanical scribbling of it and the absurdly mannered and rational sound of it that he kept on. His anxiety lessened slightly with the concentration it took to keep to the specific form of inquiry: that of Aquinas in *The Summa Theologica*. It was, then, a kind of ironic glaring at the anxiety itself, an attempt to reason it through. And the reading he did, always in Aquinas—those logical calm sentences coming from apparently calm faith—also helped to ground him, as it had when he was a boy, or he wanted to believe it did that. Yet, after putting it all away and going in to lie quietly at her side, keeping still, being considerate and thinking of himself as lovingly waiting for her to come to him, and finally drifting off to sleep at last, he would wake in the predawn hours to find that the anxiety was still there. Now he was thinking not only about the one other but about *all* the others: she had lived a life before he met her, and while he understood fully that it was no business of his to question any of it, something Marsha Trunan said one night over a dinner they were having with Iris—something about too many bad dates during her absence from the lives of friends that last winter in D.C.—upset him in a way he could not dismiss. It had started with talk about Senator Norland suffering a mild stroke and being hospitalized and how he worked too hard all the time and was so preoccupied that he hadn't even noticed the descent of one of his chief employees into desolation and despair. Faulk marked the perturbed look on his wife's face as her friend went on about it, and an image raked through him of her in the arms of other men. He was aware that this, too, was none of his business, was in fact stupidly possessive and selfish—even brutish. Yet he felt the strangeness, the otherness, of her, someone he did not really know at all, and the sensation followed him through the hours of the day and into

the nights. Of course her past had been altered by present circumstance. It meant nothing except as it related to the mystery about
Jamaica: if that was as he now suspected it was, then everything
else took on significance, and the irrationality of the thing had the
force of reason.

He could not pray. He could not think of anything else at all.
There were times when the shadow of something beyond all this,
some nameless immensity, seemed to be gathering.

He had come to see that he was the one between them who was
most changed, now, watching her and listening when she was on
the phone and looking carefully at her e-mails and whatever was
sent to her, and sifting also through the boxes that she had packed
from her time in Washington. He found nothing but the photograph taken in Chicago. There were many other photographs, but
they were all of her with Iris or with friends or people she had
known in France and in Washington—people around the senator
and the senator himself. In one little box were photographs of her
when she was small, elementary school poses, class pictures, a little
girl with a wide, lovely smile and a sadness in her eyes.

He put all this away with the care of an archeologist handling
ancient artifacts, and felt deceitful for all his suspicions. Even so,
he could not shake them.

Oh, God, help me.

She did some reading. She found that more than seven out of ten
victims of the crime never report it. She looked it up and then went
to other sources and looked it up again. The lowest estimate was
six out of ten.

It filled her with resolve at the same time that it horrified her.

In the nights, this was the thing that woke her, this knowledge.
Others managed to go on, others made their way, and she would
lie awake hearing him in the next room or breathing in the bed at
her side and think that she could make it. She could live past it and
be through with it at last.

It was the work, the painting, that she could use to learn how to
be herself again. Long ago she had written in her notebook some-

thing of Wyeth's that she had admired without realizing its true force: *I think one's art goes as far and as deep as one's love goes. I see no reason for painting but that. If I have anything to offer, it is my emotional contact with the place where I live and the people I do.*

But all the emotional contacts seemed so attenuated and frail now.

The country was at war in Afghanistan, and the master terrorist had declared a jihad on the United States. The anthrax horror was playing out on TV and in the papers. There were claims that the killer powder—which one reporter said looked like Purina Dog Chow—was "weapons grade," and a man in Florida said this was the same makeup of the biological agents the Iraqi dictator had used on his own people. Someone else said there was evidence that smallpox was mixed in with the powder.

"The mortality rate of smallpox before the vaccine," Faulk said to Iris one evening over dinner, "was something like fifty percent. You know what it was for the Spanish flu?"

"Eighty?" Iris said.

"Two."

"What?"

"Two percent. And that translated into thirty million deaths worldwide."

"God," Natasha said, low, "can't we talk about something else?"

"People will look back years from now," said her husband, "and wonder how we went through the days."

There was a sense of being threatened that was always there, like the dark outside windows in a well-lit house. Even when you didn't talk about it, the effects of it made themselves felt. The cleanup in New York and at the Pentagon continued, and each night there were more stories about all of it.

They went together and bought a small used car for Natasha, and he rode with her as she drove over to Iris's to show it off. Iris was irritable with them and said they shouldn't have spent the money, they could have taken *her* car, since she seldom used it anymore, and it was a good car, with few miles on it, only five years old. Faulk watched his wife handle the old woman's temper. She kissed Iris on the cheek and said, "You need your wheels, lady, and you know it. And we have the money." She looked at Faulk. "Don't we, honey?"

"We do," he said, delighted at the smile on her face.

It was no surprise to him that she was most comfortable around Iris. They spent a lot of time over at the old woman's house, and Iris liked the company.

At times, because they were mutually horror-struck at the history they were living through, he could believe they were coming out of their own personal trouble. Their little daily rituals were a hedge against the grief that was everywhere, and the two of them became adept at a sort of careful thoughtfulness with each other.

Each morning when they arose—sometimes separately, sometimes without much sleep—the first few seconds they were together felt easy enough, coming from the fog of dreaming and drifting, and they prepared for the day as if nothing were wrong. He would make her breakfast, and they would eat, or try to, talking aimlessly about what was in the papers. He went to work like anyone else, leaving her in her little space off the dining room, laying out her own work for the day, tubes and brushes and the small squares of hot-pressed paper.

Often, though, they were coming from hours of sleeplessness or, worse, nightmares. She kept having the nightmares. He worked at being patient and gentle. And when she would drift off, and sleep would not come for him, he would go into the little room off the master bedroom where his desk was, and the spiral notebooks, the two volumes of *The Summa Theologica*.

Sometimes he was in that cluttered, narrow room when the sun came up.

In the darkness, she would lie quiet, having awakened from the bad dreams, aware of him in the other room, and she felt small and spoiled and trifling, angry with herself for everything, even unimportant matters: her unspoken annoyance with him for minor habitual things she had never thought of before living with someone—the fact that he was squeamish about roasting a whole chicken because it made him too aware of the thing as a carcass;

his tendency to leave his clothes hanging on doorknobs or draped over chairs; his late hours, sitting up reading or writing, and his refusal to allow her into that world with him (they did not talk anymore about what he was reading or what he was writing; if she broached it as a subject, he changed the subject). But these were negligible problems, requiring adjustments that would have been necessary anyway. Withal, there were the other matters, the mud on the floor, as Iris would put it: the undeniable and increasing unease in lovemaking; the instances of recurring panic—the latest when she remembered writing Iris's address in the sand and felt it as a certainty that Constance had indeed seen Nicholas Duego at the airport. These nights, in the dark, alone in the bed, she experienced the worry about that, and then in the wooziness of half sleep actually hoped it *had* been Duego and that he was spying on her so he could see that she was not telling anyone, he would know that his secret was safe with her, and he did not have to do anything else.

And then she would wake and gasp, berating herself silently for the ways in which the fierceness of the anxiety kept her from any kind of thought about the general suffering in its terrible scale coming from the devastations of September, the horrors of the new war. She told herself that she had no right to complain about anything. She was safe. *They* were safe. From his little study there sometimes came the sound of the music he loved, Mozart's Clarinet Quintet, and the concerto, too, played softly so as not to wake her—and if she had been asleep, it would not have awakened her.

Occasionally in their mornings he would speak to her about what was in the paper, the articles about the war and about the continuing work in the rubble of the Trade Center and in Washington, the details of the passengers of Flight 93. It was all just words to her, all a matter of fighting to maintain the half smile or the look of concern, feeling the fear rise, the helpless stirring of rage at herself for it, watching him struggle with his own intuition and anxiety about what was between them.

Neither of them could find the way to break through.

One morning in the middle of November, after spending long, mutually sleepless hours apart, they sat across from each other in the kitchen, with the paper on the table between them. Each was holding a section of it open, as if neither of them wanted to look at the other, though their exchanges that morning had been quite unruffled and warm. Before he was dressed he had sat on the edge of the bed and called Iris to ask if she wanted to come over. Iris had said she was planning to sleep some more. He apologized, put the receiver down, and showered and dressed and then walked into the kitchen to make the omelets for them. But neither of them had eaten much. Minutes went by with the only sound being the shuffling of the pages and the coffee cups being set down on the table.

"This is terrible," he said suddenly.

She looked up, thinking it was something in what he was reading.

"Isn't it," he said.

"Oh, Michael," she said. "Let's not look at it."

"I don't know how much longer I can stand it."

"Honey. We—we *all* have to stand it, somehow, don't we?"

His voice rose: "I'm not *talking* about the war."

She sought to control the crying that welled up. "Please," she murmured. "Don't shout at me."

He stood and moved to the door and paused, then sighed. "I'll see you later."

"I've got a doctor's appointment this morning," she managed.

He opened the door, hesitated, but did not look back. "You all right?"

"Routine."

Now he turned. "Nothing specific?"

"It's routine, honey." She smiled and shook the strands of dark hair from her brow.

He looked at her hands where she held her part of the paper. She was trying so hard to be what he needed. "Sure you're all right?"

"Routine." She kept the smile, but a tear trailed down one cheek.

He came quickly back to the table and kissed her hair, feeling like a bully.

"I'm just tired," she got out.

"See you," he said, and her smile changed slightly, her lips trembling a little. He kissed her there and then hugged her. She stood into it, and they remained that way, arms around each other, for a long moment.

"What should I make for dinner?" she asked, wiping her eyes with the heel of her palm.

"Can't think about it now."

"No, I know. Me, too."

"Not much appetite."

"No."

"Well, spoil yourself today."

She sobbed softly, and he held her again, rocking slightly, the two of them standing by the door. "I love you," she got out. "So much."

"Honey, why are you crying? What is this with us?"

"I'm fine," she said. "Really. We're—we're fine. We'll be fine."

They were quiet again, rocking slowly in the embrace.

Finally he said, "Gotta go."

They moved apart, and he reached over and brushed the hair from her brow, set it along the side of her face. "There," he said. He thought he had never seen anyone so darkly beautiful.

"I'll call you," she murmured.

He stepped out on the small stoop and closed the screen door. She stood in the granular frame of it with her hands at her sides. "Leave the mess," he said. "I'll get it when I come home from work."

"It's nothing," she told him.

It occurred to him that they probably looked like newlyweds in the first flow of life. He thought his heart might give out.

At the job, he saw people in trouble, mostly men, all of them looking for work. And there was so little to be had. The largest local business, FedEx, had been badly hurt by the grounding of all the airplanes just after the attacks, and other companies were either laying off workers or simply unable to hire anyone new. Faulk kept trying to get interviews for people and to find some strategy for them to pursue other than simply collecting unemployment. It made him feel useful while it frustrated and saddened him for how little he could accomplish under the circumstances.

This morning, a man entered and, sitting in the chair beside the desk, looked hard at him. He was gaunt, dark, with a deeply lined face. There were pockets of darker skin under his eyes. "I know you."

"You weren't sent in here?" Pete asked from his desk.

The man turned to him. "Oh." He handed over the form.

"You recognize the padre?"

"Yeah."

"Weird to see him here, right?"

"What kind of work are you looking for?" Faulk kept his gaze on the form.

"Anything. Handyman. Anything. Yeah. Padre. I know you."

The form showed that the name was Samuel Witherspoon and that he had eighteen years of employment with the airlines, three different carriers, the last of which was Delta. And that he had spent the last two years in prison for assault and battery with intent to kill.

"The airlines," Faulk said.

"I was a flight attendant," said Witherspoon. "Haven't ever done much of anything else."

"We'll find you something," Faulk told him.

"Grace Episcopal. Yeah. Father—Father Faulk."

"He's quit that," Pete said.

Witherspoon simply turned to look at him.

"Walked away from it. Matter of principle," Pete said.

"No," said Faulk.

"You know what happened to me, Father?"

"I'm not Father Faulk anymore. It's just *Mr.* Faulk."

"Every day my wife came home late."

Faulk nodded, looking through the list of job inquiries for general repair work, house painting, and carpentry.

Witherspoon went on, "I got nobody to talk to. Christ."

"There's a couple of things here," Faulk said. "Look, I don't do that anymore."

"But I feel"—the other put one hand on the desk—"I can talk to you, you know?"

"I'm sorry, but this is neither the time nor the place."

"I saw you all those Sundays," said Witherspoon. "It hit me the second I looked at you sitting there. You were the one every Sunday when I was a good citizen." He let go a small, rueful laugh.

Faulk nodded slightly and said nothing.

"Why'd you leave, anyway?"

"Mr. Witherspoon. You're here to find work, and I'm here to see if I can help you do that."

Witherspoon wasn't listening. "She went with somebody else. The wife. We hadn't been married two years."

Faulk saw the lines in the other's forehead and at the corners of his eyes. Witherspoon glanced over at Pete as if his presence was somehow threatening.

Pete sensed this. He looked down at the page he was writing on and concentrated.

Witherspoon went on. "Father, I can't help it. I just found out last night she went ahead and married the son of a bitch."

"I'm sorry," Faulk said, thinking, *Please.*

"Excuse the language." Witherspoon sighed and sat back, putting his legs out, a hand on either thigh. It was a gesture not of trying to get more comfortable in the chair but of exhaustion. His head came against the chair back. "She came to see me in prison. Now why would she do that? I beat the son of a—I went after the—I hit him with a cane, you know, repeatedly—I thumped him with it and broke his skull. Nearly killed him. *Wanted* to kill him. Coming around like we're friends and sleeping with my wife. And I get sent up because he needs surgery on his head, and she comes to visit me. Comes to visit me, Father."

Faulk felt himself taking on the habitual mind-set of the priest, wanting to offer counsel, solace, some remedy out of the grandeur of the church he used to represent, though this urge to use his former state was also, he knew, an element of the wish to fend off the other man, keep an official's distance. "Have you talked with anyone else about it?"

"The whole time I'm there she keeps coming to see me, the

wife suffering through her husband's jail term, telling me how sorry she is, and she's living with him. The whole time. She was with him the whole goddamn time. She felt *guilty* about the trouble I got in. Christ. I *gotta* find something to do for work."

Faulk turned to the screen and cursored down to the list of contacts for handyman kinds of work: electricians, carpenters, landscapers. They were mostly contractors, seeking to hire people specializing in specific tasks. "Can you do electrical work?" He heard the quaking of his own voice. He cleared his throat and repeated the question.

"I remember looking forward to what you had to say on Sundays. Sorry. It was just a shock to see you here. Sorry. It's nothing you need to worry about anymore, is it, and maybe it never was."

"You have to concentrate on this," Faulk said, seeing his own distressing images and trying to clear his mind. It came to him that it was going to be impossible for things to keep going on as they were. He would shake her out of her denials, would get it out of her some way, the real truth. *The real truth.* He put his hands to his face for a moment, his elbows resting on the desk. His own thoughts appalled him.

"I don't know how to do electrical," Witherspoon said.

Faulk stared at the screen. "I've got someone here who needs a carpenter. Do you have any formal training in that?"

"No."

"Well, I can send you over there to talk to the guy." He wrote the address and number down and handed the paper across the desk.

"Thanks, Father," said the other, folding the paper. He shoved it into his pocket and went out the door into the bright sunlight.

Faulk turned to the computer, trying again, without success, to repress his own apprehension and doubt, seeing the mental image of Natasha with someone else, on the beach in Jamaica. He sought to shut it down, break it up into the reasons to deny it, to bring forth out of himself the belief that nothing had happened. He could not concentrate. And again he thought of forming the words simply to ask her outright: *What did you do in Jamaica that you can't tell me?*

Except that he *had* asked her about it in direct and indirect ways, and in the same ways she had steadily denied everything while pleading with him not to bring it up, not to mention Jamaica at all.

There was already someone else waiting to see him.

3

After he was gone, she worked for a time. She had decided not to use the apartment in Midtown for at least the first few weeks, wanting to be in the Swan Ridge house where, as she expressed it to him, they were home. She spent an hour trying to make progress on the picture of the sad-eyed woman—the faded color of it seemed just beyond her reach, though she had come close several times. And she had not even begun to get down to the shades of feeling in the eyes. It was going to be a long struggle, but she had been thinking about it with a kind of hunger. The necessary concentration was good; it kept back fretful turns of mind. Today she felt the practical pressure of what else there was to do.

She washed the breakfast dishes and finally went into the bedroom and lay down. For the past week, she had experienced the signs of her period starting. She was late, but she had never been regular. There had been two episodes in her twenties where she worried about being pregnant. Sometimes she couldn't bring herself to the point of concern. At that age, trouble was what happened to other people. And she was irregular. Nothing had ever happened. Lately, she had been getting up to pee in the nights, and while she knew what that meant, she still thought at first that it was simply because she was awake. But the tiredness had grown worse, and the tenderness of her breasts, more so than the usual feeling prior to a period. She did not want to think about any of it, and it was like a trap. She had been through that heavy period the last time, and so if this was a baby, it was Faulk's baby, and Faulk wanted children. *She* wanted children. A family. And having a child could be the beginning of really finding the way to get past everything and be new again.

New again.

The receiver for the phone was on his side of the bed where he had left it. With a sudden strong impulse she took it and touched zero and waited for the operator. She was going to do this. During the few minutes it took to get the number, she held the receiver between her shoulder and collarbone and put on a pair of jeans and a white blouse. Then she sat on the bed and called the number. The Orlando Police Department. Her heart was pounding in her ears. She sat down and leaned over, eyes closed. The ringing went on, and she waited, feeling sick. A recorded voice answered and recited options. Before the menu was finished, she disconnected and lay back down.

Then, lying there, she brought the receiver up and punched in the number again. She could ask somebody how to proceed; she could find out some things.

When the menu started again, she touched the zero, and a female voice came on. "I want to report a rape," Natasha heard herself say.

"Are you safe now? Can you say where you are?"

"It was—it was back in September. September eleventh."

There was a pause.

"Hello?"

"Just a minute." There was a slight static pulse and then silence. And then another female voice. "This is Officer Lorraine Brown. Who'm I talking to?"

"I just need some answers," Natasha said. "I'm—this is not a crank call—"

"Do you need someone to come assist you. You sound distraught. Are you all right?"

"I'm—it was in September."

"Yes, I was told—but you sound distraught."

"No."

"Okay, go ahead."

"I was raped. In Jamaica. On September eleventh. The night of September eleventh."

"Your name, honey?"

"Iris," Natasha told her.

"Okay, Iris. Tell me about it."

"The man—his name is Nicholas Duego—lives in Orlando." She spelled the name. "He's Cuban American."

"That's me, too, honey. I'm Cuban American. My husband's name is Brown. There are some things I've got to ask you. Are you okay with that?"

"Yes."

"Would you rather come in and talk to me?"

"I'm not in Orlando."

"Okay. These questions are gonna feel intrusive. But I have to ask them. Okay?"

"Yes," Natasha said. "Yes, okay."

"Are you in any pain right now?"

"It was two months ago."

"Okay. Not in any pain."

She waited.

"And you're not in any danger."

"No." She lost her voice and had to repeat the word. "No."

"Well, you ready, then?"

Natasha sat up on the side of the bed and put her elbows on her knees. "Go ahead."

Officer Lorraine's questions were what she said they would be: *Did you know the attacker? How well did you know him? How much time did you spend with him? Did you do anything that might've enticed him?*

She kept using the word *attacker* even after Natasha had said the name again. And the questions seemed to lead into a kind of moral test: *Were you drinking? Were you drinking with the attacker? How much did you drink? Were there any drugs involved? Did you have drugs with the attacker? How much? Did you allow him any kind of sexual advance before the incident? Did he threaten you? Did he use a weapon?*

It went on.

"These questions," Natasha said. "God! He almost—almost killed me."

"I'm asking you these questions," Officer Lorraine said carefully, patiently, "because a defense lawyer will ask them—if we can ever get the attacker to trial. And, Iris, I have to tell you the chances are pretty slim given the lapse in time, and the facts as they are. I believe you when you say nothing you did constitutes permission for the attacker to do what *he* did, but it will be a problem when it comes to prosecuting him. Honey, it just will. This is where we live. Now, I can put the name on file and watch for him in other attacks for a time, but I've gotta tell you that a lot of these cases even when we can bring the attacker in result in acquittal, especially lacking enough forensic evidence."

"I'm sorry," Natasha said.

"No," said Officer Lorraine. "You did the right thing. We're aware of it, and we have the name. And we *will* pursue it as far as we can if you want to press charges. But lacking witnesses there's not much we can do short of interviewing him and explaining his rights to him. And if you decide to press charges, then you'll have to come down here and confront him. So—I'm sorry, but I've got to tell you the chance of a conviction, even if you'd reported it that night, would anyway be in serious doubt. Drugs and alcohol. You see what I'm getting at, don't you? And the defense lawyer will want to know about your past, too—the past year or two anyway. I'm so sorry about it, but that's just how it is."

"You'll—you'll watch for him?"

"The type tends to repeat the behavior, yes. And I've made a note of it. If you wait I can put it in right now and see if anything comes up for him."

"Yes," Natasha said, sniffling. "Please." She waited, sitting on the bed and looking out into the living room and at the front door.

Officer Lorraine came back on the line, and sighed. "I'm sorry, Iris, but there's no record of anything. Not even a traffic violation. So we either have to wait, or you can decide to press charges."

"But—you're saying—it wouldn't do any good to press charges."

"Well, maybe it'd shake up his world—who knows. But then you'll have to shake up your own world pretty good, too. And as for getting any kind of justice, I'm afraid the chances of that now are between slim and none. I mean, he could have a change of heart and make a confession, but I'd bet you the farm and the land, too, that that won't happen. Like I said, under the circumstances the case would've been pretty weak even the day it happened. I wish I didn't have to tell you all this."

"Thank you," Natasha said. "You've been very kind."

"I'm only giving you what the lawyers will think and do. You want to press charges?"

"I'll decide and call you back."

"I guess it's not going to be helped or hurt by waiting a little longer. But let us know."

She set the receiver in its cradle on the nightstand. She felt strangely vacant, exhausted, even apathetic. Nothing to be done. The idea of trying to paint anymore seemed dreary and negligible, an indulgence. Something from another life, far gone. She went into the little room and looked at what she had, then took it down and put it in the stack of other attempts. Then she went back into the bedroom and lay down again.

The doctor's appointment was for eleven-thirty, but she had slept very little in the night, and so she put her arms around herself and looked at the room.

Once again she had to fight off the images: Nicholas Duego, untouchable by the authorities, arriving at the Memphis airport, renting a car, and driving into Midtown, taking a cheap motel room. Duego looking up the address she had written in the sand on the beach and finding his way there to watch her come and go, hunting her, planning something. Possessing the indemnity provided by her history and by the circumstances. But he would see that she was telling no one. Except that there was his craziness and his need to explain, his wanting her to say that what had happened was not what it was. *I do not take what has not been given.* His hands shoving the sand in her mouth, packing it there, trying to fill her throat.

Every passing car was peril.

She got up, went into the bathroom, brushed her hair, and said into the mirror, "I will *not* be a victim. I *am not* a victim. I am *not.* I'm *not.*"

Then she was sitting on the sofa in the small living room, crying softly and waiting for the time to pass. She did not even remember how she got there.

When the shadow appeared in the window of the front door she took in a breath and stiffened. The knock brought a little yelp out of the back of her throat. She rose and moved with stealth to the window in the small dining room and peered out.

Marsha Trunan.

She went to the front door and opened it.

"We were supposed to go for a walk," Marsha said. "Remember?"

It was just past nine o'clock.

"I didn't remember," Natasha said to her. "Give me a minute."

The other woman entered and sat at the table, refusing the offer of coffee but taking a clementine from the bowl there and peeling it and eating it. Natasha put her tennis shoes on, and a light sweatshirt.

"Ready?" Marsha said, chewing. Then: "You really don't remember telling me to come by at nine today?"

"I remember now," Natasha told her.

They walked up the leaf-strewn sidewalk. Neither of them spoke for a few paces. There was a cool breeze blowing intermittently, but the air was warm, still summery.

"I think I might be pregnant," Natasha said.

The other looked at her and kept walking with arms folded. "And?"

She shrugged and repeated, without inflection, "I might be pregnant."

"You don't sound very happy about it."

"I think I'm happy."

"You *think* you're happy."

"Well, it's—scary. A little scary."

"You always said you wanted a baby. You've been saying that for a while."

"I know. I do."

"Well?"

"I don't know for sure what *he* wants. I mean—he's about to be fifty."

"You don't *know* how he'll feel about it?"

"Not for sure—no."

"You're *married*. What do you talk about, anyway, that you can't be sure what he'll think about the fact that you're pregnant?"

"He's said he wants a family."

"Well, then."

"But that's talk."

"Well, hey—I mean—Jesus, if you can't trust that kind of talk—I'm sorry—but what the hell."

"Stop it, Marsha."

They went on a little without saying anything.

When Marsha spoke now, it was in a quiet, almost chastened tone. "I just mean I bet he'll be fine with it."

A car went by with the radio loud, a voice speaking in Spanish. Natasha shrank back a little, watching it go by. A woman sat behind the wheel.

"You seem a bit jumpy," Marsha said. "Part of being in your condition?"

"I guess."

Presently, she said, "So how far along are you?"

"I don't know exactly. They'll tell me. Eight weeks?"

"Must've happened wedding night, huh?"

Natasha looked at her. "Whatever. Whenever."

"If there was something really wrong between you guys, you'd tell me, right?"

She stopped, and Marsha stopped, too. They were standing on the corner where a light flashed red numbers, the seconds they had to cross. She thought of a countdown toward some disaster. She faced her friend. They were two women, paused at a crossing. Natasha had the thought that there had always been something absent in the other. "I don't understand," she said.

"You're happy with him."

"*Yes*, I'm happy with him. What a question, Marsha, for God's sake."

"Well, I mean he *is* older than you are. I don't want to pry. But something looks not right. I'm sorry. You'd tell me, wouldn't you?"

Natasha crossed the street. Her pace was that of someone walking alone. She turned and headed down to the next block, so they could come back to the house. Her friend walked along at her side, without saying more.

"I have a doctor's appointment," Natasha told her.

"Look, I'm sorry. I didn't mean to upset you."

She stopped. "How about you, Marsha. How is *your* love life?" Marsha had been seeing a pharmacy student at the university, someone she'd spoken about in rather cold terms as being good looking but not very interesting.

"Oh, let me tell you," she said, looking down. Natasha saw something uncertain in her eyes. "That's over. I sent him packing. I'm free. And loving it."

Natasha touched her shoulder. "You said he was a bit boring."

"Deadly. But he *was* pretty. I guess he thought that was all he needed. You should've seen the look on his face when I told him I didn't want to see him anymore. Like a kid being told there's no Santa Claus and for a few seconds refusing to accept the knowledge. I swear his lower lip stuck out. It about broke my heart. I almost told him I was kidding."

"Poor guy."

"Look, I really didn't mean to upset you."

They walked on. "It's okay. Really."

"Just trying to help. I mean I know depression when I see it."

"And you think you see it."

Marsha frowned. "Well, yes."

"I'm not depressed."

"Constance told me what she saw that night in Jamaica."

They had reached Iris's street. Natasha halted again and looked at her. "I should've known."

"I told her it doesn't have to mean anything."

"When did she tell you?"

"That night before the wedding."

"Oh, God. My *friend* Constance."

"She's just worried about you."

"Yes, the same way she was worried when she told you about Mackenzie and me."

"She really didn't know what to do. She told me about—it was about messing things up that day. How she wanted to let you know she believed you about it, and she got it all wrong. She was worried."

"And she told you about it."

"Please don't be angry with her, Natasha. She was really worried, and it was about what she might have done to hurt you. Really. And then Michael seemed to know something."

"Michael doesn't know anything unless she told him something. And there's nothing *to* know. It was a kiss. One fucking kiss. And I was drunk and I thought Michael was dead and he was needy and crying and I gave him a goddamn kiss."

"*Okay*," Marsha said. "*Okay*."

They went on to the end of the street, past Iris's, and turned up Swan Ridge. Neither of them spoke as they approached the house.

"Don't be mad at me, too," Marsha said. "I don't have any interest in this except worrying about you, like Constance. And Michael. All of us. Everyone who loves you."

At the entrance to the house, Natasha faced her. "Don't worry about me."

The other waited.

"Don't worry, okay? I can handle myself. *Iris* doesn't worry about me the way you and Constance have. So stop it."

"How do you stop that? How do you stop worrying about someone you love who's in trouble?"

"But we're *all* in trouble," Natasha said. "Aren't we."

"You know how I mean that," said Marsha, plainly annoyed now.

"I love my husband," Natasha told her, and as she said the words, the truth in them startled her. "I love my husband," she repeated. "And we are still in shock from what happened—like *everyone* else in this country. And Constance can take her imaginings and go straight to hell with them."

"Okay, okay. I'm sorry. *Please*."

"Now I'm going in and have a cup of green tea. You're welcome to join me if you promise to stay off the subject of my mental state and my marriage."

"I have to go," Marsha said in a small voice. She reached for a hug, and Natasha accepted it, without speaking.

4

She drove to Germantown, to the doctor's office, which was in a tall white building on Poplar Avenue. At the first-floor elevator she waited with a heavy, elderly black woman in a blue scarf, tank top, and jeans. There were darker places on the woman's large dark arms. The elevator doors opened, and she stepped in with a lumbering slowness and turned. "Where you goin', young lady?"

"Second floor," Natasha said.

The old woman pushed the button. "Baby doctor."

"Yes."

"I know her. Good doctor."

Natasha heard herself say, "This might be my first."

The door opened. "Yeah, I remember that. Coulda been earlier this mawnin', way it feels. Time goes so fas'."

"Take care," Natasha told her.

"It goes fas', honey. Make sure you 'preciate it."

The doors closed. She made her way into the waiting area of the doctor's office feeling as though the world had sent her this message through the kindly old woman. There *were* messages from the world around you if you paid attention. She signed the sheet at the window and thought about learning to appreciate things more.

The doctor was a short, blocky, red-haired woman with straight shoulders and an erect carriage as if she were trying to look taller than she was. Her name was Bass. She came in with the nurse, who looked no older than a high school student and had blond bangs that came down to her eyebrows.

During the exam, Dr. Bass spoke to the nurse, who took notes. Then she went out, and the nurse drew blood. And after a short wait, Natasha was led into the small office off the corridor. "Well, we'll know for sure in a few days, but from our little urine sample and the feel of your uterus, you're expecting."

Natasha put her hands to her mouth for a second and had to fight for breath a little.

"This surprises you?"

"Not really, no."

"You're a little pale."

"I'm all right."

"We'll set you up with some vitamins and prenatal instructions."

"Doctor—is it possible to have a . . . is it possible to be impregnated and have a period just after?"

"Well, some women have bleeding episodes."

"Like a heavy period?"

"Well, yes, actually. I've known it to happen that a woman has what she believes is a period or even a miscarriage. Enough blood to think that. And then three weeks later shows up still pregnant, with a healthy and viable fetus. Why?"

Natasha couldn't speak for a moment.

"Have you had a bleeding episode? Did you think you had your period?"

She shook her head. "But it's not common. You haven't seen that sort of thing a lot—it's rare?"

"I'd say it's quite rare. What're we talking about, honey?"

"Is there a test that can tell when conception took place?"

"Well, to calculate your due date, we count forward forty weeks from the first day of your last period. And we can make a pretty good guess at it from the amount of HGC in your blood, but that can vary from woman to woman, and so none of it's absolutely certain. It's all estimation mostly until we get a look at a sonogram—and even then we're really only guessing. Educated guesses, you know."

Natasha took a long breath, looking down at her own hands. "Why?"

"When is the latest time for aborting a pregnancy?"

"Excuse me?"

She lifted her shoulders. "Just—look. I want to know."

"You're married, right?"

"Yes."

"But you don't—you don't want to have this baby?"

"I want to want it." The tears came.

"That's a normal kind of feeling, honey. It is a big thing, and a little scary for some."

Natasha heard her own low sigh.

"How does your husband feel about it?"

"We both—we want children."

"So—"

"I don't know if I'm ready." She sobbed and coughed.

"A lot of us feel that, the first time."

"I don't know," she said, sniffling. "I don't know."

The other stood closer and put a hand on her shoulder. "Honey, do you want to talk?"

Natasha put her hands to her face, covering her eyes, and looked into the dark her palms made. She couldn't speak. She heard the door open and shut. The nurse had gone, and she and the doctor were alone.

"Tell me," the doctor said, handing her some tissues.

"I'm sorry," she burst forth. "I'm so sorry. I'm okay. Really."

There was a long space while the doctor waited for her to gain control of herself. Then: "This is a happy thing, sweetie. And it's quite normal to feel scared about it. But it's gonna be perfectly all right. You have to trust it."

Natasha nodded, wiping her eyes and her nose. "Really. I know."

"There's nothing wrong with being worried."

"Just—really scared."

"It's all going to work as it should. You're very healthy. Nurse'll give you a bottle of prenatal vitamins and a pamphlet. There's a good book called *What to Expect When You're Expecting*. And there're others. We'll call you with the results of the blood test, but I'm pretty sure. You come see me again in two weeks, okay?"

"Yes."

"And congratulations. Really."

"Thanks. Thank you. I'm sorry."

"Nothing to apologize for. Now you take it easy."

She was in a kind of daze walking out to the counter and taking the card with the date for her next appointment.

Out in the warm sunlight, she walked to her car and got into the very hot interior and felt sick. She opened the door and put her legs out and sat there for a few minutes, breathing deeply and holding her arms over her stomach.

At last she turned and closed the door and got the car started and drove with all the windows open to Iris's. When she got out she looked up and down the street. Parked cars. Nothing moving. She daubed at her eyes and nose with the tissues, then got back into the car, left the door open, and used the rearview mirror to put on some lipstick and make sure of her eyes. She walked up to the door and let herself in. Someone was talking in the kitchen. She heard a man's voice.

"Iris?" she said, suddenly filled with the urge to turn and run.

"In here, baby," Iris said.

Natasha made her tentative way in, imagining Duego sitting in there with his polite overly formal air and his speech that was so much like rehearsed phrases. But it was a man Iris's age or older. He was seated across from her at the kitchen table. The room smelled strongly of coffee. The man had a shaved head, was soft featured though a bit emaciated, his cheekbones standing out, with deep-set light blue eyes, and a well-trimmed white beard that made the hairless scalp all the more striking. He reached forward to shake hands, half-rising from his chair.

"This is Liam Adams," Iris said. "An old friend."

Natasha shook hands, staring at him. He did not look the slightest bit familiar.

"Hello," Liam Adams said.

"Mr. Adams and I go way back."

Natasha stood silent, with a half smile of greeting.

"I'm visiting from New York," he said.

"We knew each other in the mayor's office," said Iris. "When you were small."

"I remember you when you were this big." Mr. Adams held his hand out below the level of the tabletop.

"He's moving back to Memphis."

"Because of the attacks," Natasha guessed.

"Actually, I'd been planning to for a couple of years." His smile was wide, and he had small yellow in-turning teeth. His blue eyes seemed too young for the elderly features. "But the Twin Towers got me focused on it, I guess. I grew up here, you know. And—and New York requires so much energy."

Soon they were all three seated at the table. "Did you know my mother?" Natasha asked.

"No."

"It was just you and me, honey, when I took the job in the mayor's office."

"And I came in a year later, right?" Mr. Adams said.

"That's right."

He shook his head, smiling wistfully. "I got married in New York. Twenty years we were together. Never thought I *would* get married. I'd been single so long."

The other two were silent.

"She passed away in '96."

"I'm sorry," Iris said.

"March." He sipped the coffee, staring out the window.

She stood and moved to pour more coffee. He watched her and, thanking her, lifted the cup and drank again. Iris sat down, moved the flat of her hands across the surface of the table. "Well," she said. "This is certainly strange." Then she laughed. "I can't believe it. All these years—"

"You were going to say?" Natasha asked her.

"Well, it's just been so long."

There was a pause.

"I couldn't come to Memphis and not call you," Mr. Adams said.

"That would've upset me."

Natasha thought of the news she had and stared at them both. Iris asked him where he was when the towers were hit.

"I was walking my dog. Eighth Avenue, up on Ninety-First. I didn't see it until I went in and made some toast for myself and sat down in front of the TV."

"Such a terrible thing," said Iris. "Natasha's husband was there, too. In New York. But like you, a few blocks north."

"I lost a neighbor. Didn't know him that well. But I saw him that morning, and he talked about not going to work that day. But he went. There are so many ironies like that in it—people going along at the beginning of a working day like any other and something so bad coming."

"Would you like to stay for lunch?"

"No, I should go. Some other time."

Iris saw him out, then sat at the kitchen table and looked at the coffee in her cup. "Imagine," she said.

Natasha watched her, and when she put one hand to her forehead and seemed about to cry, Natasha pulled her chair around and sat close.

Iris looked at her. "What?"

"Are you all right?"

"Little headache. Had it before he got here."

"I'm pregnant."

Her grandmother turned to her and stared, eyes wide, mouth open as if she might shout or cry. "Oh, sweetie," she said. "Is it true? Is it really true?"

5

ARTICLE 3. *Whether it can be said that a person may still be in love with someone other than her spouse and decide against acting on it out of fear of hurting him, who is dear to her?*

We proceed thus to the Third Article: It seems that it can be said that a person may still be in love with someone other than her spouse and decide against acting on it out of fear of hurting him, who is dear to her.

Objection 1.
The crux of this case is against the grain of genuine straightforward honesty in my wife, who has in all other instances taken pains to be direct and truthful with me while denying that there is something more giving her these panics and night spells than the memory of having been trapped and believing she had lost me.

Objection 2.
Further, she has shown herself to be quite strong in asserting herself and her version of things when confronted or questioned, even with the lately subtle and guarded form reservations and questions have mostly taken (she will not speak of it directly), and there is clearly the same puzzlement as mine about all this in the one person she would confide in other than her husband if indeed there were such a circumstance, her grandmother, who I have come to believe continues in the same dark as I am about the cause of these confusions of feeling.

On the contrary, It is well known that in many circumstances involving a dishonesty in order to protect the feelings of someone whose well-being is in question, there exists an extreme scrutiny about matters of no bearing on the essential question, in order to preserve the deception.

I answer that, The idea itself is so contrary to the experience of being with my wife in every single other instance, and that when I watch her with her grandmother, or her friend Marsha, or our friend Andrew Clenon, it is impossible to put together this bright, intelligent, warm, expressive, and clever person with the one who seems inwardly, in spite of all her effort, to cower at the prospect of intimacy with me. That is, any intimacy beyond simply lying next to each other to read or talk. And she shows the quickest tendency to a kind of interior cringing at any suggestion that something is not the same, that something is missing. Ease is missing. She denies it and asks for time, and there seem to be moments when she comes toward me, but it all feels *produced.*

Reply Obj. 1.
The essential circumstance which is such cause of dismay is something emanating from those more than two weeks we were apart, and all the hurts and doubts stem from uncertainty about a singular event I am not privy to but about which there is undeniable evidence.

Reply Obj. 2.
What really amounts to only a few hours of fearing she had lost me does not seem at all sufficient as a cause of such a long period of lingering aftershock.

6

The two women worked on the bending exercises for Iris's knee, and some lifting with two-pound weights, and then Natasha drove her to the bank and to the store. Iris talked excitedly and happily about the new baby. "It's just what this world—just what we need now," she said. "Have you thought about a name? I bet not. Well, it's new. I wonder what you'll settle on. Have you-all talked about it? I can come over and babysit every day. It's going to be so wonderful living so close. My God, I'll—I'm about to be a great-grandmother." She was using the cane, but was clearly less dependent on it, touching it to the ground with each step. "Imagine that. A great-grandmother."

"Yes, you will be that," Natasha told her. "You already *are* that." Sometimes the bad possibilities did not play themselves out in life, and people were lucky and knew it and appreciated it. Two months. Two months. This was Faulk's child.

"I actually like the sound of it," Iris said. "Great-grandmother."

The day was cool and sunny, and they stopped for lunch at the Otherlands Coffee Bar and sat out on the wooden deck in the shade of an umbrella and were happy. With Iris's happiness, Natasha could believe that this *was* a happy thing. Suddenly she thought of sitting here with Constance the day before the wedding, and it made a little cloud of unrest in her soul. She looked at Iris's lined face and loved her for the calm that always seemed to reside there. "Come have dinner with us tonight, okay? That's when I'll tell him."

"Oh, tell him when he gets home from work."

"No, I want you there. Please?"

Iris smiled and nodded, thinking it over.

"Come help us celebrate. I want to have a party."

"Well, it's up to you, sweetie."

There was a brief pause.

"It was good seeing Liam after all these years," Iris said, and then bit into her sandwich. "He didn't remember that I met his wife. They visited a couple of times at the beginning."

"Were you in love?"

Chewing, she seemed to be trying to decide for herself what the situation had been. "We were very good friends, I guess you'd say now. Nothing happened. We had fun, though. I was grieving, raising a child alone."

The cool air and the heat of the sun was on them. Natasha realized that she did not want to know more. All of it was past, and she wanted the past to *be* past. Gone.

"I have pictures from those days," her grandmother said. "You should see your face in them—this little kid with deep shadows under her eyes and a look like grief itself. The irises of your eyes didn't touch the bottom lids. It made you look sadder than you were."

She heard this without quite taking it in. She was thinking about the fact that this was Faulk's baby and not Duego's—and then she was beset with the idea of Duego, wherever he was in Florida . . . or Memphis; that was also possible. *Two* people knew what had happened on that beach in Jamaica. The thought had not quite registered with her before she imagined him witnessing her silence and deciding to leave her alone. Perhaps this moment he was with some other unfortunate young woman, still being who he was and what he was. It seemed wrong of her not to have thought of it earlier in this way.

Iris was talking about Natasha's mother. "When she was pregnant with you she was the bloom of health. She had no morning sickness at all. No discomforts. It was like she was made to be pregnant. And that was when she got the idea of getting away from Memphis. The *grime* of Memphis. That was the way she talked about it. *Grime.* She got big as a house, and she was happy that way, and all she could talk about was finding a way out of this town. Grime. I've always loved this town and felt at home in it. It's the best of both worlds—a big city that feels very much like a small town. But she wanted out of it in the worst way. I thought it was odd."

"Well, we're all odd, aren't we? If you scratch the surface."

"I had a beau," Iris said, and gave the small nodding gesture that admitted it was Liam Adams. "For a little while when I was left alone. And I needed it, then."

Natasha reached over and touched her wrist. "You never told me this."

The old woman stared at her with brimming eyes. " 'The dark backward and abysm of time.' "

"I didn't mean it that way."

"It's all right if you did."

"I have one memory that's pretty clear," Natasha said. "The two of them sitting in the front seat of a car and snow outside the windows. I was in the backseat. They were talking low, and we were waiting for someone. But that's all. I don't know who we were waiting for. And I remember crying once because I couldn't tie my shoes, and Daddy trying to show me—and she said, 'You've hurt her feelings.' And I cried harder, milking it, but I can't see their faces, and I don't know where we were. A sunny living room somewhere and summer outside the window."

"You were the prettiest little baby, you know."

"Even with my old soul?"

"Yep."

Presently, Iris said, "I've wondered what might've happened if we *had* been in love, that man and me. He looks so old now. Well, he *is* old, isn't he."

"I think he looks nice," Natasha said.

After another pause, Iris said, "Regret hurts pretty awfully, doesn't it."

"Yes—more than anybody ever tells you."

She tilted her head, as if trying to see into what she had just heard, but also, now, gazing stonily at the younger woman. "Go on."

"No. It's—I was just saying."

"Are we talking about the same thing?"

Natasha said nothing.

"Will you please tell me what's going on with you?"

"Nothing. I'm pregnant." Too much time had passed. No one

would believe her after so much time. Or, no, they *would* believe her, and what would they do then?

"You have been so inward and not yourself," Iris said. "It's very plain. Poor Michael is painfully and obviously aware of it."

"Has he said something?"

Iris considered for a moment.

"Has he talked to you, Iris?"

"I said it's painfully obvious that he's worried about it. No, he hasn't talked to me. Not directly. I was trying to find the words to explain how it is. It's—it's in the way we speak to each other in your presence, like we're both tiptoeing around an invalid."

"Oh, well, God! That's good to know. That makes me feel so confident and strong. Thank you."

"I don't mean it as a criticism, honey."

"You could've fooled me."

"Well, I didn't. I'm worried about you, and so is Michael."

They said nothing for a few moments, Iris eating her sandwich and then wiping her fingers. Natasha watching her, but not eating.

"I've ruined your lunch."

"I felt a little nauseous before we sat down," Natasha said.

"Maybe have a little milk."

"I'm all right."

A while later, she said, "God. I'm pregnant," and she sniffled.

"Well, that explains a lot."

"I don't know what it explains. I'm having a baby, that's all."

"Look, we all love you."

"Who is 'we all'? Have you *all* been talking about me?"

"I wasn't saying it *about* anybody. Me, Michael. Marsha. Your friends. Everybody who ever really got to know you. That's all I mean."

"I feel so *watched*," Natasha told her.

ARTICLE 4 *Whether it is justified to seek answers by confronting people outside the marriage who may be possible sources of enlightenment concerning the problem, if a trouble goes unanswered for so long.*

We proceed thus to the Fourth Article: It seems that it is justified to seek answers by confronting people outside the marriage who may be possible sources of enlightenment concerning a problem, if a trouble goes unanswered for so long.

Objection 1.
It is possible that the trouble itself is colorated with imagining, and therefore might smack of the hysterical, and introduce further trouble without the benefit of further understanding.

Objection 2.
The fact of confronting anyone is by its nature extreme, and may therefore be unfeasible on the face of it, given my own character, which is to keep things inside.

On the contrary, It is impossible to suppose that one's sense of the trouble is all the product of imagining, or even partially so, though the suspicion about the former lover is imbued with what I do imagine of my wife on the beach in Jamaica, *with someone.* But there is a definite change in her feeling toward me which is unacknowledged but demonstrated in ways that she answers for with her experience of 9/11. She herself acknowledges, at least tacitly, the unease; and the panics in the night, the anxiety and trembling, are all manifestations of the trouble. They are undeniable. Therefore, I have sufficient reason to seek an answer for myself beyond our unhappy silences and the sense, even as she seems all right, that something is haunting her. It is a reasonable thing to expect a man to seek some communication with the person she was with in Jamaica, Constance, and, if my suspicions are shown to be correct, with the *someone else* my wife saw there.

    I answer that, it makes no sense to look for something that could be purely in the realm of imagining, especially if one has to confront a person who showed such clear sign of being part of the conspiracy of silence. And it would be something bordering on psychotic to seek some sort of confrontation with the photographer, because he is only one possibility, and it should be simple enough to rule him out: one has only to find out where he was during that period in the middle of September. Lacking him as the possible *other* the whole question of distrust deepens further. This is a sufficient *answer to the Objections.*

8

That evening, Iris came over to the house for dinner, as planned. She brought Liam Adams with her. She introduced him by saying, "This is my friend from the mayor's office." Faulk simply stared at them, as if waiting for some kind of punch line.

Iris said, "I guess Natasha hasn't talked to you since you got home."

For Faulk, it was another aspect of what he did not want to think about: his wife's previous life. The fact that it was from her childhood meant nothing against the rush of feeling that it was a further complication, and it made him irritable. He offered wine to them both. Natasha, returning from the store with a bag of groceries, said, "Oh, I'm sorry. I thought I'd be back before you got here." She looked at Mr. Adams and smiled.

Apparently he had come calling shortly after Natasha dropped Iris off from their lunch. Natasha put the groceries away and started heating oil to fry chicken. Faulk had poured two glasses of Rioja. Liam Adams drank his rather quickly and then spoke about taking the liberty of having another glass. "If no one minds," he said, pouring it full.

Natasha saw this, and marked it, and then went about making the dinner while the three of them talked in the other room.

They discussed the Afghan war for a while, and then Iris said, "Let's change the subject. I'm so sick of the whole awful thing."

Adams had emptied the first bottle of wine, so Faulk opened another. The new wine was a Côtes-du-Rhone, and Adams talked about how this wine seemed lighter. Natasha made the dinner with help from Iris while the two men went on about Faulk's having left the priesthood and about Adams's deciding to move back to Memphis, where he was born and raised. He reminisced about Memphis in the old days, when he was a boy and it had been a segregated city. "Beale Street then was nothing like it is now, let me tell you."

The women set the dinner out, and they all sat down to eat. Adams kept pouring wine for himself and Faulk until the second bottle was empty, and Faulk took the last bottle of red that he had, a Brunello, and opened it, feeling a little drunk himself, and watching Adams fill his glass again. Adams drank most of the glass and then poured more, talking too loud about deciding to come home and then taking five years to do it.

This was the third time he had said exactly that. Faulk looked at Iris, who looked back at him with a helpless frown. Natasha had eaten one plate and then taken seconds, surprised at her own appetite. She stood and began taking away the dishes. Iris helped her. They also exchanged glances. Iris shook her head.

"Guess I'll wait to tell him about the baby," Natasha told her.

"Well, till we're gone, anyway."

She went on clearing the table and taking the empty wine bottles. Faulk saw the sour, down-turning expression around her mouth and had the thought that a little hospitality toward Adams was not too much to ask; that it wouldn't cost her so much to be a little forbearing. He did not examine the feeling, though some part of him was vaguely aware of the resentment in it. Adams was loud, drunk, and dull as he tried once more to describe all the processes of thought that had led him to decide about moving home. And then he was rattling on again about New York and the attacks. "Nobody knew how go about an'thing." The white beard was ruffled now and wine-stained around the mouth and down to the chin.

"I felt like a refugee in a war," Faulk said to him.

"Tha's right."

"Right."

"We all were. An' strange things. Poor dumb guy—cheat'n on ez wife. S'posed to be at the office. Calls'er, tells'er he's at work. Eighty-sixth floor. Building's already c'*lapsed*. Frien' amine's uncle, died that morning, in' a hosp-eh'tal. Natur'l causes."

The two women cleared everything away and started doing the dishes. Natasha had to go sit down, and she moved past the men to get into the living room. Her grandmother finished the dishes, standing against the sink with the cane resting on it at her side. Then she made a cup of coffee and went in to where Natasha was.

"Awf'l," Liam Adams said, as if proclaiming something to a crowd. "So many refugees."

"All of us." Faulk was drunk, and did not quite know how drunk, and now he felt that he had made a wonderful new friend. He went into the refrigerator and found a half-gallon bottle of Pinot Grigio that his wife had just brought home from the grocery store. He opened it. "Mind if we switch to white?"

"Love th' whites."

He poured both glasses full, ignoring the little pocket of red in each one. The white wine was therefore faintly tinted pink. They drank, now, for some reason, with excessive politeness, setting the glasses down with great care.

Natasha murmured to her grandmother, "Did he drive to your house?"

Iris nodded. "He had a glass of wine at my house before we came over here."

"What will you do?"

"Maybe he'll stay here."

"Oh, please, no. Where would we put him?"

Faulk sat with the side of his head resting against his own palm, that elbow on the table, looking into the living room where the two women were seated side by side on the couch, talking in low tones. Adams was holding forth. "There's no hope f'rus win this one." He belched low, tucking his chin, the stained white beard. "R'lidgus wars. Las' one las-ed five hun'ed years. No fight for freed'm anymore. Bullshit." He lifted his glass, which was now empty, and seeing this, he reached for the bottle. As he poured he went on. "Fight for oil. Tha's what th' fuck it is. Scuse me." He belched. "Oil. Tha's all."

"Right," Faulk told him, though now in the back of his mind he was beginning to worry about where this night would end. Adams was in far worse shape.

"Th' buildings—terr'bull. Jus' gone. I din' see 'em come down."
He started crying now, without sound, sitting there slumped back
in the chair, looking at nothing. "Both of 'em. Gone. People dyin'
of anthrax. Boys dyin' oveh there."

"It's late," Faulk said, because nothing else came to mind.

Adams sat forward, and when he spoke now his voice was curi-
ously less garbled sounding, the words more slowly pronounced,
though plainly it was all coming from what he'd had to drink. "I
don't really handle"—again he belched—"I'm . . . I've not been so
good at be'en by myself. You know?"

"Yes," Faulk said.

"You know?"

"I know."

"You *know*."

"Yes."

"Since a long time, really."

Faulk looked into the living room and saw that Iris and Natasha had gone from there.

"You know?" Adams said.

"Yes, I *do* know."

"Wife's gone five years."

"Sorry."

"Five *years*."

Faulk was aware that sympathy was required but was unable to
feel anything like it.

"B'cause it's a man's *right*," Adams went on.

"I see."

"A man's *right*." He appeared to have settled some conflict in
his thoughts.

"Come on," Faulk said, rising. "Let's go for a walk."

In the small bedroom, the women sat on the bed and listened
to them struggle out the door, Adams still talking.

"Oh, Christ. No," Natasha said to her grandmother. "Not
tonight."

"Do you want me to stay?"

"I'm going to bed."

"Don't be too discouraged. They're entitled—it's been awful for them, I'm sure."

"Poor babies."

"*Hey.*"

"Well?"

"Give 'em a break, honey. Come on."

Natasha patted her grandmother's thick-boned wrists.

"You must be exhausted," Iris said to her. "Can I tuck you in?"

"I have to take a shower."

She looked down. "Of course. Well."

"I won't take long."

She smiled.

In the shower, Natasha got the water as hot as it would go and stood there. For a while she didn't even use the soap. She thought of being a mother, and of the child she was carrying, imagining a little girl. Someone to grow up and live in the world. She saw again the burning towers. She saw the starry quiet sky in Jamaica, and the pictures of suffering and sorrow and confusion, and she made a forlorn, hopeless effort to shut it all, all thought, away. Finally she turned the water off and dried herself and went out to the bedroom where Iris, hearing her come, had stood and with one hand pulled the blankets back. Quickly Natasha got into her nightgown and crawled into the bed, and Iris pulled the blanket up over her shoulder, then leaned down and kissed her cheek. Iris smelled of the wine and of her perfume. Her hair was strawlike, but somehow soft, too.

"My sweet girl," the old woman said. "I'm so proud of you."

"Sorry about today," Natasha said.

"Today was lovely."

"I was short with you."

"Stop it."

"What do you think they'll do?"

"They might end up in *jail* if they make enough noise."

"They wouldn't—they wouldn't get into his car . . . Mr. Adams's car."

"I don't think they'll go that far. But I'll go see. You rest. You want the light out?"

"No. I'll read."

"Good night." Iris kissed her again, then made her way out on the cane.

Alone, Natasha rolled to her side in the bed and closed her eyes, feeling suddenly almost groggy. She remembered that she was pregnant. She sat up, arranging herself in the bed with pillows behind her back, and opened a book to read, a biography of Mary Todd Lincoln. But she kept reading the same sentence, over and over. The words would not register in her mind.

9

Adams sat down on the lawn in front of Iris's house, out of breath, claiming that he was going to be sick. It had taken them some time to get this far, struggling along, Adams's arm over Faulk's neck, and Faulk mostly having to carry him, holding on to his wrist, hauling him when he dragged his feet. The night was shrouded by low clouds, and the air had become damp. The wetness of the grass made a dark place on the seat of the older man's white pants where he sat. "Neveh drink like this," he got out.

"Oh," Faulk, who was standing over him, said. "I do." He laughed and looked up at the bulges of darker shapes in the low heavy clouds. He wondered why some men slurred so when they got drunk, as if the alcohol went to their tongues. He himself was proud that the times when he had gone over the line had not been so obvious to people; he could always carry it. "Gonna rain," he said to Adams.

Adams was silent.

"How long did you say you were married?"

"Twent' years"—he made a sweeping gesture with his other arm, the one that was not holding him up—"gone."

"I think you told me that."

"You're newl'wed."

"Yeah."

"Lucky guy, huh. Your age."

"You got somewhere—can I get you a cab?"

"She's veh' pretty. Don't think she likes me."

"She's the nervous type." Faulk was surprised to hear the words come from his lips. The fact of it had a sobering effect.

Adams lay back on the grass and put one arm over his face.

Faulk had thought that they might just walk it off, but now the other man was either asleep or passed out. And here was Iris, driving up in her Taurus that had only twelve thousand miles on it. She parked along the curb where they were and got out with her cane.

For a space the two of them just stood looking at each other, Iris over the roof of her car, and Faulk standing next to the unconscious Liam Adams.

"He can't stay there," Iris said.

"Thought we'd just walk it off," said Faulk.

"Yeah. Well." Neither of them moved.

"Is Natasha—"

"She went to bed."

Adams spoke from the ground. "I b'lieve I'm be sick."

"Sit up," Faulk told him. "Sit up. You'll choke to death, for God's sake."

Silence.

Iris came around the car, slowly, using the cane. She was in some discomfort. He put his hand out. "No," she said.

Adams began to snore.

"How cold will it get tonight?" Iris asked.

"Don't know. Cool enough right now."

"I'll call a cab. He can stay here until it arrives, and then I'll wake him."

"He'll be all right laying here?"

"I can have a cab here in fifteen, twenty minutes. He won't freeze to death in twenty minutes. It must be sixty-something, right?"

Faulk looked at the sky and then back at her.

"Course, getting the cabbie to let him get into his cab. That's another story. Especially if he gets sick."

There was a pause, where they seemed to be thinking about it.

"Ridiculous," she said. "You know? The two of you."

"He seemed bent on getting plowed."

"He wasn't alone."

Faulk waited for her to say more.

"You better get on home. I think your wife's waiting up to tell you something. Something important. And son—" She stopped.

"Yeah?"

"I hope you'll be up to it."

He started down the walk.

"You want a ride?" she called.

He halted and turned. "I'll walk." Then he indicated Adams lying in his stupor on the grass. "You've got that to deal with."

"Good night, son. Remember."

"Good night." He went carefully on, concentrating. He took each step as if balanced on a ledge, but he did not sway or wobble. At the end of the street he turned and looked back and saw her still standing over Adams. She raised one hand to wave. He waved back. He thought of all the years she raised Natasha alone, grieving the loss of her daughter and son-in-law, no help. Just now, the history seemed an element of the woman's strangeness.

And then, thinking about Iris, he felt suddenly as if the difficulty inside his own marriage was in some way connected to the history: a girl raised by a woman keeping so much of her inner life to herself.

He walked up the street, full of sudden foreboding, feeling precarious, susceptible, even frail, resolving to face his anxiety and tolerate everything, determined to be kind, and not ask for more than his wife, his beloved wife, for whatever reason or reasons, could give. Probably she had done something in Jamaica that she herself considered a betrayal of him. In any case, it would have come from her belief that he, Faulk, had died in New York. So he would find a way to forgive whatever it was and go on. He faltered, nearly fell at the corner, and continued walking, overcorrecting, but then setting himself straight, being cautious with each stride, considering his own magnanimousness. Then, through the fog of what he had drunk, he saw it for what it was and felt foolish and penitent.

Lord, send my roots rain.

No. It seemed that this was all gone from him, now. The sky was only a limitless emptiness. He shook himself, stopped, and raised his fists, and then simply let his hands come back to his chest, as if praying and waiting for someone to come to him. Far off, the sound of a speeding car rose, the tires squealing.

I have believed my whole life. Help thou my unbelief.

At the house, all the lights were still on. He entered quietly and stepped into the kitchen. There was almost half of the big bottle of Pinot Grigio left, sitting in the middle of the counter. He had a glass of water from the tap, then poured the wine into the water glass and drank it down, standing wavering in the light—bereft, marooned. All these weeks he had been wanting to *know*. And now, apparently and at last, when he wanted so desperately not to, he *would* know. The wine had increased the haze of his thoughts. He took more of it, then stumbled into the bedroom, where he found her sitting up, asleep, with the book open on her upraised knees. Gingerly he removed the book. She woke, raising one hand to her face.

She was unaware of having been asleep.

"Just me," he said.

"Oh." She reached to embrace him, and he sat down and took her into his arms. For a little while, they simply sat there clinging to each other. The smell of the wine on him made her uneasy, and even so she kept her arms tight around him.

"Iris says you've got something to tell me. You don't have to tell me."

"We'll talk—let's talk tomorrow. You've had too much to drink." She was fighting the shaking in her voice, feeling the muscles of his back, his shoulder blades, the solidness of him.

He said, "You don't have to say anything. I don't care what happened in Jamaica."

"What?"

"I don't. I forgive you."

She paused, only a little. "You *what*?"

"I do. Forgive you. Whatever you did in Jamaica."

"Oh, God," she said. "This again. Jamaica again."

"You don't have to tell me about it. In fact, I don't want you to. I forgive you."

She sighed sadly. "Forgive me for what?"

"I don't even want to know who it was."

"*Who it was.*" Now she pushed at his shoulders, and when he sat back, she stared, frowning.

He said, "You had something to tell me. If it's about Jamaica, I don't care about it. I forgive you for it—whatever it was. Okay? The whole world was coming down on you, and I don't care about it anymore."

She said nothing. There was no change at all in her countenance.

For her, something had moved at her heart, a grabbing sensation. She thought she might lose consciousness.

"You thought I was dead," he told her. "It could've been that you were drunk. You got into things with somebody or ran into someone—someone you knew from before—"

She interrupted him. "What are you saying?"

He said, "Listen to me."

"No," she said. "What are you *saying*."

"I'm saying if someone you knew before—"

"Someone I—"

"I'm saying I don't care. We weren't married yet. You're human."

"I'm—"

"It's all right," he said. "Please."

"But *what's* all right. What're you talking about. Say it to me, Michael."

Now he spoke in an overly patient, almost-preening voice: "I'm saying—and I think you know quite well what I'm referring to, and I want you to be honest with me about it at last—that if you ran into someone, you know? Someone you used to be with, one of the others, an old lover, or someone *completely new*"—and with this, his voice took on the tone of an inquisitor, a lawyer prosecuting a case before a judge—"I want you to know that you don't have to tell me anything about it, because I do, I forgive you. All right? I understand and I forgive you. Whatever it was."

"You . . ." she began. But then she was silent. Glaring at him.

"I mean we're adults. We can work all this out."

"Work *what* out," she sobbed. "No. You tell me."

"Aren't you *listening*? I don't care who you ran into in Jamaica. I don't care who you had sex with in Jamaica. There. Is that clear enough? Do you *get* it now?"

"Oh." She pushed away from him, and as he stood she was out of the bed and around him, heading to the bathroom. She closed and locked the door. It was as if she were back there on the island, with a door between her and a stranger.

"Natasha?" he said on the other side. "I don't understand. I'm telling you it's all right. I'm letting go of it. It was the situation. We'll go on."

She took a breath, pressed the flats of her hands against the cool wood surface. "I want you to leave me alone now. Please. Just—leave me alone." And she was crying, sobbing. "We can talk in the morning. Please?"

Silence.

"Please go."

Fury rose in him, a hot needle traveling up his spine. So this was how he would be treated now. After the weeks of trying to look past all the signs of her failing love, and after reaching this decision to forgive her and go on, this was what he got for it, this—for his understanding and his care—*this* was what she repaid him with. He couldn't speak, standing there shivering with rage.

"Leave me alone," she moaned from the other side. "Please."

He slammed himself against the door, hurting his shoulder. Standing back, he raised one leg and kicked at it, and something cracked in the frame. She screamed.

"Stop it," he said. "Who do you think I am?" He hit the door with the side of his fist.

On the other side, she retreated to the bathtub and shower, pulling the curtain up as if to shield herself. "Please!" she shrieked, but she couldn't hear her own voice.

"You know what *happiness* is?" he said. "Does it ever cross your mind to think about that anymore? Happiness? Happiness! *Think* about it! Nobody's hurting you. Somebody's being *good* to you! Somebody *loves* you and provides for you and delights in how you laugh and how you talk. Somebody *listens* to you and *thinks* about you. You understand? Isn't that happiness?" He kicked the door again. And then again. "Well? Answer me! Isn't that happiness? *Is*n't it?"

"Oh, God."

"Who do you think I am?" he shouted. "I'll tell you who I am. I'm your *husband*, who doesn't deserve this! Who has done nothing wrong. you've *shut him out*! You've kept things from him and lied to him and let others know about it and made him feel small and nothing and weak! That's me. That's who I am. That's your *husband*. And you want me to *leave*!" He kicked the door still again with this last, and it blew open. Pieces of the frame flew everywhere, and it was as though her scream were part of the sound of the splintering wood.

Seeing her cringing against the wall next to the shower, with the curtain pulled up to cover the front of her, he thought she looked pitiable, and yet it did not make him feel for her. It made him angrier. He had the urge to flail at her, strike her. But he held himself back, moving slowly into the room. And now, amazingly, he felt a rush of something weirdly like calm purpose and righteousness. There was no need for any thinking. He would show her now; she would know what kind of man he was now. He watched his hands reach to her face, and gently he took hold, his big hands on either side. She was trembling and crying. Tightening his hold, he pressed harder, feeling the cheekbones. Then he shook her. "Stop it. Be quiet. I love you. Can't you *see* that?"

"You're—hurting—" she got out. The wine on his breath was making her sick. Gradually she began losing balance, was unable to stand, being held up by his hands. His hands trembled, squeezing, pressing.

"Look at me. Will you? This is me. This is *me*."

She said, "Let go. Let go of me!"

And he did, and she was leaning against the angle of wall and shower stall, still gripping the shower curtain, holding it just under her chin.

"God," he said. "You—my God."

"Get out," she rasped, and then coughed. "Leave me alone."

"You have to understand," he told her. But there was nothing he could find to say, nothing he could explain. "I'm s-sorry about the—door," he said, controlling himself. "I'm sorry about—this." She covered her face and turned from him, crying.

He was angry all over again. "But you've got to understand me. You listening? I don't want kindness from you. Understand? I don't want pity."

"Oh, God," she said, "Stop it. *Stop* it. Leave me alone!"

For a moment, they did not speak, standing close in the too-bright light, the door at its appalling angle and the debris at their feet, the only sounds her sobbing and sniffling and his shaken breathing.

"It doesn't matter," he said finally. "Everything's broken. *I'm* broken. This—you and me. *This* is broken."

"No," she said. "Oh, *please*! You don't know. You don't *know*!"

He said, "I know. I know."

She did not move. And she could not stop crying.

"All right," he said evenly, thinly, his voice rough and straining. "All right. You want me to leave. That's what you've wanted all along, right? So I'll leave. I *will* leave."

Through the blur of her tears, she saw him draw up as if to reach for her again. She cowered back a little more. "I don't—know—wh-what you're—talking about," she got out through the sobs and gasping.

"Ah, God," he said. "Go on, then. Go back to whoever you ran into, okay? Just—go. Why should you stay with me out of—out of—*kindness*. I'm sick and tired of *kindness*. You go right ahead. You went to Jamaica and had a high old time and you didn't know where I was and you were lonely—"

She screamed at him, "I was *raped*!" The word came in the long top of the scream. "God*damn* you! I was raped. I was raped."

He faltered back. Neither of them moved for a time. Again, there was just the sound of their tattered breathing, her crying.

Gasping it out, low, not looking at him, she said, "Oh, God. God!" She straightened, still clutching the shower curtain. And now her voice was bitter and defiant. "Do *you* get it now?"

They stood there looking into each other's eyes.

He saw the splintered and bent frame of the door, and the door itself, lying askew across the counter next to the sink. His heart was hammering in his temples, and he took another step back, one hand reaching for the broken frame. "God, baby."

"Go," she told him. "Please. Leave me alone. Please."

He started toward her, but she cowered against the wall and screamed again. "Get away from me!"

Slowly he backed out of the room. "Can we just . . ." he began.

"Get away," she said.

"Why didn't you tell me?"

"Just please leave me alone."

Searching his mind for some way through, something else occurred to him: "Who—how did it—honey—"

"There's nothing I have to say to you," she said. "God! Not now." She sobbed again. Then, sniffling, more calmly: "We'll talk in the morning. Please. Please." The words came with the crying, the struggle for breath.

"But—you can't just—did you know him? Was he with—where was—where did it happen?"

"Will you please just leave me alone."

"We can't just—" he said.

"Yes, we can." She was crying quietly. "I did."

"I'll kill him."

She said nothing, still stood there with the shower curtain pulled up. When he started toward her she screamed. "Don't you *touch* me!"

He went out and got into his car and drove to the Midtown apartment. He let himself in and moved to the little bedroom, where the folding bed still stood in one corner. There was an ache starting in his hip from having kicked at the bathroom door in the little house. He had thought his purpose in life was always to be kind and brave and good, but it was clear to him now that he had wanted more than anything else to be loved. It seemed to him that everything was over, all his plans and hopes, all his dreams and wishes and everything in which he had ever put the slightest faith. Then he thought of her and realized the selfishness of his own grief. He removed his shoes, opened the folding bed, sat down, and looked at his hands.

Do You Take This Man

I

Alone in the house, where the only sound was her crying, she had the vision: If she were a character in a movie, Duego would come back. He would leap out at her from a doorway or climb into the window of the house, and there would be a struggle. He would try to kill her. And she would kill him. The story would be over in a single cathartic moment of action. There would be the usual matters to take care of involving police and the courts and the public eventualities, the explanations. The verdict would be that her action was justified, of course: self-defense. Her life would be saved. Her husband would hold her, and they would forgive each other everything.

But in the story she was living, the hours of the rest of the night went on, while she sat, terrified, on the bed, still crying, and intermittently going to the front door to look out. She did not want him to come back; and at the same time she was afraid he would not do so. She wanted the baby, but what had happened to her glared forth, and made her want to be rid of it—shed it, push it out of herself, and be clean again.

"God," she said aloud. "No." And then she repeated it. "No."

She thought of the sixty to seventy percent who went on with their lives. She imagined them never speaking of it. And nobody noticing anything. It must be that in one way or another they found the strength to make a kind of truce with it. Somehow they succeeded in concealing it, and they smiled and laughed and went with friends and made love and they had no nightmares about it, and nobody was the wiser—or else they did have the nightmares and lived secretive, haunted lives, enduring by some means the anxiety and the scarred sense of themselves, the fear of every change, listening always in the dark, carrying the feeling of trespass and violation but showing the world only the polite, desperate lifting of a hand to wave, like that poor doomed woman in the ruin of the south tower. She worked to put the thought away, afraid that, simply by thinking it, she was depriving the dead person of her dignity. And then she thought of the men who committed these crimes and went on with their own lives, and did it over and over again. And yet too many people, men and women both, considered the thing itself a form of sexual excess, or even, awfully, in some mysteriously habituated way, an unacceptable breech of propriety. The whole culture smacked of it, smelled of it.

She sat on the bed, crying now for all those whom she would never know, as if they were all one species together, a type of creature, crouched in the failure of light all around them, estranged from where they lived, crushed by expectations and by assumptions.

And she thought about what her husband had assumed.

Finally, she got dressed and walked in the predawn toward Iris's. It was growing colder, and there was a fine mist. The mist soaked her as she walked. She let herself in, and quietly made her way upstairs, to her old bedroom, for something else to put on. Then she carried it into the bathroom, and looked at her face in the mirror. No bruising. She got out of the wet clothes and stepped into the shower. It was as it had been in Jamaica, the hot water pouring down, mixing with her tears.

"Natasha?" Iris's voice, full of alarm.

Natasha turned the water off and stepped out. "I'm all right."

Iris was standing in the doorway. "Is he downstairs?"

"I sent him away," Natasha said, wrapping a towel around herself.

"You have to go back," Iris told her, stepping into the small space with her and putting her arm over her shoulder. "You have to find him. Did you tell him about the baby? What happened? Tell me."

"He was drunk. We had a fight."

"You have to go find him."

"Let me get dressed, please?"

"I'll be downstairs. But you have to be there when he comes back. I'll make coffee, and we'll have a cup, but you must go back. Did you argue with him? You can't argue with him drunk, sweetie, you can't do anything with them when they're drunk. You're just arguing with what they've had to drink. But you have to be there when he comes home, and you *can* talk to him then. You know that."

"Please?" Natasha said.

The other shook her head, moving out into the hall. "I'll be downstairs."

She closed the door and got into the dry clothes. It was hard to breathe fully out, and she waited, trying to decide what she would say, how she would explain it.

Downstairs, her grandmother had put coffee on. She was standing at the stove, and Natasha saw the thick blue veins of her ankles.

"Sit," Iris said.

Natasha did so and put her hands flat on the table before her, sniffling. "Can I have a vermouth?"

"Coffee. It's five-thirty in the morning."

"Vermouth. Oh, please."

"So *you'll* be drunk."

"I haven't had anything to drink, Iris. I—I need something to calm me down."

"What about the baby?"

"Oh," Natasha said, crying out. "I don't *want* the baby. Not like this."

Iris stared, her mouth partly open.

"Oh, God. I can't. I *can't.*"

"Tell me," Iris said. "Come on. Tell me now."

2

He woke with a start, hearing the sound outside of a motorcycle. His head hurt. He had a swooning sense of a thing he was failing to do and then fully realized all of it, sitting up, the muscles of his abdomen twisting and cramping, his heart pounding. He had fallen asleep in his clothes.

He got out of the cot and walked unsteadily to the door of the apartment, which was ajar. He saw the street in gray light. The sky was a flat cloud screen, and there were patches of fog in the road at the end of the block. Little pockets of mist clung to the lower branches of the trees. It was a gray, chilly morning. He went back to the cot and put on his shoes. Up the street, Mr. Baines was sitting on his little porch in a bomber jacket, eating. Faulk, in his agitation, thought of him as the fat landlord. The thought was not something he had known himself capable of having. He had come to a new region of his own being and it frightened him. He wanted to break something, tear something down. Baines waved for him to come over.

"Want some?" he said, as Faulk approached.

"What is it."

"Lasagna from last night."

"Not for breakfast."

"Taking what might be my last morning outside for a while. It's gonna get cold today."

Faulk watched him eat.

"Cold front coming."

He started to move off.

"I've got somebody who'll sublet," Baines said, "if you change your mind about keeping it. So you see, old Baines will even help someone find a sublet if he wants to marry a young woman and live elsewhere and changes his mind about keeping it."

"Like I said, it'll be used as a place to work."

"Did you work all night? You don't look good." The smile didn't change. But there was a sly glint in the eyes.

"In fact, that's exactly what I did. I worked all night."

"What kind of work does a former priest do?"

Faulk hesitated.

"You in the doghouse, old son?"

"I'm writing a book," Faulk told him. "How about you? *You* writing one?"

The other man shoved a forkful of the lasagna into his mouth and spoke through chewing. "Baines likes to know how his tenants are doing."

"I asked if you're writing a book," Faulk said.

"You ever taste cold lasagna?"

"No thanks."

"You gonna be spending the night often?" Something smug about the little smile in that heavy face made Faulk want to batter him. It was the mood of this hour in the world.

"Maybe," Faulk said.

"Well." The other grinned at him. "Of course that's your business."

He walked back down the street to the car and got in and started it. And began to cry. Who had done it; why had she not told him?

Daylight had not yet cleared the trees at the horizon. Back up the street, the fat landlord was hunched over his repellent dawn meal.

At the house, he let himself in and walked through the rooms. He saw the broken door in its shocking crooked angle against the bathroom sink, and he turned slowly, looking at the windows, the furniture, all the facets of life as it was supposed to be. Then he faced again the destruction of the doorway into the bathroom. The frame, the baseboard, the lintel—crooked, splintered, and broken, bending into the space of the opening. All this had happened.

Feeling the lingering effects of the wine, he made his way into the living room and sat down on the sofa. His own rasping exhalations were the only sound. Without consciously deciding to, he began going over it all again, thinking it through, step by step, and then he remembered that she had been assaulted. She had been assaulted, and this was what she had been waiting to tell him. He saw an image of her sitting up in the bed, the book open on her knees. "Oh, God," he said.

He could not imagine a way back to her; he believed she would never want to find a way.

She would have gone to Iris's.

He drove there and then lost courage and drove by, looking at the place in the lawn where Adams had lain. Adams, the one with whom he had gotten drunk—the one whose trivial, silly descent into helplessness was one pass in a night that, if it had ended with simply going to sleep, would not even be something worth remembering. Though Adams was a man suffering, too, reliving the loss of his wife, five years ago, still afflicted with it, and Faulk had spent so much of his life trying to see into such suffering and also seeking to give help, seeking to understand it deeply enough to offer solace.

Kindness.

Through the living room window of Iris's house, he saw that there was still a light on in the kitchen, though cloudy sun was coming through the tops of the trees now. He had an image of her sitting in that kitchen talking to her grandmother, telling her, if Iris did not already know everything, about what happened in Jamaica. The secret she had been keeping all this time. He saw again the look of pure unknowing on her face as he accused her. He wanted in this moment, more terribly than he would have believed possible, to die.

3

"Why didn't you report it?" Iris said, crying. "Why didn't you tell me? Why didn't you tell *Michael*?"

"Don't," Natasha said. "Please."

They were at the kitchen table, facing each other. Iris reached across and took her hands. "Why didn't you?"

"I couldn't. Please."

There was a slight pause.

"I talked to someone in Orlando, a policewoman. It—look, there's nothing to be done."

"Oh, God," Iris burst out. "What am I saying?" She stood up and moved around the table and embraced her, holding her head against her abdomen, softly patting the side of her face.

Natasha wept, touching the back of the older woman's hand.

A few moments later, her grandmother said, "God. I should've seen it. I knew there was something else. I should've pressed you until you told me."

"It's all right now. I feel better telling you."

Iris sat down again. "You don't think Michael—he's not heading to Orlando—"

"We didn't get as far as the name."

Iris appeared to deliberate for a moment. "Honey, I've never seen two people more in love."

Natasha waited, watching her begin to sniffle.

"God," Iris went on, gaining control of herself. "I'm so sorry about it."

"Don't, please."

They did not speak for a few moments.

Presently, she breathed the words out. "He'll want to do something about it. He'll be back and he'll want to—you know he'll—you'll have to tell him all of it."

"No. I can't—I can't have him know some of it."

The other's voice was steady now. "Tell me what you think he can't know."

"I let—I let the—let him kiss me. Oh, I want to get past it. I wish it never was."

Iris waited for her to subside. "But that's such a small thing, isn't it? A moment's failing. And you were afraid. You thought Michael was—you were alone and he was alone and everyone was suffering this terrible thing. You didn't know."

Natasha sat there crying softly into her fingers. "It was hard enough telling you all that. And look what he thought. Without my saying *anything*. No, I can't. *I can't*."

"You think he went to his apartment?"

Natasha looked into her eyes but did not speak.

The old woman held the handkerchief to her mouth and then wiped her eyes and her forehead. "You'll get past this, honey. There's people—I'm sure there's people you can talk to. And you're pregnant."

"What if he can't believe it's his."

She obviously had not thought of this. "But you—"

"I know." Natasha sobbed. "But it crossed *my* mind."

"You're having Michael Faulk's baby," Iris told her. "That's what's happening."

"I feel so sick of everything, Iris."

A little later, they went into the living room and sat on the sofa facing the window out onto the street. They were quiet. The younger woman kept sniffling. The sky was darkening outside.

Iris said, "You have to talk to him, honey."

"I wish I felt different. I don't even like to think about him right now. I don't."

"No, now. Honey—there's a child. You have to try, anyway . . . you've just got to try."

"He thought I was with someone else, Iris."

"Well, he can't be expected to know what he wasn't told."

Natasha looked at her. "But he assumed—"

A moment passed.

"The assumption came from what he's afraid of," Iris said. "And he might've been right in assuming, with the rest of us, that if it was something like—if it was—that you'd have told him."

Natasha remained silent.

"Right?"

"So many never—you know?" She sniffled. "Nobody knows it happened. I read up—I—"

Iris did not respond.

"Could be—anyone. Anyone you meet."

"Do you love Michael?"

"You should've seen him. I thought he was going to hurt me."

Iris said, "Jesus." She stood and started out of the room. She wasn't limping at all, and she'd left her cane leaning against the umbrella stand.

Natasha followed her into the kitchen. "I thought the whole world was over when New York happened," she sobbed. "Oh, what happened to us. We didn't have anything to do with it. We didn't do anything wrong."

Her grandmother moved to hold her. "Baby," she said.

"Nothing makes any *sense*."

They were quiet, standing close, looking like two people unde-cided about whether to leave a room or remain in it.

"I would like to have known her," Natasha said, suddenly.

Iris blinked, and stared. Then: "Your mother."

"Yes."

There was another pause.

"I used to think about what it would've been to—to get to know her as something other than a soft blur."

"A soft blur is a pretty good thing to have when nothing is the only other choice."

Natasha wiped her eyes with a napkin from the table. "I don't mean anything about you—but I feel like I don't have anything to lean on, nothing to brace myself."

Iris said. "I'm here."

They were still facing each other.

"You'll stay here for a while?" Iris asked.

"I don't know."

4

He drove out to the interstate and along Highway 40 toward Nash-ville. He went fast, pressing the pedal to the floor, taking the car up to ninety-five miles an hour. He had no destination in mind. It was just going on. Speeding away. The road made its gradual curves before him and then was straight for miles. Away. That was what was needed. He was taking himself away. He imagined simply driving off the side, into a tree, or over one of the bridges skirt-ing a riverbed. The only sound was the wind-rush of the car as he sped on.

He drove to Jackson and pulled into a rest area and stopped, and put his forehead down on the steering wheel. He had been struggling with his faith, the whole edifice threatening to collapse, and now his marriage and this marvelous love he had been given so freely were casualties of all that. Abruptly, it came to him, with a terrible, leveling force, that she was a victim not only of the assault but of his, Faulk's, failure of trust: how wrong he had been, and he understood utterly now what that meant. Some element of his makeup had fallen into this pit of mistrust, this obsession. Last night's fit had arisen out of the crazy, synthetic, self-righteous anger of intoxication, and he was painfully aware of that. He had imagined everything from the beginning, had been wrong the whole time, and it was his suspicions about her that had magnified her unease and anxiety.

The truth of this flamed forth, here, in the closed car, in the troubled light of morning. She was innocent. She was innocent and she was beautiful and true and herself, and all of her breathing life was her own, and he had not been worthy of her.

He drove back toward Memphis. There was almost no traffic. He kept exactly to the speed limit. His eyes stung. He was out of breath. The sky before him changed to towering dark folds of cloud, and lightning flashed at the very tops of them, not going to the ground but forking, extending across.

At Iris's house he parked the car and sat for a while behind the wheel. Perhaps they were watching from the windows. The rain started, big drops splashing, then a downpour. He waited, and gradually the rain subsided and became a steady fall.

Natasha saw him from the window, and her grandmother spoke about immediately going out and meeting him, even with the rain pouring down. "Don't let him sit there." Natasha felt like hiding, going to the back of the house and letting him knock and waiting for him to leave. But she *had* been hiding, she told herself. When the rain slackened and he got out and walked up to knock on the door, Iris opened it and let him in. He stood in the light of the entrance, eyes cast down. Rain dripped from his hair onto his face, so that it looked like he was crying.

"I guess you know what I—what happened," he said to Iris, looking at Natasha and looking down again.

"I know," Iris said to him. "Yes, I know what this girl has had to deal with."

"I came to say—I don't—I'm—I can't believe I could've—"

He halted and looked at Natasha again. "Everything. It's my fault."

"Come in and close the door," Iris said. There were tears in her voice.

He took the step toward them, turned, and pushed the door shut, then faced them again, glancing at Iris and then back at Natasha and then casting his gaze back downward. His demeanor was absurd, nearly comical, that of a boy in trouble for getting wet.

"I always thought you had such a way with words," Iris said.

He left a long silence. Then: "No."

"Not much to say, is there."

"Iris," Natasha said quietly.

"I'm going to make us some breakfast," the old woman murmured.

When she was gone, neither of them moved. Natasha still felt frightened, and he had seen it. "I'm sorry," he said. "I—I'm so sorry."

She waited.

"I can't lose you. I don't know what to do now. Can't—can't I do anything?"

"I don't know."

"I love you."

"Right now," she told him, "that's hard to believe."

"I do, I swear it. Please." He saw the tears in her dark eyes and looked away. "Why didn't you—why couldn't you tell me, baby?"

His voice was so sad that for a few seconds she could not answer him.

"You were afraid?"

"No," she breathed out. Then: "Yes."

"If you'd told me—you know—"

"I should've told you," she said.

Iris came to the opening from the kitchen. "Where did I put my cane?"

Natasha walked over and got it, and when she approached with it, Iris grabbed the frame of the door, and Natasha took hold of her. "Damn thing's hurting again. Come in here and help me, will you? Both of you."

Natasha walked with her, and when they were in there, they both turned. There was the empty doorway, the living room, the rainy windows. Iris nudged her toward the sink, handing the glass kettle to her.

He went to the opening and looked in at them and saw that they were working together, Iris leaning on the cane and taking things out of the refrigerator, Natasha at the sink, pouring water into the kettle.

He walked in, hesitated, and then opened the cabinet over the stove and brought out three plates and three saucers. Iris broke eggs into a bowl and whisked them and sprinkled thyme in them, and salt and broken bits of feta cheese. Faulk laid strips of bacon in the big iron skillet, and Natasha, with trembling hands, spooned coffee into the French press.

Watching him tend to the bacon, she thought, *I don't know how we'll manage it, now, my love.* She started to speak the words and then felt the tears come, turning herself away, going on with the tasks, setting the table, pouring orange juice, laying out silverware.

He wiped his wrist across his mouth, watching the bacon sizzle. To his left, Iris, pouring the eggs into another skillet, began suddenly to cry. "I'll be better," she said quickly, standing there with the bowl in one hand, her hip against the counter. "It's not so strange, I guess. I'm thinking about my poor girl, my daughter. After all these years, it's—it's still the same pressure here." She touched her chest.

Natasha came and put her arms around her.

He looked at them, and the whole of what they had been through moved in him under his skull, a terrible pressure.

"Please," he said. "It'll never come up again. Ever."

"*What* will never come up again," his wife said. It was a challenge. And as the words came from her, she felt her own strength, her own separate being, not his, not anyone's. Hers.

He said nothing. The helplessness in his gaze was hard to look at.

They went on with the preparation of the meal, and when it was all done they sat at the table, and Iris spooned eggs onto each plate and parceled the bacon. Natasha poured the coffee and set down the small plate of buttered toast. There was a long silence. And then Iris bowed her head and extended her hands to them.

Faulk took his wife's hand, because this was grace; it was nearly habit.

"For what we are about to receive," Iris said in a trembling voice. "We pray that you will make us truly thankful."

Natasha saw the worry in his expression, the frowning anticipation. Without words, she had the rush of knowing: they were living in the new, terrible reality—war and broken expectations and suspicion and rape and masses of people dying for nothing they had done, even from a thing as harmless as the mail—and she had been frightened that she had lost him forever, and here he was, at her grandmother's table, the family table, not lost: an essentially good man carrying the weight of his blunders and failures of faith or understanding, a man full of inconsistencies and anxiety, subject to the terrors of the time, and, withal, someone who desired to be better than that and who might even find a way to make up for the things he had done and felt out of his anguish. And perhaps, through the long and difficult and—she understood this, too—doubtful journey back, she might find again the man she had fallen in love with, the one with whom she had been so happily at ease, so much at home. The one whose child she was carrying.

"There's something else I have to tell you," she said.

September 7, 2007—October 6, 2012

ACKNOWLEDGMENTS

This book was begun in Memphis; worked on and titled in Knoxville; continued in Galway, Ireland, while in the hospital with a head injury; then again in Memphis; in Ireland again; in France; and finally finished in Orange, California. Allen and Donnie Wier provided hospitality and good company throughout the composition, and my grown daughters, Emily, Maggie, and Amanda, gave nurturing and support. Lisa Cupolo was beautifully helpful through it all.